THE ANCIENT ORDER OF MORIDURA

Peter Curran

THE ANCIENT ORDER OF MORIDURA
Copyright © Peter Curran 2007

ISBN 978-184426-457-5

Cover image
'Arkimateo'
© Michael Curran 2006

Second edition published 2007 by
UPFRONT PUBLISHING LTD
Peterborough, England.

First edition published, also by Upfront Publishing, 2006

Printed by Print-on-Demand Worldwide Ltd

Peter Curran

The Ancient Order of Moridura

a novel by Peter Curran

Acknowledgements

My thanks to my family – Ivy, Michael, Maureen
and Charli for help, encouragement and proof reading.
This book is dedicated to them, and to the memory
of my mother, Moya Curran, who gave me my love
of books, and to my father, Patrick Curran, who died
when I was five years old.

Peter Curran

Peter Curran

Chapter One

"This came today. It must have been hand-delivered – there was no envelope – it was simply folded and sealed with wax…"

Paul Corr took the letter from Alistair Mackinnon, with the remains of the broken seal still on it. The heavy notepaper had a parchment-like texture, and the message was hand-written in an elegant script.

The Ancient Order of Moridura

Señor Mackinnon,

Deliver Doctor Blade to us at midday on the 10th of July in the square at Moridanza. If you fail in this, or contact any other person about the contents of this letter you will go to God on the 11th of July.

On behalf of the Grand Council,
The Magus of Moridura

Paul lifted his head and raised his eyebrows. "The Ancient Order of Moridura? I've never heard of it. Who are they?"

"Moridanza is a village in the region of Extremadura, in Spain. It's about sixty miles east of Mérida, the capital of Extremadura. I'll say more about Moridura and the Ancient Order in a moment, but I'd like your initial reactions, Paul…"

The undertone in the big Scot's voice, of most uncharacteristic uncertainty, killed the flip reply on Paul's lips. He glanced again at the letter and waved it at his friend with a dismissive gesture.

"Why treat this seriously, Alistair? It seems like a practical joke… Who is this Doctor Blade? This odd phrase - you will go to God – what does it mean?"

"Doctor Blade is the young research physicist I invited you here to interview and assess," he replied, standing up and walking to the bookcase behind his desk. The Scot was a tall man, and his erect, athletic figure belied his seventy years as he reached to the upper shelf. He pulled out a massive tome, catching its weight with his other hand. Turning, he laid it carefully on the desk, and then sat down.

"This is the Moridura Manuscript, a chronicle of the *hermandades* - the brotherhoods - in fourteenth century Spain. The original hand-lettered illuminated manuscript now lies in the monastery of Moridura, near Moridanza: this printed version was produced in Germany in the late 18th century." He opened it at a bookmarked page, then turned the book and slid it across the desk.

Paul pulled his chair closer to the desk and placed his hands gently on the volume. He shared his love of books with Alistair Mackinnon, together with a passion for classic cinema and jazz: their joint obsessions interacted with their professional relationship in a way that friends and colleagues often found baffling.

Alistair's house on the western shore of Loch Lomond in the West Highlands of Scotland was close to the research laboratories of his electronics company, Ardmurran International Electronics, in the lochside village of Ardmurran. It was built on a high spur of rock overlooking the loch, and was one of three homes; the others were a house in Edinburgh's New Town and a London flat.

Paul had spent happy times in West Craig, but the fond memories were instantly dispelled by the Latin text on the pages before him. As he translated fluently, the words of the long-dead monk echoed across the centuries and his voice seemed to fill his friend's book-lined study.

The passage bookmarked by Alistair was an account of a meeting of the Ancient Order of Moridura, comprised of two organisations - a congregation of monks and a *hermandad*, or brotherhood. The group had assembled at a pre-Roman structure known as the Portal, on the rim of *La Copa de Moridura*, a circular valley with a precipitous rock perimeter. Paul looked up from the book at Alistair, who was watching his reactions intently.

"I'm a little confused between the *hermandad*, the monks and the Ancient Order."

Alistair nodded sympathetically. "The original *hermandad*, the Ancient Order of Moridura, was a secular brotherhood of Extremaduran men, dedicated to the cult of Moridura. By the late thirteenth century, it had become militaristic and violent, but then a schism occurred in its ranks. Those of a more spiritual, mystical nature became monks, and built the monastery complex that now broods over the southern lip of *La Copa*.

"The monks of *El Monasterio de Moridura* are now a Catholic brotherhood, the Order of Moridura, more usually referred to as the Moriduran Brothers. Strictly speaking, it is not an Order, in the usual sense of a group of monasteries linked to a central superior, but rather an independent congregation of monks: it is not part of any wider group of monasteries, nor are the Brothers accountable to any superior but their Abbot; he is accountable only to the Pope. They follow most of the Benedictine rule, but don't call themselves Benedictines, but Moridurans. When the *hermandad* and the monks gather jointly for ceremonies in the monastery, they refer to themselves as the Ancient Order. Confusing, I know, but read on a wee bit more, Paul, and then you'll understand a bit better," he concluded, pointing to the book.

Paul resumed his scrutiny of the text. The anonymous author of the chronicle set down the persecution of the Ancient Order, then, with a direct narrative skill of visceral intensity, led up to a meeting around a rock formation in the centre of *La Copa de Moridura*, with the monastery as a forbidding backdrop on its the southern lip. The monks and members of the *hermandad* had assembled to witness the elevation of one of their number, Abbadocio, to Magus, a rank that had once been the pinnacle of the hierarchy of the original cult, and had survived after the schism. At the culmination of the ceremony surrounding the confirmation of the Magus, an unexpected event had occurred.

The monk's account was somewhat obscure, shrouded as it was in superstition and naked terror, but a creature of some kind suddenly appeared and attacked the Magus Elect, tearing him limb from limb in an orgy of bloody mutilation. The gathering broke up in terror: the members fled back to their homes or to the monastery, with the exception of one monk who disappeared for a time, then reappeared to become the new Magus of Moridura. The Order then entered a new, stable phase, but with the memory of the apparently supernatural events of that fateful day burned into its collective memory.

Paul leaned back in the chair, his hands still on the book. "He was there himself - he doesn't say so, but it has the feel of an eye-witness account."

Alistair nodded in agreement. "Aye, I came to the same conclusion." His tone was light, but his eyes seemed to gaze at something invisible, across a void of time, yet somehow menacingly near, almost present in the study - a primeval force.

He drew a deep breath, and said, almost flippantly, "You haven't asked the obvious question, Paul …"

Paul laughed, stood up, and grasping his left wrist with his right hand, stretched luxuriously, arching his back then pirouetted clumsily to face his friend again.

"Why do they want Doctor Blade badly enough to deliver an ultimatum like this to you? What does the wording in the note *go to God* mean?"

Alistair grunted, then reached into his desk drawer and pulled out a bound report. "The phrase means I will die," he replied, sliding the report across to Paul. "This might provide part of the answer - it is a preliminary report to the electronics company that currently employs Doctor Blade."

Paul read the report title, showing through a cutout section of the cover to the first page.

Sources of gravitational wave motion
and induced distortion in the G constant
by
Dr. A. Blade

"Before I read this, tell me this, Alistair - why should this - this Magus - send a death threat, in writing, which he must know you could take straight to the police? Law enforcement officers in every country in the world take death threats very seriously. It seems clumsy, melodramatic, wouldn't you say?"

"Melodrama isn't the Ancient Order's style, believe me," Alistair murmured. "It simply knows how ridiculous the story would seem. The death threat is encoded in their private language. To the Spanish police, the monks are a devout and respected religious congregation, and the *hermandad* is an influential fraternal organisation engaged in charitable activities, akin to the Freemasons: their stance is a bit like that of the F.B.I. under J. Edgar Hoover, denying, right up to 1957, that the Mafia existed.

"OK, but let me ask one more question before I read Doctor Blade's paper," said Paul. "How did you become involved with the Order and the monastery in the first place?"

Alistair put his hands behind his head, and leaned back. "The Moridura Manuscript was written and illuminated in the monastery. At some point in the next hundred years – a turbulent century - it was banned, and removed from the monastery by the Holy Office – the Inquisition. It should have been destroyed, but someone stopped that happening. It popped up from time to time in the libraries of various members of the Spanish aristocracy over the centuries, then vanished again in the early nineteenth century. Just over five years ago, it was offered for sale, without any prior publicity, by an anonymous collector in New York. I happened to be at the book auction, and made the successful bid.

"When I realised what I'd got, I tracked down the location of the monastery - with great difficulty, I can tell you. I then contacted the Abbot of Moridura, Brother Anselmo, and offered to gift the book to the monastery, no strings attached. I was invited to visit Moridura – a rare honour – and had a great time with the monks. In retrospect, I realise that the Spanish business contacts I used to make contact with the monastery were probably members of the *hermandad*. Anyway, that's what Santiago Manrique, my security chief in Europe believes."

Paul absorbed this, and then turned to the report. He skimmed through its technical content, then closed it and laid it flat on the desk, and leant forward, elbows on its surface with the fingers of both hands touching.

"That could be a Rosicrucian gesture, if I didn't know you better, Paul," observed Alistair dryly. "Well?"

Paul breathed deeply. "I'm not a research physicist - flicking through a complex report and then offering a superficial conclusion…" He paused. "I don't want to look a fool in your eyes…"

"Try me, wee pal," said Alistair softly, with no hint of mockery in his eyes or his tone.

Paul sat back, picked up the report, glanced at it again, and then placed it firmly on the desk. "No, it's too ridiculous for words - our friend Blade must be playing a practical joke on his egghead friends. Either that, or my school physics teacher let me down…"

Alistair gave him no comfort, but waited patiently. Paul stood up, and clasped his hands behind his head, pushing his elbows back rhythmically in a kind of callisthenic exercise. He was a small, slim man, and exuded nervous energy, in contrast to the solid composure of his friend.

"My exposition on gravity is based on a C grade in O-level physics - please treat it with the respect it deserves, Alistair - I may submit it to the Royal Society!" He adopted a rigid posture, with his arms at his sides, and looked straight ahead of him.

"Gravitation is a weak force – a very weak force - although it does great things; it can be viewed as wave motion, with waves of great length. Waves must have sources, and it has been suggested that G waves emanate from one or more points in the Universe. Questions over gravity are still holding up the development of a unified theory of everything."

Alistair smiled in spite of himself at Paul's parody of the wooden delivery of a learned-by-rote definition by a schoolboy in the science class, but he was impressed that he had retained so much. "Great! Good on you," he said. "Now, the report..."

Paul ceased his gyrations and sat down heavily in the chair. He took a deep breath, and scanned parts of the report again, and then he spoke, very quietly.

"Dr. Blade claims to have identified at least one source of gravitational waves..."

He shook his head disbelievingly and looked up quizzically at Alistair, as if to check that he had correctly understood this extraordinary statement.

"...and using equipment he has developed, he claims to be able to modulate the wave and manipulate the gravitational force. It's patently nonsense: his reputation, if he ever had one, will soon be in shreds! Does he intend to submit this junk for peer review by publishing it in a scientific journal?"

"Look at the Moridura Manuscript account again - the part about the ceremony in the Cup of Moridura," Alistair responded coolly, ignoring Paul's scepticism, "then tell me what connection there could be with gravitation."

"Connection or not, there was nothing about unbinding the planets from their orbits," said Paul sarcastically, reaching again for the ancient tome. He was not looking at the older man as he made his flippant remark, and did not see the way in which the blood left Alistair's cheeks and the sudden hollow look in his eyes. Opening the book again, Paul quickly found the part referred to, and began to translate the Latin text, fluently and without hesitation, as he would have translated Cicero not so many years ago in his Oxford college.

"...and as the brethren of Moridura prepared for the elevation of Abbadocio to the rank of Magus, a great pressure in the air came upon the Cup around the Throne: the stone moved and the rock cracked and there was a great shaking of the earth itself under their feet. The brethren cried aloud in their fear and bewilderment.

"The Throne split asunder and then the forces in the air seemed to focus and compress, and a creature formed, terrible to behold; it moved upon Abbadocio and raised him aloft; his features became flattened and grotesque to behold as his skull cracked; his veins stood out like cords, then spewed blood as they burst under the awful grip of the shimmering beast of Moridura. And then the Throne was whole again..."

Paul paused, clearly moved by account of the horrific end of the unfortunate would-be Magus. He closed the book. "That's politics for you!" he laughed shakily, trying to recover his composure, "Poor old Abbadocio - he was the victim of a squeeze play, Alistair."

"Humour's all very well, Paul," said Alistair, with no trace of levity in his voice, "but sometimes it shields us from a reality we don't want to face."

"Is that a rebuke?" said Paul lightly.

"No - no, not at all – don't get all sensitive on me: it's an attempt to bring home to you the seriousness of this matter. Now, to get back to your review of the passage in the manuscript..."

"You clearly have formed some hypothesis yourself, Alistair. Why not offer it?" Paul said soberly, lifting the Blade report and using it as a pointer.

"Because I need an independent analysis from you: because I value your objective judgement, Paul. If I may borrow some jargon from the film-makers lexicon, I need your take on it – please…"

There was a most uncharacteristic pleading note in his voice now, and an undertone of deep concern. Paul sighed, and picked up on the film metaphor.

"I'll cut to the chase - the elevation was possibly not only a status elevation, it could have been a literal raising up - to the throne of rock - and perhaps by means other than normal: a levitation, rather than an elevation. Levitation is a well-reported phenomenon, though never substantiated. Levitation could be described as…"

He paused, and Alistair Mackinnon filled the silence. "… a wee distortion of gravity, Paul?"

The question was more of a confirmatory statement than a query: Paul nodded his assent. "Go on," murmured Alistair encouragingly, "there must be more, surely?"

"The atmospheric disturbance, whatever really caused it," continued Paul, his mind's eye focused on the events at the Throne of the Magus, "would have been understandably interpreted as the materialisation of a monster - Moridura, or the monster of Moridura - which then went on to behave in a typically monster-like way, ripping the would-be Magus apart."

Alistair nodded in agreement.

"How else could the observers of that superstitious age interpret such phenomena?" he said.

"Quite - but the description could bear another interpretation, that of a field disturbance, some kind of magnetic storm…"

"A gravitational distortion?"

"You force the words from me, Alistair - but yes - the appearance of the tortured Magus-Elect could be seen as typical of intolerable G-force. Do you remember the old 1940s science fiction film, *Destination Moon*? That was the first film I recall that tried to show the effect of the *G* force during the lift-off of a rocket. It's all been done again many times cinematically, with better special effects, and we've seen the real-life version in simulators, and from the cctv cameras in the rockets themselves."

"The throne - what about the throne?" queried his friend eagerly.

"It split, or parted - to reveal what? It doesn't say..." Paul mused reflectively, then fell silent, his mind filled with the image of the rock splitting.

The pause hung heavily in the air of the study, and then Alistair murmured slowly: "It split but came together again..."

"Indeed - it opened, or split, but later closed up. A hallucination. Mass hallucination – they'd been eating mushrooms - *peyote* or something like it - hallucinogenic. The local wine had gone off - diseased bread – ergot, you name it. It probably happened all the time in the Middle Ages, and may account for a lot of religious experiences. Did you know that the visions of Hildegard of Bingen, the 12th-century musical nun, were probably migrainous in origin - shimmering star-like patterns on wavy lines?" Paul said, a note of appeal in his voice.

"Jesus Christ! A musical nun! You make her sound like something from *The Sound of Music*," said Alistair. "Why don't you want to believe it?"

He walked round from behind the massive desk and placed his hand on Paul's shoulder. He was over six feet tall and Paul Corr was five foot eight inches at most. Alistair looked down affectionately at his young friend.

"I always did subscribe to Occam's razor," replied Paul defensively. "The simplest explanation that fits the facts is usually the correct one. William of Occam was a monk too, a 13th-century British monk. If he has a Moriduran counterpart today, that monk would also advise me to make the minimum number of assumptions. You are leading me towards a conclusion that, however you care to put it, disturbs the fabric of our Universe. Why believe such an extraordinary explanation, when so many others present themselves?" He tilted his head back, widened his eyes and held out an expressive open palm. "Anyway, Blade's use of a dish aerial instead of the laser interferometer arrays now being used makes no sense at all."

"Well, for a start, leading scientists in the field are engaged in a helluva lot of speculation about gravity – a lot of theories, few facts. It remains a mystery. What cuts the Gordian knot here is that Doctor Blade has now achieved an experimental result that appears to confirm the theory," Alistair responded. "However," he added quickly, seeing Paul's disbelief, "in a way that suggests that the phenomena that can be produced are strictly limited: the Earth is not going to fall from its orbit – yet!" He gestured towards the door of the study. "Come down to the laboratory in the wee lift and I'll test your scepticism, Paul Corr."

He pressed a section of the panelling; it slid aside to reveal a plain elevator door: opening that in turn, he entered, followed by his friend. Paul was familiar with the concealed elevator, but felt the familiar frisson of boyish delight that he had experienced when he had first entered Alistair's "wee lift" many years before. The elevator, to Paul's romantic soul, was pure dime novel. It dated from the 1930s, and had been installed by the previous owner of the house to access his woodworking workshop.

It now provided access to a small, well-equipped laboratory on the lower level at the rear of the house; this backed on to a large, flagged courtyard with a low wall above a five-metre drop to the loch shore. Built on rocky promontory, the entrance hall, the main reception rooms and library of West Craig were level with the parking area at the front of the house, with a long driveway leading down to gates on the lochside road.

"Good old Otis," he chuckled, giving the elevator his pet name, although the real manufacturer was somewhat more obscure than the famous American elevator company, "he still smells of rubber, Alistair. Why don't you buy him a deodorant?"

"It's not Otis that's smelly, it's the shaft - it needs venting," replied Alistair, as they reached the laboratory

"If Dr. Blade is successful, Otis will be redundant!" retorted Paul, but Alistair seemed unamused by this remark, as he led the way across the tiled lab floor.

Paul was becoming more curious by the moment about Dr. Blade, the physicist Alistair had invited him to meet and assess as a prospective addition to the research and development staff at Ardmurran. What would this prodigy be like? Paul had a great deal of experience of young scientists, and they fell broadly into two categories – those who had chosen applied science and those who intended to pursue their life's work in pure research. The hardcore pure scientists headed for the big colleges, universities and scientific foundations, but others wanted the less-rarefied atmosphere, and perhaps the rewards, that R&D in industry could provide. Some made the wrong choice and found it hard to change direction.

It was some time since he had been in Alistair's little home laboratory, but he saw at once that it had changed since his last visit. The comfortable clutter was gone, as was the feel of a dilettante occupant that had characterised it, in spite of the fact that its owner had made his fortune in the hard-nosed electronics business. Whereas previously it had been the base for minor experiments to remind the industrialist of his roots, before the demands of international commerce had taken over his working life, it now had the distinct air of serious research. Paul was puzzled.

"Have you acquired a taste for do-it-yourself, Alistair? Why the investment at home?"

"It's Dr. Blade's laboratory at the moment - has been for the last three months or so. The good doctor is on a sabbatical from Lloyd Lonnen's company in America, and is living in a flat in the village," replied Alistair abstractedly.

"Blade?" said Paul in surprise. "But why not use the lab in your main site? The facilities are superb - and I would have thought the security was as good or better than you could deliver here." As he spoke, Paul felt for the first time that Alistair was concealing something from him, and the answer he got did not dispel this nagging suspicion.

"Well, yes - in theory, yes; but in practice, security in a large location can be patchy, and my security chief is in Madrid at the moment on other business. Too many chinks in the armour - too many people to trust. Human frailty…"

"…and all that!' Paul completed his friend's meandering reply, flatly dismissive. Something was definitely being hidden from him here.

"Anyway, there is security at the house at the moment – for tonight, really – for the party – gatecrashers and so forth," Alistair went on unconvincingly.

Ignoring the sceptical look from Paul, he took his arm and drew him towards a bench near a window that looked out on the large paved courtyard, bounded by a low wall at the edge. Paul remembered the courtyard as being empty except for some ornamental stone urns, but these had now been removed, obviously to make space for an incongruously large dish aerial, with a complex apparatus in the centre of it, pointing at the cloudless blue Highland sky over the loch.

"Are you having problems getting satellite television in the Highlands? How big is it?"

"Four metres - but it's a toy compared to say, Arecibo. It's only big compared to a satellite dish on a village house." Alistair moved towards one of the benches as he replied.

"Arecibo? The Puerto Rican one - Cornell's radio telescope?" Paul said softly. "So it's not a satellite dish, it's for radio astronomy…"

Alistair turned a knob on one of the control panels on the bench and the dish turned soundlessly through a few degrees, its central apparatus pointing into the vastness of the cosmos at an unknown destination, reaching back through the mists of time.

"It is not a radio wave aerial - you have probably guessed that it seeks another kind of wave."

"It's probing for the G source," Paul said lightly, and Alistair smiled faintly.

"Are you trying to keep my spirits up, or your own?"

Paul gazed for a moment at the dish, and then came across to the panel. "May I try?" he asked, in such a genuine, eager little boy voice that Alistair's momentary irritation vanished as he remembered the child who had first visited his library and his laboratory in the company of his father, Patrick Corr, before his premature death. Paul was glowing with intellectual curiosity and enthusiasm as he twisted the knob and rotated and tilted the dish with little grunts of pleasure.

"Having fun?"

"Yes, yes! Now if I knew what I was doing, I would have more fun still," grinned Paul. "I always like the feel of remotely controlling something."

"Or somebody. That's why you became a headhunter perhaps," said Alistair teasingly.

"I'm not at all sure what I am at the moment," Paul parried, letting go of the knob and facing the big man squarely. He fixed Alistair with a deeply solemn penetrating gaze, and stroked his chin gravely. "I am trying to find myself…"

Alistair failed to respond to his attempt at humour. "Why did you decide to go into executive search consultancy, Paul - you could have - well, you could have…" He left the sentence unfinished.

"…done something more important," said Paul, completing it for him. "I suppose I could have engaged in research into some obscure byway of classical literature or got a research fellowship in something or other, yes. But I need a more dynamic involvement with my fellow man than the traditional outlets for a Classicist permit - you know that. Anyhow, you've been grateful for my professional expertise in finding you the best brains in the business - have you not? Persuading high-fliers to come to a Highland village away from the city lights isn't easy. Anyway, I do think it's important work - it keeps the wheels of industry turning."

He looked hard at Alistair. "Go on, say it. It's not what my father would have wanted. Well, it was already too late while he was still alive."

Alistair regretted raising the subject: the premature loss of a loved one had touched them both - his wife Shelagh had been killed shortly after they bought West Craig, driving her car on the lochside road on a shopping trip to Balloch. There were no children from the marriage, and he coped with his grief by immersing himself in his work. He never remarried, although friends often urged him to do so, to his intense irritation. He placed his arm around Paul's shoulder. "Let me show you the Universe at work," he said gruffly, steering him towards the bench.

On it was a strange construction of stainless steel, in the form of a boxlike framework enclosing a small platform on which lay, of all things, an ordinary matchbox. A complex electronic rig, consisting of several printed circuit boards and banks of microchips was wired to the contraption. At its heart was a black, rocklike substance set in what appeared to be gold. A cable ran from it to a socket on the bench.

Alistair threw a switch, part of the standard power services of the bench. Paul could detect no sight or sound of power, but presumed the thing was now live. Alistair went over to the control for the dish aerial and placed his hand on the dial.

"Watch the matchbox." he said softly and began to turn the knob.

As Paul dutifully stared at it, the matchbox lifted about two inches from the little platform, and stayed there without visible means of support.

"Good God!" said Paul.

"I hope he is", said Alistair fervently, in an almost liturgical response.

Chapter Two

'When August comes, I will have been working for almost thirty-five years," grumbled Manuel Ortega, "It's enough for any man. Why must I go on?"

The broad back of Fidelicia Ortega straightened for a moment from her task. "Because you must, as I must: we work until we die."

"Soon I will be fifty, and then what? Is there nothing more? Do I deserve no more of life than this?"

Manuel's tone was querulous, and tears sprang to his eyes at the thought of his mortality, and of how he would be forced to spend the years left to him. Fidelicia sighed. These outbursts were becoming more frequent of late, and her husband did less and less in the café, and virtually nothing in bed.

Manuel had the café, the taxi, and rented out his four guest bedrooms when he could: most visitors were only passing through the village, and left after a meal or a drink. A few optimistic tourists arrived in Moridanza in the early evening, intending to visit the monastery on the following day. After driving to *La Copa* in the morning, they returned for lunch, complaining bitterly about the condition of the road, the dangers of the cliff path and the refusal of the monks to admit them to the monastery. Sometimes *hermandad* members from Mérida, usually of Grand Council status, took a room, and Manuel fussed obsequiously round them.

"Your father lived until his ninety third year and died singing in the bar - are you to go to grass at forty nine?" Fidelicia warmed to her theme. "Perhaps the brothers will take you in to the monastery: you could do odd jobs around the kitchens. Who knows, they might accept you as an *oblate*.

Or you could join the *hermandad*. With only one mouth to feed, I could run the café, maybe even learn to drive. After all, I am only forty nine, and not ready to sit in the sun just yet!" Fidelicia felt that the powerful reproach in her unyielding back carried even more force than her words.

She waited a moment, clattered the pots, and then she looked slowly over her shoulder to gauge the impact of her message. Manuel was not looking at her, nor was he gazing at the floor with his normal martyred expression: he was staring straight ahead with a strange light in his eyes. Mother of God, thought Fidelicia, he is actually considering the monastery!

She went across the room and stared down at him. He looked suddenly like an eager youth, poised on the chair as if ready to leap to the door. Her heart softened as she saw through the thickset, middle-aged man before her to the lithe, handsome boy who had whispered his plans for the future to her such a long time, yet such a little time ago. What had changed his mood so suddenly? Fidelicia carefully searched her words to find a clue to her husband's transformation. When she found it, her heart raced.

"You are considering Don Ferdinand's offer to involve you in the *hermandad*. Manuel, you must put it from your mind as you did before. *Madre de Dios*, why did I say it? Why did I mention them?"

"You said it, and now I have thought it. This time, the thought will not go away. It could be my salvation, Fidelicia."

"Your damnation. Manuel - you must not consider it. You know the things they do - besides, why would he want you? What could you offer in return?" A rising note of hysteria was entering her voice, and she could not suppress it.

"I have the car. I know the village, I know the monastery. I know many things - about many people. I speak English. I have access to my father's diaries..." Manuel rose to his feet, folded his arms, and stared proudly and defiantly at Fidelicia.

She sat down heavily on a chair, appalled at what her idle choice of words had brought to the day. From nowhere, in the heat of the day, the spectre of the *hermandad* had been conjured up by her thoughtless scolding. Her husband was like a man renewed, new purpose in his eyes, in his restless movement, a man restored to his world by a prospect which terrified her: she looked up at him despairingly.

"Manuel, you must see what it would mean! It is fine to run errands for Don Ferdinand, but to get involved in his other activities, with the *hermandad*! They have brought so many to the dust - please, not you. Do not bring this upon us. We can manage - we will change, I will change. Cristobal will help us, we could borrow money, buy a truck. There are vegetables to be hauled to Mérida. In time, maybe five years, you could hire a boy, take it easy. Esteban is a strong, willing lad – he..."

Manuel held up both hands, and glared majestically. "Stop, woman, stop! I will hear no more, no more about the Order, of trucks, of Cristobal, of Esteban. Evil! Do you question the integrity of Ferdinand of Moridanza?"

Fidelicia crossed herself hastily, and crouched on the chair, shaking her head. "Please, please, you must abandon this mad idea - it will be the end of us, I know it..."

"In five years - no - not five years - not three years: in one year – one - I can be a man of substance with their help. Have they not done as much for many? Why not Manuel Ortega? I will see Don Ferdinand today - this very day. I will give him my response to his offer – and my terms..."

"If you do," screamed Fidelicia, rising to her feet, raising her arms, and facing him "you might as well go the heart of *La Copa* and summon *La Bestia*!"

For the first time in their thirty-two years of marriage, Manuel struck her, a violent, backhanded blow across the mouth, which brought the blood to her lip almost instantly.

"In God's name, silence, woman! Have you no fear?" he gasped, his face ashen. As Fidelicia sank back to the chair, he was at her side, afraid and instantly contrite.

"Fidelicia, my love, my own one, forgive me. But to say such a thing!"

They huddled together in their first moment of sharing and tenderness for many months. At last Fidelicia pulled away and wiped the blood from her mouth with her apron. She drew a deep, shuddering breath to calm herself.

"Do it, and I will leave. I will go to Cristobal and Maria and stay with them. I cannot live in the same house as you if you do this." She forced out the words with an effort, her voice carrying both fear and determination.

Manuel's anger returned, this time cold and implacable.

"Fidelicia, you are my wife and I love you and respect you, but you do not understand men's affairs. If you go to our daughter you will shame me. But you must do what you feel is right - I will not keep you. I will explain to Don Ferdinand and he will understand, in his wisdom. The *hermandades* are an honourable part of our history: they still exist in many regions, doing charitable work. When you see that your fears are based on nothing, and you see my success, you will return, and I will welcome you. Now I must do what I have to do..." He looked at her for a moment then left the kitchen by the back door.

Walking round from the yard into the lane, he climbed into his battered Volkswagen and drove out of the small car park to the road, where he stopped for a moment, reflecting on the scene in the kitchen. He looked briefly at the front door of the café, hoping to see Fidelicia there waving to him, as she often did when he went on a trip to Mérida, but she was not there, or at least, not visible.

As he drove away, he reflected on her words about the *hermandad*: could there be any truth in her argument? Had membership of it destroyed men of Moridanza? He reviewed the obvious candidates among his contemporaries - Pepe, stabbed by a drunk Englishman; Esteban's father, a suicide who left a widow and a son penniless, and Pablo – Pablo

Miguenez, his friend, formerly a man of property who now...

As the name entered his head, he looked out of the car window and saw Carlota Miguenez, who worked as a maid in Don Ferdinand's house, walking towards the town centre. Her father, formerly a man of substance, was now a gardener for the Don. The girl was strikingly pretty. As she turned to look at the car, Manuel waved. She waved back and he felt a surge of desire. He grinned to himself at the thought that there was life in him yet, at almost fifty. And why not? His father had sired him at fifty or so, and had still been trying to grope the pretty English girls at eighty years of age.

As he drove out of the village, past the last houses, the road fell sharply and gracefully to the plain. In spite of his half a century in and around Moridanza, Manuel still felt pleasure at the sight, with Don Ferdinand's elegant house and gardens on the west of the plain - his vineyards and wheat fields surrounding it - and the monastery of Moridura lying solidly on the black ridge to the north that constituted the southern arc of the *La Copa de Moridura*.

"I am of this place, as my father was before me," thought Manuel with some satisfaction as he drove the four miles down to the gates of the estate, and turned into the first section of the long driveway.

About half a mile up the drive, he began to slow down as he approached the two stone lodges on either side of the drive. At the sound of the Volkswagen's approach, a man emerged from each lodge, walked to the centre of the drive and faced the car. Each was carrying a shotgun casually in the crook of the arm: they were relaxed and smiling, and one waved.

"Manuel Ortega, what brings you here?" one called out cheerfully, approaching the car window. His companion did not move, but grinned and shouted. "He will beg Don Ferdinand to ask Fidelicia to forgive him for his drunkenness yet again - is it not so, Manuel?"

The man at the window laughed as he casually looked past Manuel into the car, his eyes sweeping lightly across the rear seats. "The boot, *mi amigo*," he requested easily, and Manuel got out to lift the front boot lid. After a cursory inspection, he said conversationally "You must have passed Carlota on the road, eh?"

"It is hard to pass Carlota at any time. Oh, to be twenty and single! She blooms like a flower. I envy you both: you are fortunate to see her daily."

The two men exchanged glances, and there was something in their smiles that Manuel did not understand. It was not the unspoken sexual consensus in the matter of a pretty señorita that one man might establish with another, but the sharing of the knowledge of something else, something imminent and inevitable.

Manuel got back into the Volkswagen, and leaned out of the window. "*Buenas tardes, caballeros,*" he called out as the guards moved back and waved him on. Driving up the last stretch, he thought about the two men. They were not from Moridanza, but from Mérida, and although they had been with Don Ferdinand for three years or thereabouts, Manuel never called them by name. He suddenly realised that he didn't know why this was so. He knew their first names: the one who had inspected the car was called Francesco and the other Frederico, and Don Ferdinand referred to them by name all the time, as did Carlota. Yet Pablo Miguenez never did, nor, as far as Manuel could recall, did any other servant at the villa, nor did anyone in Moridanza. They were known colloquially and collectively as *los artilleros*, but never to their faces, except perhaps when Carlota teased them, but then Carlota was allowed licence to do many things, because of her beauty.

He swung the taxi round in front of the villa instead of driving round the side as he would normally have done when answering a call: he never carried passengers for the Don, for the visitors to the villa either had their own vehicles, or hired cars, or were transported in Ferdinand's Mercedes by the chauffeur.

Manuel's humble role was normally that of a carrier of packages, letters to village tradesmen and like matters. He was not permitted to offer lifts to the servants, much as he would have liked to, especially Carlota. As he got out of the Volkswagen, Don Ferdinand came on to the terrace and called out: "Manuel - *buenas tardes* - please come up!"

An imposing figure, erect, elegant and with the assurance of many generations of breeding, power and influence in his every gesture and inflection of voice, Ferdinand was almost forty-two years of age: Manuel knew that, because as an eight year old child, he had been at the greatest fiesta Moridanza had ever known to celebrate his birth. The Abbot of Moridura had come to bless the child, and a procession with many banners, statues and candles had wended its way down from the monastery, a full seven miles away, across the plain to the villa to honour the newborn son of Don Lope.

Manuel went up the steps to the terrace and followed him into the hall: Don Ferdinand gestured to the open library doors. "Please go in - I will join you in a moment, my friend."

Manuel, now full of apprehension, entered the room slowly and nervously, pausing uncertainly just inside. He had never been in the library before, but overcoming his nervousness he began to look around the room. The polished wooden floor seemed almost a seamless extension of the dark, ceiling-high bookcases. The spines of the books stared calmly back at him, secure in their timeless content, neither inviting nor rejecting inspection. Manuel would not have dared to touch them: this patrician collection rivalled the great library in the monastery. The room was sparsely furnished with reading desks, austere chairs and a huge antique globe of the world. He was tentatively approaching an open book placed on a lectern when he heard Ferdinand's voice in the hall. Pausing, he turned and moved cautiously till he had a line of sight through the doors.

He could see the Don, speaking to someone just out of view, and then he heard another voice, one that he could not identify, responding with suppressed anger to Ferdinand's words. Manuel was shocked beyond belief: who would dare to address the Don thus in his own home? He waited for an icy blast of anger from Ferdinand, but it did not come: His tone was calm, soothing and conciliatory. Then the other moved into view, but with his back to the library, and Manuel saw with astonishment the black habit of a Moriduran brother.

His bafflement increased – he knew every monk and he should have been able to instantly identify the voice, yet he could not. The fact that anyone could display anger openly to Don Ferdinand in itself was a source of wonderment, but from a Moriduran brother it was incredible: the monastery, although it had substantial financial resources of its own, was dependent for many things on the munificence of Ferdinand, and the relationship between it and the family went back as far as Philip the Second.

The monk's voice became louder. The language was English and the accent was American. Manuel strained to hear and to understand, but could just interpret isolated words.

"… not as planned … since the … airport … this time, no further delay … must have…"

Then, through his long, narrow field of vision between the doors, Manuel saw the Don's right hand dart forward. The monk's flow of words stopped abruptly and his cowl fell backwards from his head. Cropped, coppery hair was revealed, without tonsure, and the unshorn monk made a choking sound, his hands trying to break the iron grip on his throat: he fell to his knees as Don Ferdinand pressed forward and down. For a moment, Manuel was looking directly at the face of the Don, gazing down icily and fixedly at his victim.

In terror, he stepped backwards and turned around to face into the library, afraid lest Ferdinand look up and see him witness such a scene.

As in a dream, he heard Ferdinand's voice, flat and hard. "Enough - no more. Now you must leave my house and await my pleasure. You will never be allowed to pass the lodges again. If you wish to communicate with me, you may send someone to leave a message there - now go."

The unmistakable sound of Ferdinand's footsteps approaching the library was followed by harsh, heavy breathing from the hall, then, after a pause, other footsteps retreating. Manuel moved quickly to the window and looked across the veranda to the front door. A black-robed figure emerged and hurried down the steps and set off down the driveway on foot: after a few steps, the monk turned and faced the villa for a moment. The heavy folds of the cowl hid his features from clear view, but the eyes seemed to glare from its deep shadows.

"Manuel - my most sincere apologies..." Ferdinand's voice jerked Manuel around, and he fell into a half-crouch of subservience as he faced the calm, upright man who, a moment before had been throttling the mysterious visitor.

"Don Ferdinand, I - Fidelicia and I - this afternoon, we talked, and..."

Don Ferdinand pointed to a chair. "Please, sit down Manuel. You have come at last about Eduardo's diaries. I knew you would, in time, and that Fidelicia would be unhappy when you reached your decision. That is only to be expected. It is right for a man to be bold and a woman to be cautious: this is the balance we find in a good marriage, one such as we are both blessed with, my good old friend."

Manuel stared at the Don in bewilderment, his prepared words falling to pieces in his head. The crude bargaining strategy he had formulated on his way to the villa now seemed naive. The Don knew all things, saw to the heart of men - was this not the street wisdom of Moridanza? Yet he, a café proprietor, a taxi driver, had thought to try his wits against him, to negotiate from a position of strength. He moved backwards respectfully towards the chair, but could not bring himself to sit while the Don stood. Ferdinand went across to a reading desk and sat casually on one edge, motioning again to Manuel, who then sank into the chair.

"My friend, your father's diaries are very dear to you - the very thoughts of a man we all loved and respected. You cannot bring yourself to sell them like trinkets in the café: they are beyond price to you - and to me. Do not be ashamed of your hesitation and confusion: your impulse was right - trust your instincts, but also try to understand Fidelicia's fears."

Manuel, overcome by his empathy, took a long breath then began to speak.

Chapter Three

Alistair Mackinnon's house on the western shore of Loch Lomond, near the Scottish highland village of Ardmurran, was ablaze with welcoming light for his guests arriving at a dinner party in Paul Corr's honour. An invitation to West Craig guaranteed good food, fine wines, malt whisky, music, and stimulating conversation, and laughing friends arrived in cars or on foot, in a mood of keen anticipation.

The guest of honour, watching from his bedroom window as he struggled with his bow tie, wished fervently that someone else could have been the focus of the gathering. Still, he looked forward to the company of beautiful, intelligent women, also a reliable component of Alistair's parties, and to the inevitable debate on whether a Scottish single malt could be compared to a French *grand cru* in its range and subtlety. As he turned to get his dinner jacket, his eye caught the quite ordinary empty matchbox that Alistair had given him as a memento of what had been an extraordinary demonstration of anti-gravity, however modest the mass suspended.

The beginning of a revolution in materials handling and transportation, his friend had called the Blade effect, outlining with his forceful Glaswegian fluency the immense industrial potential of such a breakthrough. Paul, a sceptic to the core and familiar with Alistair's fondness for magic and illusions, had taken a great deal of convincing that he was not the victim of a clever trick, to be jeered at later over a convivial malt for his gullibility. But the electronic rig itself, and his friend's total willingness to let him try the effect personally, without let or hindrance, had finally convinced him.

"It's John W. Campbell's dream come true, Paul," Alistair had enthused, referring to the legendary editor of *Astounding Science Fiction*, the greatest pulp magazine of the genre. "It's a breadboard contraption that negates gravity."

Science fiction was one of the arcane byways in Alistair's love of books, which included the printed word in forms ranging from the *Incunabula* to a ticket from the last tramcar to run in Glasgow. He had a very special love for the classic period of pulp *scientifiction* - the original name for the genre - as he insisted in calling it. His final flourish had been to indicate that he would produce Doctor Blade at the party, having concealed the good doctor in lodgings in the town.

The apparent restoration of his friend's good spirits had not deceived Paul: it was clear that Alistair was still deeply worried, by the threat and by something else which Paul was convinced he was hiding from him. The explanation he had given was that the Ancient Order feared that Blade's discovery, once exploited commercially, would create such massive publicity for anti-gravity effects as to make their cult irrelevant, eliminating the mystical basis of its power over its credulous followers. Somehow, this didn't ring true to Paul, plausible though it sounded. Lifting matchboxes seemed a long way from bursting blood vessels and dismemberment. However, it was not Paul's way to confront his doubts: he would wait for the explanation that he felt sure would eventually be forthcoming.

The sound of Bix Beiderbecke's pristine cornet exquisitely stating the syncopated lead of *At the Jazzband Ball* rose from the ground floor, the eighty year-old recording rendered fresh and clear by modern processing techniques and Alistair's high fidelity equipment. He knew that this was to lure him down. Paul's tastes in music had formerly leaned heavily towards string quartets, baroque wind ensembles and classic rock. Alistair had brought the younger man to an appreciation of the range of jazz via Bix, by persuading him to play *At the Jazzband Ball* twenty times, against a wager that he would play it willingly for the twenty first or never play it again.

Secure in the knowledge that the taste for that uniquely poignant sound, once acquired, could never be denied, Alistair had waited out the hour complacently until his young friend admitted himself a willing loser and played it again, entering into a voluntary enslavement for the rest of his life.

The hour produced one of their timeless moments in eternity, as Paul called it, with Alistair roaring with laughter at such Southern romanticism, but in his Celtic heart secretly agreeing. Bix came to stay, closely followed by Louis Armstrong, Lester Young and Charlie Parker, although Bird proved a harder nut to crack than twenty plays: it had taken a weekend of *Parker's Mood* and Alistair, in his croaking baritone, singing the melody of *Cherokee* along with *KoKo* to convince Paul. He had coined his own name for Parker - Baroodelybebop - parodying one of the rhythmic clichés of bop - but accepted him into the pantheon on Alistair's exasperated verdict that if Paul didn't like him, it was his musical taste, and not the towering genius of Bird that was deficient.

As he tugged at his evening suit in front of the dressing table mirror in an attempt to achieve a forever-unrealisable ideal of sartorial elegance, a gentle knock sounded on the door of the bedroom. He called out.

"Yes, a moment, please…"

He went to the door and opened it, to be dazzled by a smile that wiped all other thoughts from his mind. The lips around the smile moved and the vision spoke, in a soft American accent.

"I've been sent to bring you downstairs - I'm Angeline."

She thrust out her hand cheerfully. "You're smaller than I thought you'd be…"

Paul resisted the temptation to give the caustic Bogart retort from *The Big Sleep* to a similar vertical challenge, and took her hand, moving awkwardly out of the room and closing the door behind him with his free hand.

"Are you going to let go?" she laughed.

He stared at her uncomprehendingly.

"My hand …"

Paul flushed and released it. "I'm sorry - for holding on and for being smaller than you thought I'd be."

Angeline was tall, maybe five foot nine, with glorious coppery red hair and the classic redhead's complexion. Her face was finely boned, with flat-planed cheeks and a mobile mouth that defied description, seeming to define her personality all on its own. Her eyes were green, and shone with amusement at her confused escort's discomfiture.

Paul made a desperate attempt to regain his poise. "I don't usually like American women…" he said, paused, and followed this gaffe with "Oh, Christ!"

Angeline laughed again. "That has to be a compliment - nobody could be so maladroit with an insult!" She took his arm and tugged him towards the balcony rail overlooking the big downstairs room.

"Let me show you the bear pit," she said, "They're all either Company or village – or both. I have a small flat in Ardmurran, so I know them all," and then, as they looked down into the growing crowd below, she called out, to Paul's acute embarrassment.

"Here he is, Alistair – all scrubbed up and ready for anything!"

Alistair looked up from the centre of a group of guests. "You found him, then - was he decent?"

"I guess so," replied Angeline, "but he doesn't like American women - is that decent, Jimmy, you tell me!"

Paul smiled reluctantly at Angeline's use of the all-purpose Glasgow Christian name - she had inflected it pretty well for an American. Alistair always maintained there were forty-three tonal delivery variations to Jimmy, ranging from polite interrogative to overt threat.

To Paul's further annoyance, Alistair addressed his guests in a boxing ringmaster style, raising his arms and bawling out "*Mesdames et Messieurs - attention! Voilà! Mon cher ami*, ma wee pal - Paul Corr!"

Angeline, however, gripped him firmly by the arm, flashing such a devastating smile at him that it blotted out all self-consciousness. "Let's really make an entrance - let's show them, little Paul!" she murmured. Paul got the feeling that he could do anything with this woman by his side. His shyness fell from him like a discarded cloak, and looking straight into the dancing lights in her eyes, he said "OK by me - let's do it in style."

Not even the fact that a confederate of Alistair's had now triggered a fanfare of Bach trumpets on the hi-fi put them off their stately pace, as they walked heads high with measured tread down the staircase.

"Have you starred in B-movies before?" Angeline said through her teeth, without looking away from the by now wildly applauding guests. Paul managed to hold himself together until the final step, then collapsed in helpless laughter, supporting himself on the newel post as the guests crowded round them both on the final triumphant chord of the fanfare.

Alistair didn't attempt individual introductions at this stage, but many of his neighbours and friends introduced themselves. Paul estimated the number of guests at about thirty, with ages ranging from late teens to a couple in their late sixties or early seventies. Most were Scots, and from the town: the older couple, loosely contemporaries of Alistair's, turned out to be the proprietor of the village pub and his wife. Alistair referred to him affectionately as *Le Patron*, because he was a devotee of the Quintet of the Hot Club of France, and because he spoke French as fluently as his delightful French wife spoke English. *Le Patron* spoke of hearing Coleman Hawkins as a boy in the forties, and his wife recounted fascinating anecdotes of the underground jazz she had heard as a child during the occupation.

Paul became engrossed in their reminiscences, and lost Angeline to the other guests. He finally found her again just before they went in to dinner. Alistair expertly placed his guests at the massive table, and Paul rejoiced inwardly at being seated next to Angeline.

"Fate, in the unlikely form of a large Scotsman, has thrown us together, Mademoiselle Angeline," he said, "and we must accept our destiny. Perhaps we are linked throughout eternity in ways we cannot know. Our descent of the staircase was a descent into an unknown future..." He looked expectantly for her smile at his witticism, but was met instead with a look of infinite poignancy. "Is anything the matter?" he said hesitantly.

She looked down at her plate for a moment, then up again, and a smile came again, like the sun breaking through clouds.

"You're closer than you know, Englishman," she said sternly in a mock middle-European villain's accent, "but we must speak no more of zis!"

Laughter and wine filled the evening: obscure single malts were produced and admired under threats from Alistair to lay waste to the vineyards of France. Angeline glowed and Paul felt that he sparkled. Toasts were proposed to the Auld Alliance between Scotland and France, and Paul felt left out. More toasts were drunk, then they all drifted through the lounge, to more jazz, heavy vintage rock, then bluegrass music, with Alistair extolling the virtues of the banjo, telling Angeline that it was the only indigenous American instrument.

As the night wore on, the party began to thin out: guests departed noisily at first, then more quietly. Eventually, Paul, Angeline, Alistair and Le Patron and his wife were left around a table in the lounge, with Le Patron's wife holding them enthralled with tales of the activities of the *Maquis*, the

French resistance movement, in her home village in the early 1940s.

Angeline told Le Patron that her father had been too young to be in the Second World War, but that her maternal grandfather had been in the D-Day landings in France. Paul caught a curious ambivalence in her tone in her remark about her father, something indefinable. His own sense of loss of a much-loved father had heightened Paul's awareness of the filial relationship in others; Alistair sometimes teased him about it gently.

Angeline turned to Paul. "Where are you from, Paul – London?"

Paul shook his head. "No. I live in the village I was born in, Rowley Bottom, in Buckinghamshire. But I do use a company flat in London as a *pied-a-terre.*"

Le Patron smiled. "Rowley Bottom... It sounds so – well, so English..."

"I suppose it is," Paul said slowly, "yes, it is very English, I suppose – as English as Ardmurran is Scottish."

Alistair waved his arms pityingly, and turned to *Le Patron.* "These southerners - they are so conscious of their Englishness - always parading their chauvinism!"

Paul bridled, having had enough to drink to be resentful, but was saved by the intervention of *Le Patron's* wife.

"The French must take credit for Chauvin, Alistair - and remember, I have been at Wembley when you Scots were there for the football. In every pub, in the Metro, at the game itself, I found drunk Nicolas McChauvins in abundance."

Paul roared with laughter at Alistair's discomfiture. The big Scot contented himself with a muttered aside. "It's not the Metro in London, it's the Underground..."

"Yes," added Paul, straight faced now, "and in Glasgow, it's the Subway."

Angeline clapped her hands and cried, "Why, that sounds like New York - do you really call it that, Alistair - the Subway?"

Paul, bent on revenge now, ploughed on regardless of his big friend's chagrin. "Yes, but it's a tiny little thing, a toy - a wee Victorian hole in the ground. They used to haul the cars along on a wire!"

Alistair straightened in his chair and went into a series of Glaswegian body movements; a certain flexing of the shoulders, tilt of the head and neutral focus of the eyes which Paul instantly decoded as trouble - whisky trouble. The Sauchiehall Street Syndrome, as he often referred to it. Falling backwards expertly from his chair on to the floor, he screamed in mock alarm, in an execrable Scottish accent.

"I'm too wee to fight - and you're too auld, Big Yin!"

Alistair was suddenly all dignity, mine host personified. Turning to *Le Patron's* wife, he said gravely "My dear lady, I apologise for this Sassenach - he's just a wee bit drunk!"

Laughter followed, Paul restored his equilibrium, aided by Angeline. *Le Patron* and his wife stood up reluctantly and declared that it was past one o'clock and time to be going. Paul realised moments later, to his delight, that Angeline was showing no signs of going anywhere. After much enthusiastic waving at the front door, the guests left, and Alistair, Paul and Angeline came back into the lounge and flopped down again at the table.

"A good night." declared Alistair, looking reflectively at his whisky. "It's not over yet," Paul said hopefully, still wondering about Angeline's sleeping arrangements – she had said she had a flat in the village. Then an awful thought assailed him. Angeline and Alistair? No, it couldn't be - he was old enough to be - he quickly strangled the cliché, but the thought persisted. He could not bear the prospect of playing gooseberry in such a situation: it would be intolerable, undignified. God, I'm jealous of an old man, he thought, and felt a flush rise from his neck to his cheeks.

"Angeline will stay over," Alistair said, "so we can talk all night if the mood takes us. Now, what shall our topic be, Angeline?"

Paul composed himself. For no particular reason, he thought of the conversation in Alistair's study, and the reference to Moridura as being a cult of shepherds. 'How about Spanish shepherds?' he suggested.

A pause ensued.

"Spanish shepherds?" echoed Angeline hesitantly. "Why shepherds? Why Spanish shepherds?"

"Why not?" said Alistair decisively, "they're more interesting than French shepherds, that's why. Anyway, I have urgent business in Spain shortly, so - sheep. *Oveja.*"

Angeline warmed to the game. She looked at the ceiling for a moment. "Weren't sheep important in mediaeval Spain - especially important, that is?" She looked to Alistair for an answer.

"They were, and are, important. But yes, you are right - in the 13th century, they were sufficiently important for a sheep owner's guild, the *Mesta*, to be formed. Wool was a major industry, rivalled only by agriculture. Great sheep walks, the *Canadas*, ran all over Castile. As well as peasant sheep farmers, great monasteries often maintained vast herds. They were big business, sheep!" Alistair looked at his glass ruminatively.

"Baa…" said Paul.

Angeline threw her head back and looked again at the ceiling.

"How it must have been! The lonely shepherd sitting on a rocky outcrop, under that incredible sun, in the unique light of the Castilian plain, playing his primitive flute as his flock billowed contentedly beneath his gaze…"

"Bellowed, you mean," corrected Alistair, "and he would have played the guitar…"

"… like a great fleecy cloud," continued Angeline, "under the caring eye of their protector, who in his turn was secure in the knowledge of the protection of a God of old, one who is lost to us - the one, true Christian God."

"Yes, yes," muttered Alistair impatiently, "very rhapsodic, Angeline: but, of course, it wasn't like that at all. Your shepherd would have been ignorant, half starved, suffering from various disgusting forms of invasive worms, superstitious, in terror of strange spirits and monsters - and he probably had a closer relationship with some of his flock than we would consider healthy and decent, even in these enlightened days."

Paul was mildly shocked and looked sideways at Angeline, who was apparently unmoved by Alistair's cynical interruptions.

Alistair warmed to his theme. "You must move on to the fifteenth century to catch Spain in its true flowering, in the reign of Ferdinand and Isabella."

"Hold on," remonstrated Paul, struggling erect from his sprawl. "What about the 11th century, from the dissolution of the Caliphate of Cordoba and the launch of the *Reconquista*? What about *El Cid?*"

Alistair was dismissive. "If you look at the statue erected to *El Cid* in the Plaza de Primo Rivera in Burgos, you are looking at a legend. Now, the *Poema del Cid* is a great work of art, the first epic poem of Castile, I grant you. But in Ferdinand, you have the epitome of a modern politician. Look what Machiavelli said about him!"

"--- if you consider his deeds, you will find all of them great and some of them extraordinary..." Angeline said in insinuating tones.

Paul turned to her in surprise. "Is that a comment or a quote?" he queried.

"It's a quote from *The Prince*." Alistair answered for her. "Good girl, Angeline - you tell him!"

"...his achievements and designs have always been great, and have kept the minds of his people in suspense and admiration and occupied with the issue of them," said Angeline. "I agree with you about Ferdinand and Isabella, but I agree with Paul that the 11th and the 12th centuries were fascinating. Did you know that the Knights Templar were active in Spain?" Angeline smiled at Paul, inviting his reply.

Paul, surprised by all this scholarship, replied quickly.

"I must confess that I am fascinated by them – and by Spain itself."

Alistair smiled inwardly at the echo of the eager boy seeking stories who had sat by his side on the banks of Loch Lomond not so many years ago.

"Aye – the Templars: an interesting bunch of gangsters. In those days, to survive, you had a choice of fighting, praying, or digging. The Templars fought and prayed - they didn't do much digging…" Alistair laughed at his own joke.

"…but they came to a sticky end," Angeline said gleefully.

"They did indeed," Alistair continued, "… the Order was suppressed by the Council of Vienne in 1312, and many of them were executed - poor buggers - poor, rich buggers. I always had a sneaking regard for the Templars…" He paused and shook his head sorrowfully.

"All of their property was confiscated, of course. That's what it's always all about, when all's said and done. Property, money, power. Similar objectives motivated the Spanish *hermandade*s and the military orders. Some of them are hugely influential to this day – perfectly legitimate brotherhoods, legal and moral in all respects, pillars of society. "

"Perhaps with one exception?" said Paul, raising his eyebrows. He looked at Angeline. "He has no ideals - did you know that?"

She glanced across affectionately at the man without ideals. "I know that he has - but he likes to hide them behind a wall of cynicism."

Alistair bridled. "Gie us a break! I have ideals, and I am not a cynic. Scepticism characterises my approach to the affairs of men, well-founded scepticism in most cases, I'm sorry to say."

However, Paul was growing impatient about another topic, and it showed. Why had Alistair not fulfilled his promise to produce Dr. Blade? Why hadn't he been at the party? He looked across at his big friend, the unspoken question burning in his eyes.

Alistair looked at him with amusement, pouring himself another whisky. He held the glass up and regarded it gravely, without looking at Paul. "Go ahead and say it. Where is Doctor Blade? I have no secrets from Angeline on that score," he said. He moved his mouth and chin in a way that meant he was trying to conceal his amusement.

Paul shook his head irritably, and glanced at Angeline. "Well, where is he then?"

Alistair laughed aloud, a great explosive Celtic burst of mirth.

"*He* isnae here, pal, but *she* is…"

Paul looked blankly at him, recognising the suddenly broad accent as presaging a revelation to the obtuse listener. His mind raced to beat the exasperating Glaswegian to the conclusion, but just before the half-formed thought could crystallise, Alistair gestured grandly.

"Paul, may I introduce you formally to Doctor Blade - Doctor Angeline Blade."

His gust of delighted laughter echoed round the room as Paul stared into the depths of a pair of unfathomable green eyes, melted under the power of her smile yet again, and smiled ruefully as he held out his hand to grasp the hand of the discoverer of the Blade Effect.

Chapter Four

B rother Mateo, standing on the southern rim of *La Copa de Moridura*, some fifty metres above the plain, looked down the narrow, precipitous path to the rough road that provided the only vehicular access to the base of the rock. The road, visible from where it ran down the hill from Moridanza all the way to the rocky prominence of Moridura, disappeared under the east side and met the path that wound up around the rock to the southern face and ended at the paved area in front of the great gate to the monastery.

The monastery discouraged uninvited visitors. Those who climbed *el sendero de precipio* to the gates were politely turned away, and escorted back down the path by one or more monks. Trusted traders, such as Manuel Ortega, parked their vehicles on the plain then, with the assistance of the monks, brought their supplies up to the monastery. For very large objects that could not be brought up the path, there was a rope hoist with an ancient winding mechanism mounted at a rock overhang on the summit, from which there was a clear fifty metre drop to the plain. It was still functional, but in need of maintenance.

Mateo shaded his eyes with one hand and squinted at the road, trying to catch sight of the Abbot's car, loaned to the American visitor. Brother Anselmo had asked him to wait at the foot of the cliff for the car to arrive, and guide the American up the cliff path, which was extremely hazardous, especially at certain points - a path with no handrails or walls of any kind. The young monk intended to reach the road end before the anticipated arrival time the Abbot had stated.

As he started down the path, he cocked his head, straining to catch the sound of a vehicle, but could hear nothing but the subtle noises of the plain and the ridge; birds and small creatures, the whispering of the wind and the familiar sounds from the great bulk of the monastery behind him. He had not gone far, when the noise of a car door slamming echoed up the ridge. Mateo immediately knew that the Abbot's enigmatic guest was already at the base of the path, had parked the car in the rough lean-to on the gravelled space that served as a parking area, and was now heading up the path alone. Why was he so much earlier than the Abbot had predicted?

Brother Anselmo had stated confidently that Don Ferdinand's meetings lasted an hour, neither more nor less. It was seven miles from the Don's estate to the monastery, on the rough, potholed road at least a fifteen-minute journey. *El Americano* should not have been at the road end for at least another twenty minutes, and his approach would have been visible – and audible – at least five minutes before that. Mateo moved faster than was prudent down the treacherous path. The man had either waited for him, or had been engaged in some activity in the parked car; these were the only explanations for the delay between his arrival and the sound of the car door slamming.

Brother Mateo's obsessive speculations about the doings of *el Americano* were entirely consistent with those of his brethren. The monks of Moridura had few novel events to disturb the age-old pattern of their lives, and the arrival of the mysterious transatlantic visitor, and the Abbot's strange proscriptions relating to his stay in the monastery had provided a cause for endless discussion and gossip. Brother Anselmo had personally picked up the American from the square in Moridanza early in June. Mateo did not know how the visitor had arrived in the village in the first place without a car – there was no regular coach service from Mérida.

El Americano's luggage had consisted of a small suitcase, an attaché case, and the large metal trunk, which had caused problems when being transported up the path on the cart. Only Brother Mateo was physically strong enough to handle this, and the guest had been very agitated about its safety; he met Mateo at the gate, and his angry outburst when it collided with the gate had appeared excessive to the point of sinfulness to the Brothers. Their censure was exceeded only by their curiosity as to its contents. Brother Mateo, who had carried it through the cloister and up the stairs to the guest wing, testified to its enormous weight, redoubling the already fevered speculation.

The Abbot had ushered him to his room without a word of explanation to his secretary and deputy, Brother Gregorio. The red-haired American remained in one of the six bedrooms in the guest wing of the monastery for three days, during which period, to the astonishment of the Brothers, the Abbot personally took his meals to him.

On the fourth day, the Abbot addressed the Brothers, asking for their trust and understanding. He explained that he was unable to tell them of the identity of the visitor, nor the purpose of his visit to the monastery. The visitor would be permitted to wear the robe of a Moriduran, (a rare privilege, usually accorded only to lay officials from Rome or to a *confrater*, a special status awarded to favoured lay persons) and no one must address him for any reason whatsoever. For the rest of his stay, he would eat with the Abbot, who would be absent from all communal meals. Brother Gregorio would carry out all the functions of the Abbot until further notice. The Abbot's car (the only vehicle available to the monastery) would be at his disposal at all times.

The American remained in the guest wing - a mysterious, rarely glimpsed presence - until one night Brother Mateo went to the monastery library and found him reading. The visitor glared at him in fury, and then left the library without a word. Mateo returned the massive book the American had been reading to the almost inaccessible corner shelf from which he had taken it, climbing a ladder to do so. It was only as he slid it back into its dusty place that he realised it was the Moridura Manuscript, a work forbidden to all but the Abbot by ancient custom, and by the *Index Librorum Prohibitorum*, before its abolition in 1966. The Abbot respected the rule of 1557 and the rule of the monastery, which pre-dated the Index. The long lost book had been returned to the monastery five years previously by a Scottish gentleman. Mateo involuntarily smiled at the memory of the big Scotsman.

Earlier today, without warning, Mateo had been asked to get the car ready by the Abbot, who had then appeared with *el Americano*. The Abbot raised his finger to his lips, choking back the warning Mateo was about to give about the treacherous nature of the road to Moridanza. The visitor went down the path, accompanied by Mateo, and then left without a word, moving off at excessive speed.

Mateo ruminated on all of this as he continued his descent. Half way down, he saw the American, who was forging on up the path at a hazardous rate. They met and the young monk gave a respectful greeting, but it was rudely ignored. He then turned and positioned himself on the American's left, and matched his stride. The path was barely two metres wide, and at several points it was narrower than that. The monks never walked two abreast, but courtesy and safety demanded that, when accompanying guests or the Abbot, the more dangerous outside positioning that Brother Mateo had adopted was mandatory.

When they reached the summit, *el Americano* pushed past him, strode across to the wicket gate, and entered the monastery. Mateo signalled to the resentful spirit within him, with the calm movements of external acceptance by which his body disciplined his soul, that its anger must be controlled and dissipated.

The other monks struggled to control the base promptings of their bodies by prayer and meditation, but for Mateo it was a pride as old as Spain that had to be subjugated. He was alive to the signals of dominance and submission sent by other males and his instinct was to subdue opposition, to direct, to lead. As a young man, he grappled with the inherent force of his nature, recognising that it would ultimately jeopardise his immortal soul unless disciplined. In a previous age, Mateo could have utilised this in a Church that needed soldiers of God, but today, there was little need for such qualities. He bowed his head and followed the American through the open wicket gate, locked it with his own key, then headed across the courtyard towards the cloister. As he walked, he prayed.

"O Lord, my Saviour, help me to change my feelings towards this stranger. Fill my unworthy heart with charity towards him, one of your creatures, as I am."

Mateo waited for the feeling of peace that always followed such a deep, heartfelt appeal to his God, but it did not come. Instead, a sensation of profound foreboding filled his being. He started to enter the cloisters behind the American, when a faint gleam at his feet caught his eye. On the ancient, worn stone paving slabs lay a small figurine on a gold chain. He reached for it with instinctive curiosity, then, in an instant of recognition, drew back as though from a flame. The figurine was a finely worked gold representation of a centaur-like figure, part man, part beast. *La Bestia de Moridura.*

The tiny ruby eyes glittered in the dim light, and Mateo experienced a sense of imminent danger. His instinct was to take the thing to the Abbot, but he could not bring himself to touch it. All the night terrors and superstitions of his childhood flooded back: the fearful whispers of the older monks, the tales told by the young monks of the shimmering haze which sometimes hung over *La Copa*, the mysterious prohibitions on certain topics, certain books in the library - all of them linked to the cult of Moridura, and the *hermandad* that had constituted the Ancient Order of Moridura before the monastery was founded.

Mateo forced himself to remain calm: he breathed deeply and repeated rhythmically, *O Lord, protect and guard me from evil*, and succeeded in calming his turbulent emotions. A question entered his mind. How had he recognised *La Bestia*? No representation of the mythical creature existed in his experience: no description had ever been offered, even in the most lurid tales of his brethren. Why then his certainty over the figurine?

The answer came as he recalled something that had happened earlier. He was in the library - *el Americano* was leaving, looking back at him with rage. Mateo was moving towards the reading desk and reaching to close the book the American had been reading. The illuminated pages were before his eyes in full eidetic recall: on the left hand page the beautifully lettered text, and on the right, a line drawing delicately shaded in blue, a perspective drawing of an ancient, ruined cloister. An arch of the cloister was on the left and on the right, two monks in the ancient Moriduran habits - one seated at a table with his head covered, and one standing before him. To the side stood a figure in martial garb, imperious, detached, waiting and watching as the two monks conducted their mysterious intercourse.

All of this Mateo remembered consciously, as he remembered the zodiacal overlay across the picture. But now, from a perception suppressed in the library, he saw in his mind's eye another figure, in shadow behind the wall in the left foreground, a massive, tortured figure, poised, listening...

Mateo shuddered. It was *La Bestia*, recognised and rejected in the same instant by his subconscious, an image thrust at once down to the primitive layer of his mind, to the Id, where it had lain dormant until now. He reached down and picked up the figurine on its gold chain. Clenching the object firmly in his left hand, he strode purposefully across the courtyard towards the main entrance. In the hall, he hesitated for a moment, then, with renewed determination, climbed the staircase and headed for the Abbot's room.

He stopped outside the door. What if Brother Anselmo was not in his office and it was Brother Gregorio instead? Mateo grimaced in frustration: Gregorio was an unimaginative bureaucrat - he would murmur inconsequentialities, slip the figurine in a drawer and forget about it - or worse still, he would casually return it to the American. Mateo moved closer to the door and cocked his head, listening for a familiar voice. It came, but from behind him, not from behind the door.

"Mateo - you wished to speak to me?"

He turned and faced the Abbot. Brother Anselmo was old and frail beside the tall, massively built, young monk. In his youth, it was said, he had been as muscular and powerful in build as most of the monks of Moridura. Some said he was suffering from a wasting disease, the monks' sickness. Brother Anselmo's deep eyes looked up enquiringly at him, and his gaunt features carried a warm, encouraging expression.

"I - yes, Brother Anselmo - I realise that Brother Gregorio is acting for you, but on this matter..." The words tailed away, and Mateo held out his clenched fist and slowly opened it. The expression on the Abbot's face changed very slowly. The warmth slipped from his aquiline features, the light of fellowship in his eyes was replaced by a focused gleam, and his lips narrowed almost imperceptibly. Mateo felt that the Abbot was controlling an intense reaction to the sight of the figurine.

"Where did you come by this - this pendant, Brother Mateo?"

"It is not a pendant, it is..."

"I know what it is, Mateo. We will talk about it in my room..." Brother Anselmo reached past him and opened the heavy door. Mateo followed him into the narrow, high vaulted room that served the Abbot as an office, waited respectfully as the old man moved behind his desk and sat down, then he silently laid the figurine on the desk. He neither looked at it nor touched it, but regarded Mateo in a strange, neutral manner, without expectancy, almost as if he wished the matter before them would go away and let them start afresh on some more mundane topic, like why the mail was late.

"I found it outside. *El Americano* must have dropped it as he entered."

The Abbot gave a sigh and bent his head.

"Why do you assume that, Mateo? Anyone could have dropped it."

The younger monk stared in astonishment at his superior.

"But Brother Anselmo, it cannot belong to any of the Brothers. You can see for yourself what it is; who else could have dropped it?"

The Abbot lifted his head and spoke slowly and softly, as though to a child. "It is a gold representation of a centaur, or something like a centaur, with a tentacled head, eyes formed of rubies, suspended on a gold chain, finely worked - probably Moorish, perhaps even Roman, in origin. You found it outside the monastery. These are the facts you possess, Mateo. Why should it not be mine? Why must it be *el Americano's?*"

Mateo's thoughts raced in confusion: could the Abbot be jesting - or was he testing his knowledge of the object? Could it really belong to Brother Anselmo? He was now on the horns of a dilemma - if he admitted to knowledge of what the figurine represented, he must explain how he knew the form of *La Bestia*, and this would involve discussing the encounter in the library, and his inadvertent glimpse of the forbidden book. The Abbot was about to break the silence when the door opened abruptly.

"Brother Anselmo, I must ask you to…"

The American broke off when he saw Mateo; his eyes flicked to the Abbot then to the faint gleam from the desk. Without hesitation, he strode across the room, picked the figurine from its surface and slipped it under his robe. His face was expressionless as he spoke. "I guess I must have dropped this outside, Brother Anselmo - I picked it up in a little jewellers in Madrid when I flew in. Beautiful little thing, wouldn't you say?"

"Beautiful and expensive, I would say," replied the Abbot smoothly, then, turning to Mateo, he laughed. "Mystery solved, Brother!" He made a faint gesture of dismissal, but Mateo missed it and turned to face the American, ignoring the Abbot's order that no one should address the guest.

"I found it in on the stones outside, señor – just after you entered. It is fortunate that you did not drop it on the path. To lose such a valuable object…" He let the words hang, looking straight at the other man, feeling Brother Anselmo's cold disapproval from his right.

In a nervous gesture, the visitor pulled back the cowl of his habit. The close-cropped red hair was like a flame in a cave in the dark room. The American was in his late forties or early fifties, with a large head and a strong neck. Mateo felt immediately the power of the man, recognising a penetrating intelligence and a searching curiosity in the green eyes, which scanned his features as though seeing the tall monk for the first time: Mateo was aware that he was bracing his body as though for an attack, and that his fists had clenched.

The tension was broken by a sudden smile breaking over the red-haired man's face.

"You're Brother Mateo! I guess I've been less than polite. You brought my bags and trunk up, and, yeah, I guess it was you in the library that night. Well, my name is Lonnen - Lloyd C. Lonnen. Call me Red…" He reached out a broad hand, looking up into Mateo's eyes.

Mateo grasped it and felt a powerful grip that matched his own. Lonnen released his hand and turned to the Abbot.

"This guy would have made a useful football player if the Moridurans hadn't grabbed him, Brother Anselmo. Catch 'em young, eh?"

"Brother Mateo has been with us from his earliest years – since infancy," said the Abbot.

The American whistled in surprise. He realised instantly that Mateo had probably been an abandoned child, born out of wedlock. But how had the monks managed to raise him in their all male environment? Had he been wet-nursed by someone from the village?

"You're a true son of the monastery, Brother – you've given all of your life to it."

"Not yet, señor..." There was no hint of a smile on the big monk's face, but Red Lonnen was certain that this had been a flash of humour. He looked at Mateo with renewed interest. "So you know little of the world, Brother – or of Spain."

"I have had access to the monastery library since I was a child, señor, and among my brethren are many learned men and fine tutors," Mateo replied with great dignity. " I know what I need to know of the world, and a great deal about Spain."

The Abbot interrupted him unceremoniously.

"Señor Lonnen has much to do, Mateo. Thank you for finding his pendant. Now you may go." His expression made his disapproval abundantly clear: Mateo had not observed his instructions about addressing the American. Discipline would surely follow.

Mateo left and went to a small bare room provided for solitary prayer for troubled monks and knelt facing the narrow window high on the bare wall. The sunlight streamed in, and he looked at the myriad specks of dust in the beam - as numerous as the stars in the heavens.

"O Lord, help me still my turbulent mind..." he commenced, but the motes of dust continued to hold his attention. They floated because they were lighter than air, he reflected, but the stars, the planets - they were held in their eternal orbits by God's grand design, just as the very air that carried the dust was held in its eternal envelope around the Earth.

"O Lord of all Creation," he recommenced with determination, caught up in his ecological theme, "help the race of Man preserve and cherish the great gifts you have bestowed, let them refrain from profane acts which harm the balance of the natural world. Help them to understand the delicate balance of their Universe, the invisible threads which gently link the planets in their courses..."

As he spoke the words, which seemed to spring from the depths of his soul, a profound foreboding clouded his mood, and he felt as though the very wellspring of his being was running dry. The dust specks seemed to whirl madly in the light beam, then suddenly the light vanished. He sprang to his feet with an incoherent cry, filled with a nameless panic, an apprehension of extinction, but then the passing cloud that had momentarily obscured the sunlight moved from its face, and the light flooded back into the cell.

Mateo felt the heat of the sun in the beam: he stroked his face in delight, and felt the tears course down his cheeks. Falling again to his knees, he raised his arms in supplication and cried "Lord, Lord, what must I do - help your servant understand the confusion of these days!"

Chapter Five

T he late afternoon sun made the panelled wood in the library glow softly, and the gold-tooled lettering on the spines of the books lit up as though on fire. Ferdinand listened attentively as Manuel Ortega began to speak tentatively of that which he had kept hidden for so long.

"Don Ferdinand, it is my fervent wish to tell you all that you wish to know; yet I find it very difficult. My father..." He hesitated and looked down.

Don Ferdinand reached across and took both Manuel's hands in his own.

"Of all the men of Moridanza I have known, Francisco Ortega was the finest. All who knew him are indebted to him for the example he set. Truly, he was a man of Moridanza, a true *extremeño*, and what more can we say of a man than this? Whatever you decide, Manuel Ortega, be true to his memory."

Ferdinand's face and voice exhibited a deep emotion that bore no relationship to his actual feelings. His coldly logical intention was to pre-empt as much of the bargaining strategy and tactics of the crafty peasant facing him without losing the impetus towards the disclosure he sought.

"I thank you for your words about my father – his blessed memory lives in my family and, I hope, in the district. Don Ferdinand, I will be fifty years of age soon, and I feel that I am at a crossroads in my life. Like many men in middle life, I have the growing sense that I have not achieved what I intended for myself, my wife, my children. My dreams have not been realised - life seems to be slipping away, the years go faster, and I am conscious of my own mortality. But I feel that it is not too late – that I can change my destiny even now. And this – this little thing that I have – the diaries – they are my father's true legacy to me. He would want me to use them prudently…"

His voice tailed off. The signal had been sent: an explicit condition placed on the release of the diaries would have been presumptuous and dangerous. The Don must draw from him the things he wanted in return. He waited.

Ferdinand rose slowly, turning away from Manuel and walking across to the antique globe of the world. He laid his long, spatulate fingers on it and slowly turned the sphere. Still looking at the globe, he murmured aloud, as though talking to himself.

"What might a man want as his life reaches its midpoint? He has the love of his family and the friendship of his peers, but feels that there must be more – an assured status, something that delivers respect. That can only come from a guaranteed place within a powerful group that can confer the benefits of unquestioning support in everything he does – a *hermandad*. Rights and privileges can be his if he accepts the concomitant duties that membership of such a brotherhood places upon him. A proud man will accept such obligations wholeheartedly, as the price of belonging.

"And what of a man in business, facing all the uncertainties and vagaries of commerce – what will he seek in middle life? He will hope for a reduction of risk, the security that comes from the assured custom of the most respected people in his community, so that others may observe and follow the example of their betters.

"And finally, a man in middle life, who has something of value that he has held and cherished for many years, will not expect to surrender it without a tangible token of its value, one substantial enough to give an impetus to his new plans, a token that will enable him to hold his head high among his new brothers, one that signals to the world that a sea change has taken place in his life.

"To such things, a man of respect may legitimately aspire, without any suggestion of greed or cupidity being levelled against him."

Manuel could scarcely breathe. Don Ferdinand had articulated his three bargaining objectives effortlessly and elegantly, almost as if he had read his mind. He tried to speak, but only emitted a strangled gasp. The tall man turned and looked directly at him.

"If what I have said represents something like your aspirations, Manuel, would you look to me to assist in fulfilling them?"

Manuel, no stranger to crude commercial haggling in his business dealings, was lost in admiration at the finesse of a master negotiator.

"You have so accurately expressed my hopes for the future that I risk seeming impertinent in adding to your words, Don Ferdinand. My trust in you is absolute, yet I have a problem. I know where the diaries are, but it is many years since I have seen them. They are secure, of that I am certain, but I must satisfy myself that I can fully deliver my part of our agreement, since there can be no doubt of your capacity to fulfil your commitments."

He looked at the Don, and the blood drained from his face at the effect his words had produced. From warm benevolence, Don Ferdinand's expression was now one of cold suspicion.

"Manuel Ortega, have you come me in the hope of advancing yourself without the certainty that you have the diaries? You have listened to my thoughts about your future, about the things I might do for you, without the capacity to deliver your part of the bargain? Such a posture in the marketplace in Moridanza would have earned you the contempt and distrust of your suppliers, if not their blows, yet you adopt it with me."

Manuel dropped to one knee imploringly in front of the erect, unyielding figure before him.

"Forgive me, Don Ferdinand – I did not think of it in this way, believe me. I was so anxious to tell you of my willingness to deliver the diaries that I overlooked the significance of this fact. Only as you spoke did this realisation come to me. I am not a clever man; I do not plan, I do not think beyond the moment. I am a simple man of action; I react to events, to problems, to opportunity."

Ferdinand was rather touched by the frankness and accuracy of this self-assessment by Manuel, but he still retained a suspicion that the crafty peasant in him was seeking a tactical advantage at almost a subconscious level, running on instinct rather than an analysis of the situation.

"Well, then, there is a simple solution to our dilemma. You must tell me the location of the diaries; I will send someone with you to check that they are still there, and that their condition is acceptable. You will bring them back to me and I will assess their true worth, then we can talk again about how we can satisfy your legitimate objectives. Is this not the way forward? I can call someone now who will go with you."

Manuel's mouth was dry with fear. He felt trapped – why had he not foreseen this situation? It all seemed so obvious now – why was it not evident to him before? He silently cursed his stupidity.

"Don Ferdinand, I have been a fool, but only a fool, and not such a fool as to try to conceal things from you or deceive you. All of these years you have respected my decision not to release the diaries…"

"I did not press you, Manuel," interrupted Ferdinand, "out of respect for your father and because of my regard for you."

"I know, I know – you have my eternal gratitude for your forbearance – but the fact is…" He hesitated.

"Go on," said Ferdinand icily.

"I am not alone in the matter of the diaries. My father did not entrust them only to me – there is another involved, Don Ferdinand – one whose permission is required..."

Ferdinand turned away and paced slowly up and down. He had suspected something of the sort: unknown to Manuel, his café and the homes of his family had been discreetly searched for the diaries. He recalled the words of Francisco Ortega to him, just before his death. "My son is basically sound, Don Ferdinand, but he needs someone to counsel him and stiffen his resolve in matters of importance."

He had assumed that Francisco wanted him to act as mentor to Manuel, but now it seemed that another had assumed that role. If that person was simply a friend in Moridanza, holding the diaries, unaware of, and uninterested in their content, there was no problem. It seemed unlikely that the diaries would be held by a local law firm or in a bank safety deposit box – the Ortegas had always been distrustful of professional services, and avoided using them whenever possible.

"Manuel, I agreed to meet with you on the understanding that you had your father's diaries and that you would deliver them to me if I could help you in ways to be agreed. Tell me who this person is, and the nature of the constraints, or our discussion ends now."

The notes of finality in his voice left no doubt; this was no bluff. Manuel knew that his relationship with Don Ferdinand would never be the same if such a breach occurred, and that knowledge chilled his heart. A man could survive in the district without Ferdinand's favour, he could endure his indifference, but no man could survive his enmity. A silence followed that seemed endless. Manuel could hear his own breath labouring in his lungs as he felt Ferdinand's eyes upon him.

"Don Ferdinand, just before my father died, he talked with me in a way he had never done before – he was ninety two years of age and he knew his end was near. We sat at the table in the café long after the last customer had gone, and he talked of our family, of the business, and then he took his diaries from the locked cupboard where he kept them. He said they contained the essence of his life in Moridanza – that they were a record of events in the district covering eighty six years, from the simple observations of a six-year old boy through early youth to maturity and old age."

Ferdinand's eyes glittered – he had known of the diaries, but the fact that they covered such a period was fascinating. He had intended to maintain his posture of impatient severity with Manuel, but he could not resist a question.

"How many volumes of the diaries were there?"

Manuel was relieved at the partial thawing of the Don's former glacial attitude.

"Almost one for every year, Don Ferdinand – certainly in excess of seventy-five volumes – and in good condition. The bindings vary, from simple board to leather-bound in later years. One diary simply contained a key in the hollowed-out pages."

"A key? How strange! What did Francisco say of their content?"

"He never explained the key. He said the diaries covered every aspect of his life, from the ramblings of a child to the observations of a man. He was fascinated by the rocks of *La Copa*, and the history and the legends surrounding the monastery – the old, old stories of..." Manuel broke off, realising that he was entering a dangerous area. He spread his hands apologetically.

"Of the Magus and *La Bestia*," said Ferdinand bluntly. "If you are to become a man of respect, we must be able to talk openly among ourselves about such things."

Manuel felt a surge of relief, of pride, of anticipation of things formerly only to be dreamed of.

"Yes – yes! Of such matters – of the rock throne – *El Trono* - in the centre of the *La Copa*. Of the changes the years have brought to it."

Ferdinand, recognising Manuel's relief at the shift in his tone, decided to pursue his line of questioning more gently.

"Have you read the diaries, Manuel? Have you at least opened them, sampled their contents? You must have been fascinated by your family history?"

"I am ashamed to admit that I only looked to certain times – to certain years, out of a curiosity about those events. The year of my mother and father's marriage – the year of my birth. Most of the rest I did not understand. My father used his own private cipher for some entries. A more highly educated, intelligent man would make more of them than I could. I did not have them in my possession for long - my father gave them into the charge of another before he died."

Ferdinand looked intently at the sweating, thickset man before him. "To another whom he trusted absolutely – a man of wisdom and unimpeachable integrity. One who commanded the unqualified respect of the entire district - and beyond. A man with a profound sense of duty to others. Is that not so, Manuel?"

"Yes – those were almost exactly his words were to me," gasped Manuel in astonishment. "How could you know this, Don Ferdinand?"

Ferdinand drew a long, slow, reflective breath as he contemplated the fact that only one man fitted the description of the person in whom Francisco Ortega had placed his trust: the implications of his conclusion were complex in the extreme.

Again he turned his back on Manuel, and paced slowly up and down, hands locked behind his back, then he stopped and looked at him. "So Brother Anselmo has the diaries?"

Manuel's silence was confirmation enough. The Abbot of the monastery of Moridura held the diaries of Francisco Ortega, and had done so for five years. How could Anselmo have kept this from me, thought Ferdinand, and his anger began to build. He mastered his feelings and turned again to Manuel, relaxed and smiling.

"This makes matters simple. You know I have a very close personal friendship with Brother Anselmo that goes back to my childhood. We respect and trust each other. I love him as I did my own father, and I am sure you feel the same. Manuel, you simply have to tell him that you wish to give me access to the diaries. They may be kept permanently in the monastery – they are safe there – and I can inspect them at the Abbot's convenience.

"This is indeed a happy outcome: your future is be assured. I will propose you for membership of a brotherhood whose existence you must be aware of, and your acceptance into that brotherhood, with all the benefits that it can confer, both material and spiritual, is certain. Members of the brotherhood, and their extended network of contacts, will look favourably on your business. Additionally, to enable you to maintain yourself in a manner fitting to your new status, and to secure the quality of your business services, a substantial amount of capital will be made available to you immediately, at nominal interest rates."

Manuel felt a wild surge of joy. I have been right to wait, to hold back, he thought; then he remembered the heart of the problem, and was gripped again by fear at the thought of explaining it to Don Ferdinand.

"I have always wished to give you access to the diaries, Don Ferdinand. What held me back was the stipulation my father made when he entrusted them to Brother Anselmo – a difficulty not of my own making. I never understood why my father required this of me and of Brother Anselmo. His words at the time made no sense to me – and Brother Anselmo, he also…"

The Don's words came very softly as he placed a hand on Manuel's shoulder.

"A stipulation? A constraint? What was this stipulation?"

Manuel felt as though he were shrinking into the floor of the library; the walls seemed to recede, leaving him in an infinite space with the tall man standing above him. He would have given anything not to have to say the words that fell from his mouth into the room.

"My father said that his diaries must never be shown to you or any member of the *hermandad*."

In the unbearable silence that followed he felt the other man's grip on his shoulder tighten, then relax. Ferdinand went back across to the globe, placed both hands on it and looked up at the ornate cornice of the ceiling.

He forced himself to recall his father's imperative – master your emotions or they will master you – use your anger as a controlled expression of your will at a time of your choosing.

Manuel waited in trepidation for Don Ferdinand's reaction, a wait that seemed interminable. A gentle knocking at the door of the library broke the silence. "I gave orders not to be disturbed, Antonio," Ferdinand shouted impatiently to his manservant, the only person permitted to interrupt him in conference.

"My apologies, Don Ferdinand, but it is Brother Anselmo – he says that it is vital that he speak with you."

The two men in the library looked at each other, each with the same thought; was this coincidental or had the other arranged it in advance? If coincidental, was it fortuitous, or would the unexpected arrival of the Abbot of Moridura add to the tension already present in the room?

Ferdinand looked directly into Manuel's eyes and knew that it was not his doing. He strode across to the double doors and threw them open, moving forward to embrace the frail old monk, throwing his powerful arms around Brother Anselmo's slender body.

"This is unexpected but welcome – you rarely honour my home with your presence! What brings you to me on this happy day, my old friend? As you see, we have another friend already with us…" He motioned towards Manuel, who was half-crouching in a subservient posture to the Abbot.

Brother Anselmo walked across to him with his arms outstretched.

"Manuel! How are you? I have too often been busy during your regular visits to the monastery; how is Fidelicia - and your family? How you remind me of Francisco, God rest his soul…"

The resemblance is only physical, thought Ferdinand - Manuel would never be the man his father had been. He lacked his intellect, his curiosity, and his indomitable courage. Manuel's presence now posed a problem: if the Abbot had come about the diaries, a three-way discussion would be difficult; if he had come about some other matter, Manuel could not be present. Ferdinand's complex private analysis was interrupted and instantly rendered irrelevant by the Abbot's next remark.

"Ferdinand – Manuel! It is fortuitous that the three of us are here together, for I must speak with you both about two matters of vital concern to all of us – Francisco Ortega's diaries, and an American industrialist, Lloyd Lonnen, known as Red Lonnen because of the colour of his hair."

Ferdinand was taken aback by Brother Anselmo's forthright manner, and by the mention of the American. Lonnen had contacted him in advance about the invitation he had secured from the Abbot to visit the monastery. American tourists were common in Mérida, so when he arrived in Extremadura, Ferdinand had placed him in the largest hotel there, to maintain his anonymity prior to his arrival at the monastery.

Now the Abbot's words must be interpreted quickly, before the discussion commenced. He decide to acknowledge that he knew Lonnen, since the man had been in his house just a short time ago; Manuel might have seen him, might well have heard and even observed their argument; the Abbot could have observed his car leaving the estate. Anything was possible – prudence demand the truth, or at least some of it.

"I too have met with Señor Lonnen, Brother Anselmo. Shall we speak of what we know of him?"

"It is imperative that we do: pressure of time has not permitted an earlier discussion, but now that we three are together under your roof, the moment has come," the old monk replied smoothly.

Manuel slowly assimilated what he had seen and heard. Don Ferdinand had been insulted by his mysterious guest, had physically attacked him, yet the Abbot had the American as his guest in the monastery.

Ferdinand motioned them across to a larger table close to the high windows of the library. Manuel waited respectfully for the others to sit. Brother Anselmo positioned himself with his back to the windows, murmuring that light hurt his eyes these days. Don Ferdinand remained standing, waving his hand to Manuel to indicate that he should sit on the Abbot's left. He then sat down facing Brother Anselmo and the two men looked at each other warily.

Ferdinand broke the silence.

"Shall we share what we know of Señor Lonnen, my old friend?' He laughed and added "Manuel has no knowledge of this man to share, have you, Manuel? Or are you going to surprise us?"

Manuel stammered "No, no – I saw him with you for the first time in the hall earlier." As the words left his lips, he realised his mistake, and a wave of apprehension swept over him.

The tall aristocrat's face became an inscrutable mask; he forced himself not to look at Brother Anselmo. His moment of anger, of weakness, had been witnessed by Manuel – and now the Abbot knew for certain that Lonnen had been here just before he arrived.

"Of course, Manuel – you came just as he was leaving. I kept you waiting while we concluded our business."

Manuel understood the unspoken message only too well; whatever he had seen or heard in the hall he must keep to himself. All would be revealed shortly, and whatever the outcome, it surely would be to his advantage. Yet there was a feeling of tension, of foreboding in the room that unsettled him, and the spectre of *La Bestia* lurked behind his chair.

Chapter Six

I have been guilty of the worst kind of sexist assumption," said Paul Corr, smiling ruefully at Doctor Angeline Blade, the subject of the Ancient Order of Moridura's ultimatum to Alistair Mackinnon.

Alistair was delighted by the younger man's manifest embarrassment, which he had deliberately engineered by his careful choice of words about the good doctor's identity.

"As you sow, so shall you reap, says the Bible," he quoted gleefully.

"Good quotation, wrong source," replied the classical scholar absently, still adjusting to his new perspective of his beautiful companion of the evening, "It's not the Bible, it's Cicero, circa 55 BC. *Ut sementum feceris ita metes.*"

As he enunciated the Latin precisely, there was a sharp crack behind them, the sound of breaking glass and a crash as something fell to the floor on the other side of the lounge. Paul froze, Alistair jumped to his feet and Angeline gripped the arms of her chair, staring up at Paul as if his words had conjured up the event. By this time Alistair was across the room and had switched off the lights.

"Stay low, and follow me," he commanded, motioning towards the door. They ran from the room in a half-crouch, feeling at once frightened and foolish. Outside the room, in the hallway, Angeline gripped Paul's hand tightly as Alistair talked in a low, intense voice to two of his security staff. They nodded and entered the lounge; after a few minutes, they returned, reported and left. Alistair came across and grasped the shaken couple's free hands.

"Ring-a-ring-a-roses," he sang in a broad accent, in recognition of the incongruous circle they had formed. They let go, Angeline and Paul laughing nervously.

"It was a high velocity rifle bullet – it came through the window, shattered my photograph, went through the partition wall and spent itself in the next room. My guys are searching the grounds – the police are on their way, but they'll find nothing. The shot wasn't meant to kill – it was a postscript to the note I showed you, Paul."

"How can you know this, Alistair?" asked Paul. He couldn't understand how his friend had reached these conclusions so quickly, when he and Angeline were still in a state of shock from the events of moments ago. Angeline looked up at him with the same baffled look as Paul. Alistair smiled, and the Glasgow vernacular word *glaikit* entered his mind as an apt description of their confused expressions.

"We can go back into the lounge – if you're OK with that?" He looked protectively at Angeline. "I am so sorry this happened under my roof – I should've been better prepared."

"For what?" said Angeline, and Paul realised that she knew nothing of the note and the ultimatum. They walked back into the room on Alistair's assurance that it was safe to do so – the grounds were secure, and security staff had been deployed. As they had been before the shot, thought Paul uncharitably, but he kept his counsel. They looked across at the broken window. Alistair bent down and picked up the shattered photo frame, shaking the glass from it with a small clatter on to the floor. It was a recent photograph of Angeline and Alistair. The big Scot had a large hole in his forehead, over his broad smile.

"Telescopic lens, good marksman – hit his mark spot on," murmured Alistair in admiration. "He must have been close to the house to get the angle right. He could've killed any one in the house at any time during the evening, if that had been the objective. No, this is to stiffen the ultimatum for July 10th – did they think I wouldn't believe them? That I don't take them seriously?" He scowled and shook his head, then glanced at Angeline.

"I owe you a wee explanation, Doctor Blade, don't I?"

"You sure as hell do, big fella," snapped Angeline, fixing him with her glittering green eyes. She turned to Paul. "Are you in on this too, bud? Keeping the little lady out of the loop…"

A voice from the hall called out that the police had arrived; Alistair, trying to hide his relief at the welcome interruption, apologised briefly and headed out of the room, leaving Paul with the unwelcome task of explaining to Angeline.

"Let's sit down, have a whisky, and I'll tell you what little I know," he said, shepherding her across to the big couch, well out of the line of the broken window. He went back and poured them both stiff drinks, brought them across and sat down.

"Alistair may owe you an apology, Angeline, but I don't think I do. After all, we only met a few hours ago…" He shook his head impatiently. "Dammit, that didn't come out right. It doesn't matter how long I've known you – I like you, I trust you, I feel as if I've waited my whole life to meet you. I want there to be nothing hidden between us." He broke off in such obvious distress that Angeline melted, and, leaning across, impulsively kissed him on the cheek.

"It's OK, Paul – I understand. I feel the same – it's ridiculous, inexplicable and not the kind of thing a professional woman should experience – but there it is."

Paul held up his glass awkwardly.

"To our inappropriate but wonderful emotions…"

They clinked glasses, and then spoke simultaneously "So, now?" They both laughed in embarrassment.

"All that I know dates from yesterday," Paul began. "Alistair showed me a note from a Spanish brotherhood called the Ancient Order of Moridura. It was an ultimatum: it required him to deliver you, Doctor Blade, to them at midnight on July 10th in the square of a village called Moridanza, in Extremadura."

"Deliver me? To Spain?" said Angeline slowly, shaking her head in disbelief. "Am I a package to be delivered? Who the hell are these people – and why do they want me?"

Paul outlined what he knew of the Order, the monastery of Moridura, the *hermandad*, the legend of the Beast, and the possible link between ancient phenomena and gravitational effects.

"It would seem that something in your work on gravitation has engaged their interest. They are some kind of ancient Spanish mafia, but with mystical overtones," he explained.

Angeline cupped her chin in her hands, and stared at Paul for a moment, then got up and walked across to the broken window. Paul jumped to his feet.

"Perhaps you should stay away from the window," he said quickly, moving across to her and taking her arm gently. She spun around and said impatiently "They won't try again. Anyway, they shoot photographs, not people."

"Not yet," replied Paul, "but they have promised to kill Alistair if he doesn't comply with their demand."

Angeline looked at him incredulously. "What? You can't be serious – they can't be serious! Why don't these people just approach me and tell me what they want? Why go through Alistair – I don't work for him – yet."

"I don't know. He's been hiding something from me. When he comes back, we'll both demand explanations. I don't know for certain if Alistair knows the real reason they contacted him, but I think he does..."

"Oh, he knows, alright."

Angeline's tone was on the edge of anger, an anger directed at the big Scotsman whom she had come to like and respect in the few years that she had known him. Their first meeting had been at a scientific conference in Brussels three years previously, shortly after her mother's death. That had led to an invitation to visit Ardmurran, to a widening range of business and social contacts, and eventually to an exploratory discussion about the possibility of Angeline joining Ardmurran International Electronics.

She had taken a three-month sabbatical from her company, being quite open with Red Lonnen, her boss, about her frustrations and the possibility of that she might resign. Alistair had invited her to Scotland to continue her research, with a view to her later meeting Paul and allowing him to interview her, administer some psychometric tests and give his overall assessment of her ability to fit into the R&D team.

Alistair came back into the room accompanied by a stocky Scottish police sergeant. He gestured towards Paul and Angeline. "These are my associates, Paul Corr and Doctor Angeline Blade – Paul, Angeline, may I introduce Sergeant Macdonald – he will need to take a brief statement from both of you about this incident."

The faint but distinct emphasis on the word brief, and the look he gave them clearly signalled that they should not go beyond the basic facts. Reading his thoughts, Angeline placed her hand round his wrist and gave a gentle, reassuring squeeze, and then dazzled the young sergeant with a smile

"It will have to be brief – there's little to tell; it happened and we don't know why…"

They sat down, and Alistair muttered something and left the room. They each gave their versions of the incident; Sergeant Macdonald made brief notes and then looked up from his notebook.

"Can you think of any reason why someone should have fired a shot at the house? Anything that occurs to you, anything at all, no matter how trivial it may seem?"

He fixed them with that unnerving policeman's look that manages, together with tone of voice and subtle body language, to combine politeness, encouragement, suspicion, and veiled threat in one focused stare. Paul shook his head in what he hoped was convincing bafflement.

"No – I can think of nothing, even trivial, that could relate to such an action, Sergeant Macdonald," he replied.

The young policeman sustained his basilisk stare for a moment, and then turned to Angeline.

"Doctor Blade?"

"Well, as a matter of fact, there is something, Sergeant…"

Paul's blood ran cold as Sergeant Macdonald brightened and smiled encouragingly, inviting her to continue.

"Mr. Mackinnon – Alistair – has been very active in a movement to control the activities of some power boaters on the loch – excessive speed, dangerous manoeuvres and so on. It is a matter of concern to all loch users. Perhaps he's upset someone, or some group?"

"Thanks for that insight, Dr. Blade," said Sergeant Macdonald, disappointed. "It's an outside possibility, but unlikely – but we will look into it." He closed his notebook decisively, and stood up.

"Thank you both – Mr. Corr – Doctor Blade – I am sorry you both have experienced such a thing while visiting Ardmurran. We're not exactly the crime capital of Great Britain up here, and we all feel ashamed that an incident like this could happen in our area. Thank you again for your help – I am sure Mr. Mackinnon will keep you both informed about any progress in our investigation."

Angeline and Paul made tentative motions to shake hands, but the sergeant moved back briskly, putting away his notebook. He was certainly not oblivious to Angeline's femininity; he looked again directly at her with an expression that was now not that of a policeman. Perhaps he was a virgin, like the Scottish police sergeant in the cult film, *The Wicker Man*, thought Paul, jealous again in spite of himself. This unfortunately conjured up another image from the film, of a woman writhing naked against a bedroom door, and only a supreme effort of self-control prevented Angeline being substituted in his mind's eye. He suddenly realised that this was the first time he had entertained an explicitly sexual thought about her, and he was inexplicably ashamed of it.

Sergeant Macdonald left, and Angeline said warmly, "What a nice young man!"

"I would guess that most young men are nice to you," observed Paul dryly, "Maybe most men in general…"

Angeline lifted her head, and gave him a look that made his heart thud.

"Are you jealous?"

Paul turned scarlet – he knew he was reddening, and felt a fool. "Yes, but I'm trying to be sophisticated and ironic about it."

"And failing – but charmingly!" Angeline said softly. Paul took her by the shoulders, pulled her towards him and kissed her, gently at first, then passionately. She responded for a moment, then pulled away.

"I think we must save this for another time, Paul. It's now the seventh of July – no, it's the eighth of July. At the moment, we have my freedom and Alistair's life to consider in just a couple of days from now – and maybe more cosmic matters."

Paul responded quickly.

"You're right – of course. But that was cosmic enough to keep me going."

They both laughed shakily, then Angeline, suddenly vulnerable, looked down, avoiding his eyes.

"Paul – I'm different from a lot of women of my age. I don't get involved in casual affairs. As a matter of fact…"

"Stop right there, Angeline," he said firmly. "I think I sensed it somehow, because – well, I'm no Don Juan myself and I get ribbed by my contemporaries about it. An older morality, born of an inner conviction that there would be someone uniquely right for me - and now there is. I'm sure as hell not going to rush things. Even if events weren't crowding in on us, I wouldn't want to rush things."

"But, Paul…"

"No buts – we understand each other perfectly. Let's move into friend and colleague mode till this situation is closer to some resolution."

The awkward silence that followed was broken by Alistair bursting into the room. "They've got him," he said, "they've found the marksman – I wish to hell they hadn't – they're bringing him here now!"

Paul didn't have to ask the reason why Alistair was upset, nor did Angeline: the pressure on him now from the police to reveal more, especially if the gunman talked, would be intense. Sergeant Macdonald made an entrance with another policeman; they were holding a handcuffed man of about forty-five to fifty years of age between them, olive-skinned, handsome, with black hair and dead eyes that looked past them to the bullet hole in the wall. He had an old crescent-shaped scar above his left eye that pulled the eyebrow up slightly, giving him a faintly quizzical expression.

"We found him on the loch shore, perhaps trying to signal to someone on the water. We have his confession that he fired the shot – we have the rifle, and he has implicated others. He says he came to Glasgow from the continent, seeking seasonal hotel work, and then found his way up here. I think he may be in a disturbed mental state, or under the influence of drugs. He was approached by some people, and offered money to frighten you; there was apparently no intent to kill or harm. They supplied the rifle, according to him: he had a considerable sum of money in his possession when we found him, so it appears to stack up. Would you like to speak to him, Mr. Mackinnon? He speaks reasonable English, but heavily accented – I don't know, maybe Italian?"

Alistair thought for a long moment. "Yes – yes, I would." He went across to the prisoner. "Why?" he said softly.

The man's eyes came alive. He looked directly up into Alistair's eyes and whispered, almost mouthing the words *"Recuerde julio el décimo - o vaya a Dios."* Then the light went out of his eyes, his jaw clenched, and his body slumped between his captors. A strangled, guttural sound came from his throat as he fell forward.

"He's having a fit," shouted Sergeant Macdonald, "get him on the floor – quickly!" They lowered the now jerking body of the man to the floor and laid him on his back. His eyes were closed and the veins were standing out on his forehead.

"Get his mouth open, he's suffocating!" cried Angeline, falling to her knees beside him. "We must give him mouth-to-mouth – thump his chest!"

All five of them knelt around the now motionless man on the floor.

"I can't force his jaw open – it's locked shut," panted the constable to Sergeant Macdonald, "it just won't open!"

There followed a seemingly endless period of frantic activity around the prisoner, with the constable continuing his attempts to open his mouth, Angeline pressing hard and rhythmically on his chest, the sergeant calling for an emergency ambulance on the telephone, Paul feeling for a pulse at the side of the man's head.

Eventually Paul stood up, shaking his head, a look of despair on his face. "There's no pulse – I think he's dead, Alistair."

They continued their vain endeavours until the ambulance arrived and the paramedics rushed in. They quickly confirmed that the man was dead, placed him on a stretcher and took him out of the house to the ambulance. Sergeant Macdonald gave a sigh, and spoke to the constable.

"Go with them, Colin." He turned again to Alistair in baffled frustration. "What happened? Was it some kind of heart attack – or did he somehow do it to himself?"

"I think he may have swallowed something he had in his mouth – or perhaps he had taken something before you apprehended him. He was clearly mentally deranged, poor creature – he has been unscrupulously used by some person, or some group, Sergeant Macdonald. We may never know who sent him." Alistair's tone was strong and definitive, carrying all his considerable natural authority.

"Poor bugger!' exclaimed the constable. "Sorry, Doctor Blade... I'll follow the ambulance," said the sergeant, but before he reached the door, he turned.

"He seemed to say something to you just before he went into that – that convulsion, Mr. Mackinnon – was it Italian? Did you understand what he said?"

Angeline opened her mouth to reply, but the Alistair was ahead of her.

"It was completely unintelligible – almost gibberish, Sergeant. We'll never know – it could have been an apology or a threat."

Sergeant Macdonald looked hard at him, nodded reluctantly and then he and the constable left the room. Angeline and Paul looked at each other, then at Alistair. "I don't know what he said, but it sounded Spanish, not Italian," said Paul.

Angeline went across to a chair and sat down, limp and exhausted. "Alistair knows what he said – don't you, Mr. Mackinnon?" Her tone was hostile. "He said *recuerde julio el décimo - o vaya a Dios* – remember the tenth of July or go to God."

"Aye, that's what he said," said Alistair heavily. "He was sent by either the Ancient Order or the *hermandad*. His task was to fire the shot, and if he got caught, to offer his cover story, then kill himself. That's the level of control they have. They may have offered him benefits, or made threats to his family."

Paul was astounded. Angeline was more pragmatic. "But who was he signalling to on the loch? Maybe he had a confederate to help him escape by boat!"

Alistair said wearily "It's not likely – logistically, it wouldn't make sense for them. I think that once he knew he was going to be apprehended, he pretended to signal to someone on the loch in order to remain consistent with his cover story. He knew his chances were slight, and so did whoever sent him."

"You said he was sent by either the Ancient Order or the *hermandad*, Alistair – but the letter, the ultimatum, came from the Ancient Order of Moridura, from the Magus. What's going on?" queried Paul.

Alistair shrugged. "Violence is not the way of the monks of Moridura, and is certainly not their Abbot's approach. The Magus isn't in charge of the Moriduran Brothers - the Abbot is their superior. The Grand Council is a body I've never heard of – the monastery's governing body is the monastery Chapter. The behaviour is more characteristic of the *hermandad*. I don't really know what's going on, Paul."

The two men went over and sat down beside Angeline: she had recovered something of her poise. She looked hard at Alistair, then her expression softened and she said slowly,

"Are you going to deliver your package in two days in the square at Mérida, or are you going to go to God?"

For a moment, anger flickered in Alistair Mackinnon's eyes, to be immediately replaced by an expression of great tenderness; he knelt down before her and took both her hands.

"Angeline, ma wee pal - you know I'll never do anything to harm a hair of your beautiful, clever wee head." He stood up abruptly, embarrassed by his show of affection.

"After all, I plan to invest heavily in your research..."

Paul became agitated, finding it hard to make sense of it all, deeply worried for the safety of a man he had loved and respected since childhood, and now, for a young woman he had met only a few hours ago, one who had entered his life like a bolt of lightning.

"Alistair, we must go to the police and tell them the truth; this bunch of medieval gangsters mustn't be allowed to get away with such intimidation!"

The tall, charismatic presence of Mackinnon suddenly seemed to fill the room, confident and powerful.

"No, we can't do that, Paul. What we must do, all three of us, is go to Madrid later this morning. We will grab a few hours sleep, then a car will take us to Glasgow Airport: the flight will take several hours. My security chief, Santiago, will meet us, and from Madrid, we head in the direction of Mérida, in Extremadura, by car, and from there travel east to a village called Moridanza, near the monastery of Moridura. There's a café in the village that can accommodate visitors – I know the owner, Manuel Ortega and his wife, Fidelicia - I stayed there on my last visit five years ago. From there we'll make contact with the Abbot of the monastery, Brother Anselmo."

Alistair clasped his hands together. "I have no right to ask this of either of you - especially you, Angeline - and clearly you may refuse. If you do, I'll go alone. I know that this extraordinary request demands a full explanation and I will give it to you both. I deeply regret the situation I've got you into, but I know that you'll understand when I explain, even if you decide not to come with me. An enormous amount is at stake; there is an imminent threat that has global implications for the lives of millions - perhaps for the planet itself." He waited for the full import of his words to sink in.

"Angeline, could you somehow try to give Paul the absolute essence of your work, remembering that he is a headhunter, sorry, executive search consultant, with an irrelevant classics degree."

Paul shook his head at the description; he gave Alistair a reproachful look, then turned to Angeline.

"I've read your paper and I have a rudimentary understanding of gravity, but I have to say my initial reaction was…" He broke off, and shrugged apologetically.

Angeline completed his unfinished sentence.

"…that this mysterious Doctor Blade must be nuts – that the paper has never been published because its claims are impossible to substantiate. Without proper peer review, it's almost certainly worthless…"

"Well, yes, but that was before I saw the matchbox…"

"You became a true believer. Doubting Thomas putting his hands in the wounds?" Angeline raised an eloquent eyebrow.

"Let's say agnostic. Try to help me embrace the faith!"

Alistair saw, with some surprise and a great deal of satisfaction the look that passed between his young friends. My God, he thought, has it happened this fast? But then, it did for me. The thought of his first meeting with his wife came back to him with almost unbearable poignancy.

Angeline stood up.

"OK, here goes – the core of my report and my findings. Gravity is a weak force, but one that affects everything. Newton was the first to understand it, and its effect on celestial bodies. It is wave-like, and may emanate from various sources in our universe. Scientists are scanning for sources, so far without success. I found, almost by accident, that by linking a simple electronic device to a small scanning disc aerial, I had apparently tapped into one source, but without being able to pinpoint it. There was a serendipitous element involved; I accidentally dropped my grandmother's wedding ring into the dish aerial - I usually wear it on my right hand, and it's too big for me.

"After coming to Ardmurran, Alistair, hearing the story of my grandmother's ring, produced a gold ring that he had, with a meteorite fragment set in it. We separated the rock fragment from the ring, and eventually found a way to incorporate it and the gold into the electronics. The presence of this unknown metal, similar to iridium, amplified the capture, and permitted limited modulation of the gravity wave. The logical extrapolation of this would revolutionise almost every aspect of our lives – transport, materials handling, medicine, space travel – you name it. The terrifying aspect is that the defence industry will inevitably find other applications and powerful commercial interests will take control of the technology…"

Paul thought for a moment, aware of Alistair watching him intently for his reaction to Angeline's reduction of mind-bending physics to a compact exposition.

"I think I understand – but why is the Ancient Order of Moridura involved? How did they know of this research? How do they know about Angeline? What can the Black Hand of Extremadura, the *hermandad*, do with such knowledge?" he said.

Angeline gripped Alistair by the elbow, and pulled him towards her, and looked up intently into his eyes.

"And those are the questions I want answers to, Jimmy! That's what I want to know – why, how, and what?"

"I have partial answers," replied Alistair, "plus a whole lot of speculative theories to offer. The *hermandad* see a threat to their power, which in some way is linked to gravitational effects, but they also see the potential to play on a much larger stage than a district of Extremadura: I know for certain that they are aware of the interest of a major corporation in the potential of the new technology, and they…"

Angeline interrupted his explanation.

"That could only be my present employer, or Ardmurran International Electronics!"

"There is one other – Xalatera – but, yes, it was the involvement of Angeline's present employer, Lonnen, that triggered their interest. That led them to investigate your whereabouts, then to me," Alistair confirmed. "They were approached directly by Red Lonnen himself. I got this from my contacts in America and Madrid."

As he said this, Alistair gave the young physicist a strange look, a mixture of concern and pity. The look was not lost on Paul, and Angeline's reaction confirmed that some complex emotions were in play; her face was tense, her mouth set tightly, her gaze unfocused.

Alistair looked away from Angeline and back at Paul.

"The *hermandad* have a sort of symbiotic relationship with the Moriduran Brothers – the monks. Historically, it is sometimes hard to distinguish the monastery and its interests from those of the *hermandad*, the secular brotherhood. The Church in Spain has always had to co-exist with powerful men, especially in Spain around the time of the *Reconquista* and later with the *conquistadores* in the New World. Of course, the Catholic Church has always compromised with secular power; they couldn't have survived for over two millennia if they hadn't.

Paul frowned. "But why is the monastery involved? Why would an obscure congregation of monks in a remote Spanish monastery become involved in these power plays? Why do you want us to go to the monastery, Alistair? I'm finding it hard to make sense of all this, as I am sure Angeline is."

"Then give her your explanation again, in more detail this time," responded Alistair.

Paul's reaction said it all – this was an unwelcome task that his friend had unceremoniously dumped on him. He was tired, confused, and worried about Angeline, but he expanded on his earlier brief account – the history of the Ancient Order of Moridura, the monastery, the horror story from the Moridura Manuscript, the gravitational phenomena – and the legend of the Beast of Moridura. To his surprise, the story seemed to brighten Angeline's mood; she became animated, and hung on his every word. When he finished, she spoke excitedly.

"This is wonderful! I can't wait to get there – this is going to be the big adventure of my dull, scientific life. Exotic locations, danger, monks, sinister secret societies – who would have thought studying physics would catapult me into this?"

Alistair betrayed some impatience at this reaction.

"You're right about the danger – and I'm responsible for placing you both in harm's way. That's bad enough, but there's more, Angeline. Red Lonnen is almost certainly already in Extremadura, maybe at the monastery. Do you still want to come with me?"

She looked as if Alistair had slapped her in the face – her elation vanished and there was an unbearable silence that seemed to last for ever, then she replied, almost inaudibly.

"Let's make the travel arrangements – there isn't much time, is there?" She reached out for both men's hands, and they formed their circle for the second time.

"We're off to see the Wizard!" said Angeline, and they clung together, embracing, dancing and laughing.

Chapter Seven

The *Officium Divinum* comprises the one hundred and fifty psalms from the Old Testament, recited on a weekly cycle, readings from scripture and the lives of the Saints, commentaries, and hymns. *Ora et labore* – pray and work, said Saint Benedict.

This common prayer of the monastic community of Moridura in general followed the Benedictine pattern, and the whole structure of the monks' day, both prayer and work was built around this. The Moridurans used the early 1940s' structure of the *Breviarium Romanum*. Matins and Lauds were said before dawn. Prime, Terce, Sext, and None were prayed during the first, third, sixth, and ninth hours of the day. Vespers was prayed at dusk, and the cycle of prayer and the day itself ended with Compline. The monastery displayed a degree of flexibility within this traditional structure, and practical considerations often caused the times to be varied. Overall, however, the Divine Office constituted the ancient framework of the monks' lives.

Guests at the monastery were allowed, and indeed encouraged to participate in the prayer cycle, but the monks had instinctively felt that their arrogant, ill-mannered American guest would decline this invitation. To their surprise, he accepted readily, and those who knelt near him noted his apparently genuine devotion as he uttered the Latin words; one monk claimed that the red-haired man was evidently moved, and seemed to be in tears on occasion.

Mateo continued to be uncharitably suspicious of the American, in spite of his brief conversation with him when he had found the gold figurine. On his way to the library after Vespers to do the work assigned to him by the Abbot – checking the latest missive from Rome on the involvement of the laity in the Divine Office – he turned over again in his mind the question of Señor Lonnen.

Guests of the Abbey had always been limited to Don Ferdinand, *confratres*, senior members of the *hermandad*, emissaries from the Vatican, and a few favoured local suppliers, such as Manuel Ortega, who, once or twice a year were allowed to stay over for one night and take part in prayers in the chapel. An exception had been the big Scotsman who had visited five years ago, and had stayed for a week by special dispensation of the Abbot. Being a Scottish Presbyterian, he did not participate in their prayers.

Some of the older monks seemed to remember him with disapproval – always laughing and singing, they muttered – but Mateo and the younger monks recalled him warmly for his good spirits and humour, and wished that he would make a return visit. Brother Joaquín could sing one of his songs, *Loch Lomond*, and said that he lived by the shores of this famous Scottish lake. The Scotsman had also brought an old portable wind-up gramophone, and played 78 rpm jazz records in his room. The Abbot was mildly disapproving, but did not stop him, and the pristine sound of Bix Beiderbecke had reverberated around the ancient corridors, although the Scotsman had the sensitivity not to play the records during prayers. Brother Joaquín, who had an excellent ear, still hummed the famous cornet solo from *Singing the Blues* while he worked.

Mateo had originally acquired a taste for classic jazz from some of the older men in Moridanza, listening to their records in Manuel Ortega's café. He listened avidly when Manuel tuned into jazz programmes on his old valve radio, with Manuel laughingly remonstrating with him, telling him that he should not be listening to music such as this, and that Brother Gregorio would not approve.

Mateo was fascinated by the Louis Armstrong recording of *It's Tight Like That*: he was puzzled by the title, the lyric and the verbal exchanges between Louis and the other band members, but the cornet solo played by Louis brought him close to tears, and he felt that it had a tragic, almost sacred quality to it. To Mateo, it also seemed to capture something that was quintessentially Spanish, but Manuel did not agree.

He entered the library and headed towards the section where current documents were held – letters, bills, church bulletins and general correspondence. All bank details were held by the Abbot in his room in an old Chubb safe, a massive metal construction with a combination lock.

Brother Anselmo settled most traders' bills in cash. Mateo was entrusted with the task of going to the bank with the Abbot's cheque and withdrawing money to maintain the cash float, being driven to and from Moridanza by Manuel Ortega, or more rarely, using the Abbot's car. Manuel sometimes settled small bills in Moridanza on the Abbot's behalf, receiving the cash from Mateo.

The monks, vegetarians by custom, lived well on homegrown vegetables and dairy produce from the district, but guests were served meat if they requested it. The Abbot decreed that all must participate in tilling the soil, because manual labour was one of the two essential components of the monastic life – *ora et labore* – prayer and work. Mateo did his share in this work, but his main duties were administrative and financial ones for Brother Anselmo and Brother Gregorio.

He also assisted the cellarer, Brother Alfonso, with the monastery's wines, which were obtained mainly from Don Ferdinand's vineyards at special commercial rates. The wine cellar, deep in the rear of the monastery, was one of the oldest parts of the monastery complex; it had two sections, the larger containing the ordinary wines for daily consumption, and the smaller - at the rear of the cellar - the fine wines, some very old, some of comparatively recent vintage. Brother Alfonso was in his late seventies, spry and alert normally, although he occasionally fell asleep in the cellar and had to be gently roused by Mateo. Mateo had hopes that he might succeed him one day, but the Abbot vetoed this ambition.

"That path is not for you, Mateo – your direction will be determined in the fullness of time. You will perform great services to the monastery, to your brethren – you will contribute to the higher scheme of things. God has your destiny in his hands."

Mateo found the letter from Rome and put it in the battered leather folder he used to carry the Abbot's papers, and then headed for the cellar. *El Americano* had developed a fondness for a particular wine from the Abbot's special racks, and had requested a bottle for tonight's meal. Mateo remembered that Brother Alfonso would not be in the cellar – he was with the Abbot discussing the next shipment of wine from Don Ferdinand.

Descending the winding stone stairs to the cellar, carrying a lit candle in a brass holder in one hand and the leather folder in the other, he reminded himself to take care not to drop the precious bottle on the way back. The ancient worn steps were treacherous, and Brother Alfonso negotiated them with increasing difficulty, the principal reason Mateo was assigned to help him.

Reaching the cellar door, Mateo placed the candleholder in the niche at the side of the door and pulled the heavy, outward-opening door towards him. There was no latch or lock on the door – it swung slowly and ponderously on its creaky hinges. He retrieved the candleholder, and entered the huge, low-ceilinged cellar, the poor light of the candle fitfully illuminating the relatively clean racks that held the newer wines for daily use: as he walked between them towards the cobwebbed vintage wine racks at the rear, he reflected on the generations of monks who had moved across this floor.

A powerful image swept across his consciousness, like multiple reflections in a huge mirror, of himself walking, the flickering candle lights stretching back into infinity. He felt in touch with the very core of his being: he reflected on the continuity of life, on his fundamental relationship with the monastery: he seemed to be moving towards a nebulous goal, the achievement of some objective, a great task, one that he had completed many times before, yet must perform again. Was this the feeling of oneness with God, with the eternal Universe, of infinity that his religion spoke of often? Yet a nameless dread lurked beneath the mood, a sense of something that threatened the fulfilment of the task.

He reached the rack on the left side where the vintage was stored, now showing many gaps where the bottles consumed avidly by Señor Lonnen had lain for decades. He placed the folder under his arm, held up the candle, checking that he had the right rack, and then lifted a bottle very gently from the rack. He must not disturb the sediment in the old wine – it must be decanted carefully before being served to the American.

Something caught his eye on his right, and he noticed, for the first time, that the rear wall of the cellar contained a small arch, faintly visible in the candlelight, formed by smaller stones than the massive blocks of the wall: the arch enclosed a wooden door, barely distinguishable from the wall. It was a small doorway, no more than five feet high, and its width was little more than the breadth of a man's shoulders.

Mateo had always understood that the wine cellar had been built into a deep depression in the rock of *La Copa* at the rear of the monastery, and that there was no way out to the slopes behind this wall. Some accounts claimed that the cellar was older than the monastery itself, and was a pre-Roman structure. He focused again on the little door. Was it ornamental? The craftsmen who built the monastery had occasionally indulged themselves with ornamental flourishes that served no purpose other than decoration, although their general style was austere.

Mateo looked more closely at the arched doorway. He could see now why he had missed it before. The wood was dark and rough-textured, and over the centuries it had become indistinguishable from the stone around it. There was no handle, and it was only after close inspection that Mateo found a large keyhole, covered with cobwebs, with no escutcheon. He looked around, but could find no key.

The candle was burning low, and he knew that he must get back to the Abbot, but something impelled him to lay down the wine, the folder and the candle, kneel down and put his ear to the keyhole. The wine cellar was acoustically dead because of the low ceiling, the wine rack, casks and bottles, but from the other side of the door there was a reverberation, as in the main areas of the monastery, an auditory sense of space and distance. This could not be; there was only rock beyond the walls, thought Mateo: yet there was the undeniable fact of the little door and its eerie echoes.

I will ask Alfonso, and perhaps Brother Anselmo, he decided, but then the strange earlier mood returned with great force, and with it a conviction that he should not tell anyone of the door. For a Moriduran to keep secrets from his brethren was frowned upon – to keep a secret from the Abbot, or from Padre Gabriel, an ordained priest, and his confessor, was unthinkable. Yet the conviction remained with him.

He picked up the folder, the candleholder and the bottle, and turned to leave the cellar; as he did so, a voice, a terrible voice, unlike anything he had ever heard, spoke distinctly from behind the little door.

"*Mateo - No hable de esto!*"

Mateo whirled round, causing the candle to gutter, and almost dropping the folder from under his arm.

"Who is there? Who tells me not to speak of this? Where are you?"

He stood there in the dead silence of the cellar, the hairs of his neck standing on end, and waited fearfully for that terrifying voice to answer, but there was only the silence, the light of the candle and the sound of his own laboured breathing. With an effort of will, he turned his back on the little door, walked quickly back to the entrance to the cellar and climbed the steps back to main corridor, then headed for the Abbot's room.

A monk called out to him jovially that he could blow out his candle now since there was enough illumination in the corridor. On reaching the door of Brother Anselmo's room, he paused, still with the dilemma of whether or not he should tell him of the door and the voice. He knocked, and the Abbot called out rather testily that he should enter. The Abbot was behind his desk and Señor Lonnen was seated in front of him. Food had already been brought to them, and a fine crystal decanter awaited the contents of the bottle. The American turned, and his expression brightened at the sight of the wine. Brother Anselmo gestured impatiently for the folder. Mateo surrendered both his burdens, receiving curt thanks for the wine from Lonnen, and nothing but a grunt from the Abbot. He left, relieved of his problem of communication for the moment.

On the way out he met Alfonso, who whispered conspiratorially to him.

"Did you get another bottle for *el borracho Americano*? Soon there will be none left."

Mateo flashed him a reproving glance, and flicked his head towards the door of the Abbot's office, his eyes signalling a warning. He took the old man by the arm and steered him across the floor till they were out of earshot.

"Alfonso, have you ever noticed a small door, with no handle and no key, at the far end of the cellar?"

"Yes, yes," the old monk muttered, "*La Puerta de Bestia* – no one knows why it is named thus. It leads nowhere – there is nothing but the rock of *La Copa* behind it. There is no key – it has never been opened in living memory. In any case, successive Abbots have forbidden it – Brother Anselmo himself told me never to speak of it, and now you have made me do so!" His voice quavered and his watery old eyes were reproachful.

"But why build a door to nowhere? Why is it called the Gate of the Beast? Could it be the Beast of …"

Brother Alfonso held up his hands in obvious distress, his expression now one of terror.

"Do not speak of it – do not utter the accursed name – we will be expelled from the monastery! You must not tell the Abbot what I have so foolishly revealed! *Cristo mi Salvador* – forgive me!"

Mateo tried to allay the old man's acute distress, putting his arm around his thin shoulders and murmuring reassuringly. Eventually Alfonso calmed down and departed, looking over his shoulder and placing his forefinger to his lips. Mateo was left with a feeling of frustration; he stood still for a moment and said a silent prayer for guidance, then headed for the refectory. It was time for supper, then Compline, and then bed. Prayers would be led by Brother Gregorio, the Abbot's deputy, a vigorous and intelligent man in his forties, but without humour or warmth: he was something of a bureaucrat, and ambitious – too many years of playing politics with the Holy Office had left their mark upon him. Mateo fervently hoped that food, prayer and sleep would bring peace to his troubled mind.

The sun was setting, but the last of the light filtered through the long narrow windows of Brother Anselmo's room, augmenting the light from the two candelabra, one on the massive desk on which the meal was set, the other on a large writing desk across the room. The light barely touched the high vaulted ceiling of the room.

The Abbot reached for the silver-handled corkscrew on the desk, and began to uncork the wine, moving slowly and carefully, respecting the venerable contents of the dusty bottle. The cork emerged silently, and Brother Anselmo placed the bottle down and lifted the decanter. Red Lonnen impatiently reached for the bottle, choosing to ignore the Abbot's reproaches over his cavalier treatment of previous bottles.

"No need – I'll risk the sediment! I need a drink!" he said briskly and moved to fill the Abbot's glass.

"No, thank you – forgive me if I don't join you. Please …" and he motioned the red-haired man to fill his own glass, then watched as a fine old wine was ruined by careless handling.

Oblivious, Lonnen drained the glass, and then poured himself another. Brother Anselmo wished he had not introduced the American to this wine – he would clearly have been content with any one of the lesser vintages. He thought of the big Scotsman, and wondered what his assessment of Lonnen would be: the two men were the chief executives and sole owners of companies in related fields and must have met each other in a business context.

Lonnen was much younger than Mackinnon, by fifteen years or so. Neither of them suffered fools gladly; both of them were intense, driven men, but Mackinnon had a breadth of vision and warmth that the Abbot felt the American lacked.

The two men ate silently for a while, the Abbot with a frugal meal of vegetables, and the American with his normal preference of steak, fries and beans. The meat was specially brought in for him at regular intervals - the monastery had no refrigerators. Lonnen had declared on arrival that, although he was well used to *haute cuisine* in the world's finest restaurants, plain food was his real joy.

"After you've been living on *foie gras* and wine, fries and beans and beer taste fine," he would often say. "My doctor tells me to ease up on the beef, but I can't. Anyway, I started out as a poor kid, and like most poor kids, I regarded steak at every meal as the key indicator that a guy had made it in life. I can't shake that feeling off – stupid, I guess, Brother Anselmo, but there it is!"

Brother Anselmo murmured reassuringly.

"Within the limits of our resources, we are happy to meet an honoured guest's dietary needs, Señor Lonnen."

There was another silence while they finished their meal, Lonnen draining his last glass of wine with a sigh of satisfaction, then he looked at the Abbot enquiringly.

"Will Mackinnon come here? Will he respond to the Chapter's invitation? He has Angeline Blade up there among the heather, and he plans to offer her a full-time job. His interest in this matter is at least as great as mine, with this difference – she did her key research and produced her paper on the gravitational effect within my corporation, not his. I own that research, its conclusions, and my company will exploit the patents, not Ardmurran International Electronics. Over my dead body! Well, over my lawyers' dead bodies!"

Brother Anselmo steepled his hands, an enigmatic look on his face.

"Wouldn't it make more sense to combine forces? Mackinnon seems to have won her confidence, and if she joins his organisation, her research will continue while you litigate. I am no expert in these matters, but litigation could take years."

Lonnen appreciated the force of the old man's logic, indeed, in his heart of hearts, he knew that he was right. He picked up the empty bottle then laid it down again with regret.

"Your isolation in this remote place doesn't separate you from the world, does it, Abbot – how in hell – forgive me – do you keep in touch with world events? You have no radio, no television; a single newspaper comes once a week. How do you do it?"

The Abbot judged the question to be rhetorical, and simply ignored it.

"You asked if Mackinnon was likely to come here? The answer is that he is almost certain to, and within the next few days; moreover, he will bring Doctor Blade with him. But I think perhaps you already know that, after your visit to Don Ferdinand?"

The American was thrown off balance; he had underrated the old monk yet again. In the way of some red-haired people under the grip of strong emotion, his face grew very pale, and the effect was to give his strongly chiselled features a menacing quality.

The Abbot noted his reaction. "I am sorry if I have been too direct, Señor Lonnen, but few things happen in the district that I do not know about; that is not a boast, it is a statement of fact."

Red Lonnen smiled, the colour returning to his cheeks.

"You have been straight to the point with me, Brother Anselmo – I like that even though you caught me with my – with my…"

They both smiled, and the American continued. "I came to you, as the spiritual leader of the district of Moridanza, and the person with the greatest knowledge of *La Copa de Moridura*. I went to Ferdinand as the guy who gets things done in business matters around here – the connected guy with political clout. I was – and still am – unsure exactly of the nature of the relationship between you. You have known each other for many years and I guess you are a family friend as well as his spiritual adviser, maybe his confessor?"

"I am not his confessor, since I am not an ordained priest – Padre Gabriel, our resident priest, is his confessor. The commercial and political life of Moridanza and the region affect us both, and it is not vanity to say that we influence affairs in the district," responded Brother Anselmo.

Red Lonnen pushed his chair back, stood up and paced slowly back and forth for a moment, one hand on his chin, the other on his hip.

"This area of Spain is remote – few tourists come here, in fact, few visitors of any kind. They're not deterred by remoteness – they stay away because things are deliberately made difficult for them. Facilities in the district are not inadequate by accident; the lack of proper access roads, the lack of electrical power in the monastery, the hostility extended to the hardy few who reach your gates or climb the rim of *La Copa*; the regulations that prohibit over-flying the monastery and the Cup, regulations that prohibit the landing of helicopters – none of these things are accidental."

He stopped pacing, went to the table and placed both hands on it, facing the Abbot.

"You and Don Ferdinand have the power and influence to change these things – a change that would bring great material benefit to you and to the people of the district – yet for some reason you fail to exert that power – that political clout. You are protecting something from the modern world. What is it, Brother Anselmo? What is it?"

The Abbot looked up at him. Lonnen found it difficult to read the wily old monk's expression.

"We are protecting a centuries-old way of life. Surely there is room for the old ways within this new world? We threaten no one." His look, of appealing holy innocence, did not fool Red Lonnen.

"I don't underestimate your survival instinct – I recognise that it has served the Church well for centuries," he said, "but your prompt and positive response to my letter requesting permission to visit you told me that something I said had a resonance for you that the legions of such requests by other persons and organisations did not. If I had simply stated that I wanted to study the history of the monastery of Moridura and the topography and geology of *La Copa de Moridura*, you would have, with infinite politeness, declined. The photograph of my little gold figurine got me my invitation – and I think you know I have something more substantial in my trunk that is of interest to you." He looked at the Abbot for his reaction; in the absence of any responses, he continued.

"What got your attention was my mention of Doctor Blade's research into gravitation, yet there are no scientists among your brethren, they are, for the most part, simple devout men, with the exception of a few scholars.

"I have been here for weeks and I am no further forward, but any doubts that I entertained were dispelled by my meeting with Ferdinand. He listened to what I had to say, yet gave nothing in return. He is an experienced negotiator, and you are an experienced diplomat, Brother Anselmo. But this was not a conventional negotiation – all my experience tells me that some other factor exists in the equation. When negotiation fails, power and force come into play, and you and Ferdinand exert power and influence in the district and perhaps beyond. Don't underrate me, please. We must understand each other fully if the conflicting elements in our objectives are to be reconciled."

"And if they are irreconcilable?" said the Abbot softly, getting up and turning slowly to the window, his back to the American.

"Then we will both abandon negotiation on this matter and resort to other means. I will not be deflected from my goals." Lonnen's tone was unmistakable.

"We do not make threats – we invite others to examine the consequences of their actions, the necessary implications of their decisions," said the Abbot, turning to face him again.

"Are we deadlocked?" asked Red Lonnen bluntly.

"We are deadlocked, as you put it, but it is not a deadlock that threatens breakdown. The arrival of Alistair Mackinnon and Doctor Blade will act as a catalyst in our relationship and break the deadlock, Señor Lonnen," replied the Abbot.

Lonnen exploded into anger; his face became deathly pale again and he jabbed his finger towards the old man.

"I will not deal with that man – he is a dilettante – he has built a large corporation, but he is mercurial and unpredictable in his dealings. He holds soft-centred convictions he calls principles, he indulges his enthusiasms, and Doctor Blade has fallen for this flawed persona. I will not turn what is already a three-way negotiation into a four-handed game – the complexities would multiply exponentially."

The Abbot moved round the table and stood close to the angry man, his entire manner conciliatory.

"Firstly, Señor Lonnen, you are not in a three-way negotiation – please accept that the strategic interests of the monastery and those of Don Ferdinand are identical in all matters that are fundamental to our interaction with you, although we may differ over tactics. Secondly, we do not see Alistair Mackinnon as a third party at the bargaining table; nonetheless he and Doctor Blade are necessary players in our complex dealings. Thirdly, a man's life may already have been sacrificed as a direct result of your involvement in the affairs of the monastery. You are not personally responsible for this, but the tragic event was one consequence of your arrival. Lastly, we believe that your interest in Doctor Blade goes beyond that of an employer and an employee. You have kept this from us for reasons you doubtless deem sufficient, but this fact impinges on our plans."

The impact of the Abbot's last two points upon the American silenced him completely, as he absorbed their implications. Someone had died as a result of his involvement; it could only be Pablo Miguenez, the emissary sent to Scotland to underline the invitation to Mackinnon.

How had his death come about? By accident? And there was the staggering fact that the Abbot and Ferdinand knew that his interest in Angeline went beyond a contractual relationship. How could they know this? At last, he recovered himself enough to speak.

"I do not understand your observation about Doctor Blade. I assume that the death you refer to was of the man Miguenez, sent to Ardmurran by you and Ferdinand. His death was presumably accidental?"

"Don Ferdinand arranged for him to go, with your implied endorsement – I had no part in that decision, and I would have refused to sanction it. His death was planned –

he died apparently by his own hand after he had delivered his message," replied the Abbot. Red Lonnen tried to maintain his composure as he listened to the old man's devastating revelation, but his shock at the Abbot's words was written on his face.

"But – I had no idea – I would never have agreed if I had known ..." His voice tailed off, and he shook his head, looking down. The Abbot's tone displayed warmth and pity as he responded.

"I believe you, Señor Lonnen. You are a man of great strength of will, one driven by ambition and the need to exercise power, but you are not an evil man. Doctora Blade has inadvertently released forces in our lives that compel us to act out our roles in a great drama; these forces are, in the words of someone wiser than I, without malice and without pity, they are beyond good and evil. But we are not, and we must find within ourselves the voice that will direct our choices as events unfold."

Red Lonnen looked at the old monk and spoke slowly and deliberately. "And what of Don Ferdinand's organisation – the *hermandad*."

The two men stood motionless in the fading light, now locked in their inner thoughts of what lay ahead of them. A bell tinkled somewhere in the Abbey and the sound of the monks' voices, united in the rhythms of prayer, drifted slowly into their consciousness.

Chapter Eight

Manuel stood behind the bar in his café, serving the few early evening regulars, offering them a minimum of conversation, going over and over in his mind the recent meeting with Don Ferdinand and the Abbot.

Brother Anselmo, at the outset, held firmly to his position that he and Manuel were bound by Francisco Ortega's dying prohibition relating to his diaries. Don Ferdinand was, to Manuel's surprise, conciliatory and understanding in the face of the Abbot's intransigence.

He argued that Manuel's father's intentions had been to protect the diaries as part of his legacy to Manuel, and to keep them out of the hands of those who would exploit them for gain, without recognising their historical importance. The Abbot did not reject this line of argument out of hand, to Manuel's great relief.

"I will consider this in solitude when I return to the monastery. In the meantime, we must share with Manuel our knowledge of recent happenings – he must be bewildered by allusions to events of which he knows nothing," he said.

The Abbot and the Don had then explained to him that a scientific discovery of great importance had been made by an American scientist – a young woman - and her findings involved the monastery and *La Copa de Moridura*.

He went on to say that when Manuel was formally inducted into the *hermandad*, he would bypass the normal probationary level of membership and be inducted immediately as a full member, and would be told more at that time. This was a rare honour, but one merited in the exceptional circumstances.

Manuel glowed with pride as he realised that his dreams were about to be fulfilled beyond his imaginings. But then the memory of his last meeting with his old friend Pablo Miguenez caused a darker theme to make its entry into Manuel's symphony of satisfaction. Pablo had come to the café, and confided to Manuel that he was going on an errand for the Don. It would involve leaving the country, but he could not tell anyone of his destination. Indeed he should not be telling Manuel even this much, but he had a favour to ask of him.

Pablo had shaken his hand before he left, and his words, and the blazing intensity of his gaze came back to Manuel.

"Manuel, old friend – my oldest, most faithful friend – I placed my beloved Carlota to your safe hands. I have always valued your friendship – goodbye, and think well of me, whatever happens."

His reverie was broken by the sound of the telephone ringing, and he picked it up.

"Café Ortega…"

A broad smile suddenly spread across his face as he heard the unmistakeable voice of *el Escocés grande.*

"Long time no see, *mi amigo pequeño!* Have you got room for four in your fine establishment?"

Manuel heard Fidelicia, listening on the extension, giggle with delight, and exclaim "Señor Alistair!"

"Do I hear the sweet voice of the most beautiful woman in the region? Forgive me, what if that most undeserving of men, Manuel Ortega overhears us!"

"I hear you, Señor Mackinnon. I am insulted - we must fight a duel!"

"*Mi Dios!* Manuel!" said Alistair in mock surprise, "*Soy perdido!* A duel it must be, then – with fine Toledo blades. How are you, wee man? It has been a long time. Do you have rooms for me and my two friends - and a beautiful señorita?"

"For the beautiful señorita only, Señor Alistair – you and your friends may sleep in the bar."

"We probably will anyway, Manuel – under the table. It will be for one or two nights only – we must visit the monastery and hope that Brother Anselmo will accommodate us for a time; then we may return to you before we leave for home."

Fidelicia's voice came on the line again

"I will prepare the four rooms now, Señor Alistair - I will leave you with my fool of a husband."

"Where are you now, Señor Alistair? Can I pick you up?" said Manuel excitedly.

"We are in Madrid airport – a car will take us to Moridanza and we will be with you in a few hours," replied Alistair. "Did I surprise you, Manuel?"

"Not entirely," said Manuel, suddenly cautious, conscious of his newfound duty of confidentiality, "the Abbot and Don Ferdinand did mention the possibility…" His voice tailed off.

"Did they, now," Alistair said softly, "did they really? Must ring off now, my friend – see you soon!"

The line went dead before Manuel could respond.

Alistair Mackinnon hung up the handset and turned to his companions. "He knew we were coming. I'm not surprised, but we must take great care. I don't think they'll interfere with us on the way to Moridanza, but we may be at risk when we get there, until I have contacted the Abbot. If he knows we are coming, as Manuel suggested he did, we're OK. I've arranged for my security chief in Madrid to meet us and take us to Extremedura. Ah, there he is now! Santiago! Over here!"

A powerfully built man in his early forties came striding across, a wide smile creasing his handsome face.

"Señor Alistair – welcome to Madrid – how was your flight?" he said, shaking hands briefly then turning expectantly to Paul and Angeline.

"These are my good friends – Paul Corr and Angeline Blade," said Alistair. "Paul – Angeline – I would like you to meet Santiago Manrique, my European security chief."

They shook hands, and then Santiago lifted two of their bags, Alistair and Paul the remainder. Angeline found herself walking between two tall men, with Paul behind them, a slightly incongruous rearguard. The three men had instinctively formed a protective formation around her, and Angeline, with her flaming red hair, attracted many admiring glances as they moved across the concourse towards the door of the airport.

A large black Mercedes awaited them; the man standing watchfully beside it nodded briefly to Santiago, then opened the rear passenger door for Angeline, who got in and slid across to the far seat, followed by Paul. Santiago opened the front passenger door for Alistair, before getting into the driver's seat. The car moved off swiftly and smoothly.

"Head for Mérida, and we'll take it from there," Alistair said briefly to his security chief, then looked over his shoulder from the front seat and grinned.

"Relax, we're OK now, you're in expert hands!" he said breezily. "Monks and monsters, here we come and if you're spied it's no' ma fault!"

Paul grinned at the Scottish hide and seek rhyme, and his mood shifted from apprehension to anticipation. Relaxing, he felt Angeline's head drop slowly on to his shoulder, then her small, cool hand crept into his in a grasp of childlike trust: the events of the night before had caught up with her, and she had fallen asleep.

He looked up instinctively at the driver's rear view mirror, and saw Santiago's eyes on him for a moment: Paul smiled and raised his eyebrows in faint embarrassment. Alistair turned his head briefly and murmured sympathetically.

"The poor wee thing – she's been through a lot, and she never slept on the plane. She'll have a stiff neck by the time we get there, lying like that, Paul."

Paul tried gently to adjust their respective positions without waking her. Angeline's eyes flickered briefly; she looked at him for a second with a drowsy smile, then closed them again and snuggled closer. He felt a sudden wholly irrational surge of gratitude towards the Ancient Order of Moridura for bringing them together in this way, but then the cold realisation of the danger she was in returned.

Alistair, still looking back at them, read his young friend's changing mood expertly.

"She *will* be safe, Paul, believe me."

"But will she?" said Paul very softly. "Are we underrating the dangers?"

"From the moment she made her discovery, she was at risk. The *hermandad* has a long reach. They don't wish to harm her – that wouldn't serve their ends. This is the only way, Paul."

Paul nodded, looking out of the window. "In which direction are we headed?"

"More or less south west, Señor Paul," Santiago said over his shoulder. He was interrupted by Alistair.

"Call him Paul - he'd like that better..."

"Mérida is over sixty kilometres south of Caceres, Paul, and Badajoz is about fifty kilometres west of it. Caceres and Badajoz give their names to the two provinces of Extremadura. It will take us several hours to get there."

Alistair butted in again, as was his way.

"Extremadura is one of the largest regions in Europe; it's about as big as Belgium and a wee bit smaller than Scotland. It is one of the seventeen autonomous provinces of Spain."

"Scotland's only a region now, is it, Alistair? I thought it was a country..." said Paul mischievously, winking at Santiago in the mirror.

"Watch it, Jimmy – just you watch it!" growled Alistair.

"And where is Moridanza in relation to Mérida?" asked Paul.

"East of the sun and west of the moon!" said Alistair.

"Is that a quote from the Old Testament or a line from a song? You're not going to tell me, then?" said Paul.

"We head in the general direction of the *Sierra del Pedroso*, Santiago – I'll direct you from there, if my memory serves me well enough.

"Do we know the real name of the current Magus?"

"He could be Don Ferdinand, the local politico and landowner mentioned in the 'phone by Manuel; he's certainly one of the High Heid Yins in the Order…"

Both Santiago and Paul were familiar with the Scottish term for people of rank and authority – the High Head Ones.

"…he could even be the Abbot of Moridura, Brother Anselmo," said Alistair ruminatively, "or he could be someone we don't even know."

"I know what you said earlier about the relationship of the *hermandad* and the monks, Alistair, but the Abbot is the superior of a religious order of the Roman Catholic Church, following the Benedictine rule. How could he possibly be directly involved with a secret society, especially a criminal one?" Paul was incredulous.

Santiago interjected at this point.

"If I may? I am a Spanish Catholic – not as devout as I should be, but still a Catholic. There has always been an area that is hard to define between religious orders and the Catholic laity and their organisations. The medieval *hermandad*es, or brotherhoods, were highly localised groups, protecting their own interests. In the sixteenth century, religious and military orders in Castile wielded enormous power, and they shaded into each other – soldiers became monks – monks became soldiers - and neither were strangers to intrigue and violence." Santiago stopped abruptly, feeling that he had departed from his security persona.

Alistair turned round and smirked at Paul.

"Where in Europe or America could you headhunt a security head honcho who could offer an analysis like that, Mr. Executive Search consultant, eh?"

They all fell silent; the hours slipped by and the car hummed smoothly on its way. A gentle snore from Alistair indicated that the he had fallen asleep. Paul's eyes met Santiago's in the mirror, and he smiled reassuringly.

"It's OK, Santiago – I won't drop off! How long will it be before we reach Moridanza?"

"I'll wake him when we are close to the turn off at Mérida - I need directions from there on," Santiago laughed. "I'm glad that at least two of us will be awake."

"You can rely on me," said Paul, closing his eyes reflectively and falling asleep. He was awakened by Angeline's gentle whisper in his ear.

"We're there, Paul – we're in Moridanza!"

He felt foolish – he had let Santiago down by dozing off, and had missed the mysterious part of the journey. Looking out of the window, he saw a small village square, with some sort of monument in the centre of it. He half expected men in hoods to surround the car and drag them out, but only a few people were around, going about their business and looking at the car with mild curiosity.

"Turn right just past that sign and up the hill, Santiago, and we're at Café Ortega. I'm ready for a wee goldie, a bottle of the local vino and Fidelicia's fine cuisine," Alistair said. "If there had been a reception committee in the square, you would have had to shoot them, or at least tell them to wait until we were fed and watered. Anyway, it's not July the 10th yet – the buggers will just have to wait."

Paul wondered if Santiago was in fact armed, and he thought Alistair's joke in very poor taste, now that Angeline was awake, but she seemed unfazed by the reference to the ultimatum to deliver her to the Order.

"What's a wee goldie?" she queried.

"A whisky," said Paul, looking out of the window.

They pulled up in front of the café and got out of the Mercedes, to be met by a middle-aged man and woman, both in a state of high excitement. They rushed forward, exclaiming in unison

"Señor Alistair! Welcome to Moridanza – it has been such a long time…"

They embraced him warmly, and Alistair hugged them both.

"Manuel! Fidelicia! It has been too long, far too long…"

He freed himself with difficulty, and said

"Let me introduce my *compadres*!"

Much handshaking and embracing followed, and Fidelicia took Angeline by the arm as they walked towards the back entrance to the café.

"We will not go in the main entrance, Señor Alistair. We will get you settled in your rooms; you must be tired after your journey, and it would cause too much excitement among my customers if you entered through the bar." said Manuel.

"But the bar is the very place I want to be! The very place…' expostulated Alistair.

"Later, later, Señor Alistair! There is a bottle of Cragganmore waiting for you in your room – I have kept one all these years in the hope that you would return, and now you are here."

Fidelicia, still shepherding Angeline solicitously, gave Alistair a reproachful look.

"The beautiful señorita must be exhausted – until she is refreshed and ready, the bar must wait!"

Paul noticed that Santiago had inconspicuously placed himself close to Angeline and Fidelicia, and as the thought entered his mind, a figure stepped suddenly out of the shadows at the side of the building. In an instant, Santiago crossed in front of the two women, his right hand flat on his chest, his left arm held out from his body with the hand flat and rigid. In that instant, Paul knew that Santiago *was* armed.

"Cristobal!" Alistair called out, and, half turning to Santiago, "It's Cristobal – Manuel's son!"

"And mine!" said Fidelicia sharply, "He has come to take your bags, Señor Alistair."

Alistair embraced the younger man: he was in his late twenties or very early thirties - a slightly taller version of his father, Manuel.

"It is great to see you again, Cristobal! We'll talk later... Santiago, give Cristobal the car keys..."

Santiago shook Cristobal's hand, they spoke together briefly in Spanish, and then Cristobal went to the Mercedes. Paul looked at Santiago, wondering why he had not gone to the car to help, then he realised that Santiago wouldn't be happy until he had reconnoitred the café and surrounding area, and they were all safely indoors.

Eventually they all got settled into their rooms, bags were unpacked and Angeline drew a bath; the others had to be content with a shower in their rooms, since her room had the only en-suite bathroom on the premises. The three men then repaired to Alistair's room, at his invitation, to share his bottle of single malt whisky before dinner. The Scotsman could be a monumental bore on the subject of single malts, as could most Scots. Santiago was evidently used to his boss expounding on the subject, but Paul occasionally found the subject tiresome. He was glad when Alistair took a last appreciative sip, then announced that he could eat a mouldy haggis.

"Let's get down to dinner, gentlemen," he said. "Paul, give Doctor Blade's door a knock – we'll see you downstairs."

They left the room, Alistair and Santiago turning left for the staircase, Paul turning right to Angeline's room. He knocked softly on the door, speaking softly. "Are you decent?"

A muffled voice replied.

"Give me a moment, Paul!" The door opened and Angeline came out into the narrow passageway. She was wearing a simple white blouse and a black skirt, and her long hair lay over her left shoulder, held in a gold clasp. As she reached to pull the door shut behind her, Paul leaned forward and kissed her quickly.

"Dinner awaits," he said, "...the others have already gone downstairs."

Reaching the foot of the stairs, they followed the sound of Alistair's raucous laughter, and found a happy laughing group clustered round him in the dining room of the café. Manuel had no private dining room; he and Fidelicia, and their family when they visited, usually ate in a rear section of the kitchen area where all the food for customers was prepared. There were no other customers dining that evening. The group around Alistair consisted of Manuel, Fidelicia, Cristobal, Manuel and Fidelicia's son, and two raven-haired young women, one short, plump and pretty, the other tall and strikingly beautiful.

Cristobal took the pretty young woman by the hand, and came over to them.

"May I introduce my wife, Maria? Maria, this is Señor Paul, Señor Santiago and Doctor Angeline Blade."

They shook hands with Maria, who blushed and was a little overawed. Then Manuel, beaming, brought the other girl across.

"This is the daughter of my very good friend, Pablo Miguenez – my friends, may I present the most beautiful woman in Extremadura – my own family excepted, of course – Carlota Miguenez!" They all shook hands, and Paul was struck by the quiet dignity of the young woman. While Santiago was shaking Carlota's hand, with a noticeable reluctance to let it go, Angeline whispered to Paul.

"What a classic Spanish beauty! Men have gone to war over a face and figure like that! But something seems to be worrying her – her thoughts are elsewhere."

Santiago engaged Carlota in animated conversation, and, in spite of her worried demeanour, it was clear that she liked him. Any woman would, thought Angeline, stealing a surreptitious glance at Paul in case he could read her thoughts – as well as being ruggedly handsome, Santiago exemplified the male as capable protector, something that many women found deeply attractive.

"Sit where you please, *mis amigos*," said Manuel, motioning to the dining table. Fidelicia interrupted him.

"So long as I may sit next to my favourite Scotsman!"

"That's not much of a compliment, Fidelicia," said Alistair ungallantly, but placing his arm around her affectionately, "you don't know any other Scotsmen! Anyway, if you sit beside me, who will cook and serve the meal?"

"Maria and Carlota will help – Manuel will serve the wine and get in my way. I will have time to sit beside you and talk – I too must eat!" said Fidelicia in mock reproof, and then headed towards the kitchen.

"I will wait impatiently for your return!" Alistair shouted after her plump retreating figure. He turned to his host. "Who is looking after your regular customers, Manuel?"

"They can serve themselves – I trust them – well, most of them. Esteban is in the bar – he is only a boy, but he will keep an eye on them," replied Manuel nonchalantly.

The meal was served – simple, beautifully cooked local dishes. Fidelicia blushed as the compliments rained upon her, and Manuel fussed proudly over the wine. Santiago sat next to Carlota and was having some success in lifting her low spirits.

When the last course was served, Fidelicia and Maria cleared the dishes from the table, and then went back to the kitchen. Carlota's offer of help was declined. Cristobal said he had better see what the customers in the bar were doing, and headed through the door to the increasingly noisy public area. Paul was looking intently at Carlota, who was in deep conversation with Santiago. Angeline whispered to Manuel.

"See how he looks at your friend's beautiful daughter, Manuel – should I be jealous?"

Alistair intervened.

"He is looking for the same reason I am – she reminds me of someone, and I can't for the life of me think of who it is…"

Paul nodded and looked at Alistair as if seeking confirmation of something. Alistair motioned with his hand, and turned to Manuel.

"Carlota's father – your friend, what is his name again?"

"Pablo Miguenez - my very good friend. He is away on a mysterious errand at the moment – he left the day before yesterday. I think Carlota expected him back today, but so far, we have no word of him. But women worry, and Pablo has had difficult times in the last few years," Manuel said in a low voice, looking reflectively across at Carlota.

"I don't remember him – did I meet him on my last visit?" asked Alistair, his eyes flicking to Paul and back again.

"You may have done – he was often in the café. Those were better times for Pablo. If you met him, you would remember him. He is a fine-looking man – film-star looks! Carlota takes her looks from him. Fortunately, my children take after their mother!" Manuel laughed, shaking his head.

"His looks were slightly spoiled by me – I hit him with a tankard in the café when we were young men. My father beat me – I ended up more damaged than he was. But my bruises got better – Pablo was left with a scar above his eye. It reminds us of our wilder days." Manuel chuckled.

Alistair and Paul glanced again at each other.

"Was it a crescent-shaped scar – above his left eye?" asked Alistair tentatively.

Manuel smiled broadly. "Yes, where the tankard base hit him! I knew you must have met him – you *do* remember him, I knew you would!"

Alistair put his fist to his forehead, turned his head to Paul, then away again. Manuel continued his reminiscing about his youth. Angeline had gone very pale; she looked across at Carlota, who was gradually becoming more animated in response to Santiago's gentle humour. Paul saw tears well up in Angeline's eyes and placed his hand on her wrist.

"You have reduced Doctor Blade to tears of laughter with your stories, Manuel!"

Angeline recovered quickly and laughed shakily, nodding her head. Santiago looked across at the sound of her laughter, smiling, but then his smile slowly vanished as he saw Alistair's expression. He half rose from his seat, but Alistair motioned him to sit, and turned to Manuel.

"Manuel, there is something I must speak to you privately about – perhaps in my room?"

They both stood up to leave, but Cristobal appeared in the doorway from the bar, and called out urgently to his father. "*Papá!* Don Ferdinand is here and wishes to speak with you…"

Manuel waved an acknowledgment to his son then looked at Alistair inquiringly. "Do you know Don Ferdinand, Señor Alistair?"

"I know of him, but we have never met," replied Alistair.

"If you will excuse me, Señor – it must be urgent – Don Ferdinand rarely calls at the café, and never at this hour."

Manuel scuttled agitatedly towards the bar. Alistair noticed that the noise from the bar had died away completely – the mere presence of this man had silenced the local drinkers. Cristobal and his father returned in a moment accompanied by a tall, elegant man with an unmistakeable aura of power. The man scanned the room in an instant; his gaze fixed on Angeline for a moment, then it moved to Alistair. The two men looked at each other, and Ferdinand inclined his head politely and gave the hint of a bow. Alistair nodded cautiously in return. A landed Spanish aristocrat, he thought, accustomed to unquestioning obedience and deference - he has the casual arrogance and poise of a matador. Was this the Magus of Moridura?

"Please accept my apologies for this unforgivable interruption," he said. "I regret that a matter of the greatest urgency has forced me to this discourtesy." His English was faultless, with only the faintest trace of a Spanish accent. Manuel waved his hands at his guests in embarrassment, making apologetic faces, and then he motioned urgently to Carlota to come across to the door. Alistair saw Don Ferdinand take her hand and speak to her in a low voice; her head jerked back and she stared up at him with a shocked glance, then she looked away, her eyes wide open and blank.

Manuel ran across to the kitchen and reappeared with Fidelicia and Maria anxiously following him. The two women took the now distraught girl back into the kitchen with them; Manuel and Cristobal said something to Don Ferdinand, and he left by the door to the bar, with a barely perceptible nod to Alistair, Paul and Angeline. Santiago was staring at the kitchen door. After a few seconds, the general hubbub from the bar drifted into the room. Manuel returned, his face pale and drawn.

"Oh, *mis amigos* – Señorita Angeline – an accident has befallen Pablo Miguenez, Carlota's beloved father. He is dead! I cannot believe it, I saw him only the day before yesterday. Don Ferdinand says – he said…" Manuel could not continue, and sat down heavily in a chair. Angeline went to his side, laid her hand on his shoulder and looked at Alistair and Paul, shaking her head helplessly.

Santiago had his mobile handset out and was about to dial a number, but Alistair held his hand up. "This is a dead spot for cell phone coverage – as is the entire district around Moridanza; who were you going to contact? Not the police?"

"No, Señor Alistair – I was going to check with Ardmurran," replied Santiago, then hesitated, looking at Manuel then back to his boss, "to establish if there has been any police follow-up on the incident. Do you want me to telephone on a landline from here?"

"Good thinking – yes – do that now, Santiago."

It was evident to Paul that, in spite of the hectic pace of events in the last twenty-four hours, Alistair had managed to brief his security chief of the shooting and its outcome. Santiago went over to Manuel, who was close to tears. *"Perdóneme, Manuel. ¿Puedo utilizar su teléfono?"* he said.

Manuel heaved a sigh, and got to his feet, motioning Santiago to follow him, and they both left the room. Alistair, Paul and Angeline looked at each other, then at the open kitchen door. The continued sobbing from the kitchen was in stark contrast to the sounds of conviviality coming from the bar.

"Is there anything we can do, Alistair?" said Angeline.

Alistair was staring into space. "He did that quite consciously and deliberately, while we were here – the arrogant bastard did it for maximum effect!"

Angeline was aghast – she had not made the connection between Don Ferdinand, the shooting and the suicide of the intruder. Paul had, and he was equally horrified.

"Alistair, these people think they are above the law – but surely they cannot be? Surely a link can be made? He has sent a man to his death simply to underline an ultimatum – it is appalling. Santiago must telephone the police in Mérida – they can contact Interpol."

"No, Paul – no!" snapped Alistair, his voice hard and edgy. "We are walking on the edge of a precipice; if we fall, we will trigger events of enormous significance for the lives of countless people, cataclysmic events. I'm not exaggerating, please believe me." He faced his friends. "We must play this game by their rules until we've reached the monastery and spoken to the Abbot – there's no other way. Nor can we tell Manuel – I believe that he may become a *hermandad* member, if he isn't already one."

At that moment, Manuel came back into the room from the kitchen. After taking Santiago to the telephone, he had checked on the bar, and then entered the kitchen through an external door. "Señores, señorita – I have been to see Carlota – she is calmer now, but her heart is broken. She will stay with Cristobal and Maria. Now I must tell my customers that

I am closing the bar early. They have already heard about poor Pablo..." He made a despairing motion with his hands and headed for the bar.

"Right, let's all go up to my room and talk," said Alistair

"No,' said Angeline, 'let's go to mine – it's larger than the others."

Paul gave a thin smile. "Do you always invite men to your bedroom so readily?"

"There's safety in numbers," replied Angeline lightly, but her eyes were full of sadness for the bereaved Carlota.

Chapter Nine

All of the four guest bedrooms in Café Ortega were small; the one currently occupied by Angeline was the largest, with an en-suite bathroom and shower. It was furnished with twin beds, one upright chair at the small dressing table, and a leather armchair that had seen better days. Angeline motioned them into the room, and Alistair promptly draped himself on one of the beds, piling the pillows up behind him against the headboard. Angeline went across and sat on the edge of the other bed; Santiago waited politely until Paul sat down in the armchair, then he turned the chair at the dressing table around and perched on it.

Alistair placed his arms behind his head and yawned wearily. "It's been a bloody long day – I'm about all in!"

"You're not falling asleep in my room - you have things to tell us," Angeline said firmly. "Shoot!"

Alistair looked at the ceiling. It had an old-fashioned centre light consisting of a single bulb suspended in a glass bowl shade that hung by chains from the ceiling rose. It reminded him of his childhood in the 1940s – such light fittings had been commonplace in the tenement flats. The bowl filled up with dead flies, dimming the light, and had to be emptied regularly, a gruesome task.

"Where to start?" he grunted. "There's no simple narrative here - it's a bizarre tale. I bought the book – the Moridura Manuscript – then decided that the monastery, if it still existed, had a better right to it. Spain abounds with monasteries, all well documented and accessible, but this one proved strangely hard to find. It wasn't shown on the map – *La Copa de Moridura* wasn't mentioned by name, and only a scrutiny of the contour lines revealed the formation, on an old large-scale relief map. I tried to home in on it in Google Earth's satellite view, but the area was fuzzy and obscured.

"There's no electricity in the monastery; it has no telephone system and the area is in the dead zone for mobile telephones. I wrote to the Abbot, Brother Anselmo, and after a time, I got a very cordial invitation to visit the monastery. I travelled to Mérida, and was met by Manuel and taken to Moridanza. I stayed over for two nights at Café Ortega, and then he drove me to the base of the Cup of Moridura, where the road ends.

"From there I was led on foot by a monk sent to guide me up the cliff path to the monastery, and was greeted by Brother Anselmo. He thanked me for the Moridura Manuscript, and it was returned to the library with a very moving ceremony. I then was introduced to the age-old rhythms and rituals of monastic life. But the monks weren't dull – far from it. I'd bought an old wind-up portable gramophone in a junk shop in Mérida, and some jazz 78s – classic stuff – Louis, Sidney Bechet, Bix - and the monks loved it.

"But then the fundamental strangeness of the monastery and *La Copa de Moridura* began to reveal itself. I wanted to walk in the shallow valley that is *La Copa*, but the Abbot was reluctant to agree; he gave a number of reasons – safety, nothing of interest – none of which were convincing. When I told him that I had also commissioned a Latin scholar to read passages from the Moridura Manuscript to me, and that I was interested in the Ancient Order of Moridura and the legend of *La Bestia*, he became very evasive, and withdrew into a studied politeness.

"Abusing Brother Anselmo's hospitality shamelessly, I got up very early one morning and, in the few hours before the monks rose for their first prayers of the day, I followed the route out through the gates at the back of the guest wing and found myself on a lip of rock at the rear of the monastery. There was a wide path leading down from this point, and in the faint light before dawn, I saw the vegetable plots of the monks on the slopes of *La Copa*. As I made my way down, I was aware of a curious sensation of heaviness in my limbs – it was almost like wading in water. I could see across the shallow bowl of *La Copa* to its centre, and there seemed to be a protuberant rock there – black and isolated. Then I saw what at first seemed a trick of the early light, a shimmering column of air above the rock. I picked up a piece of hard black rock from the ground beneath my feet, and realised at once that it was meteoric rock, metallic, and then it all seemed so obvious – *La Copa* was the shallow crater of a meteor that had struck aeons ago.

"The faint sound of a bell from the monastery behind me reminded me that I was behaving dishonourably to my host in being there, and that I must get back before my breach of trust was discovered. The climb back up should not have been too arduous, but I felt the additional burden of the strange heaviness in my limbs that I had experienced earlier."

Alistair paused and looked at his rapt audience of three.

"Go on, please – this is wonderful stuff, Alistair!" Angeline said excitedly.

Alistair was now revelling in his role as storyteller, in spite of the sombre conclusions to which he was leading.

"Up until that point, I had eaten with the monks in the refectory, but that afternoon, Brother Anselmo invited me to eat with him in his office. Alfonso, the old monk who looks after the wine cellar, brought us a superb bottle from his special rack. The Abbot came straight to the point, telling me that he knew of my pre-dawn visit to *La Copa*, observing, without rancour, that he realised that a powerful curiosity such as mine would not be restrained by mere good manners. I accepted this gentle slap on the wrist, and apologised as best I could. What he then said is burned into my memory, and I can repeat it almost verbatim, even after five years."

As Alistair continued, Paul, Angeline and Santiago were transported back in time to that meeting of five years ago and felt that they could hear the voices of the two men.

"Señor Mackinnon, the monastery of Moridura is in your debt for returning a book that was lost for centuries, a book of inestimable value to us – more than you realise. I am halfway through my eighth decade on God's good earth. Even in this solitary place, the world of the twenty-first century impinges on our consciousness and I have watched the relentless advance of science and technology with growing apprehension; I knew it was only a matter of time before our age-old isolation and the unusual geological formation on which the monastery stands would arouse the interest of powerful men – the media, politicians, businessmen, men of science, scholars.

"Over the centuries of the monastery's existence, the secular world has periodically impacted upon our community, like a whirlwind that comes suddenly, without warning, then leaves just as quickly. I count myself fortunate that, in this new millennium, the first of the new breed of men to find us has been one such as you, returning our most treasured possession to us. But you may be the harbinger of others with baser motives.

"The monastery of Moridura was built on the foundations of an earlier structure, one called the Portal by the Romans, in the area then known to them as Lusitania; that structure itself was built on the foundations of an even older one, the origins of which are lost in the mists of antiquity. This site was known to the Iberians as Moridura – it was sacred to them. Christianity came late to Moridura, but, as has been the way of the Church for all of its history, it absorbed the old myths and legends into its own practices and doctrines. Our own congregation grew out of an older brotherhood. But with the absorption came a terrible legacy and an awesome responsibility – a singular responsibility.

"*La Copa de Moridura* is the result of one of the many rocky wanderers of space crossing the orbit of our Earth, and surviving the fiery path through our atmosphere to become a meteorite, impacting on the surface with devastating force.

"Other meteor craters are dead monuments to ancient catastrophes: *La Copa*, however, is not dead – it lives, and with a malign potential to initiate a chain of events that could destroy all life on Earth, and perhaps even our solar system. This potential was created at the moment of impact, but the Good Lord, in his wisdom, simultaneously sent something to protect us – the rock we call *El Trono*, the Throne, which is the tip of a great spear of a rocklike substance that plunges deep into the earth; with it came something that lives, and has lived over the millennia – that regulates the instability at the heart of *La Copa* - a Guardian. That something has had many names – the one that survives was given to it by the Iberians. The Vatican and the Holy Office have regarded this legend as a heretical superstition, and it is forbidden to talk of it. But you have read it in the Moridura Manuscript, Señor Mackinnon, therefore I may speak of it…"

Alistair Mackinnon broke the spell of his account of the Abbot's words by swinging his lean body off the bed in one smooth movement, and standing up. His listeners returned with a jolt to Angeline's bedroom and the twenty-first century.

Paul broke the silence.

"The Beast," he said, exhaling a long breath, "the Beast of Moridura! *La Bestia.*'

Alistair sat down on the other bed beside Angeline, and tried to lighten the atmosphere. "When I was a boy, sneaking into the picture house by a back door to see James Whale's *Frankenstein*, I confused the monster with its maker, as did most of the audience, calling the creature Frankenstein. Moridura may have been a person as well as a place – the one who gave a name to the legend: alternatively the mythical being may have been called after the place name. Popular legend casts this creature as a monster, but from the Abbot's account, it is more like a guardian of whatever instability lies at the heart of the Cup of Moridura."

Alistair read the three faces looking at him. "You want to know whether I believed the Abbot or not?"

Paul broke the silence. "I'll speak for myself only: yes, I want to know how much you believe of what you were told. I take it you don't buy the supernatural stuff?"

"That pretty much sums up what I want to know too," added Angeline.

Alistair looked at his security chief. "And you, Santiago?"

Santiago was silent for a moment, and then he spoke, choosing his words carefully. "Señor Paul and Doctor Blade are your friends and colleagues – Doctor Blade is also a scientist. I will act on your assessment of what you were told, whatever that may be."

Alistair looked distinctly irritated. "Why the formal tone? I count you as both friend and colleague, Santiago, and I value your opinions. Speak freely."

"Yes, Señor Santiago," said Angeline, "speak freely…"

Santiago responded stiffly. "I do not mean to offend anyone, but easy familiarity does not come naturally to me. Deference to authority is something deeply rooted in my upbringing. You have been kind enough to invite me to address you on first name terms – I regret my lapse. It will not happen again." He stood up and gave a slight dignified bow.

Angeline jumped off the bed, and embraced the tall man, placing her head on his broad chest. "Oh, Santiago, how my mom would have loved you," she said affectionately. Paul tried to look amused, without success.

"Let go of my colleague, Angeline, you shameless American woman!" said Alistair.

Angeline bounced back on to the bed. "Tell it like you see it," she said to Santiago.

Santiago sat down again, more than a little nonplussed. His dark eyes swept across the others. "Alistair – Paul – Angeline," he said with deliberate emphasis, "what I believe, from all that I have heard, is this – the monastery of Moridura values its privacy above all else, and has gone to great lengths to protect it over the centuries. Their secret knowledge has two dimensions - one that men may profit by, and one that threatens them. The Order of Moriduran monks has a worldly alter ego in the *hermandad* and the two meld into each other."

Santiago looked directly at Alistair. "You penetrated their age-old defensive mechanisms, Alistair, by offering the monastery a prize beyond price, one that they could not decline – the book. But they trusted you, and they believed that their trust was well founded – then Angeline made her discovery, and you became linked to her work. Now, five years after they first met you, they must act to protect their interests. I would judge that a fundamental disagreement now exists between the Moriduran monks and the *hermandad* about the methods to be used..."

He stopped abruptly. "I have said enough – perhaps too much, *mis amigos?*' then he smiled, his great, broad, open smile that warmed the room.

Paul's earlier twinge of jealousy vanished. I like this man, he thought, and I hope I may become his friend. Alistair looked at Santiago with considerable satisfaction. When I chose this man, I chose well, he thought.

"The missing elements are the role of the diaries of Francisco Ortega, Manuel's father," said Alistair, "and who now has them. I'll talk to Manuel in the morning – meanwhile, let's get back to our own rooms and get some sleep. I think we are safe for the moment."

"But, Alistair, there is so much more we need to know," said Angeline appealingly. "Can't we talk a bit more?"

"No," replied Alistair firmly, starting to get up off the bed with a great show of fatigue, "I'm an old man, and I need to rest."

"Oh, you poor old thing!" said Angeline, helping him to his feet. "Can you find your room by yourself?"

"Get off me, lassie, or I'll skelp your bum," snapped Alistair, making a playful swipe at her rear, one that was gracefully avoided. The three men left, with goodnights to Angeline. Paul was inclined to linger, but Alistair took him firmly by the arm and steered him towards the door. Outside the room, he paused and pointed to a single straight-backed chair in the corridor.

"We'll take three-hour shifts until morning. Paul, you take the first; Santiago, you take the second; I'll take the third. I hope you can find something to read. Change into your pyjamas first, Paul – then if Angeline should pop her head out, you can say you were on your way to the bathroom."

Paul, who had been worried about Angeline's safety, instantly saw the sense of the plan. He nodded and went to his room and changed. When he came back into the corridor, Santiago was waiting for him, and handed him a small automatic pistol, a Walther .25 calibre. He offered quick, whispered instruction about its operation and the safety catch, then said goodnight and returned to his room.

Paul sat in the hard, uncomfortable chair, with the gun at his side, mentally rehearsing what he would do if Angeline decided to pop her head out of the door. The whole thing would take on the character of a Feydeau farce, he thought. Angeline would conclude that his intentions were amorous, he would jump up out of the chair, the gun would fall to the floor and go off, Angeline would scream – doors would open and close and trousers would fall down.

Faint noises came from downstairs; probably Manuel closing up for the night. I hope he doesn't check the corridors, Paul reflected, foreseeing a problem in explaining his presence in pyjamas, carrying a gun. He felt suddenly very sleepy, and had nothing to read. Keep the brain working – engage in some non-repetitive intellectual activity, he instructed himself. He thought he mentally construct all of the musical scales, visualising the piano keyboard, starting with the scales formed on the white notes, the scale of C first, and then the harder chromatic intervals. He worked through the scales, but E, A and B were harder than he had remembered them from his school music lessons.

Dammit, he thought, it would have been just as easy to do it chromatically. He did D-flat with some difficulty then fell quietly asleep in the middle of the scale of E-flat.

He awakened with a feeling of pressure on his shoulder, a body leaning over him, and something being wound swiftly and expertly around his mouth from behind. He recognised the smell of duct tape, and the ripping sound of it being unwound. As he tried to rise, something metallic pressed into his neck below his chin; the line of the shotgun's single barrel ended in the fist of a man standing over him. He grunted, and another cold, metallic pressure came on his left ear. A sense of despair overcame him – he had fallen asleep, for how long he had no idea, and now Angeline was threatened. He had no doubt about the men's intentions. Santiago's quiet, controlled voice from along the corridor cut across his train of thought.

"*Retrocede lentamente y con cuidado, caballeros, o morirá allí donde se encuentra …*"

Paul guessed the Spanish roughly as move back or die where you stand. The men straightened up, and looked at Santiago, who was calm and poised, halfway out of his room, holding a Beretta 93R machine pistol levelled at the men. In that fraught moment, the door on the other side of Angeline's room opened, and Alistair stepped softly into the corridor, his ancient Webley Fosbery .38 revolver in his hand.

"*Caballeros*! I think we have what used to be called a Mexican standoff – if anyone so much as breaks wind, World War Three will break out."

His Scottish lilt was convivial, almost affable.

One of the men gave him a speculative look. *"Pero su amigo morirá, señor."*

"And so will you, *caballeros*," replied Alistair, "and Don Ferdinand will have a great deal of explaining to do – if not to the police, then to Brother Anselmo."

The other man spoke cautiously, in heavily accented English. "We cannot surrender our arms, señor. What do you suggest?"

"Move back slowly from my friend in the chair and walk very slowly past the gentleman at the other end - towards the staircase – then leave quietly. We are both crack shots – do not test our marksmanship by doing something careless. Retreat with dignity and report back to Don Ferdinand that your mission has failed. Tell him all will be well – we can reach an agreement at the monastery. He will understand, and appreciate your good sense."

The man responded quietly. "We will leave as you suggest." He nodded to his shotgun meaningfully. "We do not need to be marksmen with these, señor."

The two of them backed away from Paul, and walked carefully past Santiago to the staircase. As they reached it, Alistair spoke softly. "Don't think of returning, *caballeros* – that would be a great mistake."

Both men paused, and looked back at Alistair, then one of them turned his head to Santiago and smiled. *"Somos ambos hombres ocupados, amigo. ¿No es así?"* The sound of their footsteps going down the stairs echoed back in the corridor, then there was the sound of a door closing.

Alistair stood still for a moment, and then walked towards Santiago. "What did he say?" he asked.

"He said that we were both hired hands."

"They won't be back. I'm amazed that Ferdinand tried such a crude snatch. Perhaps I've overrated the man."

They both stood in front of the deeply humiliated Paul, who was removing the duct tape from his mouth with some difficulty.

"Well, wee man – asleep on the job! Firing squad at dawn for you," said Alistair.

"Alistair – Santiago – I'm so sorry – so ashamed!" blurted Paul.

The door to Angeline's room opened and her head appeared, her red hair tousled, her eyes sleepy. "What's going on? Am I missing a party?"

"Sort of," replied Alistair, then he and Santiago looked at the scarlet-faced Paul, trying to hide their smiles.

Chapter Ten

At breakfast, Fidelicia moved briskly in and out of the kitchen, singing cheerfully, unaware of the intrusion in the night. Paul ate morosely, still in a chastened mood, while Angeline tried to lift his spirits with small talk. Alistair and Santiago spoke to each other in low voices, adding to Paul's feeling of failure and sense of exclusion.

Fidelicia bustled back into the room again, carrying more coffee. "Manuel had to leave early to pick up Carlota from Cristobal and Maria's house; he will take her to Don Ferdinand's house later. She works as a live-in maid there, Señor Alistair," she said as she set the coffee down.

"Yes, I knew that, Fidelicia. Aahh, who makes coffee like you!" said Alistair, noisily sipping from his steaming cup.

"You flatter me!" giggled Fidelicia, "Are all Scotsmen like you?"

"There's nobody like him, Fidelicia – he is a one-off!" said Angeline, "Isn't he, Paul?"

Paul lifted his head, nodding weakly. Alistair seized upon this sign of life. "Pull round here, you two – we need your input."

Angeline and Paul lifted their coffee cups and dragged their chairs round on either side of the two men.

"About last night..." began Paul, but Alistair held up his hand.

"You drew the short straw on first watch, Paul - we were all exhausted, and it could have happened to any one of us."

Paul shook his head and looked down; Santiago put his hand on his shoulder and shook him playfully. Had it been anyone else, Paul would have felt patronised, but he was deeply grateful for this sign of comradeship.

"To business," said Alistair. He rubbed his nose, and glanced at Santiago. "I'm finding it harder and harder to read Ferdinand. What could he hope to gain from a stunt like last night's? I don't get it. Have I overestimated these men? Are they just crude thugs, with violence their first resort? After all, we're here, Angeline's here, and the deadline not until tomorrow. What did they hope to gain by such a show of force?"

Santiago exchanged a glance with Alistair, and reached an unspoken consensus. He turned to Paul.

"I am supposed to be the security expert here, but, like Alistair, I find elements of the situation unusual. Before I offer my analysis, I would welcome your view - you were at the eye of the storm, Paul…"

Paul glanced at Angeline, and her openly affectionate smile reassured him that she had not lost faith in him.

"I know nothing of Don Ferdinand, other than what I saw of him last evening. The man is, as I understand it, a landed aristocrat with long family connections with this area and with the monastery. In Scottish terms, he is the Laird of Moridanza and district. If the *hermandad* is as influential in the area as you have indicated, Alistair, then he must at least occupy a senior position in it, and may actually be the Magus of Moridura. Yet my reading of passages in the Moridura Manuscript would lead me to believe that the Magus may occupy dual membership – of the Moriduran monks and the secular *hermandad*. This creates anomalies: if he's a monk, the authority of the Abbot is compromised; if the Abbot is the Magus, his position as head of the monastery would be untenable in the eyes of the Vatican."

"Fascinating," murmured Alistair, 'but can you reconcile these conflicting strands?"

"I don't know if I can," said Paul, "but I'm inclined to believe that the present Magus *is* a monk, and that all the Magi since the unfortunate Abbadocio have been monks. It may be that Ferdinand now aspires to the position of Magus, to consolidate his power base."

Santiago nodded. "I can see how the Holy Office – the Inquisition – could have rationalised their existence, as a non-heretical extension of Mother Church, into a loyal brotherhood of the laity. I am with your analysis so far, Paul – it makes good sense to me."

"Go on, Paul," said Angeline, "Let's have your interpretation of current views – the contradictions in their behaviour – the role of Don Ferdinand."

"Something echoes in my mind from the words of our two nocturnal visitors," said Paul, his embarrassment returning at the memory. "When Alistair told them to go back to Ferdinand, they neither confirmed or denied that he had sent them."

Angeline looked surprised. "They would avoid confirming that anyway, surely? That behaviour is characteristic of front-end enforcers in any organisation – don't implicate the Man."

"Let me finish," interrupted Paul, "Bear with me if my exposition is a little slow – I'm thinking aloud. Let's assume that the ultimatum – the letter – had originally been approved by the Abbot as a simple invitation, but that the threat was added by the *hermandad*. The incident at Ardmurran and the events of early this morning must have been their work. When we did arrive early, the Abbot was satisfied that we had come to Moridanza of our own free will, and that his objective could be achieved by discussion, but the *hermandad* decided to play hardball. If that is the case, the old adage holds good – there is no situation, however complex, that, after close, careful analysis doesn't become more bloody complex!"

Angeline and Santiago laughed, but Alistair didn't. "If you're right, Paul, I've endangered Angeline and all of you by bringing you here."

"Well, we're here,' said Angeline matter-of-factly, 'in among the High Heid Yins – if I can borrow your Scottish expression - and we must sort out the puzzle as best we can. I seem to be the object of their attentions - but why focus on me alone? My basic research work is held by my present employer and is now also in your hands, Alistair. As a matter of fact, Red Lonnen is the only absent High Heid Yin in the equation so far - we have you, me, Ferdinand, the Abbot and the mysterious Magus – only my present employer is missing," concluded Angeline, looking expectantly at the others.

Alistair looked down at the floor. "I don't think he is missing, Angeline – I believe that he's already here," he said reluctantly.

The blood drained from her face and she stared at him, aghast.

"What?" she said in a tiny voice. "Where?"

"He must either be at the monastery or with Ferdinand – or he could be in Mérida: he can't be in the village – that would be too conspicuous. I'm sorry to have to shock you with my conclusion, Angeline, but a number of things point inexorably to it."

Paul knew instantly that Angeline's reaction was not just that of someone contemplating a defection from one employer to another. The news that Lonnen might be here had touched her at a much deeper level than that.

Santiago, however, still turning Paul's analysis over in his mind, had missed the nuances. "How well do you know Lonnen, Angeline?" Alistair tried to catch his eye, but Santiago was looking intently at Angeline.

"As well as a junior research scientist can know her CEO, I guess," she said, attempting a casual air. "He's a driven man, highly-stressed, with a short fuse. His complex relationships with the defence industry place great pressures on him. He's always been a winner, and doesn't like to be thwarted. He doesn't suffer fools gladly. That's about it."

She turned to Alistair. "What makes you think he is here? Why should he come here? He thinks we're both in Scotland

– if he was going to go anywhere, it would have been to Ardmurran, surely?"

Alistair got to his feet and looked out of the dining room window at the low white houses of Moridanza.

"I don't want to distress you by what I have to say, but this is a time for frankness – for truth, above all else. I believe that Lonnen sought and obtained an invitation from the Abbot to come to Moridanza. He could only have received that invitation if he had something of great value to offer, or had made a credible threat, or was withholding something the Moridurans and the *hermandad* wanted badly. I think he has all three bargaining chips in his stack.

"The Order and the Abbot must have got their knowledge of your research from Lonnen; I didn't tell them – neither did you. Ardmurran International Electronics's security is tight, as is that of Lonnen's company. Santiago is the only other person who knows. Your colleagues in Ardmurran have no concept of the real implications of your research. So it must have been Red Lonnen." Alistair moved closer to Angeline and looked at her, desperately wishing that he could avoid giving his next conclusion.

"I also believe," he said slowly, "that Lonnen and Ferdinand were the ones who decided on the letter – the ultimatum – and that they sent Pablo Miguenez to Loch Lomond."

Angeline stood up, shaking her head violently. "No, Alistair! No! He wouldn't have been a party to that – to a man sacrificing his life. It's not in character – it's just not in his nature. He's ruthless and demanding but no – not that."

Alistair made soothing noises and sat her down gently, sitting down beside her. "Don't upset yourself, lassie, it's not as bad as I've maybe made it sound. He never meant to harm you – he only wants you back – and I don't believe he would be a party to Miguenez trying to kill himself. But I do think he has misjudged the Order, the Abbot and Ferdinand."

Paul stood up, and stretched his arms above his head. "I think we all need to get out into the open air. We don't seem to be safe indoors, so we might as well be in the fresh air if we are going to be kidnapped, shot, or otherwise disposed of."

Alistair looked at Santiago, who shrugged in a non-committal fashion. He preferred the more defensible inner space.

Angeline stood up. "That's a great idea – I'm in Spain for the first time, and all I've seen are airports, cars and hotel rooms. Let's view the scenic highlights of Moridanza!" She had recovered her verve and enthusiasm, and radiated youth and life. Her change of mood was so infectious that all of their spirits instantly lifted, and the sense of a big adventure returned.

"Why the hell not?" Alistair burst out, and even the disciplined, contained professional mien of Santiago relaxed somewhat, and his serious features split into a wide grin.

Angeline laughed. "You should smile more often, Santiago – it suits you!"

Paul stretched again, put his hands behind his head, and did his little pirouette. "Do we need a guide? Will we get lost in the maze of Moridanza's streets?" he said playfully.

"Hardly," replied Alistair, "it only has a dozen or so."

They were all heading for the door when Manuel appeared, looking harassed. "Señorita Angeline, señores – I am so sorry I was not here at breakfast time – I had to drive Carlota to Don Ferdinand's house – we were late – the Don was very angry. *Los artilleros* are nowhere to be found, and no one knows where they are…'

"*Los artilleros?*" queried Alistair.

"*Sí, señor - los artilleros* – how do you say?"

"The Gunners - *pistoleros?*" prompted Santiago.

"*Sí, señor* – the Gunners! They are called that because they always carry *escopetas* – old-fashioned shotguns, you know? They guard the estate and shoot wild dogs. Don Ferdinand has been asking everyone where they could have gone – *esta muy agitado* – upset."

"You seem a little *agitado* yourself, Manuel. Come with us – we're going for a stroll around the village – show us the sights, eh? I can't remember anything from my last visit except drinking and singing in the bar!"

Manuel relaxed a little, and laughed. "We had the good times, señor – *By yon bonnie banks and by yon bonnie braes…*" he sang, with a surprisingly authentic Scottish accent.

'You remember!' said Alistair, with evident pleasure.

"Oh, Señor Alistair!" exclaimed Manuel, overcome by nostalgia, "We had the good times – such good times!"

"Right!" said Alistair briskly. "Walk with us and tell us all about your new good times. I hear that fortune may be smiling upon you?" He put his arm round Manuel's shoulders, nodded to the others, and they all trooped out into the morning sunshine, went down the hill and turned left into the main street, heading for the village square. The people of the village were going about their business, and a number of them called out to Manuel, eying his companions with open curiosity.

Manuel swelled with pride: his café bedrooms were all occupied, his guests were very evidently important persons from outside of the area, *la chica pelirroja* was strikingly beautiful, and he, Manuel Ortega, was obviously a personal friend of the tall, distinguished man. His neighbours would be speculating about his new status. He drew a long breath of satisfaction.

One of the locals, a regular at the café bar with a long memory, recognised Alistair, and called out to him "Hey Jimmee! *¿Qué tal estás?*"

Alistair gave a cheery wave. "*Buenos días, caballero,*" he replied, then, turning to Manuel, "Let's go and sit on the bench at the monument."

They all sat down except Santiago, who strolled around the monument with a casual air. This did not fool Paul, who was sitting next to Angeline: the big Spaniard was expertly scrutinising the square, the shop doorways, and the mouths of the little streets running off the main street. He had produced a pair of sunglasses from his pocket, and when he put them on, the stereotypical image of the bodyguard was complete.

Angeline whispered to Paul. "He does make me feel safe – he's a good man! Alistair always picks good men. Were you involved with his selection, Paul?"

"No," said Paul, sharply reminded that, without the intervention of Santiago in the early hours, she would not have been safe, "he was hired before I began to work with Ardmurran International Electronics. I met him for the first time yesterday." He, too, felt safer that Santiago was around, but he also experienced a sense of failure and inadequacy. His mouth still felt sore where the duct tape had been, and the sensation of vulnerability and powerlessness came again to haunt him.

Angeline sensed his thoughts, and linked her arm in his. "Paul Corr, my nice guy. You went through an ordeal trying to protect me – you might have been killed! Were you afraid?"

Paul squeezed her arm and turned his face into her hair. "Not for myself – only for you, Angeline. I love you, and never more so than when I thought I had failed you." He became disconsolate again. "I did fail you – I fell asleep. I can't forgive myself." He pulled away, and looked again at Santiago, who was still pacing up and down.

"No – you didn't fail me, Paul. It is not a crime to be overcome by fatigue."

"Santiago wasn't overcome by fatigue – he wasn't even on watch, he should have been asleep, yet he stopped them." replied Paul.

"He had a good night's sleep the night before in Madrid. You had already been through traumatic events at Ardmurran, had only a few hours sleep, then the journey,"

Angeline said firmly. "Stop blaming yourself, it's not an attractive trait!" She softened the rebuke by kissing him on the cheek.

Alistair jerked his head conspiratorially to Manuel and winked. "They only met the day before yesterday, and now..." he whispered.

"*El amor verdadero* - it comes in an instant from God," said Manuel, "It was like that with Fidelicia and me."

"And with me and Shelagh," said Alistair sadly. "It can never be replaced. Some said I should marry again after she died, but I never considered it. We didn't have long together..."

Angeline now had one ear tuned to the conversation on her left, and her heart went out to her friend and mentor. He had spoken of his wife only briefly with her, and the subject obviously gave him pain, so she hadn't pursued it.

Alistair suddenly turned and smiled at her. "Eavesdropping, bonnie lass?" he said softly.

She blushed and took his big, gnarled hand, so different from Paul's. "Sorry – I couldn't help it."

Alistair laughed. "Young Love in Extremadura – at a cinema near you!"

Paul missed all of this – he was watching Santiago intently. The Spaniard had stopped pacing; his back was towards the monument, his legs were spread, his arms hanging loosely at his sides and his knees were very slightly bent. He seemed like a big cat about to spring. Paul scanned the busy square, and immediately saw the object of Santiago's attention.

From an alleyway between two shops, a figure in a monk's black habit was heading purposefully towards them. Even at this distance, the advancing monk created an impression of enormous physical power; he seemed to cut through the people in the street as though they were drifting leaves in his path. The cowl of his habit was large and deep, and even the bright sunlight did not reveal his features. His arms were folded low across the cord around his waist, and his hands were invisible.

Paul heard the laughing conversation of his companions coming from his left, but it seemed like a dreamlike echo from another time and place compared to the intensity of the scene unfolding before him – the relentless progress of the medieval apparition moving towards them and the coiled power of the man directly in its path. Paul remembered a phrase from the study of robotics – *uncanny valley* – to describe a perceptual phenomenon in the design of robots, where a feeling of unease, terror or revulsion was caused in the person observing a robotic action.

Alistair leaned out from the bench across Angeline to say something to Paul, and caught the line of his eye: he saw the monk, and his security chief about to confront him. Angeline was leaning behind Alistair's back and laughing as she listened to Manuel recounting something about his first meeting with Fidelica.

The monk came within three metres of Santiago then stopped. As he unfolded his arms and his hands came into view, Santiago's right arm swung up in front of his body and his left arm began to rise, open-palmed. Paul remembered the posture as the one Santiago had adopted when Cristobal had suddenly appeared from the darkness on the previous evening. The monk slowly put his palms together in an attitude that suggested deference or prayer, and then spoke in English, his voice deep and soft.

"I have a message for Señor Alistair Mackinnon."

Santiago maintained his defensive posture, but when he spoke, his voice was calm and encouraging. "Who is this message from?"

"The Abbot of the monastery of Moridura, Señor," the monk replied in a respectful tone.

Alistair Mackinnon came striding past Santiago, reaching his hand out to the monk. "Brother Mateo – my good friend!"

The monk threw back his cowl, revealing a young man with strong features, an open expression and very large, widely spaced dark eyes. His hair was jet black, and curled close to his tonsured head. He smiled and bowed, acknowledging Alistair's warm greeting.

"It is my great pleasure to see you again in Moridanza, Señor Mackinnon – many years have passed since we last met – five, perhaps?" He shook Alistair's hand.

Paul, still sitting with Angeline, was struck by the sheer size of the young monk. Alistair and Santiago were both tall, powerfully built men, but Brother Mateo was a good half a head taller than either of them, with wide shoulders that the loose habit could not wholly conceal. Santiago was shaking hands with him now. The three men turned and walked back to the monument.

Paul and Angeline stood up and were introduced to the newcomer – Manuel obviously knew him and liked him. Angeline had that look on her face that all women have when they meet a handsome, celibate and unattainable man of faith; it was the look, as Alistair had once mischievously put it, of a jockey who had lost his whip. As Paul took Brother Mateo's hand, he thought again of the uncanny valley reaction on his first sight of the monk, then, as he smilingly shook his hand, the feeling returned again, causing an involuntary shiver.

"Mateo, we all decided to take the air after breakfast. Will you walk with us back to Manuel's café? We can talk on the way," said Alistair. "Where did you park Brother Anselmo's car? Does he still have that ancient Mercedes?"

Mateo smiled as he replied. "Yes, Señor Alistair, he does. But I did not use it to get here – today I walked."

Alistair looked at him in astonishment. "Mateo, it is over ten miles from the monastery! When did you leave?"

"Eleven," the young monk said casually, "it is eleven miles – I left just after dawn.'

Alistair shook his head in admiration. "That's a fair pace by any standards, Mateo – I congratulate you."

Manuel broke in, his voice affectionate and concerned. "You have not eaten, my good friend. Fidelicia will fill your belly – we don't want you to shrink to the size of Brother Alfonso! Who would carry my heavy deliveries up *el sendero de precipio*, eh?"

They all turned up the street to the café, and as they entered, Fidelicia called out in surprise and delight. "Mateo! Have you eaten?"

"There's a woman who can recognise a hungry man at ten paces," laughed Alistair as Manuel went forward to talk to his wife.

Manuel and Fidelicia disappeared into the kitchen. As they entered the dining room, Brother Mateo looked anxiously at Alistair. "In my joy at seeing you again, Señor Alistair, I have failed to deliver the Abbot's message."

Alistair shook his head. "If he let you come eleven miles on foot to deliver it, pal, the Abbot's message can wait a bit longer." As he spoke, Fidelicia arrived bearing food, clucking solicitously. Mateo looked at it eagerly, then he looked up in some embarrassment at the group.

Alistair turned to his companions. "My wee stroll has brought my appetite back – if Fidelicia will bring me something too, I'll join Mateo in his meal, and catch up on all that has happened in Moridura." His look made it plain that he wanted to be alone with Brother Mateo, and the others drifted amicably through to the deserted bar.

Alistair made a token show of eating, but he wasn't really hungry. In contrast, the young monk eagerly consumed Fidelicia's offering. It must take a lot of food to fuel that big frame, thought Alistair. His mother used to say of big eaters that she would rather keep them for a week than a month.

When at last Mateo had finished, Alistair poured him another coffee. "And now, Mateo – what has Anselmo got to say to me?"

The monk gave a satisfied sigh, and then spoke formally. "Brother Anselmo extends his felicitations to you and your party, and invites all of you to be his guests at Moridura, Señor Alistair. He regrets that he was unable to send the car to pick you up, because the American, Señor Lonnen, is using it today, but the Abbot assumes that either you have your own transportation, or that Manuel will bring you."

Alistair laughed. "Thank the Good Lord that you and the four of us don't have to cram into Manuel's Volkswagen – we'd need a miracle to achieve that! We have a Mercedes at our disposal – a more recent model than the Abbot's venerable machine. I'm sure Santiago would be happy for you to drive us back, if you're agreeable."

"I would have been happy to walk back, Señor Alistair," said Mateo, beaming, "it would have been preferable to Manuel's transportation. But I would esteem it a privilege to drive you back – and to drive a new Mercedes. Señor Santiago - he protects you, does he not?"

Alistair remembered now the subtle sense of humour and the incisive intelligence that had made him like the young monk so much on his last visit. "Yes, Santiago protects us, and does many other valuable things for my company. Mateo, you referred to an American guest – was that part of Brother Anselmo's message?" he asked.

"I would not have presumed to add or subtract from his words, señor – the Abbot is most insistent that his words are relayed exactly."

So, thought Alistair, the wily old Abbot wanted him to know of Lonnen's presence before he accepted the invitation. Was his purpose to entice him or deter him? He decided that it was neither; he simply wanted him to know the players in the game.

"Have you met this Señor Lonnen?"

"I have, señor - he is red-haired, like the beautiful señorita," said Mateo, with an air of innocence.

Alistair ignored the implication. "Do you have a view about this American, *mi amigo* – do you like him?"

Mateo looked uncomfortable at the question; he shifted his huge body in the chair, and it creaked alarmingly. "My opinion of a guest at the monastery can be of little value, and it would be disrespectful of me to offer one, Señor Alistair. The Abbot has forbidden me to engage in conversation with him, beyond basic requirements."

Alistair put his hand across the table on to Mateo's wrist. My God, he thought, he has a wrist like another man's biceps!

"I value your opinion very highly, Mateo – I cannot think that Brother Anselmo would think it disrespectful of you to offer it to me. In fact, I think that perhaps he may want you to give me any information that you feel is relevant to my impending visit."

Brother Mateo broke eye contact with Alistair for a long moment, and a stillness settled over him. This strange quality he exhibited came back to Alistair – he had noticed it and wondered about it before, when he had first met Mateo. Was it dignity? Gravitas? Charisma? What could this young monk have achieved, had he chosen to pursue his destiny in the wide world instead of devoting his life to the cloister?

The spell was abruptly broken by Mateo letting out a tremendous belch. He got to his feet immediately, smiled and bowed gracefully. "My apologies, Señor Alistair - I have eaten too much, too quickly, and on an empty stomach!"

His standing up and bowing reminded Alistair of the way jazz musicians made their apologies for a wrong note in an ensemble piece. The young monk was totally at ease with himself and quite unembarrassed, and Alistair admired him for it.

"Now that you have disposed of that, shall we go back to my question?" said Alistair. "Do you have a view about the character of the American, Lonnen?"

"He lacks good manners; he is interested only in his own objectives; he responds well to people only when they can be of service to him. I have known him only a very short time, but on balance, I do not like him, however, I also think that in a crisis he would be a man who could be relied upon – but only if his interests coincided with one's own." Mateo looked inquiringly at him. "Do you know this man, señor?"

"I would ask you to call me Alistair, Mateo – as I request all my friends and colleagues to do – but I know the Abbot frowns upon such familiarity, so I will not press the point. In answer to your question, I know the man mainly by reputation; he heads an electronics company, as I do, in fact, he is my main competitor. I have met him at conferences, but I have had little real personal contact with him. My assessment of him is very similar to your own."

He poured another coffee for both of them. "Is there anything else about the American that you might think relevant, Mateo? Anything that would not breach your duty to Brother Anselmo?"

"Yes," replied the monk, "Señor Lonnen is permitted to wear the habit of the Moridurans and he attends Mass and prays with us regularly. When he prays, he is often overcome by emotion."

Alistair nodded, and considered this information. It seemed likely that Lonnen was a Catholic, or a lapsed Catholic. Alistair had been born into a Scottish Presbyterian family, but he was not a churchgoer.

"There is one other matter, my friend. You have met our beautiful companion, Señorita Angeline. Women are only permitted to enter the monastery in the most exceptional circumstances, as I understand it. Is Brother Anselmo aware of the presence of a woman in our party? Does he realise that I can only accept his invitation if all of us are included?" Alistair watched the monk closely as he waited for his answer.

"Brother Anselmo has arranged special accommodation at the monastery for Doctora Blade," replied Mateo. "He therefore must regard the circumstances as most exceptional, señor."

Alistair was at once both relieved and astonished. A woman in the monastery! He could imagine the frenzied buzz of gossip among the brothers and the thin-lipped disapproval that would be expressed by some of the older brethren. He shook his head, and then stood up.

"I must rally my party, pack our bags, and then we must all set off for Moridura. Manuel will be disappointed that we are leaving so soon, but I will see to it that he does not suffer financially from our short stay."

The monk rose to his feet. "I have a message for Manuel, Señor Alistair. The Abbot has also requested his presence at the monastery; but first, he must pick up something for Brother Gregorio. I will deliver this message while you are engaged with your friends." He walked across the dining room to the kitchen, and ducked through the doorway, which had been built for men smaller than Mateo.

Alistair went into the bar. Esteban was wiping the tables, and called out a greeting to him. Santiago, Paul and Angeline were talking animatedly in a booth near the door, and they looked up. "Time to go, guys," said Angeline, "the boss has returned!"

After a brief word with Alistair, they all went to their rooms to pack their things. When they assembled outside a few minutes later, Mateo was helping Manuel to load provisions on the back of a small trailer hitched up to the Volkswagen; the back seats and the front passenger seat were already crammed with boxes and baskets. Manuel was in a state of high excitement, and called out jokingly to them. "I regret your visit was so short, *mis amigos* – now I must re-let my rooms!"

"No, you won't, Manuel," said Alistair. "I'm retaining our reservations – I want the rooms kept vacant for our return, whenever that may be. Charge me full rate – I don't want to be outbid by a rich tourist who happens by!"

Manuel made effusive noises of genuine gratitude: there was little chance of him re-letting the rooms, and the money would be welcome.

Santiago was loading their bags into the boot of the Mercedes. Alistair walked across. "Mateo will drive – he is excited at the thought of driving such a fine new car after the Abbot's ancient vehicle. He knows every rock and pothole of the road, so you can take it easy for twenty minutes or so," he said.

Mateo finished helping Manuel and came across. Santiago handed him the keys with a smile, then Mateo eased himself into the driving seat, moved the seat back and adjusted the mirror. Santiago sat beside him in the front, and the rest of them clambered into the back seat, Alistair behind Santiago, Angeline in the middle and Paul behind Mateo.

The town of Moridanza stood on a prominence in the flat countryside around it. Mateo drove down the short lane from the café, turned right into the main street, and out of the village. The road dropped on quite a steep incline, and for the first time, Santiago, Paul and Angeline saw the plain of Moridanza laid out before them in the hard, brilliant sunlight. They were heading north, and they could see a large house and outbuildings on the west, surrounded by cultivated land.

Brother Mateo turned his head slightly. "Ahead on your left, about four miles away, is the estate of Don Ferdinand of Moridanza, and straight ahead, towards the northern horizon, lies *La Copa de Moridura*, with *el monasterio de Moridura* on its southern lip." Angeline whistled in open appreciation.

"What a wildly romantic sight!" she enthused.

Santiago half-turned and laughed. "Spain has many such sights, Angeline, and more spectacular."

"Don't be blasé, Santiago! I haven't seen all of your wonderful vistas. Let me enjoy this one." Her enthusiasm overlaid a strained note in her voice, and Alistair turned to her. "Are you OK?" he said softly.

She shook her head impatiently, looking straight ahead, and Alistair wondered if she realised just how much he knew about Lloyd C. Lonnen.

After about five minutes, the road passed the outer gates of Don Ferdinand's estate, and they could see a long driveway snaking towards the main house. Two stone lodge houses could be seen part way up the drive, on either side. "That's where *los artilleros* are normally stationed," said Mateo, "but I have heard that they cannot be found at the moment. Don Ferdinand will be very angry, and his anger is something to be feared."

"Even by you, Mateo?" said Alistair.

"I fear God and my own weaknesses, but rarely anything or anyone else, señor," replied Mateo in a matter-of-fact tone. But as he said it, the monk remembered the little door in the cellar, and the awful voice that had made his blood run cold. He concentrated on avoiding the ruts and potholes, even though the suspension of the superb machine he was driving was coping effortlessly with the primitive road surface.

Alistair felt a surge of pleasure as he watched *La Copa de Moridura* grow closer. It reminded him of the first sight of Edinburgh Castle on the road in from the south to the city, although the height of *La Copa* was much more modest than the four hundred feet of the spectacular Castle Rock.

"I have a thing about structures built on rocks," he said. "My own house on Loch Lomond - West Craig - is on a wee rock, and my original neighbourhood in Glasgow – Dennistoun - has a street called Wester Craigs, and there was the Fir Park, a rocky hill above a stream, the Molendinar, where the monk Mungo was instructed by his dying master, Fergus, to build a church. That's where the city was founded and it's now the site of the cathedral and the Necropolis – the City of the Dead. When we were boys, after going to see the Frankenstein movie, we would climb over the wall into the Necropolis and play at Frankenstein among the mausoleums. I was the Monster, because I was tall. There's a great Spanish movie where a wee girl thinks she's met the Monster after seeing the film – what's it called, Santiago?"

"*El Espíritu de la Colmena* – The Spirit of the Beehive," said Santiago. "It is a favourite of mine – the little girl was wonderful."

"What's your favourite film, Mateo?" asked Angeline.

"I have never been to the cinema, Señorita Angeline, and I have only occasionally glimpsed television. You must remember, I have spent my whole life in the monastery, with occasional trips to Moridanza."

Everyone fell silent at this revelation. A 21st century man who had never been to the cinema and who had only glimpsed television. Paul eventually broke the silence. "But you read a lot, Mateo – in the monastery library?"

"Those books that I am permitted to read – those that are not on the *Index Librorum Prohibitorum*, or are not specifically forbidden by the Abbot."

"Your English is excellent and presumably you read the language. Do you also read Latin?" asked Paul, his interest aroused.

"Yes, Señor Paul – I grew up with Latin as virtually a second language. Moridura has not abandoned Latin …" He broke off abruptly, and Paul speculated that the monks were perhaps breaching some Vatican ruling on the use of Latin.

"Have you read the Moridura Manuscript since it was returned to the monastery, Mateo?" asked Alistair.

Mateo deftly sidestepped the question. "We have arrived – this is the end of the road." The black rock face of *La Copa* towered fifty metres above them as the car pulled on to a small parking area at the foot of the steep path up the cliff. Three smiling monks moved forward to greet them.

Chapter Eleven

As they got out of the car, Alistair looked at the three monks.

"A reception committee?" he whispered to Mateo.

"Each one of you must have a guide on the path – you will remember from your last visit that it is very perilous for those unfamiliar with its hazards," replied Mateo, beckoning to the monks. Introductions were made; the three Moridurans were Brothers Felipe, Antonio and Juan.

"The brothers will walk on your left, and you will walk with the cliff face on your right. I would advise you not to look down, unless you have a head for heights – the view is good, but seductive – it draws one dangerously to the edge." The brothers laughed and said something in Spanish. Santiago smiled and Mateo translated.

"They say it is their job to fall off the rock if you stumble – so please be careful! We are on the eastern side of *La Copa* – the path climbs west to the monastery. I have the greatest experience of the path; I have travelled it since childhood and I have been a guide since early manhood. If you will forgive my presumption – I feel that Señorita Angeline's safety is of paramount importance to all of us, and therefore I should be her guide."

Angeline was lost for words – she didn't know whether to be outraged or grateful. Her expression showed that she was on the edge of an outburst; Paul interjected rapidly.

"We agree with your assessment, Mateo, but I take leave to believe that you are also motivated by old-fashioned gallantry and the chance to walk with a beautiful woman!"

Mateo blushed. Alistair and Santiago laughed, as did the brothers.

Angeline was not pleased. "You bunch of sexist...' she burst out, then choked back a word from her considerable vocabulary of invective, remembering the company she was in. She turned to Mateo, and gave him a smile that would have caused a saint to throw away his halo and kick a hole in a stained glass window.

"I believe you to be an Extremaduran gentleman, Brother Mateo, and I am privileged to have you as my guide."

Mateo gave a sigh of relief.

"Your guides will carry your bags."

"We can carry them ourselves, surely?" said Alistair.

"No, señor, you may not. Only those with long experience of the path are allowed to carry things; guests new to the path must have both hands completely free on *el sendero de precipicio* – forgive me – the cliff path."

"*El sendero de precipicio* conveys greater danger than the cliff path, Mateo - *the path of the precipice* would be our literal translation," said Paul, and they began their ascent. Paul went first, accompanied by Brother Juan; Mateo and Angeline fell in behind them, followed by Alistair and Brother Antonio; Santiago and Brother Felipe brought up in the rear.

The winding path curved west up the rock face. For once, Paul felt that his smaller stature and lighter build gave him an advantage over his tall, heavy male companions. The incline was very steep indeed, and fit though Alistair and his friends were, they soon found that they did not have enough breath for conversation, the dangers of the climb demanding all of their attention span. Paul found that it took an effort of will not to look down. Angeline was effectively prevented from doing so by Mateo's great bulk, and he kept her attention by chatting about the life of the monastery, but Paul felt a bit like Lot's wife trying not to look back at the destruction of the cities of the plain. He remembered a fragment of a Russian poem mourning her as one who gave up her life for a single glance, and now, at this height, Mateo's words came back to him – "The view is spectacular, but seductive – it draws one dangerously to the edge."

At certain points there were crude steps with low risers hacked into the rock. They seemed to add to the hazards of the ascent rather than facilitate it; there were one or two hair-raising stumbles by those on the inside track, and only the experience and strong right arms of the monks averted falls.

At last, they reached a flat, paved area in front of a large double gate. Paul looked at the seven-metre wall and the massive studded wooden gates, and moved close to Alistair. "This looks Roman to me, not medieval – it looks like the outer wall of a fort."

"Spot on," said Alistair. "The monastery complex incorporates structures that go back to the Iberians, and there are lower levels that I have never seen. Most monasteries were effectively forts, especially in Extremadura, when the Moors were on its borders, before the *Reconquista*."

Satisfied that his charges were all safely assembled, Brother Mateo invited them to turn and look down across the plain of Moridanza. Although at fifty metres high, their vantage point was only about the height of a modest city office block, it was the highest point in a flat plain that extended to the hill of Moridanza and beyond. The view was spectacular, but they had little time to enjoy it. There was the sound of a great bolt being drawn back, a loud creaking sound, and the great gates of the monastery began to open. Mateo turned in astonishment – he had expected to lead the party through the wicket gate. The main gates were rarely opened. The Abbot had evidently decided to welcome his guests in style, he thought, and he felt a surge of pleasure at being part of it.

As the gates opened, a monk in a black habit, with the cowl thrown back, emerged; immediately behind him were two other monks.

"Welcome to the monastery of Moridura! My name is Anselmo – I am the Abbot of Moridura." He motioned to two monks just behind him, and they both came forward. "Brother Gregorio, my deputy, and Brother Joaquín."

Alistair, in spite of the formality of the old monk's welcome, could not restrain himself, and he ran forward and embraced Brother Anselmo.

"*Mi amigo viejo!* How good it is to see you after all these years!" He turned to Brother Gregorio and shook his hand warmly. "Gregorio, it is a pleasure to see you too." He then moved to Brother Joaquín, who was grinning in delight. "Joaquín! Do you remember *Singing the Blues?*"

"*Sí,* Señor Alistair – Bix's cornet solo lives in my ears for ever!" replied the little monk, pumping his hand vigorously.

The Abbot smiled indulgently, with a hint of reproof in his voice. "You make it hard for me to maintain the dignity of my office and the formality of my welcome to you and your guests, Alistair. But it is good to see you – we have much to talk about."

Alistair stepped back, contrite. "Before I introduce my friends, may I express my thanks to the estimable Mateo, and to Felipe, Antonio and Juan who protected us on the path. Do you have any plans to have a chair lift installed, Brother Anselmo? I am sure the monastery is rich enough to finance one, or maybe you could get a grant from the Department of Tourism and Leisure?"

"You tease me, Alistair – you know that we value our old ways and our isolation," replied the Abbot. "Now, perhaps you will introduce me to your friends?"

The introductions over, the Abbot invited them to enter the monastery precincts through the open gateway. As they walked across the stone-flagged approach to the cloister, Alistair whispered to Angeline, "What do you think of *el monasterio de Moridura?*'

She looked at Alistair with an expressive shrug and slight raising of her eyebrows. He smiled at her. "It's more impressive inside," he said softly.

Angeline found herself approaching the front section of the cloister of the monastery. She counted twelve arches, and she could see through the arches to the other sides of the cloister. A few monks in black habits were walking slowly up and down, reading from prayer books in their hands. Above the cloister, she could see a higher building with a pitched red roof and long, narrow windows. There was a tower at one end of the building that extended about six metres above the ridge of the red-tiled roof, with three long, narrow windows above the roofline. There were two other buildings with pitched roofs on either side of the cloister, with the gables facing her, each with three large, narrow windows high on the gable, one small, square window close to ground level on the left, and two even smaller windows adjacent to each other on the right. The whole effect was of a plain, functional construction, with no obvious external ornamentation, although the windows were stained glass.

As they reached the cloister, Brother Anselmo turned to Angeline. "Doctora Blade, it is thirty five years since a woman last entered the monastery precincts: please forgive my brethren if they appear startled, or even stare – they do not intend any discourtesy."

Angeline smiled at the old monk.

"Thank you for your concern, Brother Anselmo. If you feel it to be appropriate, I prefer to be called Angeline, or if that seems too informal, others have called me Señorita Angeline."

"Señorita Angeline, Alistair Mackinnon once quoted me a line by the Scottish poet, Robert Burns – *the rank is but the guinea stamp – a man's a man for a' that* - a sentiment that I share," replied the Abbot, "and I am certain that the poet intended the word *man* to include both sexes."

The group entered the cloister, and one or two monks did look up abruptly from their prayer books, but most maintained a studied decorum. In the centre of the quadrangle bounded by the cloister, there were small vegetable plots, and two monks were on their knees at work. Angeline noticed that the other three sides of the cloister provided access to the main and side buildings of the monastery.

They turned left along the cloister then right, then left through a door into a large interior space with a polished inlaid wooden floor of intricate design. Angeline knew that she must be at the gable end of the building to the left of the cloister that she had seen from the front of the monastery courtyard. The light was streaming in from the three stained-glass windows high on the wall, and lighting up the hallway and the elaborate roof timbers.

Looking down the length of the building from the gable, she saw a wide wooden staircase of dark wood, about three metres wide, with ornate carvings on the newel posts at the bottom. It led to an upper landing with a balustrade on either side of the staircase; panelled walls could just be seen on either side of a passageway on the landing. Both sides of the base of the staircase were open, and appeared to lead to the far end of the building. Angeline concluded that this vast room had once been completely open and undivided from gable to gable, and that the staircase and floor above were later additions. It was a pity, she thought, because the full majesty of the intricate roof timbers could not be seen in their entirety.

"This is where we accommodate our special guests," said the Abbot. "In the centuries since the monastery was built, this space has had many functions, and even today, it must be pressed into service for many and varied uses. We have few modern conveniences, and I hope you will be able to tolerate their absence. There is no electric light – we rely on candles and natural light for all our illumination. There is no central heating. We do have a primitive plumbing system that was installed in the early 18th century, and we have our own water supply from natural springs. This is supplemented by rainwater collected in barrels at various points. Our water is safe and clean – we have never had a water-based infection or water pollution in living memory, so it is safe to drink water supplied specifically for consumption.

"Water for your ablutions will be brought to your rooms and regularly replenished by our lay brothers. We can arrange a shower of sorts, with notice. At the top of the stairs, there are six guest bedrooms, three on each side of the passageway. They have been formed by high, heavy wooden partitions, but are open at the top because of our timbered roof structure, to admit air and light. Each room has a window set in the outer wall of the building.

"One is already occupied by Señor Lonnen, our American guest; Señorita Angeline's room is the first on the left, and is adjacent to an empty room. The end room on the left is yours, Alistair. On the right, the first room is Señor Paul's, followed by Señor Santiago's. Señor Lonnen is in the end room on the right, facing Señor Alistair's room.

"On the ground floor, in the passage to the left of the staircase, is a water closet for the use of the señorita. In the right passageway, there is one for the señores. At the far end is the space where you will eat; it is also a place where you may read and relax, and where we may meet to address vital matters during your stay at the monastery. Brother Joaquín will attend to all your day-to-day requirements.

"We are in a dead zone for radio, television and mobile telephone communications, so any portable devices you have with you will not function. If you have portable computers, you will be reliant on the life of your batteries, unless you have brought solar recharging packs; to recharge the batteries will involve a trip to Moridanza by Brother Mateo. After Señor Alistair's last visit, Brother Joaquín convinced the Chapter, our governing body, that his spiritual development would be inhibited if we did not acquire a clockwork gramophone, of the type Señor Alistair had with him on his last visit.

"With the help of Manuel Ortega, we purchased one, and a small number of records chosen by Brother Joaquín, assisted by Brother Mateo. The gramophone and the records are available for your use. We would only ask that you do not play it during the times of prayer and devotion – a proscription you may recall from your last visit. If there is anything else you require, Brother Joaquín will obtain it, or will contact Brother Gregorio."

Joaquín looked pleased; Gregorio looked slightly disapproving: Alistair gave a conspiratorial smile to Joaquín, putting his arm around his shoulder.

"I cannot thank you enough for all your consideration of our needs, Brother Anselmo," he said, "I was worried about Joaquín's musical development when I left, but I see that my fears were groundless." He glanced quickly at Angeline, who looked abstracted and tense, and then looked back at the Abbot. "When will we meet Lloyd Lonnen? I look forward to renewing our acquaintance…"

"Señor Lonnen is elsewhere in the monastery on business with Ferdinand of Moridanza. The seven of us will eat together, if that is possible. Manuel Ortega will eat in the refectory with the monks – that is where he normally eats when at the monastery. He may be able to join you for other meals. Gregorio and I must leave you now; we have other business before lunch, and Joaquín will return to the cliff top to assist Mateo when he returns with your bags. I will return in about an hour and a half with Don Ferdinand," said the Abbot, "and, Señorita Angeline, with your countryman, Señor Lonnen."

Angeline's face was expressionless, but she inclined her head very slightly in acknowledgement. The three monks then left the room – glided was the word that came to Paul's mind as he observed their smooth, silent movement to the door. Santiago promptly disappeared down the left hand side of the staircase.

"Shall we follow him?" asked Paul, about to do so.

Alistair put his hand on his arm and laughed. "No, let him do his job first."

The three of them waited for a short time, then Santiago reappeared from the right passageway. "Give me a moment to check upstairs," he said apologetically, and bounded up the staircase. He turned on the landing at the top, looked down at them over the balustrade, and gave a theatrical wave, then headed down the passage between the bedrooms. They could hear his footsteps and the sound of heavy doors being opened and closed.

"Three," said Angeline, counting.

Alistair and Paul picked up her chant, and together they called out "Four! – Five…" Santiago appeared on the landing as they chanted six, and then he came down the middle of the staircase at a half run, without using the handrail of the banister. Angeline could not help admiring his catlike grace of movement.

"Clear," he said simply, and joined them.

"Then let's go through!" said Alistair breezily, and they followed Santiago's initial route down the left hand passage beside the staircase. The passageway was lit by small, rectangular windows in the massive stone wall on their left. The right hand side of the passageway was a wall of panelled wood. Halfway along on the left, a wooden construction about two and a half metres high and just over a metre wide jutted out from the wall. The dark wood was ornately carved, and there was door with an aperture cut at head height in the centre.

"It looks like a confessional box," said Angeline.

"It's the ladies' facility," said Santiago primly, "the gentlemen's facility is on the other side of the staircase."

Paul and Alistair laughed and Angeline tried to cover her embarrassment with a quip. "Where I come from, the ladies' privy *is* a confessional box if it holds more than one!"

"Don't say that to Anselmo and Gregorio," replied Alistair, still laughing, "or it will be many years before they admit another woman to the monastery of Moridura!"

"Well, Joaquín and Mateo wouldn't be scandalised," said Angeline defensively, "and with this level of domestic plumbing, neither should the two exalted brothers. I wonder if the bowl is by Thomas Crapper?"

Alistair laughed in recognition at the name of the famous American inventor and manufacturer of sanitary fittings.

"What makes you think there is a bowl, Angeline?' Santiago said teasingly.

She looked at him in horror, threw open the door and peered in, then pulled her head back out, relieved. "Thank God for small mercies! There's also what looks like a cistern and a chain."

"That may be a bell to signal that…"

"Shut up, Alistair, you nasty man!"

"You'll need a candle," said Alistair, unabashed. "Don't set fire to the privy when you do go – the entire internal structure of this place seems to be made of wood."

"He is beyond redemption, Angeline," said Paul soothingly, as they walked past the wooden edifice and past two more small windows. "Was there a window inside?"

"If there is, it admits no light," said Santiago, "but I will check later."

"Is the gents exactly the same?" asked Angeline as they reached the end of the passageway.

"Exactly the same," replied Santiago. "I don't think yours was meant for a woman - it would only be used every thirty years or so if it was…"

"I might have preferred that," said Angeline huffily.

They entered the space at the other end of the building. In size, it appeared to be a mirror image of the space they had first entered, open to the roof timbers, with three large windows, however, instead of a large central staircase, there were two smaller staircases from the bedrooms, one at each end of the landing. There was a large, rectangular wooden table on the right, with four high-backed chairs along its length on each side, and a single chair at each end, bigger and more ornately carved than the others. Two candelabra sat on the table, each candelabrum holding five tall candles. The two long sides of the table were set for a total of seven people.

Two large pieces of furniture that looked like sideboards sat beneath the windows. On the left of the room was a low table surrounded by four small wooden benches with high backs. The benches had loose leather cushions on the seats, and leather cushions tied to the back. Against the side wall stood a tall bookcase, open-fronted, and a set of library steps. A wooden lectern was placed near the bookcase. Six straight-backed chairs stood in a row under the landing, between the two staircases.

The benches around the low table looked disapprovingly at the artefacts placed incongruously in its centre – a wind-up phonograph with a large brass exponential horn, and a pile of 78 rpm records. All that was missing was a small dog, thought Angeline.

Alistair sprang forward and began to sift through the pile of records, murmuring in pleasure. "If I had picked my forty old-time greats, it would have been very close to this selection! How the hell did they do it?"

"Don't say hell, we're in a monastery," said Paul, "and don't try to play them till we get permission – it's only eleven thirty – we've got at least an hour before lunch."

Alistair straightened up reluctantly, and saw that Santiago was looking back in the direction they had come. "Something bothering you, Santiago?" he queried.

"Yes – what is in the large central area beneath the upper floor? There are no doors, and there is no obvious access to it. We have this space, the two passageways and the space that we first entered, and this in the middle of it. I reckon it must be about fifteen or sixteen metres long by nine or ten metres wide. That's a lot of space unaccounted for…"

"Maybe it's the septic tank for the privies," said Alistair, reluctant to let go of the earlier scatological themes.

Santiago went off down one of the passages, and they could hear him knocking on the walls. He emerged from the other passageway shaking his head.

"The panelling is heavy, but I think there is a void or space of some kind behind it. Monks are not known for wasting space; I'll be happier when someone tells us what's in there."

"Won't it be discourteous to ask?" said Angeline impatiently. "After all, we are guests of the Abbot; one doesn't go around the house asking one's host what lies behind closed doors. We don't want to give the impression that we expect to be murdered in our beds!"

The look that Santiago gave her was that weary look a security professional gives to his vulnerable charges when they question his judgement, but he said nothing. Angeline took the point, and smiled at him.

"I can raise it delicately with Mateo, when he comes with our bags – or with Brother Joaquín. I think Joaquín might enjoy a good gossip," said Paul. "If they clam up, then we know not to raise it with Brother Anselmo."

"Good sense," responded Alistair. "In any case, if we can't get in, whatever is in there can't get out, eh?"

"With respect, Alistair, I don't think we can rely on that principle – Spanish monasteries are full of tunnels, secret passages and God knows what else – our history made them essential adjuncts of survival," said Santiago.

Alistair grew impatient with his security chief. "We're in a large monastery complex. It's just not practicable to reconnoitre the whole bloody place."

"I must at least safeguard our sleeping area, Señor Alistair," said Santiago. "We are at our most vulnerable in the night hours, as last night demonstrated – and those responsible for that are still at large…"

"Don't start back with the Señor Alistairs, Santiago. OK, I withdraw my remarks; I defer to your judgement – it has never failed me."

The tense moment passed. Alistair returned to gloating over the gramophone and Paul and Angeline gave the big Spaniard conspiratorial winks, to which he responded with a deadpan expression. The sound of voices drifted along the passageways, then the sound of feet ascending the far staircase. More footsteps and the opening and closing of doors followed, then Mateo appeared on the landing above them, followed by Brother Joaquín. They both descended, and Joaquín rushed across to Alistair at the gramophone, talking excitedly. Mateo joined the others.

Everyone in the room seemed smaller in the presence of the big monk, and Angeline couldn't help the guilty thought that it was a pity that such a splendid specimen of manhood was devoted to a life of prayer and contemplation.

"We have taken your bags upstairs and put them in your rooms. There is fresh water, soap and towels. Hot water can be brought from the kitchens when you need it. Don Ferdinand and Señor Lonnen have just arrived and are with the Abbot. They will be joining you for lunch in about twenty minutes. Joaquín will be happy to show you to your rooms," Mateo said, raising his voice and looking across pointedly at his companion, who broke off his chatter and scuttled back, smiling. "I have other business before I go to the refectory, and must leave you now," he concluded, and with a brief respectful nod, he left.

"We can go up to your rooms from this side," said Joaquín, leading them up the right hand staircase. "Señor Alistair, the first room on the right is yours. The doors have no locks, as you see, only a latch. Señor Santiago, the second room on the left is yours, and Señor Paul, you are next to Señor Santiago on the end. Señorita Angeline, the end room on the right is yours"

Angeline entered her room, and was delighted to find that there was a stained glass window facing her, about two metres above the floor, with an upward sloping sill let into the massive external wall. The light from the window focused down at an angle into the room, adding another dimension to the light coming from above. The other three walls were of panelled dark wood; there was no ceiling, and the main roof timbers could be seen above the partitions.

In the right hand corner of the room stood a substantial wooden bed, its headboard against the rear stone wall. The bed cover was an anachronistic modern duvet. A small table stood beside the bed, with a water jug and glass, a candlestick, candle, matches and a snuffer. In the left hand corner, against the rear wall, was a wooden construction with a basin let into it; beneath it was a vessel to collect waste water from the basin. Above the basin, a mirror in a wooden frame hung from the wall; towels were draped over a brass rail. Next to the basin was a large jug containing water. Against the left hand wall was some kind of table or reading desk; on it was a small candelabrum with three candles, matches and a snuffer. A straight-backed chair stood in front of the table. The floor was uncarpeted.

Angeline heard much banging of doors, a muted Scottish curse, and came out just as everyone reappeared simultaneously, as though in a stage farce. They all looked at Santiago, who looked back questioningly at them.

"Go on, say it!" commanded Alistair, and as Santiago replied, they all chorused in unison, "There are no locks on the doors…"

Santiago was unamused; he came forward with objects in his hands, and handed each of them a small metal flashlight.

"We cannot rely on candles and matches alone," he said, "the whole of the interior is made of wood, and it's also draughty. These are small, but powerful and they can be focused to a tight spotlight or a wide beam by turning the head."

"Good," said Alistair, "I don't fancy visiting the downstairs privy with a candle in my hand. Don't tell the Abbot we have them - he might not approve. After all, the monks been using the privies for several centuries without burning the place down."

Angeline was suddenly serious. "Did you look in Señor Lonnen's room, Santiago?" she asked in a tight, small voice.

"Yes," replied Santiago, "an intrusion, I know, but my check would have been incomplete..."

"It makes perfect sense to me," said Paul, "anyway, he's not at home at present. Anything of interest?"

"I didn't go through his things, Paul, I just looked in," replied Santiago. "I did notice a large trunk, a small suitcase, an attaché case and a laptop computer, none of which are part of the standard equipment of Hotel Moridura."

The sound of footsteps below interrupted their exchange, and then they heard a strong, confident male voice with an American accent. "I guess they're upstairs, Brother Anselmo..."

The three men looked surreptitiously at Angeline. Her face was set; she lifted her head, and drew a long breath. "The Abbot has arrived with his guests – best go down and meet them," she said in a matter-of-fact tone.

They reached the landing, paused, and looked down. The Abbot was standing with two other men around the low table with the gramophone. Red Lonnen, dressed in the habit of a Moriduran monk, was stroking the brass horn admiringly, and Ferdinand was flicking through the gramophone records, a faintly contemptuous look on his face. At the sound of footsteps on the landing, they all looked up, and Red Lonnen called out to them.

"Angeline! Gentlemen! Good to see you!"

Angeline made no reply, and Alistair led the way down the left hand staircase. The three men moved forward to meet them. Brother Anselmo gestured towards his two companions. "May I present Ferdinand de Moridanza and

Señor Lloyd C. Lonnen? Señorita Angeline, you already know Señor Lonnen…"

"Hi, Angeline! How was Scotland?" Lonnen extended his hand and Angeline, unsmiling, shook it but said nothing.

"Ferdinand, may I introduce you to Doctora Angeline Blade?" the Abbot continued, "Señorita Angeline, Don Ferdinand de Moridanza…"

He took her hand, and bowed slightly. "Doctora Blade, I am delighted to meet you again – our paths crossed briefly in Café Ortega last night. Señor Lonnen has spoken of you in the highest terms."

The men then shook hands and concluded the formalities. There was something in Santiago's reaction to Don Ferdinand that struck Paul as unusual, but he couldn't quite figure out what it was. Perhaps it was just the natural wariness of two dangerous animals at close quarters. A clattering and creaking sound from the passage next to the left hand staircase broke his train of thought, and a wooden cart laden with food emerged, with Brother Joaquín behind it.

"Ah," said the Abbot, "our lunch has arrived – shall we sit down?"

He motioned them to the dining table. It was evident to Angeline that the men would wait until she had chosen her place, so she headed for the left hand chair at the near side of the table facing the windows. As she reached it, Ferdinand expertly and unobtrusively pulled it back for her, and as she began to sit down, moved the heavy chair forward.

"Thank you," said Angeline, not sure whether she liked all this old-world courtesy or not; she was used to an academic and corporate world where such etiquette at meal times between the sexes was rare.

When all were seated, Alistair's group of four was facing Brother Anselmo, Don Ferdinand and Red Lonnen across the table. It seemed to Paul that the parties had instinctively chosen to seat themselves for a meeting, perhaps a negotiation, rather than an informal lunch. Brother Joaquín bustled around, laying out an appetising array of vegetarian dishes, and two jugs of wine.

"I will now say grace before we commence our meal," said Brother Anselmo, and bowed his head. "Lord of all Creation, we give thanks for what is set before us, gathered from the fertile surface of our planet Earth – a living organism in the vastness of time and space, nourished by the star we call our sun, maintaining the life of your creatures who live on its surface and beneath its waters by its delicate and vulnerable envelope of air, and held in its place in the cosmos by invisible and mysterious forces. Give us the wisdom to interpret your Divine Will and use your gift of free will wisely. Amen."

All echoed the amen except Paul – he had always had difficulties with the grace before meals, feeling that somehow it was forcing a personal conviction on to captive guests who might not share the belief on which it was founded. It was, however, the first time he had heard an ecological grace, and the deep conviction of the old monk was impressive.

He was soon deep in the sensual pleasure of a superb meal. Whatever else these monks could do, they certainly knew how to cook.

"Brother Anselmo, this food is wonderful! I am not a vegetarian, but I could easily become one after dishes such as these. Your cook – I should call him *chef*, because his skills rival those of the finest in Europe – has my praise and my gratitude," he said with feeling.

The others murmured enthusiastic assent.

"I'm a steak and fries man, Paul, as Anselmo knows; he has been kind enough to make special provision for me in the evenings, but the lunches are slowly converting me too," said Red Lonnen.

"Thank you, you are very kind – but Joaquín must convey your appreciation to all of our brethren – all work is shared and every monk takes his turn in the kitchens. When my other duties permit, I take my turn, as does Gregorio," said Brother Anselmo. "If anyone would like me to arrange a particular meat dish for this evening, I will be happy to do so."

"I'm not converted yet, Brother Anselmo, so I would be happy with whatever you can come up with. I hear Brother Joaquín can rustle up a fine *coq au vin* – is that so, Joaquín?' said Lonnen, turning to the smiling, hovering monk.

"With the Abbot's permission, señor," said Joaquín enthusiastically, looking at the Abbot, who nodded.

"If there is enough for two, Lloyd, I wouldn't mind splitting that with you," said Alistair. Angeline looked at him sharply, somehow unhappy at his use of Lonnen's first name.

"Great! Call me Red!" replied Lonnen. "We carnivores must stick together, Alistair. Say, something's been on my mind! Have we met face-to-face before? I know of you, obviously…"

"I think we have been at one or two seminars together, and maybe the odd black tie and tux dinner," replied Alistair. "Forgive me for not bringing it up, but you know what these things are like – the faces tend to blur after a while."

"Well, I guess I'll remember you now – as the guy who is about to steal my best girl," responded Lonnen, and the atmosphere at the table instantly chilled. His smile now looked more like the bared teeth of a predator, a fixed rictus beneath expressionless, cold eyes.

Alistair laid his fork down, and the relaxed expression disappeared from his face. He was forestalled by Angeline.

"I was never anybody's best girl before, but I am now, Red," she said, and turning leaned across and kissed Paul's cheek. Red Lonnen saw the look that passed between them, and his menacing manner of a moment ago faded, and was replaced by another expression in which both loss and concern were present.

"When did you two meet, Paul?" he said finally, and his look and tone of voice came together in one blinding flash of insight for Paul. The relationship that had been implied by Red Lonnen, in referring to Angeline as his best girl, was neither contractual nor romantic, but familial, and his question to Paul was the tentative preliminary query of a father evaluating a potential suitor for his daughter.

Why hadn't he seen it before – Angeline's reaction whenever Lonnen was mentioned - the red hair? Now the question was - who else knew of the relationship? Paul was as certain as he could be that both Lonnen and Angeline knew – but why were they failing to acknowledge it? What was the explanation for the different surnames? Did Alistair know, and if so, was he supposed to know? And what of the others – Santiago, Don Ferdinand and the Abbot? Caught up in this, Paul failed to respond to Lonnen's question, but Angeline filled the silence for him.

"We met the night before last, at Ardmurran, but it already seems a lifetime ago – we've been through exciting times in the last two days, haven't we, Alistair?" She turned to the big Scotsman, who was cradling his face in both hands, looking directly at Red Lonnen, an enigmatic look on his craggy features.

"Aye, we have, bonnie lass, we have. We have at that…'

Lonnen was silent; he glanced quickly at Brother Anselmo and Ferdinand, looked away just as rapidly, retreated for a moment into himself, and then recovered his composure.

"I knew you were a headhunter, Paul, but your abilities clearly range more widely than finding high-level scientific talent. Are congratulations in order?"

"If you mean for finding the most important person in my life, yes, they are – but I would suggest that this isn't the time or place speculate about our future plans."

The embarrassment and tension at the table became almost unbearable. Brother Anselmo intervened, his voice calm and businesslike.

"I think we may now address some practical matters that concern us all, with your permission. Rather than do so at the table, we will go elsewhere. I thought we might walk in *La Copa*." He rose from the table, and they followed him to a small, inconspicuous door on the right-hand side of the rear wall, and through it to a paved courtyard with a wall about four metres high at the far side of it. There was a gate in the wall, its double doors opening into the courtyard. Monks were coming and going through it, carrying baskets that were either empty or full of produce; some were carrying agricultural implements. They were chatting together cheerfully, but fell into a respectful silence when they saw the Abbot and his party, and parted to let them through the gate.

Chapter Twelve

O n the other side of the wall was a narrow lip of rock, about two metres wide, then a wide path leading down a gentle slope into *La Copa de Moridura*. Angeline and Paul stood together and gazed at the circular, shallow valley, about a mile wide, its continuous rock perimeter broken only by the buildings of the monastery behind them. In the centre of *La Copa*, a black protuberance could be seen. The slopes directly in front of them were under cultivation. Paul estimated that this area extended in an arc of about half a mile round the lip of the valley and about a quarter of a mile down the slope. It was laid out in a series of neat rectangular plots, with well-trodden paths linking them together. About twenty monks were either working the land or carrying baskets to and from the monastery. It was a scene from a medieval tapestry, thought Paul, imbued with a deep feeling of timelessness and the eternal cycle of life. His reverie was interrupted by the Abbot's voice.

"Señorita Angeline, señores - *La Copa de Moridura*," he said, with a wide, sweeping gesture. "Let us walk down to its very heart, to the rock formation we call the Throne – *El Trono*: it is perfectly circular and about seven metres high from the ground to its peak. We believe that it penetrates deep into the heart of *La Copa*."

They followed the Abbot down the path in pairs, forming a procession; the Abbot led, followed by Ferdinand and Red Lonnen, Alistair and Santiago, and Paul and Angeline, who, as the rearguard, took the opportunity to hold hands. Paul, now with the knowledge that Angeline's father was ahead of them, felt illogically guilty about it. The murmur of the conversations of those ahead drifted back to them, but the content was not discernible.

"Paul, I believe I can feel the strange heaviness that Alistair mentioned from his first visit – am I imagining it?"

"No, you're not – I can feel it too." Paul bent and picked a stone from the ground and, cupping it in his hand, tossed it gently in the air and caught it again. There was something indefinably odd about its motion as it fell.

Angeline looked sideways in amazement. "Can I try?" she said eagerly.

He handed her the stone, and she repeated the effect several times. "My God, I can't believe it! This must be a gravitational effect – it can be nothing else. It's hard to describe…"

"Look at the stone," said Paul softly.

Angeline held the stone close to her face.

"Is it a meteorite fragment?" Paul asked.

"Before you gave it to me, I would have said that was extremely unlikely – when meteors hit the ground, they almost always vaporise on impact – in fact, some explode before they hit the ground, as happened on the Siberian meteor site. They can create so-called shatter cones from the existing rock at the point of impact, and sometimes melt droplets solidify into tektites. But this looks like no other rock I know – it could be iridium. It's fascinating! You know, I think that the lowest point of *La Copa* is beneath the level of the plain, at the start of the cliff path."

"That was my impression too – the gradient of the slope down from the monastery is steeper than that resulting from a fifty metre drop over 800 metres - but isn't that what you'd expect from the impact site of a meteorite?" asked Paul.

"Yes, a saucer-shaped depression in the plain," said Angeline. "What really concerns me is that, if this is a meteor crater, *El Trono* – the rock at the centre - simply shouldn't be there. Imagine a flat area of wet sand, then dropping a cannonball on it – what do you get?"

"A concave depression in the sand," replied Paul. "But what if there was a rock in the sand before I dropped the cannonball?"

"It would either be crushed, or driven into the sand; the end result would be the same – a concave depression. In a meteor impact, it would probably be vaporised along with most or all of the meteorite."

"What can you deduce from the presence of a rock formation the size of the Throne?" said Paul, "I'm baffled…"

Angeline chewed her lip. "Well, we know what the Abbot told Alistair on his last visit. I don't buy that. This isn't my field of science, but logically…" She looked at Paul. "You're not a scientist, but you have a logical mind – you figure it out, and see if I agree."

"OK," said Paul, "I can only think of three possibilities, not necessarily in order of probability; one – *El Trono* was, and is, an indestructible part of the meteor; two – *La Copa* was not formed by a meteor impact, but is either a natural formation or is volcanic in origin; three – the Throne arrived or was created at some point in time after the meteor impact. The last possibility - the Abbot's version - seems the most unlikely of the three…'

Angeline clapped her hands in glee. "That's my boy – they're exactly the alternatives that I see. We've arrived at the mystery itself!"

They joined the group gathered on the south side of the black rock. The Abbot and Ferdinand put their hands on it, and because the others were not sure if this gesture was proprietorial or reverential, they resisted the urge to do likewise. The Abbot relieved them of their doubts, as a spiritual advisor should.

"Touch it," he said, "it won't strike you dead – not this time, at least."

Humour was a rare event with Brother Anselmo, and even Alistair was not sure how the remark was intended, but they went ahead and touched it anyway. They all expected that the rock might be cold to the touch, or perhaps warmed by the sun; what they experienced as their fingertips and then the palms of their hands were laid on its surface was totally unexpected.

El Trono was vibrating, subtly, but quite distinctly. It reminded Alistair of the four-beat vibrato of a saxophone section in a big swing band. He estimated it to be about four beats per second, 240 beats per minute. They were at a loss as to how to react, but Red Lonnen, with typical directness, broke the silence.

"This is like a goddam séance – if we all concentrate, we can lift the rock, run around and it will spin with us!"

Everyone let go, and Paul laughed a trifle nervously. "Does it always vibrate like that?" he asked.

"Always within living and recorded memory," said Ferdinand, "We of this place call it the heartbeat of *La Copa*."

"As you can see," said Brother Anselmo, "the rock, or at least, the visible part of it, is smooth and very hard – metallic: there are fragments scattered around *La Copa* that seems to be of the same material. The part above ground is seven metres tall, circular, with a base circumference of eighteen metres. If we now walk around to the north side," he went on, motioning them to follow him, "we shall see that the stone is partially cleft and has a set of indentations in the cleft that function as steps to the summit. These indentations, or steps, have been present throughout our recorded history, as revealed by pictures and text in the Moridura Manuscript, and in even more ancient records in our library. We do not know if they are a natural formation or if they were formed by some hand."

The group reached the north side of the stone pillar, where the cleft and the indentations were clearly visible. At the top could be seen a smaller protuberance in the rock.

"What you see is the access to *El Trono* - a formation on the top roughly in the shape of a seat or throne, facing south, that gives the rock its name: you may have noticed it as we walked down *La Copa*," said the Abbot.

"May we ascend the steps, Brother Anselmo?" asked Paul. Red Lonnen was already about to do just that, but the Abbot gently put his hand on the American's arm. "We would prefer you not to," he said softly but insistently. "Access to the summit is reserved for occasions of special significance to us, and only certain individuals are allowed to ascend the steps."

Paul was not clear if the Abbot was speaking for himself and Don Ferdinand, or for the Moriduran monks, or the *hermandad* – perhaps they were all at one in this. Angeline interjected at this point.

"You regard *El Trono* and the summit of the rock as sacred then, Brother Anselmo?'

"Sacred is not the word I would use," said the old monk warily. "The ceremonies surrounding *El Trono* are not of a religious nature – they are not part of our religious observances or beliefs." He shot a glance at Ferdinand.

"Perhaps taboo – a rather pagan concept, I fear – is a more accurate word. The ceremonies related to this geological formation are very ancient, pre-Christian, in fact," said Ferdinand smoothly. "The Catholic Church has always been tolerant of ancient beliefs that do not conflict with the central tenets of the Faith, indeed, our great forefathers in the Americas adapted and incorporated local superstitions into the mainstream of their religion."

"Of course," said Alistair, "Extremadura is the land of the *conquistadores* – it was your forefathers who made Spain the great world power it became – and a centre of European culture and learning."

Ferdinand bowed gracefully in acknowledgement, and for a moment, Angeline had a vision of his handsome, cruel features looking out from beneath a helmet, his body encased in armour, a sword in his hand.

Red Lonnen was displaying some impatience with this digression, as he saw it. "If we are to achieve our objective, I must examine the summit of *El Trono*," he said forcibly. "If those present here cannot permit access, who can?"

Ferdinand turned slowly and faced him, and Alistair realised that there was a deep enmity between the two men.

"The Abbot and I have that authority but we choose not to exercise it at this time," Ferdinand said, slowly and with great emphasis. "A time will come very soon when it will be necessary for us to ascend to the summit. After that time, we will consider your request."

Red Lonnen seemed about to challenge Ferdinand's reply, but then his eyes moved to a point beyond him.

"We have company!" he said softly.

They all looked in the direction of his gaze to the north of *La Copa*. Halfway down the northern slope, about quarter of a mile away, twelve red-robed figures were advancing towards them. They appeared to be hooded, with their robes coming to high points above their heads.

"It's the Klan!" said Lonnen, "Extremadura chapter…"

He laughed. Nobody else did, and Ferdinand gave him a look of utter contempt. Santiago moved close to Alistair.

"The two men on either side are armed with either rifles or shotguns – I can't tell which at this distance. It's probably our friends from last night – if they're carrying shotguns, our weapons will be in range before theirs are – if it's rifles, we're in trouble. Give me a moment…"

He took a small spotter scope from his pocket and swiftly scanned the oncoming group.

"It's *escopetas* – shotguns. OK to act?"

Alistair nodded grimly, and both men simultaneously drew their weapons and fired into the air. The sound of the shots reverberated from the rock behind them. Angeline, Paul and Lonnen instinctively ducked; the Abbot and Ferdinand turned as one and looked at Alistair and Santiago in shocked incomprehension, the Abbot raising his hand in a gesture of protest, his face white with horror. Paul, after the initial shock, felt for the small automatic pistol that Santiago had given him on his ill-starred watch at Angeline's door, and took it from his pocket.

The line of robed men had stopped, and the end men were on their knees with their weapons levelled at the group at *El Trono*.

Ferdinand spoke first. "This is an outrageous insult to the Abbot, your host, and to this place of special significance for us, Señor Mackinnon. You are in the grounds of a monastery, a place dedicated to God."

Alistair didn't even look at him as he replied. "God will understand, I'm sure, and perhaps the Abbot also, when he hears what I have to say. The outrages directed against me and those close to me, to date have included an ultimatum and death threat by letter, a shot fired in my home, Pablo Miguenez committing suicide in my home, and last night two men with shotguns invading Manuel's café and attempting to abduct or harm Doctor Blade. If you have any influence with those men, whom I take to be members of the organisation known as the *hermandad*, then go to them and tell them to retreat, or prepare to be fired upon."

He jerked his head towards Santiago, who had produced a folding stock and fitted it to his pistol, converting it to a light carbine. Ferdinand looked at Santiago, at Alistair with his big, heavy, long-barrelled revolver, and at Paul, who was holding his tiny automatic. He turned to the Abbot, whose face was now impassive and cold.

Red Lonnen was in a half-crouch, his hands loose at his side. "Are you going to insult me too?" he snarled at Alistair.

"I don't know if you have played any part in any of these events, Lonnen, but until I know differently, forgive me if I regard you as hostile. If you have a concealed weapon, surrender it now," replied the big Scot.

"The hell I will," said the American and reached abruptly for a leather pouch around his waist. Santiago hit him hard on the side of his head with the barrel of his automatic without even looking at him, and Lonnen fell to the grass without a sound. Angeline gasped, and made as if to go to him, but Paul gripped her wrist tightly, and shook his head. Ferdinand stood as if turned to stone, then turned and set off up the slope towards the twelve robed figures, his arms outstretched above his head.

"How do you justify this behaviour, señores?" asked Brother Anselmo, moving next to Alistair and Santiago as they levelled their weapons up the slope, watching Ferdinand get nearer to the twelve men.

Santiago immediately took a pace backwards, so that he was a pace behind the old man. The Abbot glanced back at him briefly, shook his head in disbelief, and then spoke again to Alistair. "Are you perhaps over-reacting, Señor Mackinnon?"

Alistair noted the formal address and tone. "No, Brother Anselmo, we are not. We are defending ourselves in a hostile environment. We are not here of our own choosing, but under duress – an ultimatum. A man has already died, and a young woman has lost her father. The men who threatened us last night were, we believe, the bodyguards of Ferdinand known as *los artilleros*. They are on the slope now, with the same weapons."

"Do you regard me as hostile? Am I to be clubbed to the ground by your associate?" asked the old monk.

"Not hostile, but complicit in your knowledge, partial or otherwise, of these events. I want to believe that you condemn the actions of your associates, but even if you do, you have been powerless to prevent them, and remain so at this moment."

The Abbot looked deep into his eyes for a moment. "Look behind you, señor," he said softly.

All but Santiago glanced back. Advancing towards them down the slope from the monastery was a group of about twenty Moriduran Brothers, carrying agricultural implements – scythes, sickles, hoes and forks. They were no more than three hundred metres away.

"Santiago!" said Alistair, his tone urgent.

Santiago turned and looked for a fleeting moment, then turned back, still aiming his pistol to the north. "They're all yours, Alistair," he said over his shoulder.

On the ground, Red Lonnen began to stir, groaning.

"Get his weapon quickly, Paul, before he recovers. Keep him covered – shoot him in the leg if he tries anything."

Angeline stared at them both, dumfounded, with a look of confusion and betrayal in her eyes.

"I'm sorry, lassie, but this is necessary – we won't harm him unless we have to. Help him if you can once Paul disarms him – but be careful..."

Paul bent over him, swiftly removing an automatic pistol from the pouch strapped to his waist; there was blood on one side of Lonnen's head and in his ear, and his eyes were half-open.

As the monks grew closer, Alistair turned to the Abbot. "Is *El Trono* going to be our Alamo, Brother Anselmo? We are outnumbered, if not outgunned. Why are your brethren here?"

"They are here to protect me, to protect the Throne of Moridura, and to protect you, if required," the Abbot said wearily. "They constitute no threat to you – observe who is leading them..."

Alistair now recognised the giant figure of Mateo; beside him, a small figure next to his huge companion, was Manuel Ortega. Sancho Panza at the head of an army of monks, thought Alistair, and smiled in relief.

Red Lonnen was sitting upright, with Angeline holding a handkerchief to the cut on his head; Paul still stood over him with the gun, vainly trying to catch her eye. Ferdinand was now with the group from the north side of *La Copa*. He could be seen dragging one of the end men across to the front of the others, then doing the same with the man from the other end. Shouting could be heard; Ferdinand was pointing back to the north rim of *La Copa*: the main body of ten turned and headed back up the slope.

Santiago brought his pistol down from his shoulder, and gestured to Alistair, indicating the activities on the northern slope. Ferdinand had taken the shotguns from the two men, who had now pulled back their hoods. He broke the guns and put one under each of his arms, shouted again at *los artilleros*, then turned south towards *El Trono*, motioning the men to follow him.

"That looks like a definite gesture of submission to me, Santiago – what do you think?" queried Alistair.

"I think it is hopeful, but that we should be cautious until he reaches us. They refused to surrender their arms before – this time they must. There can be no negotiation…"

"We'll evaluate the position when we hear what Ferdinand has to say. He has done as we have asked and more, but this is a tactical retreat, not a surrender – he is a proud man,"

Alistair looked down at Red Lonnen, who was struggling to his feet, with Angeline's assistance.

"Well, this is a fine mess you've got us into, Red!"

"Nice mess," said Paul, instinctively correcting the misquotation of Oliver Hardy's most famous line.

Lonnen dusted himself down, leaning for support on Angeline. "Tell your guy to stop pointing that popgun at me, Mackinnon," he said weakly, "I'm no threat right now…"

He turned to Santiago. "No hard feelings, Santiago – you were doing your job. I should have had enough sense to bring my own corporate muscle with me. If you ever want to jump ship, there's a place waiting for you with my company."

Alistair indicated to Paul that he could put the gun away. "You'll understand if we hang on to your weapon, Red?" He used the nickname again with emphasis, signalling that he wanted a reduction of tension now that the immediate threat had passed. Lonnen gave him a penetrating look, then a curt nod, acknowledging the signal.

Angeline looked undecided as to what she should do next, but Red Lonnen gently removed her helping hand. "I'm OK, now – I think I can stay upright unassisted…"

"You might be concussed – are you sure?" she said uncertainly, looking at his eyes.

He smiled at her. "Yeah, I'm OK. Maybe it was worth getting sapped to get all this tender loving care!"

Angeline's expression darkened instantly, and she moved quickly to Paul and took his hand. The tension visibly ebbed out of him, and he pulled her closer.

Lonnen had a quizzical look as he watched the powerful chemistry at work between them. "I guess I should be glad it wasn't you that hit me, Paul – that really would have complicated things," he laughed, rubbing his head.

Ferdinand and *los artilleros* had almost reached them. He stopped, some three metres away from Alistair's group, and threw the two broken shotguns towards them; they landed close to Santiago's feet. The faces of the two men with him were expressionless masks, but their eyes held a mixture of fear, hate and confusion.

Santiago, still levelling his pistol, went down on one knee and retrieved the two weapons, without taking his eyes from the three men in front of him. Behind Alistair's group, monks were appearing round either side of the rock, and Manuel and Mateo came and stood respectfully beside the Abbot. Manuel looked at Alistair, and gave an expressive shrug, his large eloquent eyes showing his bewilderment.

"Manuel! Mateo! I feel better now – Mafeking is relieved and so am I," he said brightly. He turned back to Ferdinand. "I thank you for what you have done, Don Ferdinand. With your help, we've defused a dangerously volatile situation - Santiago, I think you can put up your weapon - but we are left with an unknown potential of further conflict," he said, holstering his own revolver, the Webley Fosbery that Santiago had brought from Madrid and given him at Café Ortega: his *Maltese Falcon* gun, as he affectionately called it.

"I have a view of the situation we find ourselves in, Ferdinand, but my analysis is incomplete. How do you and Brother Anselmo see things? Can we start from a position that we all regret what happened here today, whatever its causes?"

The Abbot lifted his head, and looked from Alistair to Ferdinand. "I can say that I regret it deeply – all aspects of it, and I wish to move to constructive dialogue."

The tall aristocrat was silent for a moment. He gave Alistair a long, searching look. "I can start from the position you suggest, and I think my actions have amply demonstrated my wish to move forward without a threat of force hanging between us, señor."

"Don't I have any say in this?" interrupted Red Lonnen, his tone betraying his irritation with the cautious ritual dance that was taking place before his eyes. He was not a negotiator by instinct, usually leaving it to specialists in his organisation, and relying on naked commercial pressure to back up his demands if the way of words failed.

"Not at this moment, Red, but your input will be valuable and indeed crucial at a later time," said Ferdinand softly, without breaking eye contact with Alistair. Mollified, Lonnen fell silent.

"Firstly," responded Alistair, "I need to feel that my friends and I are safe while we remain in the monastery, or, indeed, in Moridanza – and I include Manuel Ortega, his family and Carlota Miguenez among those for whom I seek this assurance. Secondly, I need your assurance, Ferdinand, that the two men known as *los artilleros* are either under your control once more, or that you immediately nullify their capacity to threaten us further."

Ferdinand flushed. "I have sent my people back to our assembly point on the north ridge. You have my assurance that the safety of you and your three colleagues will not be threatened by me, or by those accountable to me. Manuel Ortega and his family are my honoured friends: Carlota

Miguenez is my employee and is under my personal protection. As for Francesco and Frederico," he went on, glancing briefly and menacingly at *los artilleros*, "they will abide by my will or suffer the consequences." The two men were ashen-faced, their heads bowed.

"I must also make it clear, Señor Alistair, that I did not order or endorse the actions of these men, nor did Brother Anselmo," he continued, gesturing to the north towards the ten red-robed figures, who were almost out of sight, retreating up the slope. "They were not acting under the instructions of the Magus or the Grand Council of Moridura, and they will answer for that transgression. Francesco and Frederico will make personal restitution to me for their disobedience and disloyalty."

"Please give me a moment to confer with my colleagues," said Alistair. He gathered Angeline, Santiago and Paul around him. "I think we can accept his assurances, limited as they are. What do you think?" he said in a low voice.

Paul raised his eyebrows expressively. "Have we any choice? It's either that or try to leave."

"I'm inclined to believe him," whispered Angeline.

Alistair turned to his security chief.

"We are still vulnerable to this faction within the *hermandad*, even if we accept his explanation. We will be here overnight and even more vulnerable during the hours of darkness, but as Paul has said, it is either accept his word or leave – there can be no guarantees," said Santiago quietly.

Alistair nodded and turned again to Ferdinand. "We accept your explanation and assurances, but we'll take precautions against the forces you cannot control. What do you require from us?"

"Simply that, at the appropriate time, determined by Brother Anselmo, that you listen to what we have to say, and decide whether or not you can assist us in achieving our objectives."

The Abbot came forward and stood next to them. "We will meet this evening after dinner in the chapter house with the Chapter of the Moriduran Brothers. Ferdinand will attempt to arrange for one or more representatives of the *hermandad* to attend – it is unlikely that the full Grand Council can be assembled at such short notice."

"Forgive me, Brother Anselmo, but I was summoned here by a letter, signed by the Magus on behalf of the Grand Council. Is this not inconsistent?" said Alistair, looking at both men in turn.

There was a long pause; glances were exchanged between Ferdinand and Brother Anselmo, then Ferdinand spoke, almost reluctantly.

"The Grand Council is a body that co-ordinates the *hermandad* and the Moriduran Brothers in matters of joint interest. The authenticity of that letter is in doubt, although the Grand Council undoubtedly wanted you and Doctor Blade to come to Moridura. I believe that someone has either exceeded their authority or misunderstood their brief. I regret this, but can say no more at this time."

"The situation is inherently unstable, Ferdinand, and I can't hide my concern. The two men behind you – they've heard all that we've said. Should this worry us?" Alistair said, indicating *los artilleros*.

Ferdinand looked over his shoulder towards the two terrified men. "If they betray my trust again, they will either go to God," he said menacingly, "or be delivered to another power, one that resides in this place."

Francesco and Frederico rose and, came across to him and prostrated themselves at his feet, speaking in Spanish, in what was clearly a desperate plea for clemency.

Ferdinand kicked them away like dogs. "Go back to the monastery and wait for me. Leave your weapons here."

The two men got up and made their way through the group of monks, their heads downcast, and headed up the south slope. Alistair waited until they were out of earshot.

"You referred to another power that resides in this place, Ferdinand?"

"A superstition of the credulous in the district – the myth of *La Bestia*: it can be usefully exploited on occasion," replied Ferdinand.

Brother Anselmo called Mateo across to him, whispered something to him, and Mateo returned to his brethren, gesturing to them to follow the two retreating men back to the monastery. The Abbot called to Manuel to wait behind, then turned to Alistair.

"May I suggest that we all return to the monastery now. Manuel will act as your guide. Your evening meal will be served to you at seven o'clock in the guest wing, but I regret that Señor Lonnen will be unable to share the *coq au vin* with you as originally planned. Ferdinand, Señor Lonnen and I have arrangements to make for our meeting in the chapter house at eight o'clock. Please use any of the facilities of the monastery you require – Manuel will advise you. I would ask you not to enter the chapel during prayer. Brother Mateo will show you our library if you wish to make use of it – you are already familiar with it and part of the monastery from your last visit, Señor Alistair. Please play your gramophone between prayer times - Brothers Joaquín and Mateo will be disappointed if you do not use our gift to you."

The Abbot turned to Manuel. "You may eat with Señor Alistair and his colleagues, if that is acceptable to them, Manuel. Don Ferdinand and I require you to attend the meeting at eight o'clock in the chapter house."

Manuel swelled with pride, but a pride that was not unmixed with apprehension.

"Come on then, old friend,' said Alistair, putting his arm around Manuel's shoulder, "let's go and listen to some jazz, and talk about old times!"

They all headed up the slope, with Red Lonnen bringing up in the rear, a solitary figure behind the laughing group ahead of him. Angeline looked back at him for a moment, and then quickly turned away again.

Chapter Thirteen

"We'll have to squeeze our jazz in before Vespers," said Alistair eagerly, riffling through the stack of 78s. "What's your choice, Brother Joaquín?"

"*Parker's Mood*" replied Joaquín, his eyes bright with anticipation.

"My, my, Joaquín – your tastes have moved on since I was last here!" Alistair removed the gleaming, black record from its paper sleeve. "Where did you get these platters? This is in mint condition!"

The group in the dining area of the guest wing comprised Alistair, Brother Joaquín, Brother Mateo, Angeline, Paul, Santiago, and Manuel. Angeline and Santiago looked disapprovingly at Alistair's activities at the gramophone.

"Jazz is fine, but don't you think we have more important things to talk about?" said Angeline impatiently, and Santiago nodded in emphatic support. Paul tried to look neutral, but Manuel and the two monks looked shocked.

"Jazz is good for the soul," replied Alistair, holding the voice box of the gramophone arm poised over the spinning disc. "We can have our discussion during Vespers – we only have this window of opportunity. Besides, the Abbot made it clear that he expected us to use his gift, and our friends here would be *desolado* if we didn't have our wee jazz fix – eh, Manuel – Brothers?"

Paul realised at once that Alistair wanted to wait until the Moriduran brothers had gone to Vespers before discussing the agenda for the evening meeting in the chapter house. Whether he envisaged Manuel being involved was an open question.

"What you are about to hear is a definitive blues improvisation – a masterpiece. Joaquín, you are to be

175

congratulated for choosing it." Alistair lowered the needle on to the record.

Joaquín smiled ecstatically as the ineffable sound of Bird's alto saxophone followed the piano introduction, echoing from the ancient walls. Angeline, who had grown up with rock and modern popular music that was predominantly vocal in character, gradually became aware that this wordless, instrumental music was a voice, speaking in a language that articulated emotions and experiences that mere words could not express, and that the artist making the statement was the Shakespeare of this language, one who had reshaped the traditional jazz phrases and harmonies into a completely new form without sacrificing the deep, dark heart of the blues.

Joaquín and Mateo had instinctively brought their hands together as if in prayer, their faces rapt. Even the controlled, imperturbable Santiago was moved by the naked intensity of the music, and felt his mind moving along strange and fascinating paths. He remembered Carlota, how beautiful she was, and the tears in her eyes for the father she had lost.

Manuel was seated on one of the benches, his hands on his knees, his head bowed. The music stopped and Alistair lifted the arm from the shellac, and moved across to Angeline. "It will all work out for the best – you'll see…" he said comfortingly.

"You know, Alistair Mackinnon, sometimes you're not a bad guy," said Angeline, looking warmly at her mentor.

"Only sometimes? I think of myself as the good guy most of the time," said Alistair, affecting a wounded expression. "Something lively now – happy jazz!"

Brother Joaquín looked at Mateo. "*At the Jazzband Ball*" they said simultaneously.

"Brothers of Moridura, your word is my command!" said Alistair, and soon the commanding lead of Bix's cornet was ringing out, punching out the staccato melody of the old jazz standard. Paul and Angeline started to dance. Neither of them could manage a proper quickstep, but they contrived to jive and twirl in approximate time to the beat. After the first chorus, Santiago politely tapped Paul on the shoulder, and Angeline was reluctantly surrendered to him. He led her into a very expert and graceful set of steps, somewhere between a fast tango and a quickstep. Manuel and the Brothers nodded in approval, and Alistair shook his head in admiring disbelief.

When the music stopped, the onlookers burst into spontaneous applause. Santiago and Angeline smiled in embarrassment, and then Santiago led her to the bench and bowed as she sat down next to Paul, who whispered something to her, bringing a furious blush to her cheeks.

"Where did you learn all that, Santiago?" she said, to cover her embarrassment. "You dance like a professional!"

"My mother and father were – and are – keen dancers," replied Santiago. "When I was a child, they competed in local dance halls, and took me along. When I was seven, they sent me to dance lessons – it got me beaten up at school, but it toughened me up. I told my parents that I would only continue with the dance lessons if they also sent me to martial arts training."

"I remember once being thrown out of the old Glasgow Barrowland Ballroom for trying to throw a punch," reminisced Alistair fondly. " The bouncers arrived so fast that the punch never landed. They threw me into the Gallowgate with the traditional farewell – don't come ******* back, Jimmy!"

He then realised that he had sworn, and looked at the Moridurans apologetically. They were both sitting with their fingers to their lips in gestures of reproof, then Brother Joaquín burst out laughing, followed by Mateo and Manuel. To cover his embarrassment, Alistair went off at a tangent, declaring, to the evident disbelief of his audience, that shellac – a component of the old 78 records – was made from the secretions of "a wee beastie" called the lac and that the insect had featured in ancient Hindu legends.

There was more jazz, more dancing, and both Joaquín and Mateo declined Angeline's invitations to dance with her, but with obvious regret. Eventually, the Moridurans indicated that it was time for Vespers, and they left reluctantly.

"Time for the serious bit, now," announced Alistair. He indicated that they should move across to the dining table, and they all sat down. Alistair looked across at Manuel.

"Manuel, my wee pal! We've had a fine time with music and dancing, but we now have important matters to address. You'll have gathered from the events in *La Copa* that there are complex forces at work, and that we're not here for a holiday. There are many things you don't know, and I feel that you have many things to tell us. Let me start by telling you that *los artilleros* came to your café in the early hours of this morning and overpowered Paul at gunpoint, with the apparent intention either harming or kidnapping Angeline."

Manuel's shock was evident – the blood drained from his cheeks and he gripped the arms of his chair. His first thought was for his family. An act of violence had occurred in his café – in his home: but then concern for his friends took over.

"It's OK, Manuel, we foiled the attempt, and no real harm was done, but taken together with the actions of *los artilleros* in *La Copa*, it's clear that some group means us harm, a group that includes renegade members of the *hermandad*. Well, I hope they're renegades, and that the whole bloody Order isn't ranged against us!

"We came here after receiving an ultimatum that seemed to come from the Ancient Order of Moridura, but which Ferdinand implied was not legitimate. In addition, a shot was fired into my home; the man who fired it was your friend, Pablo Miguenez; he was caught by the police, repeated the threat from the letter, and then killed himself."

Manuel stared blankly and uncomprehendingly at Alistair.

"Now, I have a question to ask of you, Manuel – two questions, in fact. Has Don Ferdinand offered you membership of the *hermandad*, and if so, what did you have to offer in return? No one enters the *hermandad* without a dowry of sorts, isn't that so?'

Manuel was silent, still trying to come to terms with the news that his friend Pablo had died by his own hand. Eventually, he cleared his throat nervously. "Señor, the *hermandad* values discretion above all else," he stammered.

"And I value friendship and trust above all else, Manuel," said Alistair, his tone suddenly cold. "The *hermandad* sent your friend to his death."

Manuel's head jerked, as though from a blow. Tears came to his eyes. "Your friendship is very important to me, Señor Alistair, and the safety of you and your friends is also of major concern to me. So I will answer, though I place myself and my family in danger by doing so. I have been offered membership of the *hermandad* without the usual probationary period, a rare exception. The price of this is that I release to the *hermandad* – to Don Ferdinand – the diaries of my late father. They are held in trust for me by Brother Anselmo, but under a proviso in my father's will stipulating that they would never be released to any member of the *hermandad*. Don Ferdinand and the Abbot have been deliberating whether this condition can be relaxed in view of radically changed circumstances."

Alistair was intrigued by Manuel's answer. "What is the significance of your father's bequest? Why do they want the diaries? Do you know?"

Manuel shook his head in bewilderment. "No, I do not, Señor Alistair. I have not read much of the diaries They cover most of my father's long life, but in the main they seem to record little things – day-to-day small events and conversations, and his observations of crops and flowers in *La Copa*. Parts are encoded. Why they matter to powerful men I do not know…"

Angeline looked thoughtful. "Manuel, you have visited the monastery since you were a child, with your father, and as an adult, in your capacity as a supplier to the monastery. Tell me what is unusual about the people and the plants of the monastery?"

Manuel smiled. "Everything about the monastery of Moridura and *La Copa* is unusual, Señorita Angeline. Perhaps you have all noticed that you are all a little stiff in the legs and the joints after your walk today? We joke in the village – the monks of *La Copa* have lead in their boots, but also have the legs to lift them! All of the monks are heavily built, at least until they get old and frail, like Brother Anselmo and Brother Alfonso. Look at Mateo – a child of the monastery, his whole life spent on *La Copa*. He is a giant among men, stronger than the strongest monk. Brother Mateo can lift weights that no man can lift – I have seen him lift a loaded cart to free a wheel. His strength is legendary – it is fortunate that he is a man of God and a man of peace!" He smiled again at his recollections.

"What about the crops – the plants, the flowers of *La Copa*?" persisted Angeline.

"I am no farmer," said Manuel, "but I know they are unlike other produce – in size, in taste, in texture. We have a saying in the village – a man may live for a day on one potato from *La Copa*. The growth and the harvest times are different from those on the plain – there are many differences, too many to remember. Mateo is interested in these things – he says the monks have the bones of Neanderthal men. We have another saying in Moridanza – don't pick a fight with a Moriduran monk – he will break you like a dry twig!" He chuckled again. "The monks make the vegetables and the vegetables make the monks!"

"What is the meaning of all of this, Angeline?" asked Alistair. He had his own theories, partially formed on his first visit, and now reinforced by Manuel's observations and anecdotes, but he wanted the view of a Doctor of Physics.

"All life on our planet evolved and exists in the Earth's gravitational field," replied Angeline, "but until NASA and space flight, no one knew what the effects of microgravity would be. We now know that long-term exposure to weightlessness can produce negative physiological changes in humans, among them dehydration due to the brain reacting to the transfer of fluids from the lower body to the upper by increasing the excretion of fluids, deterioration of muscle and bone, and temporary anaemia. Cell structure is profoundly affected by microgravity – metabolic and chemical processes are adversely affected." She began to pace up and down, causing Paul to have disconcerting reactions to the combined effects of a beautiful face and body and a powerful intellect at work.

"As for plant life – well, similar considerations apply. Gravity has a key role to play in the growth of plants. Plants sense gravity by hormones, particularly hormones known as auxins. Auxins are created in the tips of the plant shoots, and then move to the roots because of the pull of gravity. This stimulates the growth of root cells. Conversely, hormones cause the shoot tips to grow upwards and away from the gravitational force. The effect of zero or microgravity on plants is to some degree contradictory, but effects there undoubtedly are…" Angeline paused. "Sorry – am I loading this with scientific jargon? It's hard to explain without the use of some scientific terms…"

"You're doing fine, lassie," said Alistair encouragingly.

"All gravitational experiments to date have either simulated gravitational variations, or conducted them in space. There is no precedent for what appears to be happening in *La Copa* – a persistent, localised *increase* in gravity over an extended period of time. In the absence of formal scientific enquiry here, the observations and notes of intelligent amateur observers are highly significant. Manuel's father's diaries seem to fit this definition. The question is – what information does the *hermandad* hope to glean from them? I don't imagine it's agrarian in nature…"

"If Manuel doesn't know, it is futile for us to speculate," said Paul.

"I agree," said Alistair, "but now we must consider what the *hermandad* and the Moriduran brothers want from us, to prepare for this evening's meeting. What do we know for certain?"

"They want me here, but for what?" responded Angeline.

Santiago stood up and began to pace up and down. "I think they have an urgent problem: they are confronted by an opportunity or a threat, perhaps both. There is some sort of deadline facing them. The role of Red Lonnen in this remains undefined," he said, glancing at Angeline, then pointedly at Alistair. "We need more information about his motives."

Alistair took a long breath, and then he went across to Angeline. "I don't want to place you in a difficulty, or intrude in highly personal matters, Angeline, but this is a time for absolute frankness and openness. The events of earlier today were observed by all of us: in the situation in which we find ourselves, I regret that there is no place for privacy. Can I suggest that you confer with Paul and decide what you feel able to tell us?"

She nodded briefly, took Paul's hand, and drew him towards the far corner of the room. Alistair went over and sat down with Manuel.

"They need to talk, Manuel – the poor lassie has had a traumatic two days, and she has to confide in Paul before she can decide what she want to share with all of us."

"Love is in the air, Señor Alistair, even in troubled times such as these – love will not wait for the right time – love's time is always right now."

In the far corner, Angeline was on the verge of tears, being comforted by Paul. "You're among friends, and I'm more than a friend. The relationship between you and Red Lonnen – well, I reached an inescapable conclusion from his behaviour and reactions earlier, in *La Copa*. Do you want to confirm what I believe, Angeline? Don't feel compelled to if you don't want to…"

"Oh, Paul," she sighed, and stroked his cheek, "was it so obvious? He's my father…"

Paul pulled her close in his arms. "I guessed it, and I'm sure Alistair has known for some time, although he's never confided in me. Santiago has probably figured it out too – only Manuel will have been oblivious to the relationship."

They parted from their embrace, and Angeline composed herself. "Red Lonnen and my mother, Hilary Blade, worked together as young research assistants in R&D in the firm that he later came to own. They had a very brief affair in the late 1970s – my mother left the company when they broke up, then found that she was pregnant. She raised me on her own and never told Red that he had a child. I graduated, got my doctorate; and my first job, with an international computer corporation. Meanwhile, Red Lonnen climbed the corporate ladder, led a management buyout, and subsequently acquired a controlling interest in his company. My mother never told me who my father was – she said it was the result of a brief liaison, and that she saw no useful purpose in telling me his identity; she begged me not to pursue it."

"Didn't you want to find out?" asked Paul.

"Of course, but it wasn't high on my agenda – my studies took up all my time - and I respected my mother's wishes, especially since she contracted cancer just after I found my first job; my priority was to look after her. Then I was headhunted by Lonnen's company – my mother was so ill by that time that the fact that I was changing jobs barely registered with her. I joined the company, and was able to pursue my research into gravitation. A few weeks before my twenty-fifth birthday, my mother's condition moved into the terminal phase, and just before she died, she told me who my father was. I was dumfounded, but didn't tell her that I was now working for him."

Paul shook his head in sympathy. "What happened then?" he asked.

"I agonised over whether or not I should approach him. There was no way of proving that he was my father, short of a DNA test – my birth certificate didn't identify the father. I wanted to stay with the company. I liked my work and I had good, supportive colleagues – we were a team. From what I had heard of Red Lonnen - confirmed by my own observations - he was a ruthless man who let nothing stand in his way. He was also very rich, and I could envisage how he might react to what he would see as a claim on his fortune. Nonetheless, I decided he had a right to know. To my knowledge, he was unaware that he had a child, since my mother never told him…"

"So you did tell him, and the outcome was not a happy one," said Paul sympathetically.

Angeline's eyes clouded again, then she got a hold of her emotions. "I approached him, told him what I knew, and said that I had no wish for a public acknowledgement of the relationship, nor did I intend to make any financial claim on him. If he required it, I would resign, but I was happy in my job, and would prefer to continue my research."

"He must have been thunderstruck," observed Paul.

Angeline gave a short, harsh laugh. "Not exactly. He said that some years after my mother left the company, when he had the resources and the contacts, he traced her through a private enquiry agency, found out that she had a child, and deduced from the birth details that I was probably his daughter. He then decided not to contact her or me – he said he was respecting what he believed to be her wishes. However, he kept track of my career, and was responsible for the executive search that brought me to his company. During the pre-employment medical, he illegally arranged for a DNA sample to be taken without my knowledge or consent, and matched it with his own, confirming that I was his daughter."

Paul shook his head incredulously. "What a rat! What happened then?"

"He displayed no emotion or affection, maintaining a purely business tone during the conversation. He said that he wanted me to stay with his company and continue my research. Neither of us was to acknowledge our blood relationship – that would be damaging to his reputation and my relationship with my colleagues. His lawyers would draft an agreement that precluded my revealing the relationship in his lifetime, one that required me to remain with the company for a minimum of ten years. In return, he would deposit one million dollars in my bank account, and name me as sole heir to his controlling shareholding in the company in the event of his death. He did not wish any contact between us other than that required by our professional relationship."

Paul could not hide his contempt and disgust. "What kind of man is he? My God, the man is a monster!"

Angeline laughed, a genuine laugh this time. "That's my father you're talking about, Paul!"

"What did you do?" said Paul, knowing with absolute certainty what her answer would be.

"I told him to go to hell," replied Angeline, her eyes flashing, "I said I didn't want his money or the controlling stock, but that I would abide by his other conditions regardless of whether I remained with the company or moved on. I refused to sign anything. That was about three years ago – shortly afterward I met the Big Fella at a convention."

Paul pursed his lips. "I can see why Lonnen felt vulnerable when you went to Ardmurran on your sabbatical leave. He has only a conventional contract of employment with you; you have signed nothing, but have made a major scientific breakthrough while on his payroll. Most of your options are open, although he could claim the rights to your research findings."

"His problem in regard to my gravitational rig is greater than he realises," said Angeline. "My report omits key elements in the circuitry. By now, he will have attempted to duplicate my gizmo, and have realised that it won't work. I wouldn't like to be in the shoes of my colleagues right now – without the rock fragment and the gold, they will be sweating blood trying to replicate the experiment, and failing." Angeline seemed in some way ashamed.

"That bothers you – I can see why... It's not in your nature to conceal something from your colleagues, from a team you worked closely with. Why did you do it? I know you must have had a good reason," queried Paul.

"I alluded to it in my earlier discussion with you guys. Everything hinges on the piece of rock – I believe that the scale of the gravitational distortion is directly proportionate to its size, and to the amount of gold in the rig. Somehow, they act as a focusing beacon for the gravitational wave, and if the quantities were larger, the induced distortion would be greater," said Angeline.

"The rock is the limiting factor in the effect; if there is no more of it, then, unless an identical mineral or metal substitute can be synthesised in the lab, only matchboxes will be lifted; if greater quantities of the rock can be found, then the effect is potentially unlimited. I removed the rock sample from the rig before I left, and substituted a conventional piece of quartz. I had two reasons for doing this. Firstly, the rock belongs to Alistair, or more accurately, to the Monastery of Moridura. Secondly, an unlimited effect could destabilise the planet's gravitational field – perhaps even the solar system's balance. I am in the position of Oppenheimer during the Manhattan project." She looked very grave.

"*I am become Death: the destroyer of worlds...*" quoted Paul softly. "He took the gamble, and Hiroshima, Nagasaki and nuclear power were the consequences...."

" ... and Three-Mile Island and Chernobyl," added Angeline.

"Let me figure this one," said Paul reflectively. "Your father knows your rig won't work without you and he knows you have continued your research with Alistair; you almost certainly plan to jump ship and sign on with Ardmurran International Electronics. He found out that there is a connection with *el monasterio de Moridura*: somehow he has got the Abbot's attention – he had something to offer - or threaten - that got him his invitation to come. On arrival, he finds that the Abbot's motives are not just commercial ones, so he latches on to Ferdinand as a man of the world, none too scrupulous, and with a power base through his membership - and perhaps control - of the *hermandad*.

"Ferdinand and the Abbot are uneasy allies, as the *hermandad* and The Moriduran Brothers have been since the schism. Manuel's place in the equation rests on his father's diaries; but the Abbot has them in his possession already, and under his control by the terms of the bequest: up to this point, he has refused to release them to Ferdinand. He fears what he will do with the information – he sees some danger. But in some way, they are both being driven by the same imperative, the same fear, perhaps the same deadline." Paul stopped. "I have run out of steam," he said, 'and I need Alistair's input – and yours - and Santiago's. Are you ready to tell your tale to the others?"

"Yes," said Angeline decisively. "I have the distinct feeling that our time may be numbered in weeks, if not days – a nameless apprehension of an impending cataclysm. Do you think I'm nuts, Paul?"

"No," replied Paul, "and neither will Alistair. When he first broached this the day before yesterday – already it seems a lifetime ago – he was deeply worried, more worried than I have ever seen him. Let's rejoin the group…"

They walked back to the others, Paul with his arm around Angeline's shoulder; he released her and sat down, nodding to Alistair. They looked at her expectantly.

"I have something to tell you all…" And so Angeline told her story, recounting how she had found a father who had consciously rejected the possibility of a loving paternal relationship with her. When she finished, her friends gathered round her, offering words of sympathy and support.

Alistair mussed her hair affectionately, and asked Paul playfully if he really wanted a woman who had turned down a million bucks; Santiago simply gripped her wrist and smiled; Manuel assured her that she was now part of his family and kissed her hand.

Eventually, she broke free of her fan club, and raised her arms above her head, like a boxer claiming victory, and indeed, she had a feeling of release - of catharsis – as if she had emerged from a long, dark tunnel. "I love you all," she said, "and now you know my secrets. What's next?"

Alistair was showing some concern, however, and turned to Manuel. "You are now privy to all we know, Manuel. I realise that you have obligations towards the Abbot and Don Ferdinand, but I must ask you to respect our confidence in you, at least until after the meeting in the chapter house."

Manuel was silent for a long moment; he moved back from the group and faced them. "*Mis amigos*, I have known most of you for a very short time; Señor Alistair for five years, but only for one short period in those years. But I feel that you are truly my friends, and that we have each other's best interests at heart. But I am a man of almost fifty years of age with a family to support from a variety of business endeavours that yield meagre returns. My father's diaries have now given me an opportunity to prosper beyond my wildest dreams by giving me entry to the *hermandad*."

He looked directly at Alistair. "I will attempt to preserve confidentiality as you request – I have been honoured by your faith in me – but I am not a clever man, I am not familiar with the ways of powerful men of business. I will do all that you ask, to the limits of my ability, but try to understand those limits. Please…" He looked appealingly at Alistair.

Alistair took his hand. "I do understand, wee pal, and I offer my thanks to you for what you've said. Whatever the outcome of tonight and the next few days, I promise that I will protect you and I'll give you financial help to develop your business: you and your family will be secure. There is evil at work, Manuel, and the bad things that have happened are not just the result of the misguided zeal of some members of the *hermandad*."

He stopped speaking as the sound of footsteps came from one of the passageways. Mateo and Joaquín emerged, fresh from Vespers.

"Señores – Señorita Angeline – we are not interrupting, we trust? There is a facility available in the far corner of the courtyard that leads to *La Copa* that some of you may wish to use," said Joaquín tentatively. He looked at Mateo for support.

"It is a water shower facility," said Mateo, "and there is enough space and water for four at a time to use it. We climb to the top of the structure and fill the tank – with cold water only, I regret to say. A wheel mechanism releases the water through a perforated iron grating; the waste water drains to the slopes of *La Copa* and helps to irrigate our fields. Joaquín and I have filled the tank, and if you would like to use it, we will take you there," said Mateo, with grave solemnity: it masked his urge to smile, thought Paul.

"Well, this is a bonus – what do you think, guys? Ladies first, then maybe a refill can be managed for the rest of you?" laughed Angeline.

"I don't think we are being offered a choice here, guys – the decision is made," said Paul.

"Can we no' squeeze five in at once, Joaquín?" said Alistair mischievously. Manuel looked shocked, and then said a quick prayer to inhibit the images that came to his mind. Joaquín blushed and stammered, and was rescued by Mateo.

"Regretfully, Señor Alistair, we are a male congregation and not used to modern ways, and the presence of a woman in the monastery is a rare event. The knowledge that four men and a women were in the shower simultaneously could be a cause of scandal to my brethren, and affect their concentration in times of solitary contemplation."

Mateo's tone and expression exactly matched Alistair's, Paul noted. The big monk was being gently ironic, but clearly meant business. Alistair gave him a long look, resisting his urge to smile.

"Of course, we understand, Mateo – forgive me. My only thought was to conserve water, and save you the labour of refilling the reservoir. If we can help with that, of course we'll be glad to!"

"Then it's decided," said Angeline jubilantly. "Show us the way, Brothers!"

"There is enough water for two sessions, if the señorita releases the water for no more than four minutes," said Mateo. "If I may, I will instruct one of the señores in the operation of the release mechanism, which must be operated from outside the shower area. It would not be appropriate for Joaquín or me to be present while the señorita is in the shower. Of course, we will be happy to release the water for the señores. Joaquín will bring the large towels and soap."

"Let's draw lots to see who gets to operate the wheel," said Alistair.

"Don't be silly, Alistair! Paul, you go with Mateo," said Angeline, then, with a sudden afterthought, "Is there a changing area, Mateo?"

"Yes, Señorita Angeline, it is adjacent to the shower area, but it is very basic, and will be a little damp," replied Mateo, and then gestured to Paul to follow him. They went off through the small door to the courtyard. Brother Joaquín had disappeared along a passageway to fetch the towels, relieved to be out of a conversation that he found embarrassing.

"I wonder if the Abbot felt we needed a bath before meeting the Chapter and the Order tonight?" mused Alistair, sniffing his armpit.

Santiago looked worried. "We will be very vulnerable if we shower together," he said. "I'll forego my shower to ensure security, Alistair," then seeing from his boss's expression that he was about to make fun of him, added quickly "I know we are being light-hearted, but the danger has not lessened; please trust my judgement."

Paul reappeared with Mateo, beaming. "I am now the Master of the Wheel!" he said. "Everything depends on me!"

Joaquín emerged from the passageway, almost invisible behind an armful of huge bath towels.

"I guess this is it," said Angeline, holding out her hand to Paul. "Oh, great Master of the Wheel, lead me to my fate!"

Mateo spoke. "I will leave you now. Dinner will be served here at seven. After dinner, I will conduct you to the chapter house." He bowed gracefully, and left. Joaquín headed for the door to the courtyard: after a few minutes, Angeline and Paul followed him.

"I haven't looked forward to a shower so much since after my junior prom," said Angeline. They walked across the courtyard to the stone building built in the centre. A wooden ladder led to the stone reservoir on the top. There were narrow apertures about two metres above the base to admit light and air. Paul opened a door and Angeline entered, to find a tiny changing room with a bench, with Joaquín's towels and bars of soap lying on it. There was an inner door; Angeline peered in and saw a space about three metres square and three metres high, with a grating on the ceiling and a damp, stone floor.

"Tell me when you're ready!" called Paul from outside. He waited patiently, then a door banged from inside the structure and a moment later Angeline called out. He began to turn the iron wheel: a scraping, grinding noise came from above, followed by loud squeals and giggles. The system was working; he looked at his watch. "Four minutes – no more!" he shouted, not sure if she had heard him. After three minutes, he gave a one-minute warning to rinse, feeling like a car wash attendant. Santiago was prowling around on watch.

When the minute was up, Paul turned the wheel again, and then went off to fetch the others.

Alistair was about to play a record, but laid it down reluctantly, and followed Paul to the courtyard, where they waited for Angeline to come out. She emerged, laughing, with damp hair and a radiant expression.

"I hope you left us enough water," Alistair called out gruffly.

"Speak to the Master of the Wheel – that's his responsibility," said Angeline imperiously, sweeping past them, emitting a soapy perfume.

Paul, Alistair and Manuel headed for the shower. Mateo appeared and went to the wheel. Santiago watched him operate the mechanism. When delighted shouts came from within he felt envious - and dirty. When they came out, Mateo went up the ladder and checked the reservoir, then came back down and said that there was enough water left to give Santiago a brief shower. The offer was gratefully accepted, and Santiago went in. Alistair, Paul and Manuel stood watch. As they waited, Brother Joaquín's cheerful voice came from the door of the guest wing, informing them that their evening meal was ready.

Chapter Fourteen

Alistair surveyed the dining table, and then pointed to the throne-like end chair.

"Manuel, I want you to preside over the meal, and keep this unruly lot in line! Santiago and I will sit on your right, Angeline and Paul on your left."

The astonished Manuel obediently went to the end place and stood behind the chair, ill at ease, until Alistair had shepherded the others to their assigned places.

"Now we can all sit down," he said. "You are a thorn next to a rose, Manuel!" Manuel looked at the smiling Angeline and visibly relaxed: he began to twinkle a little and enjoy his exalted position. Brother Joaquín hovered around his cart until they had all settled, then served the soup.

"Manuel, will you say grace?" Alistair requested.

Manuel took a deep breath. "Lord, to eat is a blessing; to eat among friends is a privilege. We give thanks for food and for friends. Help us, Lord, to meet the challenges that lie ahead of us, and protect us in our difficult hours. Amen."

The others chorused their amens: Alistair gave him a nod of approval, and Manuel smiled happily.

"Before we start – who is going to share the *coq au vin* with me?" asked Alistair. "Perhaps it should be Angeline, since Red was unavoidably detained?"

"I willingly forego it – I am now a committed vegetarian," laughed Angeline. "I bestow my share of the unfortunate fowl upon Manuel!"

The meal was superb, but Alistair decreed that only a modest quantity of wine be consumed – they had work to do. Santiago abstained completely, drinking only water. Joaquín served each course briskly, conscious, as they all were, that the meeting in the chapter house was scheduled for eight o'clock. After the last course Alistair stood up and moved towards the gramophone, intent on ending a fine meal with some jazz. He selected a record, placed it on the turntable, and lowered the needle on to the record. It entered the groove and jumped out again, and he felt the big brass horn vibrate.

"Sorry!" he called back to the dining table. "Clumsy!" He tried again, with the same result. He gave a muted curse, and glanced back at the others, ready to apologise again, but saw them looking at each other in puzzlement. He straightened up from the low table, and placed his hand on the back of one of the benches: it was vibrating steadily, and he recognised the frequency of it instantly – it was the same as the heartbeat of *La Copa*.

Angeline stared at her glass of wine: the liquid in the bowl was showing ripples. Paul placed his hand on her arm, and looked at Joaquín enquiringly. Manuel rose from his chair apprehensively. Alistair walked back to the group.

"Joaquín – can you explain this?" he asked.

The monk ignored the question, his head turning from side to side as if in search of something or somebody. Paul grasped Angeline's hand to reassure her, but then he suddenly had the feeling first experienced in the square in Moridanza, the uncanny valley sensation - a sudden awareness of an alien presence, of the unnatural.

On instinct, he looked at the left hand passageway, and there stood Mateo, massive and motionless. Paul hadn't heard his footsteps approaching, but put this down to his concentration on the strange vibration. Joaquín looked across at his brother monk in evident relief, and Alistair followed the look, saw Mateo, and put his question again.

"Mateo – can you explain this phenomenon? The vibration…?"

"I recognise it, but I cannot explain it, Señor Alistair. It resonates to the heartbeat of *La Copa*, and it has been happening with increasing frequency and intensity for some weeks now. I have never experienced it before this period, but many of the older brothers remember it happening once before, many years ago." His imposing presence and his totally calm demeanour were reassuring, and the others relaxed a bit.

"Whatever it is, it has scratched my record," said Alistair. "Perhaps we'll get an explanation from the Abbot and the Chapter when we meet."

The vibration stopped as suddenly as it had started, and the group began to chatter, relieved that it was over. "Mealtimes can never be taken for granted in the monastery, I can see that," laughed Angeline. Manuel came across to Alistair.

"My father has mentioned this twice in his diaries, señor, and I have experienced it once before. I was fifteen years of age, and had just made my first delivery to the monastery for my father – my first job. It frightened me then, and it frightens me now. Am I a coward, Señor Alistair?" he whispered.

Alistair placed a hand on his shoulder. "No, knowing fear doesn't make a man a coward, Manuel - brave men feel fear. Come and sit with me at the gramophone table and tell me all about this recurring event..."

He took his arm, and they went across and sat down next to the shining brass horn. Santiago went across to Mateo at the mouth of the passageway. Angeline and Paul remained seated at the table as Joaquín discreetly cleared it and loaded his cart.

"You felt this vibration before, when you were fifteen?" said Alistair.

"Not quite fifteen," replied Manuel, his big, liquid eyes looking into upwards into the vaulted roof timbers and into old memories. "It was in the July – I had left school before the summer holiday because I would be fifteen years of age before the holidays ended and school resumed. That makes it almost exactly thirty-five years ago – I will be fifty in August.

Many of the younger monks were frightened, and thought it was an earthquake – they had never felt the heartbeat of *La Copa*. Only a few monks – usually about twenty in number - are allowed to go to *El Trono* – the rest never go there. It is forbidden, except on the day of the Ceremony."

Alistair digested this information, then called out to Santiago. He came across and sat down and Alistair quickly summarised Manuel's information.

"Was there anything else happening at the time you mention – the previous occurrence of the vibration? Anything unusual?" asked Alistair.

Manuel racked his brains, his brow furrowed in concentration, and then his face cleared. "I remember the older brothers saying that the Ceremony of the Elevation of the Magus Elect was close. I asked my father about it, but he would tell me nothing. Oh, yes – there was something else!" Manuel brightened, and chuckled. "The baby arrived shortly afterwards – maybe a week after!"

Alistair and Santiago looked mystified; Manuel looked conspiratorial and jerked his head towards the two Moriduran brothers as they finished clearing the long table. "Mateo arrived – he was the baby!"

Manuel was delighted at the impact his reminiscences were having on his audience.

"The Abbot, newly elected by the Chapter, told the brothers before Vespers, one day in mid-July, that a baby had come to the monastery, with a wet nurse, and would be brought up as a monk: he would be called Mateo, after a young monk of the same name who had left the monastery suddenly. Young monks do leave," he said, tapping the side of his nose, his eyes twinkling. "They decide that the celibate life is not for them anymore – they see a pretty girl, and their vocation vanishes like a leaf in the wind."

Santiago was puzzled. "I would have thought the Abbot would disapprove, and would not call the baby after such a monk."

"The explanation is simple, señor," said Manuel. "Only one monk may bear a name at any time. One Mateo had gone – a new Mateo had arrived! Do you see?"

Santiago nodded. "Of course, that makes good sense, thank you," he said. "What do you know of the Mateo who left?"

"I only met him once. *El Gigante*, the monks called him. His strength was legendary, in fact, boy that I was, I didn't believe the stories I heard about him. Now that I have seen what our Mateo can lift," he said, looking fondly across at the big monk, who was standing patiently waiting to guide his charges to the chapter house, "I can believe that the old tales were true."

Alistair looked down, his brain working furiously. He opened his mouth to ask a question, but Santiago beat him to it. "When was the even earlier instance of the vibration, the first one that your father experienced? When did it occur?"

Manuel thought for a moment, then named the year of the diary that recorded the event. Santiago's eyes met Alistair's, then both men looked at Manuel. The significance of what he had told them had obviously escaped him – he was still caught up in his own thoughts about his boyhood and his father, Francisco.

"And there was another strange thing," he said, a faraway look in his eyes. "Over the years, young, unmarried mothers have abandoned their babies, but always on the steps of the church in Moridanza. It would be dangerous, almost impossible for a young woman with a baby, distressed, to ascend *el sendero de precipio* to the gates. Also, in every case of an abandoned baby, the identity of the mother has been discovered quickly thereafter – the village is small, and word spreads quickly – but where the baby Mateo came from is a mystery. The Abbot has never offered any explanation."

"Has our Mateo never been curious about his parents?" queried Alistair. "I would have thought that he would want to know…"

"When he became a young man, he asked the Abbot, but Brother Anselmo told him that when the time was right, he would know," said Manuel, "and he was satisfied with that. In spite of his proud nature, Mateo has the gift of obedience, a quality highly regarded in the monastery."

Manuel looked past them; he signalled to them by flicking his eyes and jerking his head; they turned round to see Mateo bearing down on them.

"I guess it's time to go, Santiago – gather the flock!" said Alistair, standing up.

"Señores, Señorita Angeline - may I escort you to the chapter house? Manuel, you are to wait here until you are called," said Mateo.

"Are we ready for this?" Alistair looked at the group. "Our team discipline will be as follows – one singer, one song – I'll initiate all interaction, and respond to all questions or proposals. Listen and evaluate, but do not intervene spontaneously."

They followed Mateo down the passageway to the other end of the guest wing, and out into the cloister, turned left towards the central building of the monastery, and entered through its imposing main door. The monk led them through another door into the interior of the chapter house, with its high, vaulted stone roof and massive corbelled pillars.

At the far end, two long wooden tables had been placed at right angles to another of the same length, but made of stone. At this table, facing them as they walked down the room, sat the Abbot, flanked by three monks on either side of him, with Gregorio on his left, and Joaquín on his right. At the left hand table sat Ferdinand, dressed in a red robe with the hood thrown back. On his left sat Red Lonnen, looking out of place in his black monk's habit; on his left were three red-robed figures, their faces hidden behind their hoods. On Ferdinand's right, another three red-robed and hooded figures sat, silent and menacing, the eyeholes in the red hoods revealing nothing. Behind Ferdinand stood the two figures of *los artilleros*, dressed in ordinary clothes, without their *escopetas*, and apparently unarmed. Their stance was nevertheless that of bodyguards, and they exuded menace.

All of the seated men rose as Alistair's party moved to the right hand table. Mateo moved the heavy chair back for Angeline, and then pushed it forward as she sat down in accordance with Alistair's seating plan. Alistair had instinctively positioned himself directly across from Ferdinand; Angeline was on his right, facing her father, with three vacant chairs on her right. Paul and Santiago sat next to Alistair, with one vacant chair on Santiago's left.

Alistair was unhappy with the arrangement, but it was too late to change it. It suggested an adversarial relationship between him and the man across from him, and placed the Abbot in a position that suggested neutrality, or even chairmanship of the meeting. Mateo, to his surprise, did not leave, but had moved to the door, and stood there, a statuesque figure in the dim light of the chapter house. The others had remained standing until Alistair's team sat down. The Abbot raised his arms.

"May I welcome Señor Alistair Mackinnon, Doctora Angeline Blade, Señor Paul Corr and Señor Santiago Manrique? In the entire history of the monastery, a woman has never entered our chapter house – we are delighted and honoured that you should be the first, Señorita Angeline."

He then bowed gracefully to Angeline, as did all of the others. She half-rose from her seat in embarrassment, acknowledging his words and stammering her thanks; she nodded to the others, but avoided her father's eyes. Red had an enigmatic half-smile on his face.

"Before we examine what our formal agenda might be," said the Abbot, "I would like to clarify how I see the role of the Chapter – which comprises my six colleagues and myself – but first, I will introduce them. On my left is Brother Gregorio - already known to you. Next to him is Brother Alfonso, then Brother Diego. On my right are Brothers

Joaquín, Ramón, and José." Each brother stood and bowed briefly as his name was mentioned.

"I speak only for the congregation of Moriduran Brothers, represented by the Chapter. I am their superior – we are not a democratic institution - but our decision-making process is normally that of consensus seeking. If consensus cannot be achieved, then my decision is final, and it then represents the view of our brotherhood. I claim no right to chair this meeting, and no such role is envisaged by Don Ferdinand or myself. Ferdinand, I ask you now to explain your role." The Abbot gestured to the Don, who rose to his feet and bowed. He began to speak, in a highly formal, almost declamatory tone.

"I am the *primus inter pares* of a secular brotherhood representing the economic and social interests of its members in Extremadura and beyond. Our history reaches back to the time of the Romans and beyond. Our respected brethren in the congregation of Moriduran monks are part of that history: once we were one brotherhood, but since the religious order was formed centuries ago, we have become two independent groupings, but with a common history and tradition. In our unified form, we were known as the Ancient Order of Moridura, and that name survives on ceremonial occasions and is also used when our objectives coincide, and must be pursued jointly. At such times, we are united under the office of the Magus of Moridura…"

His statement was brought to a sudden halt by the return of the mysterious vibration, this time intense enough to shake the heavy wooden tables, cause the candelabra on the tables to rattle, and the candle flames to flicker. Ferdinand leaned forward and braced himself with both hands on the table, and waited for the vibration to subside. Brother Anselmo and the monks of the Chapter sat motionless, but Red Lonnen was looking around apprehensively, as were the hooded members of the *hermandad* and *los artilleros*.

Alistair reflected that their pointed hoods would not protect them if the great vaulted ceiling and its massive pillars crashed down on them. The image of Sampson bringing down the temple of Dagon flashed into his mind, and he looked across at Mateo, still standing motionless at the door. Aye, you could destroy a temple, if you wanted to, big man, he thought, but there's no Delilah to encourage you.

The vibration ceased as suddenly as it had commenced. The hooded figure on Ferdinand's right was pulling urgently at his sleeve and some of the others were bending forward and looking along the table at him, seeking an explanation. He shook the hand from his sleeve impatiently.

"The heartbeat of *La Copa* is most pronounced at the moment," he said. "It is a recurring phenomenon that is familiar to those who have had a long association with the monastery, but some of my associates have not experienced it before."

Alistair seized the moment. He had not intended to interrupt Ferdinand's formal introduction, but the hiatus caused by the vibration, and the Don's unplanned words, gave him his chance.

"Forgive me, Don Ferdinand, but your reference to your associates prompts me to make an observation…" He paused, waiting for the other's reaction. Ferdinand held out his right hand, palm upward, and tilted his head inquiringly.

"I assume that you plan to introduce your colleagues, and that they will reveal their faces. I respect your traditions, but I would find it unacceptable to engage in a dialogue with hooded participants." Alistair was polite but firm.

Ferdinand did not reply for a moment; Red Lonnen was looking at him intently, and the heads of the hooded men were turned towards him. The Abbot and the monks of the Chapter sat motionless at their stone table looking straight ahead. Angeline, who was closest to them, thought they looked like a medieval relief carving, part of the stone wall behind them.

At last, Ferdinand spoke. "Our traditions demand that when we meet in formal session, we wear the formal robes and hoods of our *hermandad*. I have departed from this personally because I have met you and your colleagues before. My associates are all prominent men in business and political life in Extremadura and appear here incognito, as it were. They would find it unacceptable to reveal their identities. It is a great deal to ask of you and your colleagues, Señor Mackinnon, I know, but I must request your indulgence in accepting this constraint, however alien it is to your normal business methods."

The tall aristocrat looked directly at Alistair as he concluded his reply, and there was an unspoken message in his eyes and in his entire physical posture that the big Scot interpreted at a subliminal level.

He stood up, and the two men faced each other for a tense moment. "I had not anticipated a requirement to confer with my colleagues this early in the proceeding, Don Ferdinand," Alistair said, "but I must ask you and Brother Anselmo to give me a moment to do just that."

He then indicated to his team that they should rise and join him, and walked to a point out of earshot of the main group. They gathered round him, and Angeline, unable to contain herself, spoke first, her voice low, but filled with suppressed anger.

"I will not talk to hooded men – it's outrageous. All this old-world courtesy doesn't make it acceptable. I won't do it – we must *not* accept it, Alistair!"

Alistair's voice was calm and soothing. "We're playing for big stakes, Angeline – don't secede from the Union just yet - we can't afford a Civil War." It was a shameless attempt to tap into her American heritage, and she recognised it as such, but it worked, and she calmed down.

"My best judgement, and my instincts as a negotiator," Alistair continued, "tell me that this is a non-negotiable posture – a deal-breaker. They'll walk out rather than disclose their identities; in fact, I suspect that they know that either Santiago or I would recognise some or all of them. These guys are not all locals – some of them are from Mérida, maybe Madrid."

Santiago nodded in assent. "When I first met Ferdinand, I felt that I recognised him, and that he recognised me. Now I remember where – it was a conference in Madrid. I was there with your brief to monitor seminars addressing distribution channels. Somebody pointed out a group at a table in the dining room and referred to them as the Mérida mafia, and there was much laughter at our table - but nervous laughter – there was fear in it. One member of the group was Ferdinand – I am sure of it now. I also think that the heavy-set man in the robe on his right was also in that group in Madrid. If it is same person, he is a major political figure in Extremadura, with strong connections to the defence industry in the U.S.A. There is no way he is going to pull his hood, Alistair."

"OK, we must reach a decision fast – are we prepared to live with Ferdinand's constraint?" Alistair searched their faces, and saw reluctant agreement. "Right – back to the table!"

They all sat down except Alistair. Ferdinand was seated and conferring with his associates. He looked up expectantly, his face tense. Alistair made the most of the tension, and paused before he replied – he wanted his concession to be valued.

"We have considered your request, Don Ferdinand. Although it violates our deepest instincts to conduct a discussion with hooded men, out of respect for you, the Abbot and the Chapter, we are reluctantly prepared to accept your position."

Ferdinand rose to his feet and bowed, and the Abbot raised his head and looked warmly at Alistair, nodding in approval.

"You have my thanks and that of my associates for your understanding of our difficulties, señor," began Ferdinand.

"If I may, I will now continue to set out our desired agenda for this meeting. I speak only for the *hermandad*." He paused, as though gathering his emotional and intellectual resources.

"It is our belief that *La Copa de Moridura* possesses two unique characteristics – its topography and the nature of its rock, including the spear of rock we call *El Trono*. A gravitational anomaly has existed in this area since time immemorial, resulting in the pull of gravity being higher in *La Copa* than elsewhere on the planet. We believe that this is caused, at least in part, by its concave topography and metallic rock acting as a kind of giant dish aerial, akin to a radio telescope.

"When my associates and I became aware of the discovery made by Doctora Blade," – he bowed to Angeline – "we immediately appreciated its commercial and scientific implications. We have access to high-level scientific expertise through our network of associates, in Spain and elsewhere, but none of them could explain how the Blade Effect worked, nor could they replicate it. They did, however, conclude that it was likely that the inventor had incorporated a metallic element in the electronics that was unknown to science. If such a metal had an extra-terrestrial origin, it could only have come from a meteorite.

"All of this pointed inexorably to *La Copa de Moridura* and *El Trono*, and opened up the possibility that the age-old gravitational anomaly could be controlled and applied on a vast scale. This would make *La Copa de Moridura*, the Moridanza district and Extremadura the focal point for scientific research and industrial and commercial developments of world significance. It would, regrettably, end our historical isolation and involve a change in our culture, but this is a price we must pay for embracing the future."

Ferdinand paused to let the full implications of his exposition be absorbed by Alistair and his team before turning to Red Lonnen.

"Shortly after we became aware of Doctora Blade's discovery, Brother Anselmo was contacted by Señor Lloyd Lonnen, and later, he contacted me. I now invite Señor Lonnen to offer his perspective." He sat down, and Red Lonnen rose to his feet. He looked across at his daughter for a moment, and then turned his gaze to Alistair.

"The research was commissioned and funded by my company, and the discovery was made by Doctor Angeline Blade, a salaried employee of my organisation. My company owns the Blade Effect, and all that results from it," he said bluntly, in his harsh, combative tones.

Disregarding Alistair's rules of engagement, Angeline started to display anger and disagreement, shaking her head emphatically, and making small noises of dissent, but his right hand gripped her wrist, and she settled down, with a huge effort of self-control. Lonnen watched the ripples from the stone he had thrown in the pond, and waited for a reaction from Alistair or Angeline, but none came: he looked disappointed, and continued.

"In spite of our clear legal right to this scientific breakthrough, my company behaved ethically, responsibly and with generosity. I allowed Angeline to take a sabbatical; I did not protest when she went to Ardmurran in Scotland, to work with my main competitor, recognising that the Scottish universities were carrying out major research on gravitation; I did not demand that she return when her research team back home failed to duplicate her results because of information - and perhaps something more tangible - that she had withheld from them.

"She is a brilliant young scientist, at the outset of what undoubtedly will be a distinguished career – who knows what she may achieve? As it stands, her research has not been published, nor has it been submitted to peer review. The whole history of anti-gravity research is infested with cranks, and, without the support of a large corporation such as ours, I fear that Doctor Blade will also be dismissed as such, on a par with those who develop perpetual motion devices."

He looked again directly at Angeline, then back at Alistair. "I could have destroyed her professionally with ease. I did not do so, for two reasons: firstly, I acquired two artefacts that originally belonged to the monastery of Moridura.

"You found the Moridura Manuscript, Alistair, and it gave you a way in to the monastery; but the manuscript was not the only thing that was taken from the monastery. Something else of even greater value was stolen, and was lost for centuries. Unlike you, Alistair, I'm not an altruistic man – my gift to Brother Anselmo, when I make it, will be conditional – it's a bargaining chip. To those who might contemplate seizing it by force, let me warn them that I've secured the artefact by a device that will destroy it if it's stolen. Like Alistair and his associates, I realise my own vulnerability during my stay, and I've taken precautions to protect myself."

Ferdinand's face was expressionless as the American spoke; he looked straight ahead, but without making eye contact with Alistair. The heavy-set hooded man on Ferdinand's right half-turned in his chair and leaned forward, looking across Ferdinand to Red Lonnen. Even under the loose robe, the aggression in his body posture was apparent to the onlookers, and the hood added to his distinct air of menace.

Red, oblivious, turned again to Angeline, and his hard expression softened. "My second reason for not destroying Doctor Blade's scientific standing is a more personal one, and this is not the place to discuss it. It is sufficient to say that Angeline's wellbeing and safety is of first importance to me. Anyone who attempts to harm her will have me to reckon with." Angeline looked down at the table in front of her, and then she felt the reassuring pressure of Alistair's hand. She looked up again, her expression neutral, and waited for her father to continue.

"I believe that Ferdinand and Alistair Mackinnon want essentially the same things that I do, namely, to be involved in the development of the Blade Effect, to protect the intellectual property rights to the discovery, and to profit from the exploitation of its commercial and industrial potential. Brother Anselmo, however, has very different priorities..." He turned to the Abbot, nodded to indicate that he had finished, and then sat down abruptly.

"Thank you, Señor Lonnen. Your position and that of Ferdinand is very clear to me and I am sure to all of us. Señor Mackinnon, do you wish to respond, or may I state the position of the Chapter?" asked Brother Anselmo.

Alistair shook his head, and gestured to the Abbot to continue.

The old monk stood up slowly, a look of deep weariness and sadness on his lined face as he gazed straight ahead. His voice was drained of emotion, flat and expressionless.

"We are close to an event that has always had great significance for the monks of Moridura and for the *hermandad*. It is a cyclic event, occurring every thirty-five years, and is of great antiquity. We call this event *El Partir del Trono* – The Splitting of the Throne. It is an event that we mark by a ceremony, and our archives show that this ceremony has been taking place since the time of the Romans, and it may have been celebrated before records began. The Magus of the Ancient Order of Moridura conducts the ceremony, assisted by the Abbot of the monastery, and the ceremony is observed by the monks of Moridura, members of the *hermandad* and *confratres* of the monastery."

The old man paused, and then he spoke very deliberately, as if choosing his words with great care. "The Ceremony has no religious significance: it forms no part of the observances of Holy Church. The Chapter of the monastery regard this event as a recurring natural phenomenon, one that has been marked by a ceremony for over two millennia. It is therefore worthy of our respect and our attendance. Any beliefs that my brethren and I hold about the event are rooted in the two natural physical manifestations: the vibration that we call the heartbeat, and the splitting of the rock formation that we call *El Trono*. Those of my brethren who pursue scientific enquiry have theories about the origin of *La Copa de Moridura* and the central rock formation: the monastery is isolated geographically and culturally, but not intellectually. Others may place different interpretations on the phenomena..."

Ferdinand looked down at the table and his hooded colleagues shifted uncomfortably as the Abbot spoke these words. Alistair half-expected an interruption from one of them, Brother Anselmo's pause after his last statement seeming to anticipate such an intervention. But there was only silence from the *hermandad* – a leaden, sullen silence.

"It is my belief, and that of the Chapter, that whatever natural event created the topography of *La Copa* – we believe it to have been a meteor impact and *La Copa* to be its impact crater – also created a gravitational anomaly, an instability in the mysterious force that pervades our Universe. Modern science has only a very partial understanding of this force, and, in its speculations about dark matter and black holes, sometimes seems no better equipped than a medieval theologian or alchemist to give an account of it." For a moment, a lighter note entered his voice.

"My scientifically-inclined brethren tell me that one current of thought in the world scientific community is that gravity and the three-dimensional nature of the observed universe are but illusions, and that we are in fact two-dimensional creatures inhabiting a two-dimensional world. It gives us some harmless amusement to consider that the very scientists who sometimes dismiss religious belief as superstition now seem to be the flat-earthers!" Brother Anselmo looked quickly at Alistair to catch his reaction, and was gratified to see a wry smile of acknowledgment on the Scot's face, but then the Abbot's expression changed and his gaze seemed to become fixed on a point beyond the confines of the chapter house.

"Both the event that is now imminent, and the variation in the heartbeat of *La Copa* that heralds it, are aspects of this instability – an instability that creates the gravitational anomaly that is part of our daily experience. We believe that the spear of rock - of which *El Trono* is the visible part above ground - is a control and regulating device that was embedded in *La Copa* aeons ago by a cosmic intelligence beyond our imagining – sentient beings, from another solar system, another galaxy, perhaps from another dimension of the space-time continuum. These beings, created by the living God, as all things are, were the representatives of a civilisation at a level of scientific development that we cannot conceive of, a civilisation capable of monitoring and influencing cosmic events – a civilisation that has now vanished."

The impact of his words on his audience was profound; there was total silence and a sense of heightened expectancy in the vast room as they waited for the climactic statement that they knew instinctively the old monk was about to make.

"*La Copa* has a nascent singularity at its heart – the potential to become a black hole of infinite mass that will suck everything into its maw – our world, the planets, our sun. It will become the destroyer of worlds. All our experience, all of our scrutiny of the records of previous events, lead us to believe that the regulating mechanism is failing, has been progressively failing for six hundred years, and is now at the crisis point. The unique event, documented early in the fifteenth century by the Moridura Manuscript, was the beginning of a process akin to a nuclear chain reaction. It was triggered by the removal - the theft – of a crucial part of the regulating mechanism."

The Abbot knew there was a question burning in the minds of the scientists in the room. "There is something you all want to put to me, is there not?"

Angeline turned to Alistair, seeking his permission. He nodded and smiled. Angeline thought for a moment, and then her eyes met Brother Anselmo's.

"I find it difficult to frame my question without seeming discourteous to you and the Chapter, Brother Anselmo, but it is this: how can you be so certain on such a complex scientific issue as a singularity – a black hole – without access to state-of-the-art equipment and expert knowledge? The best theoretical physicists in the world are tentative in their conclusions on this subject, and often disagree on fundamentals – how can a brotherhood of monks be so positive? Is it simply a matter of faith – of belief?"

The Abbot looked in turn at each of his brethren, as though seeking their approval for what he was about to say, and then he looked again at Angeline.

"Señorita Angeline," he replied, "it is most certainly a matter of belief, but of rational belief, not faith. We have access to sophisticated technology, beyond the capacity and understanding of your most esteemed colleagues, and to an extra-terrestrial intelligence that comprehends it fully. We have been in the presence of this technology and this intelligence for centuries, but have only begun to understand it in comparatively recent times. And now, early in the third millennium, four elements have come together, by the will of God, at our time of greatest need, to assist our understanding – the Moridura Manuscript, the artefacts recovered by Señor Lonnen, your discovery of the Blade Effect, and the diaries of Francisco Ortega."

Brother Anselmo fell silent and looked at his audience. It was not clear to them whether he had concluded his statement, or was simply gauging the impact of his words. Whatever the old monk's intentions had been, the silence was ruptured by the man in the robe on Ferdinand's right, the one identified by Santiago as a senior politician.

He stood up, and shook off Ferdinand's attempt to restrain him by placing his hand on his arm. "*Esto es inaceptable!*" he said in a harsh, aggressive tone, "*Estas personas no son extremeños!*" He pointed towards Alistair's group, then to Red Lonnen. "*Hemos revelado más de lo que debriamos! Debemos tomar lo que es nuestro…*"

Santiago leaned straight across Paul to Alistair. "Trouble! We're foreigners, too much has been revealed to us already – he wants the Ancient Order to take what belongs to it…" His voice held a note of urgency and signalled imminent danger.

Ferdinand seemed to be in an agony of indecision, but then he stood up. "I regret this, but it is necessary…" He made a signal with both hands, a turning, flicking motion. Instantly, the six hooded men drew automatic pistols from their robes; all the guns were pointed at Alistair's team, with one exception. The hooded man on Red Lonnen's left had pressed his gun against the American's left temple. *Los artilleros* had also drawn pistols from their jackets, and they moved round swiftly to position themselves behind Alistair and Angeline.

"Stay calm!" Alistair said softly to his team, holding his arms out palms downwards in a conciliatory gesture.

Ferdinand addressed himself directly to Alistair. "Please do not do anything foolish – you will not be harmed. We simply want to secure what is ours by right."

"I think you're the one who has done something foolish, pal…" Alistair's voice was cold and menacing, the voice of the Glasgow streets, and his eyes had narrowed to slits. "You've risked an outbreak of uncontrolled violence that could have led to Doctor Blade being injured or killed. You've jeopardised your own interests. I can't easily forgive this fourth act of violence against myself and my friends."

"Hey, Alistair!" Red's tone was jocular, in spite of the gun at his head. "You thought I was one of the bad guys! Whaddya make of this?"

"Aye, I might have got you wrong, Red – but you've been hanging around with bad guys - this is what happens when you keep the wrong company," replied Alistair curtly.

Red grinned. "Yeah, well, a guy can't get everything right. Take this guy with the gun at my head – he was brought up in the wrong neighbourhood. Nobody told him that if you put a gun on a guy, don't get too close – or get behind him..."

In one swift movement, his right hand came up across his chest and seized the wrist the other man's gun arm. He thrust it away from his head and down, simultaneously placing his left hand under the gunman's elbow and thrusting upwards. The hooded man screamed in agony as his shoulder and elbow were dislocated and the gun landed on the table. In a swift movement, Lonnen had the gun in his left hand and his right arm round Ferdinand's neck. He jabbed the automatic into his ribs and rapidly pulled him back from the table away from his armed associates.

"Don't try anything, fellas, or your *primus* will be *mortuus*," he said calmly. "Brother Anselmo, can you do anything to settle these guys down? They seem to be predisposed to violence – it ain't seemly in a monastery."

Alistair looked along to Santiago, who indicated by a jerk of his head that Alistair should look behind him. Angeline and Paul turned at the same time. Behind them stood the giant figure of Mateo; at his feet lay *los artilleros*, their arms and legs splayed at random angles. They made no sound whatsoever. The big monk held their two guns loosely in his hands. No one had seen him move from the door or overpower the two gunmen. It must have happened at lightning speed while the others were distracted by Red's manoeuvre, thought Alistair.

There were now six guns held in the room, one by Red Lonnen and the others by the five hooded members of the Ancient Order. Their sixth member was moaning in agony, slumped over the table, his robe in some disarray, its pointed hood at a faintly comical angle. The heavy-set man who had set the whole process off had turned and was facing

Ferdinand, who was being held as a shield in front of the body of Red Lonnen.

There was almost total silence in the room, apart from some heavy breathing. The Abbot picked up a small bell from the stone table and shook it; its tinkling echoed gently through the great chapter house. Almost at once, monks began to enter the chapter house from many directions, appearing soundlessly from behind pillars and through doors that were invisible in the recesses of the room. They flooded around those at the two tables like an overwhelming black tide, surrounding the hooded *hermandad* members, pressing against them from all angles. Ferdinand and Lonnen disappeared in a clutch of black-robed figures, and Alistair's group found themselves isolated from each other by a press of Moriduran Brothers around them. Mateo picked up *los artilleros* as though they were rag dolls and bore them away through the main door.

The monks melted away silently, leaving behind five hooded men and Red Lonnen without guns. Ferdinand was rubbing his throat, and the injured hooded man was still lying moaning over the table. After some time, Mateo returned and resumed his impassive stance at the main door of the chapter house. Alistair, on an instinct, checked for his revolver; it had gone. He looked at Santiago and then at Paul; they both tapped their chests with both hands, and then held out their empty palms, smiling ruefully. They too had been silently and expertly disarmed.

"I abhor violence," said Brother Anselmo with a sigh, "It achieves so little, yet does so much harm." He turned towards Don Ferdinand, and his tone was paternal and regretful. "If you continue in this fashion, Ferdinand, it will destroy you – it will destroy all of us. In the name of God, put your greed and lust for power behind you, and repudiate the men who have brought you to this – they are alien to our traditions."

He then looked at the hooded man whose outburst had triggered the display of force. "Señor, you initiated this violence by your intemperate remarks. Your inability to exercise self-control threatens us all at a time of crisis. I must separate you from your associates, and detain you in a secure place until the crisis is over. I regret this infringement of your liberty, but you have left me with no choice."

The hooded man looked at the Abbot as if to protest, then he saw the figure of Mateo advancing on him from the door, and thought better of it. As Mateo reached him and grasped his arm, he turned to the Don.

"Ferdinand, this is outrageous. You must stop this, take necessary steps…" His voice tailed off as Mateo forcibly marched him towards the door.

"Am I next, Abbot? Have I been a bad boy too?" said Red, but his light tone lacked conviction.

"You risked the life of your daughter," said the Abbot flatly, "You must answer to your own conscience for that."

Lonnen looked as though he had been struck across the face. He glanced at Angeline, then away again. "I would have preferred to reveal that in my own time, Brother Anselmo – perhaps Angeline would have liked to pick her moment also."

The Abbot made no response to this; he looked at Alistair, then at Ferdinand.

"Where do we go from here, Brother Anselmo? Such little trust as I had in Ferdinand has been completely destroyed by this act of naked aggression – not only do I distrust his motives, I have now no faith in his judgement," said Alistair.

Ferdinand remained completely still, stonefaced.

"Trust is a desirable element in negotiation, but not an essential one," replied the Abbot, "and this undoubtedly regrettable episode has shifted the parameters of our discussions in a way that can yet prove positive. We are called upon by God to perform great things in the face of an impending crisis. Let us withdraw with our people to reflect in private on what is possible, with the thought that we cannot succeed unless we find a way to work together.

"Ferdinand, I suggest that you and your associates return to the dormitory of the *confratres* - the necessary arrangements have been made, and a member of the Chapter will conduct you to it. Señor Mackinnon, will you and your friends please return to the guest wing with Mateo – and you too, Señor Lonnen, if you will. No one should attempt to leave the monastery – to descend the path in darkness would be folly. The main gate and the wicket gate will be locked in any case. Your weapons have been put beyond reach; they will be returned to you at a propitious time."

He bowed gracefully to Alistair and Ferdinand in turn. Alistair gestured to his group and they joined him at the door and left for the guest wing. Paul looked back and saw Ferdinand's group leaving through another door.

Chapter Fifteen

B rother Mateo conducted Alistair and his party back to the guest wing. As they entered, Alistair pulled him aside. "What did you do with *los artilleros*, Mateo? You must have hit them hard for them to stay unconscious so long."

"Harder than I meant to," said Mateo, "I banged their heads together. I have put them in our shower facility and barred the door. In a moment, I will turn on the water to revive them. The Abbot has decreed that they must leave the monastery tonight – they are not members of the *hermandad* and cannot be trusted – they are mercenaries."

"It seems to me that none of the *hermandad* can be trusted after tonight's debacle, Mateo," observed Alistair dryly.

Mateo paused for a long moment before replying. "It must seem that way to you, Señor Alistair – our ways are difficult to understand. Violence is part of the heritage of the *hermandad*, as the way of peace is part of the heritage of the Moriduran Brothers; both behaviours are deeply rooted in our natures. It was a Scotsman, was it not, who captured this duality - in Dr. Jekyll and Mr. Hyde? The monks and the *hermandad* understand each other, and certain things are accepted between us. Don Ferdinand is of the ancient *hermandad* tradition, and he will ultimately submit to the discipline of the Ancient Order – our joint identity – and to the authority of the Magus. The person who created the disturbance represents part of the *hermandad*'s accommodation with secular power – he owes his membership to his political influence rather than his respect for tradition. He has the support of some members of the Grand Council. The Moriduran Brothers have had to compromise with such men throughout the ages – it is the way of our world, and perhaps of the wider world."

"Hate the sin and love the sinner," observed Alistair. He put his next question hesitantly. "Mateo, who is the Magus? There have been many references to him, yet his identity is unknown to us. He must have been present tonight. Are you able to enlighten us?"

"That is a question that you must put to the Abbot, señor – it would be inappropriate for me to respond," replied Mateo. "If you will excuse me, I must leave now to attend to the men in the shower facility…" A faint smile lightened his serious mien for a fleeting moment.

Alistair thumped him playfully on the arm. "You're looking forward to giving them a drookin, eh, Mateo?"

"If you mean dousing them with cold water – of course not – it is a duty that I must perform." Mateo bowed politely, then turned and went ahead of the others along the right-hand passageway, through the small door in the rear wall and across the courtyard to the shower facility. He listened for a moment, but there was no sound from within. Grasping the wheel, he turned it effortlessly, and the metal groaned as the grating slid back, and the water cascaded down. Almost immediately, there were startled curses from within, scuffling footsteps, then banging at the barred door and more shouting.

Mateo removed the iron bar that secured the door, opened it slightly, and held it firmly against the onslaught from within. "Calm yourselves, caballeros. I am to escort you from the monastery and down *el sendero de precipio*. Great care and a tranquil spirit are necessary to accomplish this safely in the fading light – please prepare yourselves."

He released the door, and the two men emerged, truculent, wary and dripping wet. They looked up at Mateo, then at each other, and then visibly relaxed. "Brother Mateo has given us sore heads, eh, Francesco!" said Frederico, the taller of the two.

Francesco made no reply, but simply looked away. "What are we to do when we reach the path end, Mateo – cross the plain to Moridanza as darkness falls?" asked Frederico appealingly.

"You may either do that, or sleep in one of the *hermandad* cars till morning – the doors are unlocked, but there are no ignition keys," replied Mateo, indicating that they should follow him as he headed towards the cloister.

"We could hot-wire a car and leave anyway," laughed Frederico.

"That would be unwise. Don Ferdinand would not be happy if you did that – you have already incurred his displeasure once," responded Mateo.

They went through the cloister to the main courtyard and towards the wicket gate. Mateo produced his key and opened it, ducked through and waited on the other side for the two men. Francesco looked at the big monk, scowling.

"We must postpone our reckoning with you, Brother Mateo – forgiveness is not in our nature," he said icily, exchanging a look with Frederico, who laughed again.

"We must not part in anger! Mateo was acting under the Abbot's instructions – is that not so, Brother?" he said softly and ingratiatingly.

"Stay in single file on my left – exercise great care - you do not know the path as well as I do," said Mateo, as they set off down the steep incline. As they began the descent, Francesco, who was in front, slowed down, until Frederico was almost touching him, then as one, they turned and pushed hard against the body of Mateo. His huge frame barely moved in face of their onslaught, and his voice was calm as he spoke.

"This is folly – you place all our lives in danger."

The two men ignored his words, pulled back as far as they could against the rock face, then rushed him again, arms outstretched, palms flat. But there was nothing there – Mateo's great, black-robed bulk had simply vanished. As they went over the edge, they saw the setting sun, blood red on the horizon and screamed their farewells to life as they plunged towards the plain. Mateo, his back flat to the rock face, crossed himself and bent his head. There was no point in descending to the plain – they could not have survived the fall. Their bodies would be recovered in the morning.

"May God have mercy on your souls," he intoned, turned and headed back to the monastery, a great sadness in his soul. As he walked, he examined his conscience over the incident. He had resisted their first onslaught, but even with his strength, he could not have kept his balance on the precarious path at the second, more forceful attempt; if he had come to grips with them, it was likely that all three of them would have fallen in the struggle. His lightning sidestep had been an instinctive response, one that he would have used to avoid violence on safer terrain. How was he going to explain this to the Abbot? What would be Don Ferdinand's reaction?

He reached the summit, entered by the wicket gate and locked it behind him. On his way through the cloister, he met Brother Alfonso. The old monk was muttering to himself; he looked up and grasped Mateo's habit.

"Mateo – oh, Mateo – why do we live in such times? What will be next? Is there worse to come?"

"I have been responsible for the deaths of two men, Alfonso," replied Mateo, grasping the old monks hand. "*Los artilleros* have fallen to their deaths from the cliff path."

Brother Alfonso looked up at the distressed young monk. "My beloved brother – Mateo, my son – this is terrible news. But however it happened, you cannot be to blame."

"I was their guide, I am to blame." His voice broke, and remorse swept over him again. "I was responsible for their safety – Brother Anselmo put them in my charge, and now they have gone to God. *Mea culpa, mea culpa, mea maxima culpa…*"

"You must go to the Abbot at once. I have just come from him - he is in his study with Don Ferdinand. Go to him now, Mateo."

"Thank you, dear brother," said Mateo, and headed towards the Abbot's room. Alfonso watched his departing figure for a moment, then turned, shook his head, and resumed his muttering as he paced the cloister.

Outside of the Abbot's room, Mateo braced himself, and then knocked. Brother Anselmo's voice called upon him to enter. Both men were sitting at the Abbot's desk and Ferdinand looked impatiently over his shoulder as he came across the room.

"I hope this is something urgent, Mateo," he said, his voice hard and hostile.

Brother Anselmo gazed into Mateo's eyes, and instantly recognised the young monk's distress. "Ferdinand, will you leave us, please. I sense that Brother Mateo has something very pressing to impart to me. We will continue our discussion shortly. Forgive me…"

Ferdinand rose, his movements betraying his irritation at the interruption, and his peremptory dismissal by the Abbot. He left, trying to slam the door forcefully, but its massive construction resisted his show of indignation, and it swung shut majestically and soundlessly. He stood outside for a moment, feeling once again diminished by his lack of self-control, and tasting bile in his throat.

"Mateo, take a moment to recover your composure, then tell me that which you must," said the Abbot softly. "I have the feeling that *los artilleros* have gone to God; I pray that I am wrong."

Mateo looked at the floor, then placed his great hands on his forehead. "They attacked me on *el sendero de precipio* – twice. The first time, I resisted them, but the second time…" He shook his head despairingly.

"Poor Mateo – you are not to blame," said the Abbot, his voice full of compassion. "I must take responsibility for sending you on the path with these two men of violence, these hired assassins. May God have mercy on their souls. You must make your confession to Padre Gabriel as soon as possible; absolution is certain. Your penance will be your grief: I am less easily absolved of culpability for their deaths."

Mateo fell to his knees; Brother Anselmo moved swiftly round to him, and reached down and took his hands, lifting the young monk to his feet. "I will tell Ferdinand, and others who need to know, what has happened. The bodies of the unfortunate men will be recovered at first light and taken to Moridanza. Their deaths will be recorded as accidental, their burial swift. There will be no inquest – they are men without an identity, part of an anonymous criminal culture. You and I will mourn them, Brother Mateo, but few others; we will offer our prayers for their immortal souls. You must not allow any shadow of doubt – scruples - to deflect you from the great task that lies ahead of you. Now you must leave me – I must speak again with Ferdinand. Go to the guest wing and tell Señor Mackinnon and Señor Lonnen what has happened."

Mateo bowed, turned and left the room, his soul lightened by the words of the Abbot. Alfonso was hovering anxiously just outside the door, and he looked up into Mateo's eyes and saw that all was well.

"Mateo, at such a time I hesitate to ask you to perform a mundane task, but perhaps it will occupy your mind. Señor Lonnen is in the guest wing and has requested a bottle of his favourite wine - again – would you get it from the cellar and take it to him?"

"Willingly, Brother – I am on my way there now on an errand for the Abbot" said Mateo, relieved at having something tangible to do. He headed for the cellar steps, took the candle holder from the niche at the side of the door, lit it and descended the winding stone stairs. At the bottom, he pulled the door towards him and entered the cellar. Moving towards the rear racks, he tried to keep from his mind the memory of the little door and the awful voice, but it kept returning to his thoughts. When he reached the end rack, he could not stop himself from looking again at the arched door. What he saw caused him to jerk back, as though from a blow.

A key was protruding from the keyhole of the wooden door, and the edges of the door were clearly defined where it met the stonework, instead of being encrusted with dirt and cobwebs. The door had been opened since he had first noticed it on his last visit. The very name of it chilled his heart – *La Puerta de Bestia*, Brother Alfonso had called it. He tried to turn away, to ignore the little door, but a compulsion drove him to place his hand on the key.

A strange calmness gradually possessed him and he felt a sense of inevitability, almost of familiarity, as he slowly turned the key. There was no handle on the door, but the oval key handle was large; Mateo pulled it, and the door swung inwards. As it did so, a cold blue-green light flooded into the dark cellar, and terror swept over him. He let go of the key as if it were red hot, and jumped back from the doorway, almost dropping his candleholder.

He tried to master his mindless fear: he pulled the door wide, then, with a supreme effort of will, bent down and looked through, with a nameless dread of what he might see. What lay before him was a long, narrow circular tunnel cut into the rock of *La Copa*, the uneven surface of the black walls reflecting light in a way that showed the texture of the rock: the tunnel ran in a downward slope then curved left, and he could see no further. The source of the cold light was invisible – it simply pervaded the tunnel.

Then a question entered his mind – why had the light not been visible through the keyhole? He pulled his head back and closed the door; no light was visible. He pulled the key out and peered through the keyhole; there was only darkness. He replaced the key, opened the door again, and the light returned: it seemed to be controlled by the opening and closing of the little door – there was no other explanation.

Mateo's fear began to dissipate, replaced by a powerful curiosity, but then he remembered his dual errands – get the wine for *el Americano* and report the deaths of *los artilleros* to Señor Alistair. He closed the door reluctantly, locked it, retrieved the bottle of wine, and then headed back to the cellar entrance. As he left the cellar, climbed the steps and went towards the cloister, he reflected on what he had seen. Someone either had possessed the key or had found it, and had opened the door. It could not have been Alfonso; he was terrified of the legend of *La Bestia*, and even more frightened of the Abbot. A more unsettling thought then occurred to Mateo as he reached the guest house door. What if the little door had been opened from tunnel? The implications of that explanation made his blood run cold.

As he entered the guesthouse, he could hear the sound of the gramophone echoing along the corridor and he stopped before the main staircase to listen. It was Louis Armstrong's solo on *It's Tight Like That*. The sheer power and emotional intensity of the music touched him at the deepest level, as it always had since Alistair had first introduced him to it. How had this jewel come to be set in such an ephemeral little song in a minor key, with its strange verbal exchanges?

He began to walk along the left hand passage beside the staircase. Could the angel Gabriel have manifested himself at the beginning of the 20th century in human form, as a little fatherless black boy in a New Orleans slum? The talent was so evidently God-given, sublime – it spoke of humanity and eternity. He reached the candle-lit end space just as the music was ending and stood there motionless, his head tilted to catch the final notes.

As the music died away, Paul turned from the gramophone table around which they were all grouped. His instinctive capacity to sense the presence of Brother Mateo had once again alerted him before the others to the monk's silent arrival – almost a materialisation, Paul felt. He smiled at Mateo, who was standing at the mouth of the passageway, holding a bottle of wine, his open features transformed by his ecstatic response to the music.

They all turned, smiled and waved, except Red and Manuel, who were engaged in conversation. Manuel was looking somewhat forlorn. He had not been invited to the chapter house because of the disruption of the meeting, and his anticipated elevation to the *hermandad* had been postponed – temporarily, he fervently hoped.

Alistair beckoned Mateo to come across, but then saw that he was reluctant to join them for some reason, so he walked across to him.

"Did you catch all of Louis's solo? You know, many jazz critics don't rate it highly. They say the melody is too simple – not enough harmonic variation in the chord progression. But what the hell do they know? Any four bars phrase that Louis ever played was worth more than their whole lifetime's critical output."

Mateo nodded, then turned his head to the side as though in pain.

"Do you have something to tell me, Mateo?"

The big monk met his eyes, and then turned his head away again. After a moment, he spoke, the words coming slowly and with great difficulty.

"I have been responsible for the deaths of two men, señor – I have failed in my duty to the Abbot."

Alistair knew at once what must have happened. In his essential innocence, the young monk had not appreciated the malice that *los artilleros* bore him for their humiliation in the chapter house, and subsequently in the shower facility. Something must have happened on the cliff path. He turned and beckoned Paul, Santiago and Angeline to join him.

"Brother Mateo has something to tell us – I think *los artilleros* have met their Maker. Am I right, Mateo?"

The pain in the monk's eyes induced a great wave of affection in the others; they clustered around him solicitously, and Angeline took his arm.

"I was guiding them down *el sendero de precipio*, observing the Abbot's instruction that they must leave the monastery. I warned them of the dangers of the path – I assumed the customary protective position on their right. We had gone a very short distance when they attacked me. I repelled them, but then they rushed at me again, and I acted on instinct…"

"You stepped aside…" said Paul, comprehending in an instant what Mateo, in his attempt to avoid further violence, would have done.

"Oh, poor Mateo!" breathed Angeline, stroking his arm sympathetically, "No one will blame you – they were violent, dangerous men – they brought it on themselves."

"They were children of God, with their lives ahead of them. Now they are lying in the darkness, broken and lifeless…" Mateo shook his great head again, as though trying to expunge the memory. "I must make my confession to Padre Gabriel as soon as possible. Those men – they were not able to seek forgiveness…" His tone was despairing.

"Who knows what happened in their last moments – your God is a merciful God," Alistair said brusquely. "They may have reached out to him in perfect contrition before their lives were extinguished. Trust in your God and your Abbot – you mustn't blame yourself - don't dwell on it - that would really be a sin, Mateo!"

The monk looked at Alistair in gratitude. He had never known a father, and in spite of his brief knowledge of the Scotsman, he felt an almost filial attachment to him, similar to his love and respect for Brother Anselmo and one or two of the older monks he had known for all of his life in the monastery. Mateo relaxed, and lifted the bottle of wine he had been holding at his side.

"I must take this wine to Señor Lonnen," he said. As the words left his lips, he looked at Angeline, recalling the Abbot's words to the American in the chapter house. He held out the wine to her. "Perhaps you would prefer to take the bottle to him, Señorita Angeline?" he said casually.

Angeline looked up at him, then at the bottle, and knew that a momentous decision was facing her, and that Mateo was fully aware of the implications of what he was inviting her to do. Still holding Mateo's arm, she took the bottle with her other hand.

"We will take it to him together, Mateo," she said decisively, and as they walked towards her father, she was grateful for the reassuring presence of the monk beside her.

Red Lonnen looked up from his conversation with Manuel as they approached. He opened his mouth to say something, and then thought better of it. Angeline held out the bottle, still gripping Mateo's arm.

"You favourite wine, Red – courtesy of the Abbot and my friend Mateo…"

As her father reached for the wine, their fingers touched at the neck of the bottle, then their eyes met for a long moment. "Thanks, Angeline," he said, his voice subdued, "and thanks again to you, Mateo – what will I do without you when I leave this place – if I leave this place…" He stood holding the bottle, and there was an awkward silence. Alistair, Paul and Santiago joined them; Alistair glanced at the bottle of wine, then at Paul.

Paul recognised what was expected of him. "Unless you plan to drink alone, Red, I'll get some glasses – we should manage a glass each, with luck."

"I'm sure Mateo can get us more if we need it," laughed Red, returning to his normal breezy tone, "although I think Alfonso disapproves of me drinking his best wine. We must console Manuel – he's had a frustrating evening, sitting here waiting for a call that never came and missing all the action!" As Paul returned with both hands full of wine glasses from the dining table, Red looked up at Mateo.

"What have you done with Laurel and Hardy – those guys whose heads you banged together? That was as neat a piece of action as I've seen – quick as a flash, down they went…" He grinned, then the grin faded as he saw the effect of his words on Mateo and the others. "Oh, oh! – what's the story, guys?"

"They attacked Mateo on the cliff path, and went over the edge – they're dead." replied Angeline.

Red sucked in his cheeks, and looked up at the silent monk. "I guess that changes things – yeah, that will give Ferdinand something to chew on. Yeah…"

Paul had uncorked the wine, and was carefully filling the glasses at the gramophone table. Mateo caught his eye, and signalled that he did not want wine. "An extra glass for you, Red!" said Paul, "Brother Mateo is opting out!"

They gathered around Paul, picking up their glasses: Alistair held his up in front of him. "Here's to Mateo," he said, and the others chorused the toast. The monk acknowledged it with a graceful nod.

"Thank you, my friends. Now I must leave you and make my confession to Padre Gabriel before the day ends." He bowed, and walked away into the darkness beside the stairs.

Paul shook his head disbelievingly. "How does a man of that bulk walk so silently? I can't even hear a board creak, never mind a footstep?"

"Mateo has always had a light footfall, even as a child," said Manuel, glad of an opportunity to talk and lift his own gloomy mood. "The monks have a saying when they are startled by something: *it came upon me like Mateo*, they say. Poor Mateo, I am so sad for him! He will brood about the deaths of *los artilleros*. If only they could have died at someone else's hands!"

His observations were interrupted by the return of the vibration, this time with greatly increased intensity. The gramophone horn resonated in sympathy, hands holding wine glasses shook as if with palsy, and the great timbers of the roof far above their heads creaked and groaned alarmingly. Alistair had a look of intense concentration on his face, performing a count.

"The frequency has changed, not just the amplitude; it's a six-beat vibrato – listen!" he said, looking to Angeline for her endorsement of his conclusion.

"I agree," she responded, "It would seem that the Abbot was right to be worried."

Suddenly, they all experienced a feeling of weakness; it was difficult to hold their arms up, and their heads slumped to their chests. As they turned to each other for reassurance, their movement were strangely delayed, as though in a slow motion film sequence. Angeline gripped Paul's hand, and her anxiety was heightened by the way that the slowing down of the head movements of the others, together with the expressions of fear on their faces, lent an eerie quality to their appearance.

The vibration ended as abruptly as it had started. Red stretched his arms and flexed his shoulders as though he had just laid down a heavy burden. "*La Copa* is heading for a coronary if this keeps up. In the chapter house, I thought the Abbot was laying it on a bit thick about a crisis, but if this continues…"

Everyone looked at Angeline, and Alistair articulated their expectations of her. "Doctor Blade, you're the only real egghead among us – can Anselmo be right? Are we sitting on a nascent singularity, and about to be sucked into a black hole?"

"I haven't been called an egghead since high school," said Angeline. She clasped her hands together, then unclasped them and took a sip of her wine. "Much of what science says about black holes is speculation – the same holds good for gravity waves. Something triggers a singularity – the collapse of a star is one theory. There is also much talk about so-called primordial black holes, ones that were formed during the big bang – if there was a big bang…. The whole thing is complicated by the fact that our three-dimensional universe – if it *is* three-dimensional – may be what is called a *brane*, floating in hyperspace, one of what may be an infinite number of parallel universes. It is also possible there may be points at which these universes break through into each other – the wormhole concept of hyperspace.

"The site of *La Copa de Moridura*, before the meteor's impact, may be have been a kind of rip in the brane, a rip that connected to a black hole in another dimension. If the Abbot is right, then the force of even a comparatively small meteorite could have created the instability that he believes in. There is just no way of telling. Even if we drafted in a world task force with unlimited resources, we could probably do nothing – certainly not in the time scale that Brother Anselmo forecasts. He says his convictions are rationally driven, not faith driven, but can we believe this? What about all this stuff about access to superior technology and an extra-terrestrial being with super powers? We're in Flash Gordon land – ray guns and super-heroes…"

Alistair thought for a moment; he looked at Red. "How do you see it? Is the Abbot in fantasy land?"

"I'm with Angeline in her general assessment, but as for the superior technology, well, there I have to take a different view to my daughter…"

Angeline looked up in astonishment at her sceptic father's last remark, and Paul saw an unfathomable look in her green eyes.

"The reason I disagree is that I have a piece of the superior technology in my trunk upstairs – two pieces, in fact."

With this devastating remark, Lonnen paused, and his eyes swept over his stunned audience. He looked satisfied with the impact of his revelation. "I guess you all want to see them now – well, all in good time. There's something else you may have missed. Mateo, our big friend. What's your assessment of him? Notice anything odd about him?"

Manuel was the first to reply, and his tone was defensive.

"Brother Mateo is a fine man – a child of the monastery, strong, devout, faithful to his friends, loyal to his Abbot. Everybody likes and respects Mateo," he said, "and I am proud to call him my friend."

"*Los artilleros* might not have shared your opinion of him, Manuel," said Red Lonnen, "but I reckon most of us would endorse your assessment. But what else?"

Angeline looked at Paul, then back at her father. "He has great physical strength, even by the standards of the monks of Moridura. There are anecdotes of feats of strength – Manuel recounted some." Manuel nodded enthusiastically.

"There is a special aura about him at certain times," said Paul slowly. "I seem to be aware of his presence just before he arrives. I first noticed it in the square at Moridanza, and I have felt it several times since then. He regularly creates what was once called an uncanny valley moment – a sudden eerie feeling that something alien – robotic - is present."

Angeline glanced at Paul, and she too became slightly defensive. "Alien? Robotic? He's one of the nicest men I have ever met, Paul – gentle, courteous, and with a sense of humour. If he were representative of all men of faith, I could lose my agnosticism and embrace the Church again!"

Red laughed. "He wasn't gentle when he banged heads together in the chapter house," he said, "and two guys went over the edge trying to get revenge. I wouldn't like to get on his wrong side…"

"That's unfair," snapped Angeline, "He did what he had to do…"

Alistair had been listening reflectively to the discussion. He was still not quite sure what he could safely share with Lloyd Lonnen, but he decided that there was no time for caution.

"Are you aware of the significance of the time frame surrounding Mateo and the recurring instability of the heartbeat of *La Copa*, Red?" he asked.

"I sure as hell am. He arrived as a baby at the same time as the last event, thirty-five years ago - and there have been other Brother Mateo's. I've looked at records in the monastery library. There's a long line of Mateo's stretching back to the foundation of the monastery, at the time of the schism in the Ancient Order. Everyone of them arrived as a mysterious baby when the previous Brother Mateo disappeared - always vanishing at the age of thirty-five, and always close to the time of the Ceremony. There is no coincidence here – something very odd is going on. But there is something else, something that will give you all an uncanny valley moment – it sure as hell gave me one!

"You've used that rackety arrangement they call the shower facility, and so have I, before you came. Mateo initially operated it for me, and insisted that I should not use it alone, since that wasted water. He also let it slip that he, in contrast, always showered alone, never in a group of four monks - the usual arrangement. I asked him why, and he said that it was the Abbot's wish, and that he had never questioned this prohibition.

"Anyway, I got tired of always having to call Mateo when I needed a shower, and one afternoon I went out to the courtyard with my towel, ready to go it alone. I heard the water cascading, and concluded that some of the brothers were performing their ablutions; I figured they wouldn't mind a fifth bather, so I stripped off in the changing area and went in. Brother Mateo was there on his own, showering. He was shocked at my arrival, not from any sense of false modesty, but because I had caused him to breach the Abbot's prohibition. He requested politely, but insistently, that I leave immediately. I did so, but not before I noticed something extraordinary…"

Red knew how to deliver a punch line; years of presentations to senior industrialists, government officials and stockholders had taught him to use key disclosure to maximum effect. He made his audience wait, and then he lowered his normally slightly strident, harsh tone.

"He had no navel," he said softly, "a magnificent physique, a fine figure of a man – but he had no navel."

Angeline shook her head in disbelief. "But everyone who is born has a navel – without a navel, there would have been no umbilical cord, and if there was no umbilical cord…"

"…there was no womb – no mother," said Alistair. "Either you were mistaken, Red, or Mateo has had some operation that covered or eliminated his navel. Perhaps, if he was heavily muscled, the navel was invisible? Concealed in a six-pack?"

Red nodded. "They are both possibilities, ones that any rational man would accept as the explanation – but I am as certain as I can be, given the circumstances, that there was no scarring and no possibility of a concealed navel. He was stretching upwards towards the water – his abdomen was clearly visible. There was nothing there…"

Everyone was feeling a sense of bewilderment, loss and regret, and Manuel, in his direct and innocent fashion, put their feelings into stumbling words.

"But if all this is true, if Mateo is not – if he is – if the dates and the records are true, then Mateo…" He looked desperately to the others for reassurance, for a straight denial of the thought that was forming in all of their minds.

Red sensed the deep affection and respect of the group for the young monk, even though everyone but Manuel had known him for a very short time. "He may not be a man born of woman," he said evenly, "and his days may be numbered. Well, I prefer to seek a rational alternative explanation, in spite of the way the facts stack up. I haven't got an answer, but there must be one. I'm not going to let the closed atmosphere of this place suck me into believing mumbo-jumbo!"

Manuel impulsively wrapped Red in a warm embrace, to his laughing embarrassment, and Angeline felt an abrupt surge of respect and even affection for her father, emotions that unsettled her. Paul put his mouth close to her ear. "I'm beginning to think that your father may be almost human, even if Mateo isn't…" he whispered. Angeline dug her elbow viciously into his ribs, and he winced, still grinning.

Alistair had something on his mind. Might as well get it all out, he thought. "Red, there *is* something you can clear up, for me at least. Why have you been wearing the habit of a Moriduran Brother during your stay here?"

Lonnen met his eyes with a rueful grin. "You sure get right to it when you're in the mood, Alistair – is that a Scottish trait?"

"It's certainly a Glasgow trait," replied Alistair, unfazed by the implied rebuke.

Red shrugged fatalistically. "I guess all my secrets are coming out tonight," he said, looking at Angeline as he spoke, "so why not this one. I'm what the faithful refer to as a lapsed Catholic, except that description doesn't accurately represent why I abandoned the Church. It was a conscious decision to be free of moral constraints in conducting my business affairs – I wanted to screw the competition with a clear conscience." He saw the barely concealed disapproval of the others, and laughed.

"You're scandalised! Well, believe me, it's a common reason among those brought up in a religion where the moral rules are tightly drawn – it's an instinct to do a Houdini and wriggle out of the ethical straitjacket."

"I thought Catholics could sin happily and then wipe the slate clean by confession," said Alistair, his Scottish Protestant beliefs about Roman Catholics in his native country coming into play, "Isn't that the way it works? I always envied them that…"

Lonnen shook his head. "Wrong – the dominant emotional mindset of Catholics is guilt. Absolution gets you off the immediate hook, but you've still been a bad boy. Three Hail Marys or even the Rosary won't erase the feeling you get when you destroy a man, his business and his future for competitive advantage, or sell a weapons product that will be used to kill thousands of people. I thought being free of the religion would wipe it out, and it did, for a while - but long-term, it doesn't work…" He exhaled in a sort of heavy sigh. "Some things are even closer to home than that – some things are harder to live with…" He looked again at Angeline, as though trying to tell her something profound.

"The habit – the Moriduran habit?" said Alistair softly.

"You don't let a guy lose the question, do you?" He paused. "After I get all of this gravity stuff sorted, I may stay in the monastery - permanently. I have the Abbot and the Chapter's acceptance of me as an *oblate* – it's a voluntary attachment to the monastery, without taking religious vows. I still control my property and can leave any time I like. I'm kind of on probation…"

"Jesus Christ!" said Alistair with feeling.

"Yeah, He kinda comes into the equation - He might have something to say about it! I will have to decide at some point whether I want to go the whole hog and take my vows, or simply be a *confrater* – a lay person who retains a voluntary connection with the monastery. It's an honourable status – a number of kings have been *confratres*. I might even join the *hermandad*.

"Meanwhile, we have a question to address. What is the *hermandad* going to do? They don't really believe that a crisis is imminent. *La Copa* has been acting up for all of their history – they're like people who live on the slopes of a volcano – they don't believe it will ever erupt. Don't be fooled by that fat clown in the chapter house tonight; there are hard-eyed guys back in Mérida, in Madrid, and the defence industry brass that we both know back in the States, all of them scenting a huge, incalculable opportunity - they won't be put off by a little local superstition. If they descend on us, it will be too late, one way or the other. Either the black hole zonks us all, or they do."

Alistair couldn't help admiring Red's stark and economical analysis of the situation. "Not much of a choice, but the logic of it is that we act fast," he said. "Whatever interest group gets the upper hand, Angeline is the key – and, make no mistake, they could compel your cooperation, Angeline," he added, turning to her with a concerned expression.

"Nobody can make me cooperate," said Angeline defiantly, her mouth set.

"Oh, yes, they can," interjected her father, "maybe not by hurting you, but by a threat to harm those close to you..." The implications of his statement were all too clear, and Angeline looked less sure of herself.

"Señor Lonnen, it seems to me that the sooner we see the devices contained in your trunk, the better. They will be significant determinants of our course of action, perhaps even the crucial determinants," said Santiago.

"If you want to see my secrets by candlelight - fine," replied Red, "but Angeline will need to make a close examination of the devices in the morning light. And we have the not inconsiderable problem of getting the main device downstairs – it is very heavy. I still marvel at the fact that Mateo pushed it up the cliff path on the monks' rickety cart and then carried it up to my room unaided – the man is a modern Hercules!"

"I think we would all like a sight of these devices," said Alistair, "even by candlelight."

"If it is extra-terrestrial in origin, that will add to the romance of the situation," said Angeline excitedly.

"Listen to our objective scientist! You sound like Pollyanna. Oblivion is just around the corner, Angeline – let's have some gravitas," said her father; for once, his daughter was not offended by his bantering tone.

"Have we all got our electric torches?" asked Santiago, "The monks didn't take mine when they took my automatic."

After a quick check, the others confirmed that they still had the flashlights, and they headed for the staircase. Alistair looked back and saw that Manuel was hanging back, undecided as to whether to follow or not.

"Come on, Manuel! It's your party too..." he called out, motioning him to accompany the group. They went up the left-hand stairway and Red opened the door of his room, got a match, struck it and lit the candles. Alistair, Paul and Santiago produced their torches, but Angeline shook her head.

"Let's do it by candlelight – please. Let's not insult the ancient objects with artificial light."

Her father shook his head disbelievingly. "These things have been knocking about the globe for a few hundred years and have been back and forth across the Atlantic Ocean more than once! But if that's what you want, Angeline..." He laughed indulgently, enjoying the new, relaxed relationship with his daughter.

He went across to his trunk. "Before I open it, guys, try and lift it by the handles at each end." he said.

Alistair and Santiago positioned themselves on opposite sides, grasped the handles and tried to lift the trunk; it moved a fraction, but they couldn't get it off the floor; they squatted in best power-lifter's style but still failed.

"A quick route to a hernia - it took four baggage handlers with equipment to move that thing. I had to bribe the right guys in the States and in Madrid to get the damn thing through Customs and on and off the flights. It has almost screwed the suspension of the automobiles it's been in, yet Mateo lifted that out of the boot of the Merc, on to the cart, pushed the cart up the cliff path, then carried it single-handed into the monastery and up here, with no complaints." He shook his head at the memory of the feat. He took a key from his pocket, opened the lock of the trunk and lifted the lid; inside was a plain wooden box, dark and stained. They held the candles over it as Red lifted the lid, then there was a collective gasp.

Inside the box was a rectangular object, with two handles on the top at each end and lugs projecting from each of the sides. It was made of gold and a black, metallic material that looked similar to the rock of *La Copa*. The gold gleamed in the candlelight as the fascinated onlookers bent over to peer more closely at the object, and a drop of candle wax fell on its surface. Lying loosely on the surface was a small figurine, in the form of a centaur-like creature, with gleaming ruby eyes.

"It must be worth a fortune," said the awe-struck Manuel, and reached out in an irresistible impulse to touch the golden surface. Following his cue, the others all placed their hands almost reverently on the object's surface; it was cool to their touch, and they found themselves stroking it as if it were a living thing.

"Kinda gets you, doesn't it," said Lonnen, "the question is – what in hell is it? There's no way to its insides – it's been poked, prodded and X-rayed, without success. My best guess is that it is the core module for a much larger device, and that device must be somewhere in the monastery or within *La Copa* – perhaps underground. These lugs on the side look like placement devices to me, to fit it into the mother device. The handles on the top are for lifting and placing it. As for the little guy – the centaur – well, who knows? It frightened the hell out of Mateo. I dropped it, and he found out and returned it to me in the presence of the Abbot. He sure pissed Brother Anselmo off with his questions!"

Manuel was staring at the little golden object with a look of fear on his face.

"*¿Por qué tienes miedo, Manuel?*" asked Santiago.

"*Es la Bestia de Moridura, Señor Santiago,*" he said, his voice shaking with fear.

"He thinks he has recognised the Beast – but how, Santiago?" asked Paul, as the big Spaniard tried to calm Manuel with soothing words.

"It's a childhood memory, I think," replied Santiago, "there is a legend of the Beast as a centaur – half-man, half beast - children drew pictures to frighten each other, even though their parents disapproved."

Red closed the box, shut the lid of the trunk and locked it.

"Time for some shut-eye, I guess. We'll try and move the trunk downstairs in the morning – best to take the whole thing. I don't trust that wooden box."

Santiago came across to Alistair. "We must set up a watch system, as at Manuel's café. There are four men, so we can each do one two-hour stint, if Lonnen agrees." Alistair glanced across at the still frightened Manuel.

"Manuel, we're going to bed now. You have your own place to sleep in the monastery. Are you OK to go there alone?" he asked, "One of us can accompany you if you wish – or you can sleep here, in the vacant room."

Manuel pulled himself together. "No, thank you, Señor Alistair – God will be with me." He smiled at the others, then left, his small, stocky figure seeming somehow forlorn. They heard his heavy footfall on the stairs and across the ground floor, then the sound of the main door closing behind him.

Red was busy securing his trunk. Alistair looked at Santiago, then towards the American. Santiago shrugged, and Alistair said softly, "I think we can trust him now."

He went over to Red and swiftly explained his proposed rota – Red first watch, Paul second, Santiago third, himself fourth and last.

"Sure – I was going to suggest something similar myself. I've survived a few weeks alone up here, but I guess the game has changed after today's events," Red replied.

Alistair went to Paul, spoke briefly, then he explained it to Angeline. She looked truculent. "Why can't I stand watch?" she asked combatively.

"Because you're the prize, lassie – if they come, it will be for you and the gold gizmos. It wouldn't help if you were sitting in a chair with a candle waiting for them and we were all asleep, now would it?"

Angeline muttered indignantly, but seemed to accept his logic. However, Santiago returned, his brow furrowed. "This corridor can be approached from the stairs at either end. I think, to be safe, we must double up for two stints of four hours duration, with a man on each landing. I'll pair with Alistair, just in case."

Alistair saw the sense in this, although he was very tired and looking forward to his bed. He signalled his agreement and they quickly confirmed the new schedule. Santiago explained it to Paul - who was relieved that this time he would have company on watch - then to Red: it would be Paul and Red, then Santiago and Alistair in the pairings, covering each four-hour block. Red and Paul both grabbed chairs from their bedrooms and headed respectively to the dining area landing and the main landing. As she went into her room, Angeline called out to their retreating backs.

"If the bad men come, beat them to death with your little torches!"

Red, holding his chair in one hand, snorted and waved his other arm above his head dismissively as he walked away from her, but he did feel naked without his automatic. Angeline entered her bedroom with the thought in her head that, for the first time in her life, she was going to sleep in the knowledge that her father was watching over her. Tears came to her eyes, and she wept silently into her pillow.

Chapter Sixteen

Benedictine monasteries had accepted lay people in a special relationship with the monastery as *confratres* since the ninth century. Since the foundation of the Moriduran Brothers, after the initial animosity over the schism in the Ancient Order, most members of the *hermandad* had been *confratres*, but sometimes the Abbot of Moridura and the Chapter refused to confer the status of *confrater* on the more violent and extreme elements in the *hermandad*. In recent years, Brother Anselmo and the Chapter had even blackballed some Grand Council members, who nonetheless continued to sit on the Council, at Ferdinand's insistence.

The dormitory of the *confratres* in the monastery of Moridura was adjacent to the main dormitory where the monks slept. Ferdinand and four of his associates sat round a table at the far end, the only occupants of a huge room that could sleep many *confratres*. Of the six who had been with him in the chapter house, one was confined in a secure room by the Abbot's order and the other was in the monastery infirmary with a dislocated shoulder and elbow joint. All of them had taken off their robes and were informally dressed.

"I cannot endure this humiliation, Ferdinand. We must act soon to restore our authority and credibility, otherwise we are a spent force." The man who spoke was over forty years of age, small but powerfully built, with sharp, black eyes. He looked at the others for support, but they were watching Ferdinand intently for his reaction.

Their leader was calm, and his level gaze scrutinised each of their faces in turn. He had mastered his previous frustration, and was free of the intolerable feeling of impotence that had overcome him after the violence in the chapter house: in its place was an implacable resolve.

"I understand your emotions, Vasco, and the frustration and anger that all of you feel, but this was a temporary reverse, not a defeat. Before we determine what our response must be, we must examine our own part in creating the situation," he said, his tone placatory.

"Do you believe that we are to blame for what happened, Ferdinand?" The words came from the thick-lipped mouth of Casimiro, a man in his early thirties, with heavy-lidded, expressionless eyes.

"It is not our way to blame ourselves, or apportion blame to others, my brother. We have suffered an undesirable outcome – a tactical reverse. It is necessary to objectively analyse the factors that contributed to that outcome, including our own decisions and actions, then decide upon our next move," replied Ferdinand firmly. "I seek your views, offered without anger or resentment."

"Ferdinand is right. What brought us to this was an intervention that formed no part of our strategy or tactical plan – the outburst by our absent brother, now confined against his will. That resulted in the injury of one of our number, and our temporary confusion. Let us not compound that error by giving in to a desire for revenge, for reaction, rather let us carefully consider a course of action." The speaker was a man in his late sixties; his voice was calm and conciliatory, in spite of his stark analysis.

"Thank you for your wise counsel, Severino, my most esteemed brother," responded Don Ferdinand. "Now, Domingo – we await your invaluable input to our decision-making process." He looked along the table to a tall, spare man, with narrow shoulders. He was leaning back in his seat, and his long arms were stretched out in front of him, hands flat on the table. He had a detached air, yet there was a sense of controlled force in his posture.

"We have a great prize within our grasp, and we must not allow temporary reversals to deflect us from our purpose, nor must we permit our necessary involvement with those who are not of our brotherhood to exacerbate tensions between us and the Moriduran Brothers. The things that bind us together have always been greater than the conflicts of opinion that have threatened that unity throughout our turbulent history." Domingo looked straight at Don Ferdinand, and then stood up.

"Our absent brother was responsible for the ill-considered and abortive attempt to abduct the American woman from Moridanza: he was also responsible for gathering an undisciplined group of members and *los artilleros* at our meeting place on the north ridge, for inducing them to advance on *El Trono* earlier today, and for the humiliating outcome. His indignant outburst was the catalyst for what happened in the chapter house, but it was compounded by your misjudgement of the situation, Ferdinand. You should not have endorsed his actions. Indignation is the least productive of the emotions – it yields no dividend.

"We carried our hidden weapons in the certain knowledge that the outsiders were armed: their use should only have been sanctioned by you if an attack was imminent. We violated the sanctity of the chapter house without justification because one of our number lacked self-control, and another's judgement was flawed. We also polarised the American's loyalties prematurely – he would have been useful as a mediator with his daughter. He is now firmly in the camp of the outsiders. We have been humiliated three times in twenty-four hours, on our own territory, by the errors of our absent brother, and by your error, my esteemed brother. That is my objective analysis, offered without blame or recrimination." He resumed his seat, and his air of detachment.

A long silence followed; all eyes were turned to Ferdinand. Eventually he rose to his feet, controlling his anger with difficulty.

"Thank you, Domingo, my brother. I accept and endorse your analysis. My judgement *was* flawed – I misjudged the situation created by Jaime's outburst, which I deplored. But I thought that the Scotsman and his protector would react to it as they had earlier during the ill-advised advance on *El Trono* this afternoon. It was a split-second decision, but I now see that it was wrong. I accept your censure for this act."

"Who knows what anyone of us would have done had the decision lain with us," said Severino, the elderly man. "Censure is not appropriate for you, Ferdinand – but the actions of our brother Jaime are of a different kind. They show repeated failures of judgement, and moreover, they are characteristic of his personality. Our way has been to use violence only when other methods of achieving an objective have failed, or were likely to fail. In different circumstance, our brother Jaime would be sent to God by our joint verdict, but his political influence in Mérida and the region makes this impossible. He is the main contact with our friends in the defence industry – he has their confidence."

Casimiro cleared his throat. "I have a suggestion to offer. Ferdinand, you must ensure that the Abbot releases Jaime early tomorrow morning. He does not yet know of the deaths of your men who fell from the cliff path. You must convince him that his life is threatened if he remains, and that he must return to Mérida at once. Show him the bodies on the plain if he is unconvinced – after all, he suborned their loyalties to attempt the abduction from the Ortega café. From this point on, his contribution must be his liaison with our defence contacts – he must be kept away from the monastery until the Ceremony. We all have business in Mérida before then. When we return for the Ceremony, we will reconsider how we may show our displeasure for his three errors"

The others nodded approvingly, and Ferdinand was relieved that his own authority was intact, in spite of Domingo's criticism of his judgement. But then the small, black-eyed man, Vasco, rose to his feet abruptly.

"I cannot endorse this course of action – I cannot be part of any consensus on this. Jaime is an influential and powerful man, and he has my loyalty. I cannot countenance this approach – it is a denial of his position in the *hermandad* and implies a threat to his life," he said, looking around the table. "I feel I must tell him of this discussion."

Ferdinand paused before replying, evaluating the non-verbal reactions of the others, and then made his judgement. "Thank you, Vasco, your input is relevant and timely, but because of your dissent we must now defer our decision on Jaime until we have consensus. I have urgent business with the Abbot tonight. My brothers, let us retire now."

He rose to his feet and nodded to Domingo, who moved swiftly behind Vasco, gripped his head between his hands and expertly broke his neck. As the dead man fell forward on to the table, Ferdinand motioned the others to stand. They showed no surprise at Vasco's fate – his challenge to Ferdinand and the Grand Council members had been blatant. Severino alone showed regret and pity on his face. They looked silently at the body for a few seconds, their heads bowed respectfully.

"I believe that we now have achieved consensus, my brothers," said Ferdinand. "We will drop Vasco's body from *el sendero de precipio*, at the rope hoist, before the monks have risen for Matins. His body will land close to the others. Mateo will assume that he died trying to descend the path without a guide during the hours of darkness."

With Domingo's help, he lifted the body and carried it across to one of the beds, laid it out and covered it with a blanket. He moved to the door.

"Goodnight, my brothers. Pray for Vasco's immortal soul, and then sleep well. I will return before Matins to assist you."

He left the dormitory of the *confratres*, went through the cloister, and headed for the Abbot's room. He paused in front of the door and raised his fist to knock, but Brother Anselmo's voice came from within before his knuckles touched the wood. "Enter, Ferdinand – I am alone."

The old man has a keen and discriminating ear in spite of his years, he thought as he opened the heavy door. The Abbot was holding rosary beads in his hands, with large black beads for the *Aves* and rubies for the *Paters*, linked by a gold chain, with a heavy golden Benedictine cross on the end.

"I regret that I have interrupted your devotions, Anselmo," he said. "It seems that all of our lives have been thrown into chaos by recent events. The behaviour of Jaime, my brother and the deaths of Frederico and Francesco – these regrettable episodes have cast a dark pall over our community. I bear Mateo no ill will – these men betrayed my trust twice: their deaths were perhaps inevitable."

He searched the Abbot's face in a vain attempt to divine his thoughts. The old monk had an inscrutable quality when he chose to keep his counsel, a quality that Ferdinand envied. Brother Anselmo kissed the cross on the rosary and laid the heavy beads on his desk.

"You were unhappy when the Chapter refused to accept the man known as Jaime as a *confrater*. The latent flaws in his character that influenced that decision have now manifested themselves. We cannot continue to hold a man of power and influence against his will – it would bring the monastery to the unwelcome attention of the authorities in Mérida. You have come to propose a solution to this, have you not?" It was more of a statement than a question.

"Yes," replied Ferdinand. "If you will release him to my custody, I will take him before dawn to where the bodies of the two men lie. I will convince him that his life is in danger if he stays. With your permission, Mateo will act as our guide down *el sendero de precipio*, and I will then drive Jaime to Moridanza, where he may arrange transport to Mérida. Mateo will follow in your car with the two bodies. I will meet him in Moridanza and together we will make the necessary arrangements. Is this acceptable to you, Anselmo?"

The Abbot stood up and turned away from him for a moment, and then spoke without turning round. "Do you intend to repudiate Jaime – to expel him from the *hermandad*, Ferdinand?"

Ferdinand looked uncomfortable. "At this time, no, Anselmo, for the reasons you have already given – his political power and influence – and because he is our main contact with the American and European defence industries. If we are to manage the opportunity presented by the gravitational anomaly and by Doctora Blade's discovery, we need him. Without his mediation, the Americans could withdraw." He drew a deep breath; what he now had to say would be viewed with deep suspicion by the Abbot.

"Vasco has been missing since the meeting in the chapter house. Our first thought was that he had tried to find Jaime, but now, it is my fear that he has attempted *el sendero de precipio* alone. His loyalties were to Jaime and he may have feared for his safety. There may be a third body on the plain, Anselmo."

"Your father warned you many times that the consequences of the use of force could never be fully foreseen. Three deaths have now resulted from your actions – Pablo Miguenez, *los artilleros*, and now perhaps another. Where will it end?"

The Abbot came from behind his desk and stood directly in front of him. "Ferdinand, are you so blinded by power and greed that you cannot see the greater threat that faces all of us – that may face all of mankind? Did my words in the chapter house mean nothing to you?"

"We have experienced instabilities close to the event throughout our history, Anselmo. It is vital that we maintain a sense of proportion. If we overreact, if we allow ourselves to be deflected from our purpose, we may lose control of developments that will determine the future of the region and of Spain. The entire purpose of our ancient brotherhood will be rendered meaningless if we fail at this moment. *La Copa* will recover its stability after the Ceremony – it always has – it always will. It is self-regenerating."

Ferdinand's voice was filled with urgency and conviction, yet in his heart he felt a deep unease, as though he were averting his gaze from something too awful to contemplate.

"When did Padre Gabriel last hear your confession, Ferdinand?" asked Brother Anselmo.

"It has been some time – I have been occupied by many things..." he replied, startled by the question. He recovered and spoke confidently and decisively. "I have been thinking that perhaps it is no longer appropriate for Padre Gabriel to hear my confession, and that I should seek a new confessor in Mérida. It places Gabriel in a difficult position to hear my confession. If only you were a priest, Anselmo..."

The Abbot looked grave. "You and your family through the generations have always confessed to a Brother of Moridura – it has been an inevitable and necessary part of our unique relationship with the *hermandad*. How can you contemplate such a course of action, Ferdinand? Men in your position have always required a special relationship with their spiritual advisor. I find your rationale unconvincing. Is there a question of trust with Gabriel? His holy vows are sacred and inviolable; he would willingly die rather than betray them. Surely you do not doubt him?"

"I will consider your wise counsel, Anselmo – I will reflect on the matter with great care," replied Ferdinand, but the memory of Vasco's lifeless body in the dormitory of the *confratres* increased his resolve to confess elsewhere. A busy city church in Mérida, a tired and overworked priest – he would be just another face in the shadows behind the grille to be given absolution for his mortal sin and receive his penance. The next time, he would confess his venial sins to Padre Gabriel, and the Abbot would be happy. He would have to tell a small lie to Gabriel about how long it was since his last confession, but this was a small thing. He had used this method many times. Mother Church would not approve, but his contrition was genuine each time, and the absolution was valid in the eyes of God. After all, the ritual of confession stressed the confidentiality and anonymity of the process. Had not this been the way of men of action throughout Spain's often bloody history?

He looked at the Abbot with new resolve. "Anselmo, my thoughts are these: Mackinnon, with his security chief, Manrique, Doctora Blade, and the Englishman Corr could leave at anytime and return to Scotland – or Madrid. The American, Lonnen, will stay – he is confident in spite of his vulnerability, and would not break his word to you. If he does not cooperate and permit us to examine and to take what is rightfully ours, we will take it anyway. As for his threat that he could destroy the regulator core and key – we know they are indestructible. But his daughter is another matter. Without Doctora Blade, we can achieve nothing. She and her father must be bent to our will, Anselmo – they must be compelled to face the reality of their situation."

The Abbot shook his head wearily, and steepled his hands. "Force is not the way, Ferdinand – you will jeopardise everything that we hold sacred. They are people of high integrity - intelligent, moral and principled – they have an understanding of the situation that faces all of us, as I fear you and the Grand Council do not – the prospect of total annihilation. When *El Trono* splits, there will be no elevation of the Magus Elect: the instability will suck us, the monastery, and all life forms into a minute body of infinite mass, or into another dimension. Nothing will survive. Our solar system will be destroyed, perhaps even our universe.

"Our history, our knowledge, our entire species, every animate and inanimate thing - all will vanish. If this is God's divine will, we cannot avert this outcome, but it is our destiny, under God, to try. We will use the free will and the intelligence that He has granted to us to attempt to preserve our world. We have been given the right to choose, to shape our future and the Lord will help us to choose well. This is our great test, Ferdinand."

The proud man before him bowed his head, but not in acquiescence. "Anselmo, I must act on my own judgment and my own conscience. I profoundly respect your wisdom and value your counsel, but in this, I believe you to be wrong. As Magus Elect, I must prepare for the event and the Ceremony in my own way – it has always been so. I will keep your counsel in mind at all times, and I will avoid the use of force if that is possible – but I will do what I believe I must."

The Abbot turned away again, and his frail form was motionless in the candlelight. "At least wait until morning, Ferdinand – do not use the hours of the night to pursue your objectives. I ask this of you. I will summon Mateo and tell him of the possibility of another body on the plain, and of what he must do. Go to the place of confinement before Matins: he will release Jaime, and together you will descend to the road," he said, and then he swung round abruptly.

"Make sure that foolish, cowardly man submits to Mateo's guidance during the descent," he said. "As is the way with cowards, he is prone to displays of bravado. We do not want yet another body at the base of the rock." With that, he turned away again, and it was clear to Ferdinand that the discussion was at an end. With a quiet goodnight, he left the Abbot's room and went back to the dormitory of the *confratres*.

He entered the room quietly, and saw that the body of Vasco had gone: the others were in bed fast asleep. Ferdinand lay down on his bed fully clothed and closed his eyes. He would waken and rise before dawn. He had done so all of his life: it was one of the disciplines Don Lope had inculcated into his son.

Paul and Red were close to the end of their four-hour stint. They had placed their chairs on the landing at the mouth of the corridor between the bedrooms, so that they could see each other while standing watch. They periodically paced up and down, observing the doors and looking over the balustrade to the mouths of the passageways.

As Paul was checking his wristwatch a few minutes before the changeover, he heard two doors opening almost simultaneously, and Alistair and Santiago emerged, yawning and stretching. They came together in the middle of the corridor.

"Anything?" asked Alistair softly.

"I heard a faint sound like someone crying out, just before midnight," said Lonnen softly, looking at Paul, who nodded in agreement. "It could have been an animal, but it sounded human to me."

"I heard it too," said Alistair, "it was human alright – an angry sound – a sound of protest or pain. Do you think the Abbot has been putting the thumbscrews on the fat man in the hood?"

Red laughed. "More likely that Ferdinand would put the iron on him – I think he was stampeded into a show of force by that guy's outburst." He turned to Paul, still smiling, but saw that he was looking down at the floor. All of their eyes instinctively followed his gaze.

"Do you see it?" whispered Paul.

In the faint, flickering light of the candles, a minute line of blue-green light could be seen through a fractional gap in the floorboards. The light was absolutely steady, and it looked almost like a tiny fluorescent strip at their feet. Alistair signalled them to put out their candles by licking his finger and thumb and then bringing them together. Red and Santiago extinguished the flames, and the light on the floor looked more intense. Paul took out his torch and shone it on the boards, but the light became invisible. He switched off the torch and got down on his knees, peering at the gap as closely as he could.

"I can see nothing but the light," he whispered.

"I knew there had to be something in that space, I knew it," breathed Santiago, feeling vindicated after the teasing he had received on the previous day for his suspicions. "That is artificial light – electric light - in a monastery with no electric power."

"So they say," said Red, "so they say…"

"Do we investigate, or do we do our watch stints as planned?" asked Santiago.

"If we start clumping down the stairs and up and down the passageways, banging on partitions, we risk waking Angeline. Let's wait till morning," replied Alistair.

Santiago tapped him on the shoulder, then bent down and began removing his shoes, looking up at Alistair and inviting him to do likewise. The big man shook his head resignedly, and as he pulled his shoes off, he looked up at Red and Paul. "You can go to bed," he said softly.

"Like hell we will!" replied Lonnen in a hoarse whisper, and Paul nodded in support.

"Then go back to your watch stations and Santiago and I will investigate," said Alistair, his voice betraying some irritation. Alistair padded after Red to the rear staircases, and Santiago followed Paul to the main stairs.

As they reached the staircase, Red put his hand on Alistair's arm. "Stairs and stocking feet don't mix – watch how you go!"

Alistair's annoyance at this advice disappeared swiftly when he almost slipped on the second step and had to grab the banister. He gave a muted curse, to Red's amusement, then descended swiftly to the bottom and turned into the nearest passageway, pulling out his torch. He switched it on, and then, remembering Paul's failure, he switched it off again, letting his eyes become accustomed to the faint light in the passageway. A sudden flicker of light came from the other end, and both he and Santiago realised they had both chosen the same passageway to investigate. Alistair waved at him, gesturing that he should move to the other passageway.

He walked slowly down the passageway, looking closely at the wooden panelling, feeling it and pressing hard on the surface of each panel. The wood was solid and unyielding and there was no sign of light. Halfway along, he came to the wooden enclosure of the gentlemen's privy. He looked in and lifted the wooden cover of the lavatory bowl, half-expecting the bowl to be suddenly lit by a blue-green light, but he was disappointed: there was only darkness. A continuation of his visual and tactile exploration of the panelling along the second half of the passage revealed nothing. Emerging, he looked up and saw Paul looking down at him from above, candle in hand, and Alistair gave a thumbs down sign. Walking under the main stairway, he came to the mouth of the other passage. Santiago could be seen silhouetted in the faint light that was coming from Red's candle above him, completing his exploration of the panelling.

Alistair went along the passageway to him, shrugged expressively and Santiago shook his head. They both padded up a staircase to where Red was sitting in his chair, with the candle on the floor beside him. He looked at them both, leaned over and lifted the candle holder, then stood up and handed it to Alistair.

"I guess I can hit the sack now," he said, and headed for his room. Paul was looking along from the main staircase landing, and Red placed his palms together and laid them on his cheek, indicating that their joint stint was over. Santiago went along and took his candle and Paul too headed for his room. Alistair and Santiago put their shoes on and took up their posts.

The rest of the night passed without incident, but in the last part of Alistair and Santiago's watch, about half an hour before dawn, they both heard voices and far off footsteps. As their stint ended, dawn was breaking, and the voices of the monks of Moridura were raised in their morning prayers, as they had been since before discovery of the New World and before the men of Extremadura had set sail in search of *El Dorado*.

As the sun rose in the sky, and its light spread over the monastery and *La Copa de Moridura*, two cars headed across the plain towards Moridanza. The one in front was driven by Don Ferdinand, with a terrified fat man sitting beside him: following close behind was the Abbot's old Mercedes, driven by a stone-faced Mateo, with three broken bodies lying in a tangle of lifeless limbs in the rear seats.

Chapter Seventeen

A listair and Santiago, having ended their watch stints and made their ablutions, sat and compared notes at the gramophone table as they waited for their companions to rise.

"Joaquín will be arriving with breakfast shortly after Matins, and the others will be down soon – let's see where we think we're at," said Alistair. "Red has been OK – I think there has been some kind of reconciliation between him and Angeline, and I'm glad of it, for her sake at least: I think I trust him." He looked hard at his security chief: Santiago hesitated for a moment, and then nodded.

"Insofar as we can trust anybody in this situation, yes. The Abbot believes we're all going into a black hole; Ferdinand doesn't, and wants to secure control of Angeline's discovery for profit. If the Abbot is wrong, and is just in a superstitious panic about the vibrations, then we have a straight commercial power play to resolve before the U.S. defence guys get here, and that means negotiation. The only one who can tell us whether the Abbot is right or wrong is Angeline, and to do that, she needs access to whatever Brother Anselmo is hiding from us – and I do believe he still has something vital to reveal."

Alistair thought for a moment, stroking the brass gramophone horn. "The Abbot is no fool – and yes, he may be grinding axes we don't know about. There's also the question of Manuel's father's diaries. Today will be decisive – there is a list of questions we must get answers to. Manuel may know things but be unaware of their significance, like the details surrounding Mateo," he said, then clapped his hands together and rubbed them vigorously, a street gesture from his early years, indicating imminent and decisive action.

"The wee man will be with us for breakfast – I'll quiz him then!"

The familiar rattle of Joaquín's cart came from along the passage, and the voice of Manuel could be heard. They emerged, smiling.

"*Buenos días, señores,*" they said in unison. Alistair smiled and thumped the bench beside him in invitation. "Come and join us, Manuel – did the Big Bad Bogy Beast come and get you?"

Manuel's smile vanished, and he sat down with a grave expression on his face. "When we are as close as this to an event, and to the Ceremony, it is not good to joke about such things," he said, with a quiet dignity that left Alistair feeling more than a little foolish.

"I'm sorry, that was stupid – sorry, wee pal," he said, laying his hand on Manuel's shoulder. The sound of doors opening and closing, laughter, and footsteps heralded the arrival of the others. They called out their good mornings as they came down the staircase. Manuel's good humour was restored, and Joaquín indicated that breakfast was now ready. As they moved to the table, Alistair invited the monk to join them, but he smilingly declined, and went off down the passageway.

By unspoken consensus, they kept the conversation to small talk while the meal was in progress. Eventually the chatter died down of its own accord, and Alistair judged that the time was right to broach weightier matters.

"The night yielded little but a mysterious light and some noises off," he said, "unless anybody has anything new to report?"

"I slept like a log," said Angeline, smiling fleetingly at her father, "but tell me about the mysterious light – that sounds exciting!"

Having heard the account, she raised her eyebrows. "So Santiago was right – there is something in there…"

'Nothing that we could find," said Santiago. "The light was faint enough in the darkness – we're unlikely to see anything in the daylight."

Red cut across his words. "I'm used to a heavier breakfast than this, good as it was." He stood up and looked across at Brother Joaquín's cart. "There's still something on the trolley, covered with a cloth – maybe our friendly waiter has left us a little extra," he laughed, and went across to the cart. His back was turned to the group at the table as he pulled the cloth off, then they heard him give a low whistle.

"Brother Anselmo has sent us a little something to liven up the morning, guys," he said, turning and walking over to the table with the serving dish. As he laid it down, they saw three automatic pistols and Alistair's big Fosbery revolver lying demurely on the silver dish. "Help yourselves," he said, "this will round off the meal nicely."

"He did say he would return them at the appropriate time," said Alistair, reaching for his revolver. Santiago, Paul and Red also retrieved their weapons.

"I've never had a gun given to me on a silver salver before. Isn't that what they used to do with a member in an English gentleman's club, when he was caught with an ace up his sleeve? A polite hint…" said Red.

"The question is," said Alistair, "has the Abbot returned the weapons to the men in the pointy hoods?"

Angeline looked at them with barely concealed contempt. "You all feel safer now you've got your guns back – toys for boys. Well, I don't – I wish the Abbot had thrown them down a well, or something."

Manuel cleared his throat apologetically. "Señores – señorita – I have a message from the Abbot, relayed to me by Brother Joaquín. He will send Mateo to join you shortly; he will answer any questions you may have, and he will also carry the trunk containing the artefacts down from Señor Lonnen's room. The Abbot will join you before Terce - at nine o'clock - if circumstances permit."

Alistair grimaced. "It would seem that the old boy is up early and on the ball," he said. "Not much passes him by!" Manuel looked shocked at such a disrespectful reference to the Abbot.

Paul laughed and was about to say something, but suddenly he paused and tilted his head. Angeline recognised the look on his face. Paul was having an uncanny valley moment – Mateo was coming.

"*Buenos días, señores, señorita,*" said the familiar deep voice, and there he was, framed in the passageway, smiling. They called out their good mornings as he came across to the table.

"Take a chair, Mateo," said Red.

"I hope you slept well, and that nothing disturbed you in the night hours," said the monk. "I had to leave for Moridanza before dawn with Don Ferdinand – perhaps you heard us departing?"

Alistair nodded, his mind racing. Why had the monk and the Don headed for the village at that hour? Red put the question for him with his customary bluntness.

"What in hell took you to town at so early, Mateo?"

"Don Ferdinand was taking a Grand Council member – the man known as Jaime - to Moridanza. There were three dead men to transport to the village, so we had to take two cars," replied Mateo.

Alistair eventually broke the total silence that followed. "*Three* dead men, Mateo?" he said softly, "*Los artilleros* and…?"

"Vasco, a member of the Grand Council, attempted to leave the monastery after dark, and fell from the cliff path – or at least, that is how Don Ferdinand believes that he met his death," replied Mateo enigmatically.

"What do *you* believe, Mateo?" asked Paul.

"From the position of the body, he must have fallen from a point at the summit close to the rope hoist," said the monk.

Paul visualised the summit as he had first seen it on their arrival the previous day. The rope hoist was some way from the end of the path: someone heading for the path from the monastery gate would have had to go right rather than left to reach that point. "It seems an unlikely place to fall from, Mateo," he said. "This man – Vasco – would have had to make a detour to get there. Can you think of another explanation?"

"I can think of three, Señor Paul - that he was disoriented in the darkness and thought he was walking towards the path, that he went to the hoist for some other purpose, or that he did not fall accidentally," replied Mateo. He paused for a long moment. "Our records show that the rock overhang was a place of execution in ancient times, and also a place to dispose of the bodies of those who were not to be buried in consecrated ground. The body was left on the plain to be eaten by scavenging creatures. These were primitive practices that pre-dated the foundation of the monastery."

Alistair looked reflectively at the monk. "There are many questions that my friends and I must put to you, Mateo – and to Manuel – and they may seem a wee bit intrusive. May I ask you what guidance Brother Anselmo offered you in this regard?"

"I cannot speak for Manuel, señor, but my brief is clear. I am to give you any information of which I have certain knowledge, with the following constraints – I may not voice opinions about my own origins as a child of the monastery, and I am free to decline to answer questions that I feel are matters for me and my confessor. I may offer my own informed conclusions about matters of which I have direct knowledge, but I may not engage in loose speculation. Is that helpful to you, Señor Alistair?"

Alistair's admiration for the young monk grew as he listened to him, as it did for his superior, the Abbot. "Thanks, Mateo – no man could ask for more," he said, with feeling.

Red stood up, looking at Alistair, then Mateo. "Before we get to question time, Mateo, Manuel has told us that you will help us bring my trunk down from upstairs?"

Mateo stood up. "It is best if I bring it down alone, Señor Lonnen, and that no one attempt to assist me – it is very heavy, and I need a clear path." His voice was polite but firm.

"You're the boss, big guy," said Red, "you know where my room is..." He gestured towards the staircase. "I'll go ahead and at least get the door open for you."

Mateo followed him up to the room. The others waited downstairs expectantly, remembering the weight of the trunk. Mateo appeared at the head of the stairs carrying the metal trunk with no evidence of strain. Red hovered anxiously behind him as he began his descent. Below, the observers held their breath. The staircase creaked loudly at each step the monk took, careful, measured steps.

As he got close to the bottom, Alistair indicated to Paul and Santiago to clear part of the table, and Mateo walked across and placed the trunk down on the floor. He didn't appear to be out of breath as he released his grip on the handles and waited for further instructions. Red produced the key of the trunk and, as he was opening it, spoke over his shoulder.

"I'll need you again to lift the thing out and put it on the table, Mateo," he said apologetically. He lifted the lid of the wooden box, removed the small figurine and held it in his hand as he stepped back to allow the monk access. The room was full of light from the huge stained glass window, and the little gold figure shone and its ruby eyes glittered. The monk stared at it for a moment, and then bent over the open trunk. As he looked in, the reflection from the gold artefact shone upwards on his face, and Mateo straightened up, without lifting the object to the table.

Those watching him all experienced the same chilling sensation – a feeling of the presence of something profoundly alien and terrifying. The face they were looking at was transformed – it was still the young monk they knew, but the expression on his features was that of a creature suddenly conscious of being surrounded by living beings of another species, yet aware of its own power and dominance. Mateo heaved a great sigh.

"The core and the key," he said, almost to himself, "they are restored to us. Thanks be to God." He crossed himself and bent his head, and it was only with great efforts at self-control that the onlookers resisted the urge to kneel down. The uncanny moment passed as quickly as it had come, and they looked for confirmation in each other's eyes that they had not been alone in the experience.

"You identified the artefacts as the core and the key, Mateo – will you explain this to us?" asked Alistair.

The monk smiled, his big, open, warm smile, and it was hard to believe that a moment ago he had induced sensations of awe and fear. "Gladly, Señor Alistair. The core is a critical part of the device we call the *regulator*, and the key links the device to the core – it activates it in some way. The regulator has been on the site of the monastery since time immemorial; we believe it pre-dates even the most ancient parts of the original structures on which the monastery was built. The regulator monitors and stabilises the heartbeat of *La Copa* and the phenomenon known as the splitting of the *El Trono*. Since the core and the key were removed from us many centuries ago, the regulator has been locked in the last monitoring status, and the heartbeat of *La Copa* has become increasingly unstable."

"Kinda like a heart pacemaker," observed Red, "one that's got stuck on its last reading."

"That is an almost exact analogy," smiled Mateo, then the smile left his face suddenly. "If a pacemaker fails, the person who has the implant may die, but if the regulator of *La Copa* fails, we all may die."

Angeline had been listening intently to the monk, and she now moved closer to him; tall as she was, she looked small and fragile next to him. "Mateo, do you understand exactly what the regulator is doing – can you give a scientific explanation?"

Mateo smiled down at her, and she felt a great surge of affection and respect for him. "Señorita Angeline – Doctora Blade - compared to your scientific knowledge, I am as a child in infant school, but I will offer my understanding, gleaned from what I have read of physics, and what the Abbot has told me. At the heart of *La Copa* is some form of matter that came with the meteor, or was generated by the collision, aeons ago. This we call *El Corazón de La Copa* – the Heart of the Cup. *El Corazón* is independent of the gravitational force of the Earth – it recognises only its own gravitational field. The critical initial strength of the field that was formed on impact is poised between weakening to the point that *El Corazón* expands to nothingness, or increases to infinite mass. If the latter occurs, *El Corazón* will collapse into a black hole. It performs an infinite number of oscillations in a finite period of time, and although we cannot experience this oscillation directly, we feel some shadow of it through the heartbeat of *La Copa*." He stopped, and blushed a little.

"I know this may seem like nonsense to someone of your scientific eminence, Señorita Angeline, but it is the best that I can offer. However inadequate my explanation, it describes something real," he said, shrugging expressively, eyes widened, palms turned upwards.

It was Angeline's turn to blush, a blush that was all too visible on her pale cheeks. "I am in no way eminent, dear Mateo, and your explanation is in no sense inadequate. The phenomenon you describe is known in theoretical physics, and has been graphically represented. If what you describe is the essential nature of the heart of *La Copa*, then we are in great danger." Then a thought struck her. "My device for modulating the gravitational wave uses gold and a fragment of the rock of *La Copa*: the core, as you call it, also seems to be made of gold and an identical rock. What do you conclude from this?"

"I have no idea, Señorita Angeline," he replied, then smiled his big, open smile. "We *extremeños* have always been fascinated by gold, and it does not surprise us that something of enormous value and significance would be made of gold. The Holy Catholic Church has not been indifferent to gold either..." His features became serious, but Angeline knew his tongue was in his cheek, and she laughed, then turned to her father, an inquiring look on her face.

He scratched his head, and looked at Alistair. "There's something in the back of my mind – an experiment in the early spring of 2005 – in the Brookhaven lab in New York, I think – something about particle acceleration."

Alistair nodded. "Got it – aye, I remember it, but I never related it to Angeline's work. They created a collision in the particle accelerator, using gold atoms, at close to the speed of light. It fractured the gold nuclei into the basic building blocks of matter – gluons and quarks. But there was an unexpected outcome -theoretically, at least, they created a mercifully short-lived black hole." He looked at the monk. "Mateo, now that the core and key have been returned to the monastery..."

Red cut across Alistair's words. "Just hold it right there," he said, "I haven't returned them just yet – there are conditions on the return, remember?"

Angeline looked at him in astonishment. "How can you think of imposing conditions in the situation we are in? In any case, how are you going to stop Mateo, or anyone else for that matter, removing the core and the key? Are you going to run down the cliff path with your trunk on your back?"

"She has a point, Red," said Alistair. Everyone was looking at him. Lonnen made a dismissive gesture.

"You guys must have missed what I said in the chapter house – if anyone tries to remove this without my agreement, the core will be destroyed. Of course, they can have the key," he said, waving it about in his hand, "but it won't be much use to them. In any case, it won't come to that – the Abbot is an honourable man – if he can't meet my conditions, he will let me leave, and will require the estimable Mateo to assist me with my luggage," he said. "Ain't that so, Brother Anselmo?"

They all followed his gaze to the passageway, from which the Abbot was just emerging.

"That is indeed so, Señor Lonnen - *buenos días, señores, señorita*," he replied, smiling at the group. "I see that Mateo has brought the objects downstairs – may I look, Señor Lonnen?"

Red was discomfited by the Abbot's arrival in the middle of his little speech, but he managed to grin, and waved to the open trunk on the floor. The old man came over and looked down at the core and glanced at the key in the American's hand. He crossed himself, bent his head briefly, and then looked up again.

"May Brother Mateo be permitted to place the core on the table, señor?" he said softly. Red nodded his assent. The young monk bent his legs, crouched in front of the trunk, grasped the sides of the wooden box and started to lift it. There was a splintering sound as the ancient box disintegrated inside the trunk.

"It's OK, Mateo," said Red reassuringly, "that had to happen sometime – the old wood was rotten."

Mateo picked out the fragments of the box and laid them on the floor. He bent his legs again, grasped the core by its handles, lifted it and laid it on the table, all in one smooth, apparently effortless motion. Something was bothering Alistair, and Santiago was also looking anxious. Alistair spoke before Santiago could utter what was on both of their minds.

"Red, your anti-theft device – I can only hope that you didn't interfere with the integrity of the core to fit it. What is it? An explosive device?"

The Abbot spoke before Lonnen could reply. "Señor Lonnen would have no need to compromise the integrity of the core – there is a rectangular cavity on the base that could hold a small device without penetrating the body."

Lonnen looked surprised. "You're spot on, Brother Anselmo – but how could you know that? You have never seen the object before now..."

"As Mateo will confirm, we have a very detailed knowledge of the core and the key from our records, and it has been depicted from every angle in our illustrated manuscripts. The core is also depicted on the body of the main device – the regulator," the Abbot said. He turned to Alistair. "I thank you for your concern, Alistair, but have no fear. The core has its own defence mechanisms..." He looked again at Red. "I regret that you have put yourself to a great deal of trouble for nothing, señor – your device will be ineffective."

"I don't think you would want me to demonstrate that you are wrong," said Red uneasily, a note of bluster in his voice.

"Please activate your device if you doubt my words," said the Abbot amiably, to the consternation of the others.

"Do you think I'm bluffing, Abbot?" Red responded, his voice harsh, his eyes flicking to his daughter, who was staring at him with a mixture of horror and contempt.

"No, señor, you are simply mistaken. Even if you were right, we would have what I believe negotiators call a *Mexican standoff*. However, you have no need to take such a position. You have restored the core and the key to us and for that we are indebted to you, and bound in honour to meet any condition that you stipulate. It is surely evident to you that if we do not resolve the instability of *El Corazón*, none of this matters anyway."

"I have never thought of my father as a fool," said Angeline angrily to the Abbot, "but on this showing, he is a dangerous fool."

Red's face was pale and drawn – he was unable to meet his daughter's eyes, and the contempt of the others was evident from their expressions.

The Abbot came over to Angeline, who was near to tears, and took both of her hands. "Your father is not a fool, Angeline – he is a man on a painful and difficult journey towards fulfilling his true destiny, towards spiritual self-knowledge. Do not judge him - help him to open his heart, as only you can."

The old man released one of her hands, and held his hand out towards Red Lonnen. Her father slowly moved across to his daughter and took her hand tentatively. She was blinded by tears, and returned his grasp passively, her arm limp. The Abbot released her other hand, and then she was in her father's arms, sobbing uncontrollably. He drew her gently away from the group, murmuring softly. The others turned away from the intensely private moment: Paul was in a state of confusion and high emotion. Angeline called to him, and as he went across to join them, Red turned his head towards him, still holding Angeline against his chest, and held out his hand. In it was a small rectangular trigger device. "Be careful with it, Paul - Alistair will know how to disable it, and remove the gizmo in the base of the core," he said. "That was the last gasp of the old Lonnen…"

Paul took the device and acknowledged with a nod, and put his hand gently on Angeline's back. She turned her tear-stained face to him, managed a weak smile, and pulled away slowly from her father, placing her hand on his cheek. They looked at each other for a moment, and then Paul went across to the table.

Mateo was enlisted to turn the core on to its side: something was embedded in the cavity in the base. Alistair took the trigger device from Paul, looked at it briefly, then levered it open with a fingernail and, without hesitation, broke a slender wire. He then removed the putty-like substance from the cavity, with a detonator, a tiny electronic board and the battery embedded in it, and handed it to Santiago, who moved well away from the group and made the device safe. Mateo tilted the core and laid it flat on the table again.

"Thank you, señores," said the Abbot, "It could not have harmed the core, but perhaps it would have been dangerous for those close to it. Señor Lonnen, I am glad of your change of heart."

"I guess I'm the bad boy of the class," said Red. "Judge me as you find from here on in." He handed the figurine to the Abbot. The old monk kissed it reverently as if it were a crucifix, then handed it to Mateo. Paul had his arm round Angeline's shoulders; she had recovered her composure, and was looking at the core.

"Brother Anselmo," she said, "where is the regulator device? Is your knowledge of it purely theoretical, from ancient records, or have you actually seen it – do you know its location?" She touched the black and golden surface of the core in fascination. All eyes turned to the Abbot.

"No human being has entered the chamber of the regulator and survived. Those who removed the core and the key centuries ago ultimately paid for their transgression with their lives. The Magus of Moridura and I have detailed knowledge of its location - it has always been so - although another has a deep knowledge of it, yet is unaware of this knowledge," replied the old man.

Santiago, for once, lost his customary restraint. "Are you telling us that Don Ferdinand has detailed knowledge of the location of the regulator?"

The Abbot smiled. "Ferdinand is not the Magus – he is the Magus Elect. He will become Magus, if he is deemed worthy, when the Ceremony and the event take place two days from now. When *El Trono* splits, he will be elevated to Magus."

Alistair sucked in a long breath then blew out his cheeks. "I must ask, Brother Anselmo – who is the Magus?"

"That is not information that I may give to you, Alistair – I regret the discourtesy, but I am constrained by tradition.

Only members of the Ancient Order of Moridura who witness the Ceremony know the name of the Magus. Monks who are not members of the Ancient Order do not know his identity: members of the *hermandad* below a certain level do not know his name."

Paul looked at Alistair for permission to speak, then at the Abbot. "Is there an inconsistency here, Brother Anselmo?" he asked cautiously. "All of us here know now that Ferdinand is the Magus Elect. If he is elevated, we, as outsiders, will then know the identity of the new Magus of Moridura."

"Yes, I have confirmed the identity of the Magus Elect," replied the Abbot, "but that has been an unavoidable result of the circumstances in which we have found ourselves. We urgently need your help – we are bound together by what lies ahead."

"I must raise another question," said Alistair. "We believe that there is something contained in the space below the staircases and between the passageways in this building. Last night we saw a tiny, faint strip of blue-green light under the boards of the corridor between the bedrooms. Is that the location of the regulator?"

The Abbot glanced at Mateo, and then made a small motion with his hand, heaving a sigh. "I will show you what lies behind the panelling: it is not the regulator, but something that relates to it in a fundamental way. The structure you are now in was built around a more ancient structure, the Portal, and that structure was built around something that has been part of *La Copa* throughout its history."

The old man looked infinitely weary and strangely vulnerable. "Forgive me," he said weakly, "I must sit down for a moment…"

Mateo sprang forward solicitously, and helped him to a chair. The Abbot was very pale, and his skin looked almost translucent, his eyes cloudy. "Please – if you would all sit, I would feel less conspicuous," he said, smiling wanly. "At my age, these moments come without warning…"

They all sat down at the table, Mateo on the Abbot's right. The young monk had a look of deep concern on his face. Brother Anselmo had always been the central figure in his life, and this reminder of the Abbot's frailty made him fear the loss that he knew was inevitable one day.

The old monk rallied a little; two spots of colour came to his cheeks and his eyes brightened. "There," he said, straightening up in the chair, "the moment has passed – God will give me the strength to make my contribution. Angeline, only you can offer the insights we need to stabilise *La Copa*'s heartbeat. Your discovery captured and modified the gravity wave – modulated it to create a partial and localised anti-gravity effect."

"Yes" replied Angeline, "but I cannot wholly explain my discovery or my device, or at least, I haven't been able to until now. There were serendipitous elements in what I achieved – the rock fragment, the gold. The connection to *La Copa* is now all too evident, and the fact that the core incorporates both gold and rock appears, empirically, to confirm this." She looked at her father and Alistair for support. Red nodded to Alistair to speak.

"Whatever Angeline is capable of doing can only be done if she has access to a well-equipped laboratory. No such facilities exist in the monastery, not even electric power. She must relocate the core in the regulator device, and utilise the key, whatever its function may be. But if this is extra-terrestrial technology of great antiquity, it will be alien, and, assuming it still functions, beyond the capacity of our species to understand and operate. Red, do you agree with that analysis?"

"In its entirety," said Lonnen emphatically, "with the additional problem that we don't know the location of the regulator unless you tell us, and no living being has entered its chamber and survived."

The Abbot lifted his head. "It is located beneath *El Trono* and above *El Corazón*…"

"Beneath the Throne and above the Heart," said Angeline softly, almost unaware that she had spoken aloud. Manuel was listening with rapt attention, proud that such secrets were being revealed in front of him, things that only the most exalted had known. The Abbot noticed his expression, and he paused, a thoughtful look on his face. He motioned to Mateo, who came across and bent to permit the old man to whisper something in his ear. The big monk then went across to Manuel and drew him to his feet and across to the Abbot.

"My friends, do you recognise the concept and practice of a battlefield commission in wartime?" Brother Anselmo asked, rising slowly from his seat.

Alistair nodded, puzzled. "Yes, I do - an enlisted man or a non-commissioned officer is promoted to commissioned rank on the spot without the usual bureaucratic formalities. It is warranted by the exigencies of battle…"

Brother Anselmo smiled. "Manuel was promised membership of the *hermandad* by Ferdinand in return for access to his father's diaries. I am authorised, as Abbot of Moridura, in situations that threaten the very existence of the Ancient Order, to grant that membership, and more, without the presence of the Grand Council or the members of the Chapter of the monastery. This is such a moment." He turned to the white-faced Manuel, who was supported by the mighty arm of Mateo.

"Manuel Ortega," he said solemnly, raising his right arm above his head, "in recognition of the services that you and your forefathers have rendered to the monastery of Moridura and the Ancient Order, I propose you for the rank of Brother Elect in the *hermandad* of Moridura, and for the status of *confrater* to the monastery and the Moriduran Brothers. Brother Mateo stands as your seconder. I offer the rank and status to you now: if you accept, you are bound for life to both organisations. Manuel Ortega, do you understand your obligations?"

Manuel stood bolt upright, his face shining. "I do," he said simply.

"Do you accept the rank and status conferred upon you?" asked the Abbot.

"I accept, Brother Anselmo," Manuel replied, his tone firm, yet ecstatic.

Mateo turned to Manuel and enfolded him in his arms, as a parent would a child, then the Abbot came across and embraced him. After a moment, the others spontaneously clapped their hands, and then gathered round him, shaking his hand and congratulating him.

"Well, my wee pal," laughed Alistair, "now you don't need my money, only my friendship!"

Manuel looked at him reproachfully. "Your friendship was always enough, Señor Alistair." Then he smiled. "But your money will still be welcome – you must not be too proud to offer it, for I am not too proud to accept it."

Alistair guffawed, and slapped him on the back. "With your new status and influence, you'll be a good investment, Manuel," he grinned.

"Perhaps we may all sit down again," said the Abbot, moving back to his seat and motioning the others to do likewise. "Alistair, you know the value of a summary given by an objective observer at times like these. My feeling is that Señor Paul and Señor Santiago have sufficient objectivity to contribute a perspective that will be valuable to myself and to the three scientists among us – yourself, Señor Lonnen and Doctora Blade. Do you agree? Señor Lonnen? Angeline?"

They were in obvious agreement. Paul glanced at Santiago, who motioned to him to speak first.

"We have today and tomorrow – the following day will be taken up by the event and the Ceremony," he said. "There are two aspects that we must consider – the work that Angeline must do to stabilise the heartbeat of *La Copa*, and the actions that Ferdinand and the members of the *hermandad* may engage in that could threaten her work.

"Brother Anselmo, I believe that to be of assistance to you, Angeline will have to place herself in danger – great danger – and although this concerns you deeply, you believe you have no choice in the matter. Nevertheless, you recognise that she must accept this challenge of her own free will, and you will resist any attempts to compel her to cooperate. It is therefore vital that she is made immediately aware of the resources available to her, and the nature of the risks involved in utilising those resources." Paul stopped speaking and waited for the Abbot's response.

"Your analysis is accurate in every respect, Paul. Thank you." The old man turned his gaze to Santiago. "Señor?" he said politely.

"You have returned our weapons, Brother Anselmo. That leads me to believe that you fear more violence from the *hermandad*. It also means that, however reluctantly, you accept that the threat, or even the actual use of deadly force by us might be justified in ensuring that Angeline can complete her work. Your battlefield commission of Manuel means that he must urgently assist in interpreting his father's diaries, and you want him to exercise influence with the moderate, probably local, members of the *hermandad*. That is my analysis," said Santiago.

"It is accurate in all respects. Thank you," said the Abbot. "Angeline, I must now explain to you the dangers that you will face if you undertake this task. The regulator is located deep in the rock of *La Copa*, beneath *El Trono* above the point where it enters the area of the heart - *El Corazón*. We do not know the nature of the power source for the regulator, but we do know its location. We know that there is radiation in the area of *El Trono*, of a kind that can damage human tissue – an unidentified type of radiation. We believe it to be the kind of diffuse, high-energy radiation that pervades space, sometimes called the cosmic X-ray background, but highly concentrated at this location. Some of this radiation pervades the area around *El Trono*, but it is weak in that location: only exposure over many years is dangerous to health."

"Will Magus lead me to the chamber of the regulator?" asked Angeline.

"The Magus is unable to lead you to the regulator, Angeline," responded the Abbot, "but someone else will take you there."

"Who?" Angeline's question was put forcefully, and it was clear to everyone that she would not accept an equivocal answer.

"Brother Mateo will take you to a place where your question will be answered," replied the Abbot, "and we will accompany you to that place."

Angeline felt a sense of relief, and turned to Mateo. For once, the young monk was nonplussed – he was looking at the Abbot in astonishment. "But Brother Anselmo – forgive me – I do not know who can answer this question, nor do I know of the place to which you refer…"

Brother Anselmo looked at him with great affection and sadness in his eyes. "My beloved brother, trust in God. You will find the answer within yourself when the moment comes," he said gently.

Mateo bowed his head, and his normal composure returned. "It will be a great privilege to assist you, Doctora Blade," he said simply. "May God guide us both."

Something was bothering Angeline; she was looking down at the table in front of her, her brow furrowed. She felt Paul's hand on her wrist, and she felt that special empathy that had been present since their first meeting – an almost telepathic understanding.

"Say it for me, Paul – please…"

Paul gripped her wrist tightly and looked at his friends, then addressed himself to Brother Anselmo. "*La Copa* has a heart - *El Corazón*– and a heartbeat. *El Corazón* is monitored by the device you call the regulator. The question in

Angeline's mind is this – does *La Copa* have a brain – or is the regulator its brain?"

The Abbot smiled at Paul and Angeline. "You are indeed fortunate to have found each other. Yes, *La Copa* has what you call a brain. The regulator and its core are, to use the jargon of our earthly science, pre-programmed slave devices: the core links the regulator to an active, central control point. An inexact, imperfect analogy can be made with your radio telescope in Scotland – the regulator and the core are akin to the electronics within the dish aerial, and the device that lifts the matchbox. But it takes your active involvement, using the equipment in the workshop, to modulate the gravitational wave. In *La Copa*, the matchbox has been lifted on the last instruction given to it centuries ago, but is now quivering unsteadily between collapsing into inertia, or flying out of the device into space. Regrettably, our matchbox has infinitely greater destructive power if the process fails."

Alistair whistled appreciatively. "I could almost believe that you have visited my home, Brother Anselmo – your knowledge of Angeline's rig is impressive!"

The Abbot inclined his head. "It is all there in Angeline's paper – she described it with great clarity."

Paul's mind was racing – he turned to Angeline, then back to the old monk. "But there are two factors at work in Angeline's – Alistair's – laboratory; the dish movement control and Angeline herself."

"And those same elements will be present when we attempt to stabilise *La Copa* – the brain of *La Copa* and Doctora Blade," said the Abbot.

Alistair felt a sudden sense of unease. The Abbot was leading them inexorably towards something that in some way threatened Angeline. He could see that her father shared his fear – Red Lonnen's body language signalled a growing concern for his daughter's safety. Angeline was very calm and composed; she realised that Alistair, her father and Paul were on the brink of some kind of defensive argument on her behalf. She decided to forestall it.

"I control my dish aerial and electronic devices in Ardmurran by manually operating switches, but the technology that controls the heartbeat of *La Copa* had moved far beyond such crude methods aeons ago, had it not, Brother Anselmo?" She drew a deep breath. "My brain and the brain of *La Copa* will have to somehow be synchronised – to meld – to achieve the necessary control." She held up both hands to silence to chorus of incoherent protest that was rising from her father and friends. "I am willing to do this, Brother Anselmo, if it is the only way," she said.

"My child, it *is* the only way," said the Abbot gently.

"Angeline – no!" said Red hoarsely, rising to his feet. Alistair and Paul had both turned to her and were shaking their heads in emphatic negatives.

"The decision is mine, and mine alone," said Angeline quietly, "and I place my complete trust in you, Brother Anselmo, and in Brother Mateo. I have one request – it is not a condition, it can't be that. Where feasible, I want my father, Alistair and Paul to be with me. I would ask for Santiago also, but I realise that he will need to protect us in other ways."

"Thank you, Angeline, for your trust in Mateo and myself – your courage is exemplary. Those whom you choose can be with you when the fusion with the brain occurs, but when you go to the regulator to replace the core, only the person who leads you there can be with you." The Abbot observed the concern in everyone's eyes.

"My friends," he said, "there is no other way - the alternative is the extinction of all that we know and love. The time has come to demonstrate to you that my words have not been the superstitious utterances of a credulous old monk. But first we must return the core to the trunk..." He motioned to Mateo, who lifted the golden object from the table, with the key lying on top of it, and placed it back in the trunk, on top of the wooden base that was all that was left of the box.

The Abbot stood up and motioned towards the left-hand passageway. "Brother Mateo, please carry the trunk to the entrance to the passageway and place it on the floor."

He did so, and then they followed the old monk to the mouth of the passageway, walking around the trunk on the floor, expecting him to continue along the passage, but he stopped just past the staircase, causing them to bunch up behind him. Mateo was at the rear of the group, reluctant to abandon the trunk, but the Abbot called him forward to where he was standing. The morning sun was still flooding along the passage from the great windows on the end wall, but there was a section just behind the staircase where the light did not penetrate.

"Mateo," said the Abbot softly, "reach up and you will feel a small protuberance – God will guide your hand…" The big monk looked at his superior in bewilderment, but groped upwards. After a moment, he turned awkwardly, his hand still out of sight.

"I can feel something that feels like a small wooden wheel, Brother Anselmo," he said.

"Grip it firmly and turn it clockwise, Mateo," responded the Abbot, "but not too hard! Your great strength could break it." There was a brief pause, then an audible click. This was followed by a creaking sound, then those behind the Abbot felt a draught of very cold air from the passageway that brought with it a musty smell, and another, indefinable odour. The Abbot pointed towards the right hand side of the passage and they followed him to the point indicated: there was now a gap in the heavy panelling, one and a half metres high and no more than five centimetres wide. The cold air was coming from this aperture: behind the opening was total darkness.

"Place the fingers of both hands in the gap and pull it hard to your left, Mateo; do not release the pressure until you hear a click..." said the Abbot. Mateo stood in front of the partition, to the left of the gap, forced his fingers into the gap and as he pulled, a section of the partition slid soundlessly to the left for two metres until the sound of something clicking into place was heard. The blackness within was impenetrable, and the chill air swirled around the group in the passage, making them shiver.

"The mechanism is operated by catches and a heavy counter weight – opening it raises the weight, and demands considerable force. It is designed to close very rapidly after entry, as the weight descends. This space was used as a hiding place and refuge in ancient times," said Brother Anselmo. "Before we enter, I ask you to prepare yourself for what you are about to see. It will call in question many of the certainties of your life and your scientific training."

He looked at them all for a moment, his old eyes penetrating, yet compassionate. "God will protect us. For those of you who are of a more secular disposition, Mateo will protect you," he added.

"Do we need candles – our flashlights? It looks kinda dark in there," said Red peering at the inky black aperture.

"No," replied the Abbot, "there will be light. Brother Mateo will enter first, taking the trunk with him then we will follow..."

The big monk went back for the trunk, carried it to the opening and placed it on the floor: he bent his head and upper body, and went through the opening. Around his body, a blue-green light appeared, silhouetting him, then he vanished inside, and the opening was now a square of cold, eerie light against the dark panelling. Those in the passage could not see inside because the top of the opening was just below eye level. Mateo reappeared just inside the gap, and reached forward to grasp the trunk and dragged it towards him. It tilted slightly forward and down, then went through. He lifted the trunk fully inside, then the Abbot bent and slipped through silently and easily, and the others were left staring at the aperture and then at each other.

"I'll go next and make sure you all get through OK," said Santiago briskly, and promptly ducked through, then turned and held out his hand. Alistair went next, then Paul, Angeline and finally Manuel. There was an appreciable step down as they went through – the floor on the other side was lower than the passageway.

They were standing on the black rock of *La Copa*, in a space of about fifteen metres by ten metres, enclosed by the rear of the dark wood panelling of the guest wing, with the underside of the floor of the bedroom level forming a ceiling about four metres above their heads. A blue-green light faintly illuminated the area. The trunk was standing on the black surface just to the right of the opening. In the centre of the space was a stone building, about five metres long by three metres wide, simply constructed of large stone blocks, with an arched stone roof. Some loose stone blocks lay against the base of the structure. The roof was just below the underside of the wooden floor above it. It was windowless on the side that they could see, but at the gable nearest to them was an open doorway about two metres high by a metre wide, and the faint light that was around them came from within it.

They grouped around the Abbot and Brother Mateo, feeling a bit like tourists with their guides on a coach tour of historical sites. "How old is this building, Brother Anselmo?" asked Angeline.

"We don't know exactly, but it has been here since before the monastery was built. It was constructed by the Ancient Order, before the schism occurred. It is depicted in the earliest records we have of the Order, as Mateo will confirm. He has no memory of this place at this time." He smiled at Mateo, who was staring in fascination at the stone building. Paul glanced at Alistair, who gave an almost imperceptible nod: both of them had noted the unusual phraseology used by the old man.

"What is in it?" asked Red. "What is its significance? It looks like a mausoleum."

Mateo spoke softly, his eyes never leaving the stone doorway. "There is nothing in it, señor, it simply covers a stairway – its significance lies in the place to which the stairway leads."

Brother Anselmo whispered something to Mateo, who turned a small wheel at the right of the opening: the partition slid shut almost instantaneously as the invisible counterweight silently descended.

Chapter Eighteen

Ferdinand stood in the foyer of the hotel in Mérida, impatiently tapping his hand against his thigh. He disliked being kept waiting - Jaime had been upstairs with the Americans for more than fifteen minutes, having insisted that he had to speak to them before introducing him. Calming Jaime down during the drive to Mérida had been difficult and tiresome. How had he come to allow himself to be involved with such a contemptible creature?

The answer was, of course, that he had no choice – the man's political clout and his contacts with American, British and Spanish defence contractors made such a liaison inevitable. And now he had to allow this man to translate his objectives to the Americans, a man ignorant of elementary negotiating practices, possessed only of the primitive populist skills to sway ignorant voters. His reverie was broken by the desk clerk calling to him.

"You may go up now, señor," he said in a faintly patronising tone. Ferdinand looked directly at him, and the half-sneer was wiped abruptly from the clerk's lips as he belatedly recognised the man he was dealing with. "Señor, my most sincere apologies... May I escort you to the suite?" he stammered. Ferdinand waved dismissively and went across to the elevator. The doors opened and he pushed imperiously past those leaving, entered and pressed the button for the penthouse suites. On the way up, he reflected on the fact that he had not spent enough time in the capital in recent months, had not made his presence felt in all the focal points of the city.

The elevator doors opened and he walked the few steps to suite four and stood in front of the door. He did not knock, but simply waited. There was a flicker at the peephole on the door, then it opened, and he went in. The man inside moved to frisk him, and found both his wrists pinned by Ferdinand's steely grip. Before the situation could develop, a voice came from across the room. "OK, Nico, no need for that – Don Ferdinand is our honoured guest."

The speaker was a man in his fifties, of medium height and slight build, with thinning grey hair. He was standing near the window with Jaime and three taller men, heavy-set and in their late thirties or early forties. He strode across to Ferdinand and shook his hand, then led him over to the group at the window.

"I'm Pick Carter, President of Xalatera Industries Incorporated. Pick is a nickname – I used to play guitar in my college days, and it stuck! My colleagues are from three branches of the United States military – they must remain incognito, as you will appreciate. With your permission, we'll keep it to first names – OK? Gentlemen, may I introduce you to Don Ferdinand de Moridanza?"

Each of them shook his hand, introducing themselves as Larry, Jim and Peter. Don Ferdinand smiled inwardly at their attempt at anonymity – he had thoroughly researched the identities of the senior officers who might be at the meeting, including photographs. He recognised all three – they were senior ranking officers from each of the services.

"Let's sit down and discuss what you have to offer us, Ferdinand," said Carter, "Jaime here has already outlined the possibilities. You will forgive our friends if they need a lot of convincing – there are no prizes for getting things wrong." They all sat down and looked at him expectantly. Jaime made as though to speak, but was silenced by a look from Ferdinand, who spoke first.

"We are dealing with a branch of scientific research where theory and speculation dominate and empirical evidence is slender, one that attracts charlatans, perpetual motion cranks and their like. The Blade Effect, however, is of a different nature entirely. This is the first true breakthrough in the detection, modulation and control of gravitational waves, experimentally verified, albeit on a small scale."

"The rumours about Dr. Blade's paper have leaked into the scientific community – it is regarded with derision by most of his colleagues." The speaker was the man calling himself Peter - Ferdinand knew him to be a senior officer in the United States Air Force.

"They are wrong about the conclusions of the paper – and you are wrong about the sex of the author. Dr. Blade is a woman – Doctor Angeline Blade," he replied bluntly.

Carter laughed. "Yeah, I knew that – you military guys are all sexist when it comes right down to it, Peter."

The other two smiled, and Peter tilted his head and grinned in rueful acknowledgment. "I stand corrected, Ferdinand. As I understand it, you are the number one guy in an organisation that carries a lot of weight in the region – and beyond…"

"Not number one – you might say that I am the Chief Executive, accountable to a chairman."

"It's an all-male organisation, Ferdinand – so Jaime tells me. I guess the military haven't got a monopoly on sexism," said the man called Jim.

"That is our tradition," replied Ferdinand stiffly.

"Our Army traditions are under attack," said Jim, "Maybe yours are too?"

"Only from the world of technology," said Ferdinand, "but we intend to embrace our attackers as friends – we must adapt to inexorable realities. That is why I am here."

The third man – Larry – had been listening to the exchange, and he now walked forward and looked directly at Ferdinand. "What do you believe you have to offer us, sir?' he said quietly. Some old-fashioned and welcome formality from the U.S. Navy, thought Ferdinand.

"We have Doctor Blade and her associates under our protection at the moment; her discovery is wholly dependent on our unique knowledge, and a unique substance, one that only exists in *La Copa de Moridura* – a place in the heartland of our organisation. In combination, Doctor Blade and my organisation can deliver control over the force of gravity on a scale that will revolutionise every aspect of life," he said, gauging the effect of his words upon his audience.

The three officers looked at each other, then Larry spoke. "We understand that the CEOs of Ardmurran International Electronics and the Lonnen corporation are in the Moriduran monastery at this time. Are they the associates of Doctor Blade that you referred to?" He turned to Carter. "And if so, why should we deal through your organisation, Pick? We have long-standing relationships and contracts with both of these corporations: if they have the woman's confidence, where do you come into the equation?"

"I will answer that," said Ferdinand, "if Señor Carter will permit me. I have good reason to believe that Mackinnon will resist dealing with the defence industry on this – he is a maverick, and on occasion follows his sentimental beliefs and prejudices rather than sound business practice. Lonnen's position is more complex – under normal circumstances he would be the man to deal with, but there is another factor at work - his relationship with Angeline Blade. He is her father."

Carter looked at him in astonishment. "Is he, by God! Why has he never acknowledged her as his daughter?"

"She was born out of wedlock: she is an employee of his company, but for most of her life she was unaware that he was her father. Now that they both know, their relationship is strained to breaking point," replied Ferdinand.

Larry shook his head and glanced at his colleagues. "It still seems to me that this is a powerful reason for dealing with Lonnen: however strained their relationship is, or was, they'll get over it, surely? Blood is thicker than water…"

Ferdinand shook his head. "Doctor Blade will be opposed to using her discovery for military purposes – she could even put her discovery into the public domain by releasing her knowledge to the world scientific community. Consider your history, gentlemen. What if the scientists on the Manhattan Project had done that over sixty years ago?"

"Hell, we were in a World War back then!" Peter exclaimed, "and those guys were patriots of the highest order..."

Carter took his opportunity. "This gravity thing is maybe bigger than nuclear energy. We're in a world war now, only the combatants aren't as clearly defined. Do you want to see a terrorist device levitating over the Pentagon?"

The Navy man, Larry, picked up on his colleagues point. "Pick, how do you know that these guys can deliver?" He gestured to Ferdinand. 'No offence, Ferdinand, but we know Pick – you and Jaime here, well, I guess we don't know you well enough..."

"I understand your position – you only have my word for what my organisation can achieve. Let me put it as directly as I can," responded Ferdinand. "On the day after tomorrow, I will be confirmed in the highest office of our organisation. I will become the superior not only of the *hermandad*, but also of the Moriduran Brothers, the religious order that owns *La Copa de Moridura*, including the undisputed mineral rights to the unique substance required by Doctor Blade's device. At that ceremony, which is of great antiquity, there will be a demonstration of our ancient power over the force of gravity. I can arrange for you to observe this, and our total control over Blade, her father and Alistair Mackinnon. You may be present, incognito, dressed in the robes of our brotherhood. By the end of the Ceremony, you will be left in no doubt of my capacity to deliver what I promise." He paused and looked at each of the men in turn.

"If you reject this offer, there are representative of other defence establishments ready to fill your places. There will be no negotiation on this – it is what I believe an American negotiator would call *a last offer first* proposal. Jaime will make the necessary arrangements if you wish to attend the ceremony. I bid you good day, gentlemen."

He turned on his heel and walked towards the door. As he placed his right hand on the handle, Carter called out to him to hold on, and he felt the hand of the bodyguard at the door on his right arm. He half-turned and his open left hand moved like a striking snake, the hard outer edge striking the man in the centre of his throat. The bodyguard fell back with a choking cry, and Ferdinand opened the door and left the room. By the time those inside had moved to help their stricken colleague, Ferdinand was on his way down in the elevator.

He left the hotel and called a taxi, directing the driver to a church in a run-down district of the city. Entering the old building, he found a row of four confessional boxes, each accommodating a priest in the central compartment, with a penitent in each of the cubicles on either side of it. A few poorly dressed people were sitting patiently on the pews at three of them, but the fourth pew was empty, and the door to the left hand cubicle was open, indicating that it was vacant. He moved swiftly into the cubicle before one of those on the other pews could move across, and knelt down. The priest's voice giving absolution came faintly through the closed grill, and then he heard the door of the far cubicle opening and closing. After a moment, the sliding panel moved aside, and he could see the priest's face faintly through the apertures in the grille.

"Bless me, Father, for I have sinned," he whispered, "it has been three months since my last confession." When he recounted his complicity in the death of a man, he saw the priest's head jerk into alertness. He continued with a few venial sins, made his act of contrition, received absolution and his penance, and then he left swiftly, a half-smile on his face. Sometimes it was beneficial not to be too well known in the city, he thought as he went into the street and hailed another taxi. As he sank back in the seat, his mobile phone rang. "Yes?" he said.

"Pick Carter here. Hey, Ferdinand, was that really necessary with Nico? The guy was doing his job – now he needs emergency treatment…"

"No man puts his hand on me with impunity."

"Yeah, but I had to settle these guys down – they were all for going after you. Anyway, it's over. We have agreed to go to your ceremony the day after tomorrow. Where do we go from here?"

"Jaime will arrange for you to be picked up at dawn from the hotel. Facilities on the vehicle will permit you to change into the robes of the Order: you will be driven to Moridanza, and you will be able to discuss anything relevant en route with a senior member of my staff," replied Ferdinand.

"If Nico has recovered, they will want to bring him," said Carter plaintively.

"No – absolutely not – there is no place for him at our ceremony," said Ferdinand flatly, "Goodbye." He ended the call. The mobile rang again, and he switched it off.

Chapter Nineteen

As they walked towards the door of the little stone building within the panelling of the guest wing, the enclosed space and the eerie light reminded Alistair of the fossil grove on the west side of Glasgow - the uncovered fossilised tree and root formations from a primeval forest, sitting incongruously in a pleasant city park. As a boy, it had been one of his magical things and places, together with the jawbones of the whale in the People's Palace, and the giant statue of Osiris in the Art Galleries. He felt a great surge of gratitude that he was now experiencing more magical moments at threescore and ten.

At the door of the structure, Brother Anselmo stopped and faced them. "I must caution you to take great care in descending the stairs – the risers are deep and there is no handrail. Mateo and I will go first – you may wish to observe and emulate our mode of descent." He indicated to the young monk that he should go through the doorway: Mateo had to duck a little as he entered, followed by the Abbot. Alistair entered next and was followed by Santiago, Paul, Angeline and lastly, Manuel.

The inside of the structure was completely empty and without ornamentation. The floor was the bare, black rock of *La Copa*. Just in front of where they stood was a rectangular hole in the floor, about two metres wide and two-and-a-half metres long, with sharply defined edges: The strange light emanated from it more intensely. They could see a stairway going down, although the total blackness of the rock made it difficult to distinguish its features. The Abbot stopped at the opening, on the left, and held out his right hand to Mateo. They began their cautious descent, and Alistair saw the difficulty – the steps were indeed deep, and for the first few steps there was nothing to brace themselves against. The others clustered behind him to observe the two monks. Their free arms were extended as they slowly descended: they gripped the floor at each side when they were low enough, then braced themselves with the palms of their hands against the walls.

"OK – has everybody got it? It makes good sense. Paul, you go next with Angeline. Santiago, you partner Manuel, and I'll follow with Red," said Alistair. He watched Paul and Angeline tentatively begin their descent, then Santiago and Manuel.

Red extended his left hand. "Bet you didn't anticipate holding hands with me," he laughed, as Alistair gripped his hand and they started down. The stair risers were as deep as the Abbot had indicated, and the pairings quickly developed a strange, balletic synchronisation. The combination of the blackness of the walls and stairs and the blue-green light was disorientating for all of them. Angeline's voice floated back up.

"If we fall, we'll all land on Brother Mateo, so we'll be alright!"

As his eyes became accustomed to the surroundings, Alistair saw that the steps were perfectly smooth and even, but the walls had a rough texture: this somehow relieved their blackness, and it also gave a reasonable grip to the flat of his hand. "Notice anything about the steps, Red?" he asked.

'They weren't hacked out by primitive people, that's for sure – they've been formed by sophisticated tools or processes. They could almost be laser-cut – and the walls – they're rough-textured but in an absolutely consistent pattern, like a textured wallpaper. It makes no sense – no damn sense at all…" he replied.

"Unless you buy the Abbot's version of history," whispered Alistair conspiratorially.

"I don't – yet…" said Red, "but maybe I will when I see what's at the bottom of these steps. Have you been counting?"

"Aye, as a matter of fact, I have – I've been a compulsive counter since I was a wee boy. I can count and talk at the same time without losing it. We're at forty: on a nine-inch riser we've descended thirty feet in forty steps." replied Alistair.

"How high is the rock perimeter of *La Copa*?" asked Lonnen.

'From the plain to the cliff top, about fifty metres, say a hundred and sixty feet or so. I hope we don't have to go that far down – or even deeper – the centre of the Cup is below the level of the plain."

"I'm glad you still mix your metric and imperial – unusual in a scientist… How in hell is the place ventilated?" asked Lonnen, "Surely whoever cut this hole didn't rely on air from above?"

"I hope not," said Alistair, then a thought struck him. "If it was an extra-terrestrial, the entity may not have been an air breather."

"Now you've really given me a boost! Are you Scots always this pessimistic?"

"It's our weather – it pays to be a pessimist. You're never disappointed, but sometimes pleasantly surprised," laughed Alistair, "- seventy-nine, eighty…"

"Why in hell couldn't the spaceman have built an elevator?" grumbled Lonnen.

They fell silent as they continued the descent. The light was becoming more intense, and as Alistair reached one hundred, he could see that they were close to the bottom. The Abbot and Mateo were on a flat surface and moving forward. He heard gasps of astonishment as Paul and Angeline, and then Santiago and Manuel reached the bottom steps. Alistair released Red's hand and they both stepped forward. The eight of them were standing in a chamber of about three metres square by four metres high, with floor and walls of the same black rock as the stairway. Facing them, set into the rock, was a rectangular panel, two and a half metres high by a metre wide, made of a brilliant blue-green material that appeared to be metallic. It was absolutely smooth, with a matt, non-reflective surface.

Brother Anselmo turned to the group. "Please prepare yourselves for what lies on the other side – there is no physical danger, you will not be harmed, but your most cherished beliefs and concepts will be challenged by what you will experience." He looked at Mateo. "Trust in God, my beloved brother – stand directly in front of the door, and place both palms on its surface and wait…"

Alistair saw that Mateo was uncharacteristically apprehensive, but he lifted his great arms and placed his hands flat upon the surface. What followed sent a chill through those grouped behind him. A terrible voice, utterly alien in timbre, reverberated in the confined space as it uttered a single word - *Mateo*. Alistair felt a fear of the unknown that he had not experienced since early childhood, and he saw from the faces of the others that they were experiencing the same terror. Angeline was gripping Paul's hand and Manuel looked as if he was about to fall to his knees.

The panel began to slide noiselessly upward, disappearing into the rock above it. Mateo's great frame was silhouetted in the open doorway for a moment, and then he walked slowly forward into the space beyond. The Abbot was standing by the doorway. "Please follow me," he said.

Alistair went in behind Brother Anselmo, followed by the others, and they found themselves in a circular chamber, some twenty metres in diameter and seven metres high. The light that pervaded the area seemed to emanate from the walls and ceiling, which were of the same material as the sliding panel in the rock. The eyes of the group were drawn instantly to the object that occupied the centre of the otherwise empty chamber – a gleaming gold and black structure on a black platform. The structure was in three sections; in the centre was a large iridescent slab – a screen of some kind, thought Alistair – three metres high by a metre and a half wide, framed in black, then an outer structure of gold; the other two sections, on either side of the screen, were angled at fifteen degrees towards the onlookers. Each of these sections was about two and a half metres high by four metres wide, with the main structure containing an array of dials and graphical displays, with smaller screens of similar appearance to the centre screen. Alistair's overall assessment was that the structure consisted of two instrumentation consoles angled to a central master display screen. It struck him that, from an ergonomic standpoint, whoever operated the consoles would either be very tall, or have very longs arms – or both. Like the old capstan lathes of the 1940s – not designed for normal human beings - a thought that made him uneasy.

The left-hand console showed no signs of light, power or any electrical activity: the right-hand console showed only a tiny red light, pulsing steadily at the same frequency as the heartbeat of *La Copa*, four beats per second. Facing the central section, side by side, were two raised platforms, about half a metre high, but of very different shapes. The left hand one was about a metre in diameter, and circular; the right hand one was rectangular, a metre wide by over two metres long.

Mateo, who was ahead of the group, had stopped just short of the platform edge, his back to the group. Brother Anselmo faced the group, and held his arms out at his sides, smiling. "Behold the brain of *La Copa*, my friends – but not a sleeping brain, as it might seem at first sight. It has been in this place since time immemorial. I think you will agree that it can only have been constructed and placed here by an intelligence from beyond our beautiful little planet. Its current activity is limited to monitoring the heartbeat of *El Corazón*– but it cannot act on the information it receives from the regulator because the core is absent. With Angeline and Mateo's help, we hope to restore its active role."

"Is that structure solid gold?" said Red. "If it is, its worth must be astronomical..."

Alistair gave a nervous laugh. "You can still see a dollar sign even at a time like this?"

Brother Anselmo interrupted. "The main casing is solid gold, yes, and its worth is indeed astronomical, but in a different sense to the one you suggest. The survival of our solar system may be dependent on the restoration of its full function. The gold construction is not for aesthetic reasons – it serves a vital purpose in the operation of the consoles."

"May we go forward and examine it, Brother Anselmo?' asked Angeline respectfully.

'In a moment, yes – but before that, let me ask all of you a question – did the voice you heard frighten you?"

They all nodded, slightly shamefaced. Alistair decided to speak for the group. "Did we hear Brother Mateo's name? That seemed to be what the voice articulated..."

"...and whose voice was it?" asked Red.

The Abbot smiled reassuringly, and gave a special look of reassurance to Manuel, who was still clearly in a state of terror. "You heard the sound *Mateo*," he said, "although strictly speaking, it was not uttered as our Spanish forename. It is from a language that has never been spoken on Earth, and perhaps not in our Universe – rather, *Mateo* is our approximation of the word. It was spoken by the Guardian, known to the superstitious as *La Bestia de Moridura. La Guardia* was recognising Mateo, and his right to enter the chamber."

Alistair looked at Mateo, who still had his back turned to the Abbot and the group, a posture that in normal circumstances would have been disrespectful. He seemed to be rooted to the spot, facing the golden structure, but at the Abbot's last words, he slowly turned.

"Brother Anselmo, how can *La Guardia* recognise me? I have never entered this chamber until now."

"My beloved brother, you have no memory of entering the chamber, but you have entered it many times, and you are known to *La Guardia* – you have always been known to *La Guardia*," replied the Abbot, his voice tender and filled with his love and respect for the young monk. Mateo seemed to Alistair to be troubled by the reply, but he bowed his head respectfully to his superior.

Alistair tried to relieve Mateo's distress by asking another question. "Brother Anselmo, you referred to *La Bestia* and *La Guardia* – is the Guardian feminine?"

"The gender of the nouns in Spanish is feminine, Alistair," replied the Abbot. "As for the gender of the Guardian..." He let his voice tail off, and gestured expressively with his hands. He turned to face Mateo.

"Please mount the platform, Mateo, and ascend the smaller of the two plinths – the one on the left. Face towards the centre portion – the screen. You will need no further instruction from me." The Abbot turned back to the group. "Prepare yourselves – there is nothing to fear. Manuel, come and stand with me, my brother – stand proudly and bravely as a member of the Ancient Order of Moridura and a *confrater* of the Moriduran Brothers."

Manuel moved forward and the Abbot took his left hand in his right, and they both faced the golden structure: Mateo stepped on to the black platform and moved towards the left-hand plinth.

He mounted it and stood motionless, looking like a great statue; Alistair's childhood memory of the statue of Osiris came back to him.

"Speak your name, Mateo," commanded the Abbot.

Mateo uttered his name in a strong, firm voice, and then the terrifying voice came again, reverberating around the chamber.

"Mateo!"

Almost immediately, tiny sounds, almost inaudible, began to come from both consoles – the dials gradually lit up, showing strange symbols; the graphical displays became animated, with changing diagrams appearing, and the large central screen began to display brilliantly coloured, moving patterns. Suddenly a burst of light came from the screen and enveloped Mateo's motionless figure, swirling around him, drawing back, then surging out again, as though seeking something.

The others looked anxiously at the Abbot, and Alistair walked forward and placed his hand on his shoulder. The old man was still holding Manuel's arm, but he turned his head at looked up at the big Scot. "He is not being harmed, Alistair, he is being welcomed," he whispered. The coloured patterns on the large screen cleared and were replaced by a mass of symbols and shapes that appeared and disappeared with great rapidity, and then the great voice came again, as alien and terrifying as before, repeating the name Mateo, but at each repetition, the timbre, inflection and amplitude of the voice changed: the volume dropped gradually, the harshness was modulated, and as the tonal shifts took place, the listeners felt a growing sense of security – of warmth and peacefulness: the voice fell silent for a moment, and then uttered the name again in a warm, reassuring, welcoming tone, filled with affection.

"Mateo..."

Even Manuel had lost his fear, and Alistair saw him turn his head and smile at the Abbot. Paul and Angeline were holding hands, Red was grinning, and Santiago looked almost relaxed. Alistair became aware that he himself was beaming inanely, and felt more than a little foolish. As he tried to compose his features, he saw the big monk begin to turn slowly, and then he was facing them, his face radiant and smiling. His large, lambent eyes swept across them, and his natural warmth of personality seemed to be intensified a hundredfold as he looked at each of them in turn.

"Brother Anselmo," he said, as though recognising the Abbot after a long separation, "Manuel Ortega - Alistair Mackinnon – Angeline Blade – Paul Corr – Red Lonnen – Santiago Manrique... Welcome – Mateo and I bid you welcome!"

Alistair felt the hairs on the back of his neck stand up. All of his rational education was being challenged by the simple words of the monk before him: they were either the victims of an elaborate trick, he reflected, or else they were being welcomed by the Guardian. He looked across at Paul, and saw that he was in the grip of one of his uncanny moments – his young friend was staring fixedly at Mateo.

"I understand your fears and your doubts," said the voice coming from Mateo's mouth, "but try to accept what you see and hear. For the moment, Mateo and I are as one, in the hope that you may find my voice and my presence easier to accept. For some of you, scepticism is beginning to overcome your fear, and that is good. Only through doubt can truth be fully apprehended. Let me help you in your doubt – observe, and fear not..."

They all drew back as one, with the exception of the Abbot and Manuel, as Mateo slowly rose above the platform, rotated slowly a full 360 degrees until he was facing them again, and then floated forward and descended gently the floor until he was next to the Abbot. The monk placed his great hand on Manuel's shoulder, and smiled down at him.

Alistair realised that he was holding his breath, and then Mateo's voice came, with the characteristic deadpan dryness that preceded humour. "Please, my friends, I must ask you to treat my demonstration with due gravity," he said, and his words were greeted by nervous laughter. My God, thought Alistair, either we have Mateo back with us, or the Beast has a sense of humour. Mateo's next words came like a thunderbolt into his consciousness.

"We share the same sense of the ridiculous, Alistair – humour is an attribute that is not peculiar to *homo sapiens* – even a Beast may smile…"

This cannot be happening, Alistair thought, reaching frantically back into his Glasgow street wisdom for a rejoinder that would relieve the intolerable intellectual conflict he now felt. He went into automatic pilot mode, and heard himself speaking as though he were an observer. "Are there any more like you at home, Jimmy?" he said. "If there are, God help your Mammy!"

There was a sudden feeling of great sadness in the chamber, and the voice coming from Mateo, when it spoke, had some of its previous alien quality. "Alistair, I am the last of my species," it said simply, with an inflection of intolerable grief and longing that touched the hearts of all of them.

Alistair cursed himself for a fool – the bad old street habit of trying to reduce a high intensity emotion to a gutter level. What followed removed his lingering doubt, instantly and forever.

"If Ah wiz back wi' ye, Ah wid huv skelped yer erse fur yer cheek, Alistair Mackinnon!" scolded *La Bestia*. It was his mother's voice – heart-wrenchingly recognisable, completely authentic and undeniable.

The tears came unbidden, great, tearing sobs, and then he felt the arms of Mateo enfold him, as he cried unashamedly, oblivious to his concerned friends clustering around him. Brother Mateo's familiar voice murmured soothingly to him. "Forgive us – but now your doubts are dispelled. We hope we did not cause you too much pain."

Alistair straightened up and composed himself with some difficulty: Paul and Angeline were looking anxiously up at him. "I'm OK – really, I'm alright now," he said, attempting a weak smile. He could see that they had all heard the voice and understood the fundamental nature of what had happened to him, and its implications. "Enough, Mateo," he said, "I'm convinced – no more, please!" He held up his hands in mock surrender. "May we get a closer look at the consoles now? Angeline and Red must be as eager as I am..."

Brother Mateo nodded and motioned towards the platform. "Do not expect to understand the symbols just yet. We have some work to do before Angeline can help us. Do not be afraid to touch the consoles – you cannot inadvertently activate anything."

Alistair stepped up on to the platform and moved towards the left hand console, and he saw Angeline go to the right with Paul. Her father was obviously fascinated by the large display screen in the middle, and strode towards it. Manuel mounted the platform tentatively, still staying close to the Abbot. Santiago disappeared round the back of the structure on a reconnoitre. Alistair looked back over his shoulder at Mateo, who had remained on the floor of the chamber: the big monk was smiling at the enthusiasm of those moving around the platform, stroking and probing the gold and black consoles, looking up at the high-set displays and dials, shaking their heads in wonderment and bafflement. Red was standing directly in front of the large screen, apparently hypnotised by its coruscating lights.

A cry from above suddenly made them all look up, and Alistair was astounded to see his security chief floating over the top of the left hand console. Santiago floated above them for a few seconds, a look of impotence and acute embarrassment on his face, and then he swooped down gracefully and landed among them, looking for all the world like a large bird that had been forced to make a sudden landing.

"My apologies, Santiago – my intention was to extend your experience of the function, not to startle you. As you can see, we have control of micro-gravities within this chamber," said Mateo. To Alistair, the confident and non-deferential nature of his tone suggested that it was *La Guardia* who was being a little mischievous, not Mateo.

Santiago gave Mateo a mildly reproachful look, then turned to Alistair. "The rear of the structure is simply a wall of gold and rock, without features of any kind. I was investigating its surface more closely when I was, shall I say – uplifted? It was a startling but not unpleasant experience. With a little warning, I could almost have enjoyed it..." He gave Mateo a sidelong glance.

Red turned to say something to his daughter, but saw that, on an impulse, she was mounting the plinth that Mateo had recently occupied. He moved quickly towards her, about to urge caution, when the great voice filled the chamber, in its previous awe-inspiring tones. "Angeline," it said, and the same light that had enveloped Mateo sprang from the console and surrounded her. Red and Paul reached the plinth at the same time, and both reached towards her body, but their arms were thrown back, and they almost fell. The light withdrew into the screen as quickly as it had emerged. Her father and Paul helped the startled Angeline down from the plinth: she was obviously unhurt, but a little shaken by her experience.

"That was quite something! Mateo, should you have warned me about that?" she said, wagging an admonishing finger at him, and then, to her evident astonishment, she levitated from the platform and floated down to the floor where he was standing, setting down gently next to him. Her father and Paul were left looking at the space between them where she had been, then down to where she was now standing, like volunteers from the audience on stage in a magic show when the lady in the leotard vanishes.

"This is the only way to travel, Red," she called out, smiling happily.

Brother Anselmo held up his hand. "Playtime is over, my children – there will be time enough to experience the effect. We have important matters to discuss. There must be many questions in your minds, especially about Brother Mateo's relationship to the Guardian. First, let me warn you that, when we leave this place, Mateo will have no memory of any events that took place while he was here. He has been in the chamber many times and while he is here, his mind is linked to that of *La Guardia*."

Mateo was smiling at them as the Abbot spoke. He seemed to be the Mateo that they knew, but Alistair could see from Paul's reaction to him that the other presence was still very much in the young monk. Although they had all experienced the uncanny valley effect to some degree, Paul seemed especially susceptible to the phenomenon, and attuned to the changes in Mateo. Thinking back to the first occurrence of this, in the square at Moridanza, when Mateo had first appeared, another question arose in his mind.

"Brother Anselmo, is the Guardian only present in Mateo while he is in the chamber?" he asked.

"No, Alistair – *La Guardia* is also present fleetingly at other times, but Mateo is not aware of the presence. Only when he is here are their two minds fully synchronised," replied the Abbot. "Angeline, you have observed the link between *La Guardia* and Brother Mateo. Does it offer you any reassurance about the need for a similar link to be established with you?"

Angeline thought for a moment, and then she spoke, slowly and deliberately. "I have considered what the nature of this intelligence called the Guardian might be. Everything that has been said by you - and by Mateo and *La Guardia* - suggests a living entity, but I have considered another possibility, that of an entity that once lived, but which now exists only in the circuits of the structure – the brain in the consoles – in the same way that some part of the brains of software engineers exist in a computer's firmware, even after their deaths. With a level of artificial intelligence technology infinitely beyond ours, such a programme could interact with us, almost as a living being could."

"That is a perfectly reasonable hypothesis, Angeline," answered the Abbot, "since you have seen no evidence of a corporeal creature; even if you had, you could have speculated that it was some kind of holographic projection, infinitely more sophisticated than anything our earthly science could achieve."

Red butted in, shaking his head impatiently, and addressing himself to Mateo. "Why is the Abbot speaking for you, Mateo, or Guardian, or whoever you are? You're asking my daughter to take great risks to achieve your objectives. All that we have seen could be a high-tech magic show – we're in an environment totally controlled by you, we've been made suggestible by clever demonstrations – forgive me, Alistair – and by floating some of us around the room. A Las Vegas magician could probably duplicate all of this. I still need a lot of convincing. I'm a scientist – I believe the evidence of my senses only when I can subject it to verification." He paused, and turned to his daughter. "I'm sorry for breaking in on you like that, Angeline, but we need hard answers here before we can move forward. This must rest on matter of fact, not faith…"

Brother Mateo looked at the Abbot, who nodded, and then back at Red. When he spoke, the voice was not that of Mateo, neither was it the terrible voice that had first greeted the big monk, but a voice of immense power and authority.

"You speak as a father, not just as a scientist. Your scepticism is a valid reaction to what you have seen and heard. There is nothing I can do to create certainty in your mind without interfering with your freedom of thought. I can offer more demonstrations within the limits of my power in this chamber, but they would be received with the same doubts, however impressive. I am neither omniscient nor omnipotent. I can normally only function within the limits of this place and this technology. I need Mateo as my human link to the physical environment, as a kind of avatar. I am constrained by my purpose, confined on this planet through the ages to avert a catastrophe beyond your race's imagining."

Mateo's face displayed great pain and sorrow, and the voice conveyed a powerful longing for something unattainable. "I can manifest myself as the physical presence I agreed to surrender aeons ago: it is necessary for me to do this through Mateo at intervals, but it involves great pain and great danger for both of us. Whether Angeline agrees to help us or not, we must act. I have been bound to a cycle of duty since the first of your species walked this planet, but my release from bondage is close, either by a final completion of the purpose of those that sent me, or by the total destruction of your universe. I too had a father – a father faced by a choice, as you are now. Speak with your daughter. The ultimate decision is hers, not yours, but make it jointly if it is possible."

Red looked intently at the face of Mateo, as though trying to see beyond it to the creature that spoke through the monk. Alistair placed his hand on his shoulder, and he turned slowly to face his business rival.

"What do you make of all this?" he said gruffly. "You seemed convinced by your experience, yet you're a sceptical scientist like me – forgive me, but surely you don't believe that you actually heard your mother's voice?"

"No, I don't, Red – but I do believe that I heard my memory of my mother's voice, and that could only have come from my mind. If the rest of you hadn't heard it, I could have put it down to suggestibility and hallucination, but the undeniable fact is that *La Guardia* had the capacity to retrieve that memory from my consciousness and play it back to all of us. The power to do that is far beyond anything that modern science can do – it was not a cheap medium's trick. Face it, Red, we are in the presence of something extra-terrestrial in origin. Add to that the characters of Mateo and Brother Anselmo. I would trust these two men with my life."

"But I'm being asked to trust them with my daughter's life, Alistair," replied Red, "and even more is being asked of Angeline. If I – if we – could share the risk with her..." He fell silent, unable to look at his daughter. She came forward and took his hand.

"Red..." she began, "if we don't agree, we'll all die and live to regret it!"

In spite of himself, her father smiled, shook his head ruefully, and then he began to laugh. Alistair was unable to stop his own laughter at the old joke, and the others joined in. Even the Abbot permitted himself a smile.

"Angeline has encapsulated her dilemma, and that of all of us, in a light-hearted way. To be asked to save the world is a heavy responsibility indeed. Perhaps only humour can make it bearable," he said. He looked up at Mateo. "There is one more thing you can do to help Lloyd and Angeline to make their decision..."

Mateo nodded, and pointed to the large display. "Behold - *El Corazón* – the heart of *La Copa*."

The screen clouded, swirled, then it cleared. At first, those watching felt as if they were staring into a sea of fire, then gradually, at the centre of the screen, they could see a black ball, pulsing and shimmering. There was no sound coming from the display screen of the consoles, but they all felt a vibration that was beyond description: it was as if they had placed their hands on a great machine, of inconceivable power and latent destructive potential.

Alistair knew that they were the first human beings to observe a singularity in the making – a nascent black hole. He shuddered involuntarily. Red and Angeline, redheads together, had gone their particular whiter shade of pale.

"How big is it?" asked Angeline, her voice quivering with fear and excitement.

Mateo spoke, or rather *La Guardia* spoke through him.

"What you see is not *El Corazón* itself, but a sophisticated visual representation of it. At this moment, it is no smaller than a ripe olive," the awesome voice replied, "but it oscillates on the brink of infinity. It is without consciousness, without malice, without pity. I can stabilise it – perhaps only for a time, perhaps for aeons – but only with your help, Angeline Blade. May I offer you and your father a moment like Alistair's, but for your ears only?"

Angeline and Red knew instinctively what was coming, as did the others. Alistair saw that she was still gripping her father's hand, and they both looked up at the tall monk and nodded in acquiescence. Suddenly they both jerked as if they had been struck in the face; their lips parted simultaneously and tears sprang to their eyes, then they embraced. Alistair looked across at Paul, whose face was naked with concern for Angeline, and he tried to signal his personal understanding of the unique moment that they were experiencing. For a brief, intense moment, Angeline and Red had been united in a shared memory of someone lost to both of them, and in that moment, there was total understanding and complete forgiveness.

The Abbot broke the silence. "It is time for us to leave this place – it is also time for us to eat," he said, motioning towards the door. "Once we are outside of the door, Mateo will have no sense of the events in the chamber: he will only be aware of standing in front of the door after descending the steps. Please do not refer to your experiences while he is present – they would have no meaning for him."

Everyone looked at Mateo, feeling strangely complicit in a deception, but he smiled at them, and spoke in his normal tone of voice. "Don't feel guilty, my friends – this is a situation that I am totally familiar with: think of it as forgetting a dream immediately after waking."

Angeline could not resist posing the question in her mind.

"When I help you – help you both," she said tentatively, "will I remember my experiences?"

The voice of *La Guardia* came in all its force. "Do you want to remember, Angeline?"

"Yes – yes, I do – very much…" she replied simply.

"Then you shall."

"And will Mateo share the memory with me?" she persisted anxiously.

There was a long pause, and then the great voice came again.

"At this time, I cannot answer your question in a way that would be meaningful to you." There was a note of finality in the reply, yet a hint of a resolution to come.

Mateo stood in front of the metallic door, and it lifted silently. He waited in the area at the foot of the stairs till they had exited, one by one, then the big monk faced the door again, and it slid shut. He placed his hands flat upon the door, as he had when entering the chamber, on the Abbot's instruction. After a moment, he turned and looked enquiringly at Brother Anselmo.

"Thank, you, Mateo," said the old man, "and now we must climb the stairs again, my friends, sustained by the prospect of lunch." Mateo looked confused, wondering why they had come down to this little chamber, only to leave it again, but the habit of unquestioning obedience was strong. He walked to the foot of the black steps with his superior, took his frail, bony hand in his own powerful grip, and they began the ascent, followed by the others in their original pairings.

"That was quite something - yeah, quite something…" said Red to Alistair as they set foot on the first step of the steep ascent.

Chapter Twenty

Angeline cranked up the machine, laughing. "I'm winding up the phonograph to unwind!"

"Phonograph – gramophone," remarked Alistair, "it's funny how we're separated by a common language…"

"An American invented it, so I guess it has to be phonograph," said Angeline.

Alistair, Angeline, Red, Paul and Santiago sat listening to records, relaxed after a substantial lunch. Manuel had gone off with Mateo and the Abbot on mysterious business.

"Yeah, good old Thomas Alva," added her father, "I envy him his list of patents."

"You'll be telling us he invented the telephone next," declaimed Alistair, waving his arms. "Where would we have been without American inventors? No steam engine, no antiseptic, no logarithms, no television, no tartan, no bagpipes – the list is endless…"

Red shook his head pityingly. "The bagpipes are an Irish invention. Just ignore him, Angeline - let's get back to what's to be done. We've got tomorrow - the day after is the big event. My sense of the various predictions and explanations offered by the Abbot and Mateo, not to mention our invisible friend in the chamber, is that if the Throne splits before we've got the gizmo back in place, we're all toast…"

Angeline looked pensive. "They didn't exactly say that, but I share your instinct about *El Trono* and the elevation: there is also the question of how we get to the regulator at the heart of *La Copa*. Unless there is a secret passage from the chamber of a half-a-mile or so, Mateo is going to have to totter down through the fields carrying the core. Don't they have a barrow or something?"

Her father laughed. "Angeline, this whole place is the epitome of low tech, except for the chamber, which seemed to be a sealed oasis of high technology. Alistair – Paul – what do you make of it?" As he posed the question, he became aware of a slight sense of resentment emanating from Santiago, and he turned quickly to him. "Santiago, your feel for it would be very welcome – break us out of our narrow scientific and managerial mindsets – give us a more practical view…"

Santiago smiled inwardly: it was the closest the American had come to a graceful recognition of other people's sensibilities in the brief period he had known him.

"The chamber of *La Guardia* is the control centre, and must have been implanted in the rock after the impact of the meteorite created *La Copa* and the instability at its heart. The control centre must have a communication and control link with the regulator: this must either be hard-wired or rely on radio or some other wireless model beyond our knowledge. If it *is* hard-wired, there must be a conduit of some sort to the regulator and core; if not, physical access is still desirable, at the least, for direct maintenance. Based on interpreting *La Guardia's* words, he, she or it normally has no active physical presence, but can somehow re-create a physical presence through Mateo…"

Santiago looked at Angeline as he spoke these words. "Angeline, I think that you are going to have more than a mind-link with *La Guardia* - you will be accompanied along an unknown route by a physical composite of Mateo and the alien, acting as your guide and protector, to the heart of *La Copa*."

Angeline pursed her lips and her widened her eyes. "Beauty and the Beast," she said, fluttering her eyelids.

Red shook his head in irritation. "Don't trivialise it, Angeline – if Santiago is right, this is even more disturbing."

"Let's get one thing straight, Red," snapped Angeline, "I am going to do what I have to – we all are. I've been making my own decisions for a lot of years now – I need your support, not belated paternal concern, however welcome it is."

Her father gave a wry smile, grateful that the rebuke had been softened by the final remark.

"OK – sorry! I'm new at the fatherhood game, Angeline," he said, with genuine humility in his voice. Angeline gave him a brief smile, and he turned in relief back to Santiago.

"I'm with you in your analysis, Santiago. So this physical joining, the manifestation of *La Guar*dia – is it the root of the legend of the Beast?" Santiago nodded in confirmation, and was about to elaborate, but Paul broke into their exchange.

"If the Guardian was here when our species was just appearing on Earth, who or what did he use as his avatar? Could he have used a primitive man ape for this purpose?"

"Maybe he didn't need an avatar at first: maybe the regulator was doing its job till the core was stolen, and that was in comparatively recent times – fourteenth century or thereabouts. So the Mateos could date from then," said Santiago, "but that begs another question: if conditions close to *El Corazón* – where the regulator is located – are so inimical to normal humans, how was the core stolen in the first place? The Mateo of that time obviously didn't steal it – so who did?"

"It could have been a previous Magus," said Paul, "maybe Abbadocio, the unfortunate Magus Elect – or a greedy *hermandad* member."

Red shrugged fatalistically. "We will know the answers soon enough, unless the Abbot is prepared to give them to us before the ceremony. Let's move on…"

"To where, Red?" asked Alistair. "The timetable is in the hands of Brother Anselmo."

"There's another matter," interjected Santiago, "namely, what are Ferdinand and his friends up to? He's the Magus Elect, and wants to control events. My guess is that representatives of the military/industrial complex will be at the Ceremony. He will want to demonstrate his total control over the anti-gravity discovery, the monks, *La Copa* and Angeline – he already has the political clout in the region…"

"Who would he approach in the defence industry, Santiago," asked Angeline, "the military – or defence contractors? What countries would he target?"

"Well, the Spanish military wouldn't be his first port of call," said Santiago, "and probably not Russia – they don't have the resources he needs to tap into: but he will need to involve Spain at some point, otherwise his political base will be unsustainable. He will want to present them with a fait accompli – a deal with…"

"The United States, or NATO – they are the only choices, really. As for defence contractors – since it isn't going to be Ardmurran International Electronics or your company, it has to be…"

"Xalatera and Pick Carter…" Red spat the words out. "It's got to be Xalatera, dammit! That guy's got no principles, no ethics…"

Alistair gave a cynical laugh. "I thought that's what you always held against me, Red – that I have principles."

"Only that you have the wrong damn principles. You're like all Celts – hard and businesslike on the outside, and sentimental mush on the inside. No offence…"

Alistair smiled seraphically. "How could I possibly be offended, Red? You put it so delicately…" He drew out the first vowels of possibly and delicately in a way that underlined the irony in his words, and grinned at Angeline, who was shaking her head in mock despair at her father.

"We both know the people he's likely to bring from each service, and they're all good guys," said Alistair. "I hope Ferdinand doesn't put them in harms way…"

Red remained rigorously unsentimental. "It's their business to get in harm's way – that's what they're paid for."

"Just hold on a moment!" said Angeline, breaking in to the exchange. "These are our guys, Red – they're Americans! Surely we're not going to treat them as hostile?"

"We won't recognise them if they're wearing the robes with hoods down, Angeline," said Santiago, "and the danger to them may not come from us."

Her father was still dismissive of the risk to the military personnel. "If I know senior officers, they'll be wearing full dress uniform under the Ku-Klux-Klan regalia in case anything goes wrong. They'll whip off their nightgowns at the first sign of real trouble...."

Alistair laughed raucously. "...and then they'll produce the Stars and Stripes, and wave it, and you'll all sing *America the Beautiful* while the world ends..."

Angeline and her father glared at him with identical expressions of outrage on their faces, and Alistair quickly held up his hands. "Just funnin', folks – just funnin'..." he said hastily, but still had to expertly dodge an open-handed swipe from Angeline with a swerve of his hips.

"OK, OK!" he said, laughing, and trying to avoid more blows from Doctor Blade, "I shouldn't have mentioned the flag. Jeez-oh, you Yanks – you take these things so bloody seriously."

"Nobody seems very worried about the civilian – Pick Carter," observed Paul sardonically.

"If he was dismembered by the Beast, neither Alistair nor I would shed any tears," said Red, and Alistair nodded in vigorous agreement.

"But he's an American, too," said Angeline, still patriotically combative.

"Yeah, well..." said her father dismissively.

Paul was fidgeting in a manner that Alistair recognised as trouble brewing. "Spit it out, wee pal – you've been building up to it for the last half-hour," he said with a resigned air.

Paul scowled. "You know damn well what's bothering me, Alistair," he said angrily.

"Aye, I do - you think we're being too light-hearted when Angeline is in danger."

"We're all whistling in the dark," said Angeline, "and I, for one, am glad of anything that lightens the gloom. To get back to fundamentals – my travelling companion and I will have another problem as we approach our destination on our journey to replace the core – the event horizon."

"Angeline, I have some idea of what that is, but please explain a bit more for my benefit," said Santiago, "and maybe Paul's?" He looked apologetically at Paul. "I'm hoping that I'm not alone in my ignorance, Paul – forgive me if you fully understand."

Paul laughed. "You're not alone. All I know is that it is some kind of boundary around a black hole – a kind of edge to the gravitational abyss?"

"Cross the event horizon and you're sucked in..." added Santiago.

They shuffled about a bit under the politely impenetrable gaze of the three scientists, feeling like schoolboys facing a panel of examiners.

"Not bad," said Alistair, looking at Red for confirmation.

"For laymen..." said Red, and would have continued in a similar sarcastic vein but for Angeline cutting across him.

"Shut up, the pair of you – you patronising bastards!" She smiled at Paul and Santiago. "The event horizon is a theoretical concept – we don't really know if it exists, or acts in accordance with our present beliefs about it. It was once thought that nothing could escape from a black hole, but that theory has now been modified – and remember, there is no black hole – yet! What is certain is that I am going to experience and observe a nascent singularity and some kind of event horizon at first hand. I can only hope that Mateo and his pal will know more than I do when we approach it."

There was a familiar rattling sound, and Joaquín appeared with his cart to clear away the dishes. Alistair looked at the smiling monk with an affectionate grin, but then paused, and looked more closely at his old acquaintance: beneath the ever-present smile on the monk's face there was something else, something disturbing.

"Is something the matter, Joaquín? Are you alright?"

The others glanced around, and Angeline stood up, an expression of concern on her face.

"What is it, Joaquín? Is something bothering you?"

The monk's smile became a rictus of pain as he tried to control himself, then he groaned, bending over involuntarily and bracing himself by holding on to the cart. Angeline and Alistair sprang across simultaneously to support him, led him gently to a chair and sat him down, Angeline continuing to hold his hand. Gradually, he straightened up in the chair and a weak smile returned, but the pain still showed in his eyes.

"My friends – I am sorry. Sometimes it comes without warning, but it will pass in a moment. Thank you for your help and concern."

"May we ask what the problem is, Joaquín?" asked Paul.

Joaquín stood up shakily. "I have a form of leukaemia," he said, his tone matter-of-fact and brisk, "and, to anticipate your inevitable question, my friends, it is essentially untreatable - the prognosis is six months or thereabouts. I am in God's hands now, but then, we all are, are we not?"

Alistair shook his head. "There must be something else that can be done, Joaquín – a second opinion. You must seek the advice of a top specialist – I can make all the arrangements for you."

The monk laughed, touching his friend's shoulder affectionately. "I'm sorry – I am grateful for your concern, I do not mean to sound ungracious – but none of us may live beyond the day after tomorrow. Should we seek a second opinion on that?" His eyes twinkled as he looked at his friends. Seeing that his efforts to make light of his condition had not allayed their concern, he offered an additional perspective.

"My affliction has a history: we call it the monks' condition – its incidence among my brethren has been high, both currently and historically. We believe it to be a radiation cancer. Its incidence correlates with how often a monk has been close to the centre of *La Copa* – to *El Trono*. It occurs only among those whose duties require frequent attendance."

As his listeners digested this information, footsteps heralded the arrival of the Abbot, Manuel and Brother Mateo.

"I caught the last of your words, Joaquín," said the Abbot. "There can only be one reason why you revealed your affliction. Have you recovered from the episode? Was it more severe this time?" He moved across to Joaquín and took his hand. Mateo was now beside him also, a massive, reassuring presence. Joaquín leaned his head against his brother monk's upper arm. Manuel fussed around the three monks, clucking sympathetically.

"Yes, much more severe – and sudden: there was no warning," he said. "But I will not fail you at the Ceremony, Anselmo, God willing…"

The Abbot came and stood beside Alistair.

"Radiation – it causes cancer and sometimes it can cure it. One of life's many contradictions," he said.

Alistair persisted: he did not want to surrender Joaquín too easily. "There must be other expert opinions that can be sought," he said quietly, but intensely. "Cancer treatment moves on daily. If there is any financial question…"

"Thank you, my friend: no, it is not a matter of money – we have ample resources…" Brother Anselmo looked up at Alistair. "No brother has ever survived this condition – we hope and pray, we keep in touch with new developments, but…" He spread his hands in a fatalistic gesture. "In Joaquín's case, we have other, more immediate difficulties, relating to the Ceremony."

A thought struck Alistair – his mind rejected it, but it returned insistently. He looked into the Abbot's eyes, and sensed confirmation there. "Can it be?" he breathed softly, looking across at Joaquín, still pale and leaning for support on Mateo. Brother Anselmo smiled.

"A sense of fun, a joy in living – the performance of humble tasks: these things are not incompatible with great responsibilities and high office," he said gently.

Alistair continued to look at Joaquín, who seemed small and vulnerable, an impression accentuated by the sheer size of the monk by his side. Joaquín had been looking up at Mateo, but, almost as though he was aware of Alistair's gaze, he turned his head, and almost imperceptibly his expression was transformed: wisdom, power and authority were revealed as though a veil had been lifted, yet the familiar gentleness and warmth were still present.

Alistair knew now, with an astonished certainty, that he was looking at the Magus of Moridura. It all came together now - he recalled that Brother Anselmo had said that the current Magus no longer had the physical strength to endure the conditions at the regulator, and he remembered the Abbot's refusal to answer him at another time, when he had bluntly asked for the identity of the Magus.

He looked down at the old monk, and nodded. "I will respect the confidence, Anselmo, but my friends are observant and intelligent – they may see what I have seen, although I will not give them the information unless you deem it fitting to do so." He paused, weighing carefully the appropriateness of his next query, but the Abbot was ahead of him, demonstrating the Moriduran capacity to anticipate the question in the mind of another.

"My frailty is not due solely to old age, Alistair: all Chapter members are vulnerable to this affliction. It has been the cause of death for many Abbots and most of the Magi throughout the Order's history, give or take the occasional fatality when the Ceremony goes wrong…" He saw Alistair's shock at his light-heartedness and moved swiftly to relieve it.

"What is there to do in the face of death but make light of it, my friend?" he said.

Alistair gave a hollow laugh. "I've recently been taken to task by my colleagues for doing just that," he said.

"Then you understand. That which we fear most, that which we cannot influence or control – we can always deal with it by laughing at it. We cannot remove its power, but we can deny it its victory, because we know that, beneath the surface of events, however terrible, is the all-encompassing power and love of God. Ultimately, all is well."

"I envy you your certainty, Anselmo – I wish I could share it," said Alistair, "but I am a prisoner of reason, of logical processes, of scientific scepticism. Pray for me…"

"I do – and I will continue to do so, for as much time as I have left to me," said the Abbot, "but now Manuel and I have urgent work to do. Tomorrow, members of the *hermandad* will arrive at various times in Moridanza from all over the region and beyond; they will be brought to the monastery by coach over the course of the day and they will be accommodated in the dormitory of the *confratres*. Ferdinand will arrive with the first group. Early the following day – the day of the Ceremony – two members of the Order, will arrive with four other persons. Ferdinand has informed me that they are *hermandad* members who could not reach Moridanza by tomorrow."

The Abbot paused. "Regrettably, he has lied to me and to the Chapter – these persons are not of the *hermandad*," he said sadly. "This is yet another betrayal of trust by Ferdinand. From any *confrater*, this would be unacceptable – from the Magus Elect, it is almost unforgivable…"

"Anselmo, I must tell you that Red and I believe that Ferdinand has contacted an industrialist called Pick Carter, of Xalatera Industries, and that he may try to smuggle this man and three American senior officers into the monastery to observe the ceremony. That is consistent with your information."

The Abbot looked grave. "If you are right, Ferdinand's betrayal is even greater than I thought," he said. "He will inevitably place himself and his guests in danger."

"From what?" asked Alistair. "From the *hermandad*? From the Brothers of Moridura?"

"No – from *La Guardia*," replied the Abbot.

"You mean that the Guardian punishes interlopers?"

"It is not as simple as that: you must remember that the physical phenomena that occur during the ceremony have been occurring for millennia. *El Partir del Trono* is regarded by the Order as a natural phenomenon, but the Magi of Moridura have known since Abbadocio's time that when *El Trono* splits, it stabilizes the processes at the heart of *La Copa*. The parting of the rock has a purpose – but this time..." He placed his hand on Alistair's arm.

"But enough of explanations – Manuel, Mateo and I must take our brother Joaquín to the infirmary and attend to his condition: he is weaker than he realises and must rest. I would prefer you not to reveal the identity of the Magus to your friends at this time, but do not feel compelled to deceive them if for any reason they suspect the truth."

"Never lie, but don't tell all that you know," said Alistair, quoting an old bargaining maxim. The Abbot inclined his head politely and rejoined Manuel, Joaquín and Mateo. In spite of Joaquín's protestations, they led him away down the passageway, Manuel pushing the cart. "Look after yourself, Joaquín," Angeline called out as they departed, and he turned his head and smiled at her. Paul and Santiago waved and gave thumbs up signs: Red was deep in thought.

"Let's all sit down," said Alistair. "I have something I want to put to you"

Angeline had started piling the lunch dishes and cutlery at one end of the table: Joaquín had been unable to commence clearing off the table, and now he and the cart had gone.

"Someone will come back and do that, Angeline," said Alistair impatiently, and she reluctantly stopped and moved over to join the group at the gramophone table.

Paul looked at his friend with a slightly suspicious air. "Was something going on there between you and the Abbot and Brother Joaquín? There seemed to be a lot of looks and meaningful glances in Joaquín's direction."

"Yes, of course – we were discussing Joaquín's condition, which is not unique to him. Let's sit down…"

The others reacted quickly to Alistair's remark, and Angeline was first in the ring.

"Brother Anselmo suffers from it too – that's my guess," she said decisively.

"… and probably anyone who gets too close to *El Trono* regularly, or for long periods," added Santiago.

Alistair nodded. "Over the centuries it has killed most of the Magi of Moridura, most Abbots, and…" He hesitated for a fraction of a second, avoiding eye contact with everyone except Santiago. "…almost certainly a lot of Chapter members."

Paul was listening attentively and observing Alistair closely: he had not been entirely satisfied with the answer to his earlier question; the undertone of irritation in his friend's manner was always a reliable indicator that he was concealing something. There was something in the way he had added that the radiation cancer also affected Chapter members – it seemed almost designed to deflect the inevitable question that would have followed the information that it had killed most of the Magi and Abbots, namely, "Why Joaquín?"

The afflicted monk was a Chapter member, of course, but somehow Paul felt that something else was at work. A thought entered his head: he dismissed it as fanciful, but it wouldn't go away. He realised that Alistair was looking at him slightly apprehensively. Paul tilted his head and raised his eyebrows: Alistair shook his head, an almost imperceptible movement, and Paul knew that it was a *don't go there* signal, not a denial of his intuitive conclusion.

"Christ!" he said involuntarily. Angeline and Santiago turned to him in surprise: they had missed the significance of the silent exchange between him and Alistair. But then a new concern took over, relegating his previous insight to a lower level.

"Alistair, if there is a risk from an unknown type of radiation, what are the implications for Angeline of getting so close to the source?"

"Exactly," interjected Red, echoing Paul's concern. "The monks experience it only on the surface of *La Copa*: Angeline must go right to the regulator to replace the core – how is her extra-terrestrial companion going to shield her from a high-level, intense exposure?"

Angeline looked very pale and tense: they all expected an indignant rejection of their concerns on her behalf, but abruptly her face crumpled and she bent forward. A suppressed sob escaped her lips, and Paul and her father were instantly on their feet and at her side: she did not look at them, feeling ashamed of her display of weakness. Paul looked over his shoulder at Alistair, a look of utter desolation on his face.

Her father spoke. "Angeline, you don't have to do this – if you give Alistair and me enough detail, we can go with the damned creature to the Throne – to the regulator…"

"Red is right," said Alistair, "but I can do it alone. After all, I'm older if not wiser, and if there is a radiation effect, then it will work more slowly on old bones. Let me convince the Abbot and *La Guardia* that this is the better alternative, Angeline."

She looked up, and a faint grin began to appear on her pale face. "Hey, Don Quixote – don't go tilting at windmills on my behalf!" she said.

Alistair reddened, and turned abruptly away from her, and she sprang to her feet, grasped his arm and spun him around.

"Don't go all sulky on me – it was meant as a compliment. But you know I have to do this..." She turned to Paul and her father. "You know it has to be me. I'm scared, sure, I'm scared – I've got a lot of living to do yet," she said, looking at Paul and then at Red, "and a lot a catching up to do..."

Alistair saw his chance to pose the question the Abbot had left hanging in the air.

"The bold Don may be in danger from forces other than ours," he said conspiratorially, looking around him and rolling his eyes dramatically.

"What forces?" said Red, unimpressed by Alistair's histrionics. Since his attempt at humour had fallen distinctly flat, Alistair continued in a more serious tone.

"In my conversation with Brother Anselmo before he left, he indicated that, while it is the belief of most members of the Order that the event known as *El Partir del Trono* is a natural recurring phenomenon, it is in fact, as the Abbot put it, part of an age-old maintenance cycle – the Throne is split for a purpose every thirty five years, presumably either actively by the Guardian, or automatically by the regulator."

"Sounds like some old manufacturing plants in the boondocks back home – maintenance is either non-existent or infrequent," laughed Red, his good humour restored by the return to more practical matters. "Does Ferdinand know this, or does he still believe it is a natural event? Can we expect a team of monks in coveralls with spanners to appear at the Ceremony"

"Very droll, Red," said Alistair dryly, getting his own back. "No, I don't believe he does. He expects that *El Trono* will open, he will be elevated in front of the assembled crowd – which will include three hooded men with Army, Navy and Air Force shoes showing under their robes, and one keenly observant industrialist – and then be confirmed as the new Magus of Moridura. Remember, he doesn't really buy into the Abbot's view that the world will end unless Angeline does her stuff tomorrow."

"What is the threat to him?" asked Angeline, intrigued.

Paul laughed. "He's forgotten his history – he's forgotten the fate of a previous Magus Elect – Abbadocio. Those who forget their history are condemned to repeat it…"

"Aahh," said Angeline, "*La Guardia* will pull him apart…"

Santiago shook his head, in puzzlement. "But why?" he asked.

"Yeah, why? The Magus Elect is his guy – he is going to mind the store for the next thirty-five years, or until he goes to God," said Red. Paul was engrossed in this new question, and for the moment, Alistair's earlier evasiveness over the radiation question was forgotten.

"Forgive me for thinking aloud," he said, "Why was Abbadocio ripped apart at what should have been his triumphant elevation? Did he steal the core? Why should Ferdinand be in danger from *La Guardia*?"

"Well, if the Beast is a good guy, and he knows that the guy who will be responsible for the whole shebang for the foreseeable future is a bad guy, then he ain't gonna let him become a made man, as they say in the Mob," said Red. "He'll whack him."

"You've hit it on the nose, Red," said Paul, "it's as simple as that…"

"If he is unworthy of the office of Magus, he commits a kind of sacrilege by seeking elevation," said Angeline reflectively.

"Aye, that's it – that must be it," said Alistair.

Santiago held up his hands in despair.

"I am sure we'll all be delighted to see Ferdinand meet his end, but there will be no ceremony, no day after tomorrow unless we ensure that Angeline is protected. May I return to my analysis?"

They all looked a bit crestfallen, and nodded in agreement. He acknowledged their response graciously.

"I see only two main options: the first is for us to protect Angeline until she is required by *La Guardia*: the second is that she seeks the Abbot's permission to go to the control chamber, accompanied by Brother Mateo and at least one of us, and remains there until *La Guardia* is ready to go with her to the regulator."

He waited for their reaction to his words, and, as he had anticipated, there was a clamour of voices, Alistair, Red and Paul trying to simultaneously demand that they be chosen to accompany Angeline. When they had calmed down and stopped arguing indignantly with each other, Santiago spoke.

"It has to be Alistair."

The clamour broke out again, and he waited patiently until it subsided again.

"Why?" asked Red, his face grim.

"You know why," said Santiago calmly.

Paul nodded in rueful acknowledgement.

"Alistair has the most recent scientific knowledge of Angeline's work – he can make the greatest contribution. Damn it, I want it to be me that goes with her into that place with that - with *La Guardia* – but it has to be Alistair," he said. Red looked at him then stared at the floor. Santiago seized on the grudging consensus.

"Now that we've settled that, let's consider what roles the rest of us will play tomorrow. Angeline, Alistair and Brother Mateo will be totally secure within the chamber of *La Guardia* until they are ready to transport the core back to the regulator. The rest of us must remain in and around the guest wing until they emerge with the core. We need some kind of a signal that they are coming from behind the panelling; my thought is that Alistair comes up first and gives an agreed signal from behind the wall – some kind of coded knocking."

Angeline raised a finger. "Santiago, when you were analysing the logistics of it earlier, I understood you to say that there had to be a route to the regulator for direct maintenance, and I thought you gave the implication that this might not be a direct route from the chamber. You seem to be assuming that as a fact now, expecting us to emerge with the core. Am I right?"

"I am assuming that outcome as one possibility, and preparing for it, because it is the most hazardous outcome, although I have the feeling that those stairs were not designed for *La Guardia*, but for humans only. If there *is* a direct route from the chamber, then Mateo has to take the core down to the chamber and you and your companion will go directly to the regulator; Alistair will then emerge from the chamber alone. Either scenario is supported by my knock on wood plan," he replied. "There could of course be another scenario that we haven't envisaged..."

Angeline gave a little shiver. "Just what kind of composite creature I will be holding hands with - some kind of fusion of *La Guardia* and Brother Mateo - is something that I would rather not contemplate at the moment. Let's just hope it looks like Mateo..."

"You won't be holding hands: *La Guardia's* avatar – probably looking just like Mateo - will be carrying the core," said Alistair lightly, smiling in what he hoped was a reassuring manner at her and trying to conceal his anxiety.

"The worst case scenario, if you all emerge, is that you have to move through the guest wing and across open ground down to *El Trono*; almost as bad is that you have to move through the monastery precincts to find some hidden access point," Santiago continued. "I, too, hope the avatar is not too spectacular in physical form, and simply looks like Mateo: we can then camouflage the core in some way to make it inconspicuous."

"We can't camouflage Angeline – that is who the *hermandad* members will be looking for," said Paul. "A beautiful red-haired woman won't exactly be inconspicuous as she moves amongst an all male population..."

"Unless..." said Red ruminatively.

"Of course!" exclaimed Paul, "She will have to wear either a monk's habit or the robes of the Order."

Red grunted in confirmation. "Yep – that's it."

"I agree," said Santiago, "and that's all I have for the moment. How do we spend the rest of today?"

Alistair looked at the others. "Are we endorsing Santiago's second option - that we get the Abbot's permission for Angeline and Brother Mateo to go to the chamber at first light tomorrow?"

"Why not tonight?" asked Santiago.

There was a long, strained silence, eventually broken by Angeline.

"Frankly, I'm not keen to stay overnight in the chamber," she said uneasily.

"No way!" said her father.

"It's just not on," said Paul adamantly.

"OK," said Alistair, "then we set up our watch stints for tonight again, but changed pairings. It will be Santiago and Red, then myself and Paul."

"Try not to shoot anybody – you might waken *La Guardia*," said Angeline, with an attempt at a smile. "I need time on my own now to do some hard thinking about the options open to us in replacing the core and stabilising the heartbeat of *La Copa*, and how I might relate this to an unknown technology."

"...and I need to talk to Brother Mateo," said Santiago. "We have the problem that he remembers only what happened up to the door of the chamber, and after we all emerged. He has no memory of what went on inside during our visit, nor indeed of any previous contact he has had with *La Guardia*; that is going to make it difficult to explain the logistics to him."

"I see the problem," said Alistair. "I'll have to talk to the Abbot about the plan and how to handle Mateo."

"Consult me about what?" said the voice of Brother Anselmo, as he emerged from the passageway with Mateo, startling the others: they had been so engrossed in their analysis that they had not heard the monks approaching.

Alistair pulled the Abbot aside, quickly outlined the plan for Angeline and explained his concerns about Mateo. The old monk listened carefully, nodded approvingly, and then called Mateo to their side.

"Mateo, tomorrow you will accompany Doctora Blade and Señor Mackinnon to the chamber of *La Guardia* at first light. Follow their instructions in all things. Defend them with your life, if necessary."

Mateo was baffled by the Abbot's words and his emphatic tone, and was about to say something, but Brother Anselmo held up his hand. "I know it is hard for you to understand, Mateo, but all will become clear to you in God's good time" he said. "I entrust you with this task, and I know you will not fail me. There is something else you must do. Obtain a Moriduran Brother's habit, one of moderate size that Señorita Angeline may wear, but one with a large, deep cowl that can conceal her face."

The young monk could not conceal his surprise at the request, but nodded submissively. Alistair grasped his arm reassuringly.

"We will meet here at dawn, just before Matins. Make sure you have eaten something, Mateo – it may be sometime before our next meal," he said.

Mateo turned to his superior. "Brother Anselmo, I have many duties today and tomorrow relating to the Ceremony..." He looked bewildered.

"You are relieved of all duties but the ones I have just given to you: Brother Gregorio will reassign all your other duties. Focus your mind on these tasks. Pray for guidance: God has given you a fundamental role in his plan for mankind, and He will be with you in your time of trial." The Abbot looked up at him, and placed his thin, gentle hands on either side of Mateo's face. "You have my love and my confidence, my son. You must not fail in this..."

Mateo was deeply moved, and his voice was full of emotion as he responded.

"With the help of God, I will not fail," he said, grasping the Abbot's wrists. Brother Anselmo turned to Alistair.

"Mateo faces a trial greater than he knows,' said the Abbot sadly, 'but it must be…" He extended his hand to Alistair, who grasped it warmly. "Mateo and I must leave now; he will return before dawn. I may not see any of you until late tomorrow."

With that, they both left quickly without any further farewells. Their footsteps had barely died away when the room and everything in it began to vibrate; the vibration grew steadily in intensity; objects began to move on the surface of the table; the stack of records next to the gramophone started the shake and slide and the horn of the machine rattled.

Alistair rushed to steady the pile of 78s, and as he stood, half-bent over the low table, holding them, he realised how utterly incongruous his actions were, and he smiled foolishly at the others, who were attempting to steady themselves by grasping chair backs and the table edge. The door to the courtyard swung open abruptly, swinging wildly as though in a violent wind. Then, as suddenly as it had begun, the vibration stopped.

"I hope there is no repetition of that while I'm in the chamber tomorrow," said Angeline. "Our patient needs open heart surgery as a matter of urgency."

Red looked at his daughter; she seemed composed, but he knew the underlying anxiety that possessed her about what lay ahead.

"The chamber might be the safest place to be if old masonry starts coming down all over the place up here," he said, looking uneasily around him.

"That's a great comfort," said Angeline, "*La Guardia* and I will play with the consoles and fly around holding hands while the monastery falls down above us. I can devote the rest of my life to research underground. Of course, there will be the little matter of food and water…"

Paul moved to her side; she turned to him and stroked his cheek affectionately. "Angeline…" he said tentatively.

"I know, I know. You want to protect me, to do something…" she whispered softly.

"I feel so bloody helpless. I have no role to play, no expertise to contribute – I won't be with you when you need me most…"

Alistair, her father and Santiago moved discreetly away from them, respecting a very intimate, private moment: they started an inconsequential conversation, talking loudly. Angeline drew Paul by the hand over to the rear door and they walked out into the courtyard. The unearthly dead silence following the vibration had been replaced by the gentle sounds of the birds and the voices of the monks, who had resumed their work in the fields on the slopes of *La Copa*. The sky was a brilliant clear blue, and the rays of the sun bathed the courtyard in light.

They held hands and walked slowly through the open gate in the wall, passing monks coming and going in both directions. The Moridurans smiled at them, gave quiet greetings, sighed inwardly at the sight of two young people so obviously in love, reflected for an instant on what might have been, dismissed their nostalgia, and moved on.

Angeline and Paul found a bench to the left of the gate, and they sat down and looked at the medieval scene before them – black-robed monks moving slowly about their work on the fertile slopes.

'Do you remember when we first met?' asked Angeline, then laughed out loud as she realised how ridiculous her question sounded. The monks in the fields raised their heads at the sound, and a wave of joy in living swept across them; they beamed at each other and exulted in the moment, offering silent prayers of hope and gratitude to their God.

"Yes, a few days ago – how could I forget, even after all this time…" said Paul, squeezing her hand.

"Don't make fun of me, Paul - I'm serious!" said Angeline reprovingly.

"I know what you're going to say, and I agree completely,"

"Oh, do you?" said Angeline teasingly.

"Back in Ardmurran we agreed – well, we agreed to wait until this whole thing was over before – before we..." He blushed, and then said brusquely, "I don't want to wait – I want to be with you tonight, Angeline."

"Last dance, last chance?" she said, with an exaggerated pout, looking deep into his eyes.

"Yes," he said, then grasped her and kissed her passionately on the lips. Eventually, and reluctantly, she broke free of the embrace.

"We mustn't scandalise the monks, Paul – they have enough to contend with – tomorrow is their big day. But you're right, I agree; it was what I was thinking, and I hate you for reading my mind, Paul Corr!"

"There is a logistical problem, however," Paul said, "I am on watch tonight. It exactly doesn't fit with a romantic dalliance."

"We have all afternoon," said Angeline, her tone practical, "and afternoons are more exciting – more illicit."

They both stood up and walked back through the gate.

"We'll have to keep the others at bay," said Paul uneasily.

Angeline smiled confidently, and tossed her hair.

"I think they have already read the runes – we'll be OK," she said decisively. They entered the guest wing, and Alistair, Red and Santiago were nowhere to be seen.

"I told you so," said Angeline triumphantly, and they went up the right-hand staircase to the bedrooms.

Chapter Twenty-One

T he first faint sounds of dawn came as Alistair and Paul
    met on the north landing, in the glow from rising sun
through the great stained glass. There had been no further
disturbance of the heartbeat of *El Corazón de La Copa*, no
sound or sightings of intruders – in all, an uneventful night.

Alistair looked at his young friend and gave a low chuckle,
shaking his head.

"What?" said Paul.

"For a man who is about to surrender the love of his life
to an alien being for a day, you are looking remarkably
cheerful," he replied, with a conspiratorial, all-boys-together
glance.

Paul made a feint as though to punch him: this produced
a sparring bout, which was interrupted by Angeline emerging
fresh and smiling from her room. She held up her arms, open
palms facing the boxers. "Break!" she commanded as she
walked towards the landing. Red and Santiago came out of
their rooms almost simultaneously.

"You could have had a lie-in, guys – I don't need a
farewell party," she said, and they followed Alistair and Paul
down the staircase. As they reached the bottom, Brother
Joaquín clattered in with the cart, accompanied by Mateo.

Red yawned noisily, stretching luxuriously.

"Anything on your watch, Paul?"

Paul, still feeling a slight embarrassment after the previous
afternoon's dalliance, avoided his eyes and looked instead at
Alistair.

"No – it was uneventful, wasn't it, Alistair?"

"Boringly so," said Alistair, "disappointingly so…"

Angeline moved to Paul's side and took his hand. "I'm
starving," she said. "I plan to eat a hearty breakfast." She

looked up at Mateo. "Do I have to take a packed lunch into the chamber? Will *La Guardia* object to crumbs in the lab?"

Mateo looked in bewilderment at Joaquín. The Magus grinned broadly, but offered no insight as he carried the food to the table. They sat down, and Mateo hovered uneasily, carrying a black Moriduran habit over his arm. "May I join you for breakfast?" he said eventually.

Angeline sprang up, flustered. "Of course, Mateo – you are coming with us – how could I forget!"

Mateo gratefully eased his bulk into a chair beside Angeline, still carrying the monk's habit.

"Here, let me have that," said Angeline, taking it from him and carrying it across to the bench at the gramophone; she returned to the table, smiling at Mateo. "I hope it's a reasonable fit," she said.

They ate quickly and silently, aware that very shortly members of the Ancient Order would start arriving, ferried by coach from Moridanza. Mateo finished first and stood up, with a brief apology. He looked down at Angeline, and she took a last hasty gulp of her coffee.

"I'm just coming, Mateo – I know – we must get moving. Alistair?"

Alistair stood up and motioned to the others, who were also about to rise. "Sit down, please – finish your breakfast – we don't want a crowd in the passageway."

Red ignored him, and went across to his daughter, followed by Paul. He embraced her and whispered something softly; she kissed his cheek, and then turned to Paul. He held her tightly, kissed her on the mouth, then the cheek. "I'll be OK – honestly…" she said firmly.

"Is nobody going to kiss me?" asked Alistair petulantly. "Red? Paul?"

Red and Paul came and shook his and Mateo's hands, followed by Santiago. Mateo went across to the bench and lifted the black habit.

"Shall I put it on now, Mateo?" asked Angeline.

"No – it would not be safe during the descent; walking in a habit demands a lot of practice, Señorita Angeline, and this one is large, and will hang very loosely on you, creating an additional hazard. I will keep it for you until our return."

Red put his arm around Paul's shoulder and called out to Alistair, Mateo and Angeline as they walked to the mouth of the left-hand passageway.

"Look after our best girl, guys! See you later!"

Mateo reached up behind the staircase, found the wooden wheel and turned it clockwise. There was a click and a creak, and they walked along to the narrow gap in the panelling. Mateo slid the panel along to the left until it locked open with the counterweight raised, and they bent down and entered, one by one, stepping down to the floor of the inner space. Once they were all inside, he operated the mechanism and the partition closed, rapidly but smoothly, as the weight dropped. They glanced briefly at the trunk lying just inside the partition, and walked across to the small stone building, entered, and headed for the aperture in the floor that led to the stairs.

Mateo turned to face them. "I will go first with Señorita Angeline on my left, Señor Alistair, and then pause part way down. Please do not commence your descent until we have stopped, then descend carefully until you are right behind me. You have no support but your right hand on the wall."

Angeline gave her delicate hand up to the monk's powerful grasp and they tentatively commenced their descent. Alistair stood watching them go down; their free hands touched the floor at the edge of the aperture then slid on to the rough textured wall. When the monk's tonsured head was level with the floor above, he stopped, and Alistair started to descend, his right hand on the wall. Alistair considered making small talk to reassure Angeline, but decided against it, and they continued in total silence, the light becoming brighter as they descended. At last they reached the bottom and stood before the metallic door to the chamber. Brother Mateo looked at Alistair for guidance.

"Do as you did before, Mateo – stand in front of the door and place the palms of your hands on its surface."

Angeline shivered involuntarily, anticipating the awful alien voice; when it came, and uttered Mateo's name, it was even more awe-inspiring than before, and the sound seemed to penetrate to the very core of her being. They waited but the door did not slide upwards as before; Mateo looked over his shoulder at them both, the monk's habit slung over his arm, his eyebrows raised.

"Maybe you didn't knock loudly enough, Mateo," said Angeline, her voice shaky, "try again…"

The monk removed his hands from the surface, and then placed them back again; nothing happened. Alistair thought for a moment; he walked forward, indicated to Mateo that he should step aside, and then placed his own hands on the metal surface.

"Alistair," said the great voice. The tone was not quite so intimidating this time. The panel, however, remained obdurately closed.

"I think it wants all our thumbprints," said Angeline, "make way, Alistair!"

She placed her hands on the cool surface, and the voice rang out in warm, welcoming tones.

"Angeline!"

The panel slid up silently and they entered the chamber for the second time. The great screen and the golden consoles gleamed in the cold light, with no activity showing except for the red light on the right-hand console.

"Remind me, Angeline - what happened at this point last time?" said Alistair.

"Mateo mounted the platform and stood on the left-hand plinth, then I did, although I don't know if I should have done…"

Alistair saw the confusion on the monk's face; his friends were discussing events of which he had no recollection.

"I know this must be very frustrating for you, Mateo: there is a gap in your memory between the moment you arrived at the external door and the time we left. Please mount the platform, then the left hand plinth."

The monk stepped on to the platform, then on to the plinth. After a moment, the consoles gradually came to life and the central display lit up and began to display swirling coloured patterns, then the brilliant burst of light came from the screen, enveloped Mateo, surged back and then forward again. When the great voice came, it was immediately warm and peaceful – the gradual modulation from the terrifying initial voice of the previous occasion was absent.

"Mateo…" it said, and the monk turned slowly and beamed at his friends on the floor of the chamber. They both felt weak, happy and strangely respectful, like children before a beloved, powerful adult. The incredible force of the combined personalities of *La Guardia* and Mateo was almost overwhelming, and Alistair fought against feelings of awe, deference and subjection.

"Angeline… Alistair… my friends - we have a great task to perform, one that will demand all our combined physical and intellectual resources. There are three possible outcomes: the first is that we succeed in replacing the core in the regulator, restoring communication from the control centre here, and stabilising *El Corazón de La Copa*: the second is that, using the new insights and discoveries of Angeline, we permanently remove the gravitational instability that we may call the nascent black hole: the third outcome is that we fail to do either of these things.

"Our task is not, however, just a scientific one – we must get the core and the key physically from this chamber to *El Trono*, facing the hazards caused by human fear, greed and frailty on the way. I can use force to protect our party, but its use involves danger to me and to those around me."

"Why is that?" said Angeline.

"Those who brought me to this place had to place limitations on my thought processes to protect me in an alien environment, partly to enable me to tolerate the loneliness and separation from my own kind across the millennia, partly to ensure that I fulfilled my purpose. I have been programmed with certain autonomic actions that are triggered by perceived physical threats to me and to my purpose in controlling the gravitational anomaly."

"Can you be more specific?" asked Alistair.

"You have a more specific question in your mind, Alistair," said Mateo. "Please ask it."

Alistair drew a deep breath. "When a Magus Elect presents himself at the Ceremony, do you make a judgement on his fitness for office?"

"In part, the judgement is made by my programming, but I have some discretion in the matter," said the voice speaking from the mouth of the monk, and something of the alien timbre returned to it, chilling the hearts of Angeline and Alistair.

Angeline looked distinctly uneasy at the implications of all that *La Guardia* had intimated to them; she looked at Alistair to see if her unease was shared – it was.

"Mateo, either come down here, or we'll join you on the platform. We're beginning to feel intimidated by being talked down to – I mean in physical terms…" said Alistair

The monk gave a great laugh, and leaped straight from the plinth, across the platform and on to the floor beside them, stumbling as he landed. Alistair caught him and steadied him, and the monk straightened up, grinning.

"I thought I would give old-fashioned gravity a chance. I hope I didn't alarm you, my friends," he said. "Forgive me if I rejoice in my physical presence in the person of Mateo; it is exhilarating in a way that you cannot fully understand. Now to your concerns - what can I say to reassure you both?"

Alistair and Angeline exchanged glances.

"I guess there's nothing we can ask for in the way of guarantees," she said. " My safety is not the main consideration."

As she spoke, she became aware that Mateo seemed to be experiencing some inner conflict: his expression and the neutral focus of his eyes suggested an inner dialogue with *La Guardia*, and he shook his head impatiently. He spoke suddenly and abruptly, as though breaking a constraint that had been placed on his utterance, now looking directly at her.

"You may not only have yourself to consider, Angeline…" He broke off again and turned away from them and moved towards the platform. As he mounted the platform, he spoke, but not to his friends behind him.

"I sense it – we must know – she must know…" he said, walking towards the plinth. As he attempted to mount it, he seemed to be thrown back, and he turned round in a way that suggested that he was being compelled to do so against his will. He faced Alistair and Angeline, his features contorted by some great effort, and then a terrible voice came from his mouth.

"It is better not to know – such knowledge can only threaten the task." As though with great effort, he held out both of his hands to Angeline in a gesture of appeal.

Angeline instinctively moved towards the base of the platform, but was restrained by Alistair. "Mateo, what is it?" she said, looking up at the monk. Mateo sank gradually to his knees, and bent his head. His voice sounded faintly, murmuring in Latin; it sounded to Alistair like a prayer, with rhythmic cadences, but he could only catch occasional words.

"Alistair, we must help him – what can we do?" Angeline said desperately.

"Nothing, Angeline – nothing…" he replied in tight, anxious voice, pressing her arm.

The great central display screen suddenly burst into life, and Mateo was lifted, turned and deposited on the plinth, still kneeling. The light surged out and enveloped him, whirling and twisting around his body, and then it retracted into the screen. The monk stood up slowly, turned and descended from the plinth, walked across the platform and down on to the floor. As he faced them, they saw that his features were drawn and tense; he slumped a little and would have fallen if Alistair and Angeline had not supported his great weight until he steadied himself.

"Are you all right, Mateo?" asked Angeline anxiously.

"Yes and no," he replied shakily, "I have had a difference of opinion with *La Guardia*: at this moment we are separate, but our difference is resolved – we are now agreed on the matter that was in dispute."

"What in God's name was the cause of it, Mateo? You've got us seriously worried…" Alistair's voice held a mix of concern and reproach.

"It was in God's name that I did what I did," said the monk. He looked down into his friend's eyes with great respect and affection in his gaze. "Central to our beliefs are the concepts of truth and the free will of the individual. A Moriduran accepts authority and discipline, but freely and willingly. We are prepared to sacrifice anything rather than deny truth or constrain free will." He looked down at Angeline, and gave her his great, warm smile.

"Angeline has freely offered to assist us in our time of trial, and places herself in great personal danger in undertaking this great task. She can only continue to fulfil this commitment in the full knowledge of all the facts, and now there may be a new consideration – a new element."

He took her hand gently. "I must ask you to briefly mount the plinth – there is something we must determine positively before we can continue, Angeline. May I assist you?"

Alistair demurred. "I am not sure that I can agree, after all that has just happened, Mateo. I think what we saw was one of *La Guardia's* defence mechanisms being used against you. How can Angeline expose herself to this?"

"Alistair, I trust Mateo absolutely, and, for the moment …" She placed her hand on the monk's arm. "…this is Mateo. In any event, we have no real choice – we must continue." She pulled him towards the platform. "Lead on, Brother!"

Alistair waved an arm impotently as he watched them climb on to the platform and walk to the plinth. The monk lifted Angeline up in one swift, effortless movement and placed her on it, facing the screen, then he stepped back.

The light came, surrounded her, and withdrew. She turned, Mateo extended his hand to her, and she stepped down and rejoined Alistair: Mateo remained on the platform, facing the screen. It flickered briefly, and then the display was at rest. He turned and walked to the edge of the platform and stopped. After a moment, a subtle change came over him, and it was plain that the monk was again united with *La Guardia*.

"Doctora Angeline Blade," said the great voice, "you must reconsider your involvement in the task of replacing the core and the key, and re-assess the risks involved. Mateo has convinced me that you must be given new information that will affect your decision. I reaffirm your absolute freedom to choose."

Angeline was looking completely bewildered.

"What in hell is going on?" she whispered to Alistair.

The great voice continued. "I now release Mateo to explain to you directly what you must know…"

Mateo relaxed visibly, and moved to join them. He tried to smile, but the strain of what had happened was still evident in his face.

She moved beside him and pulled at the sleeve of his robe. "Tell me what you have to tell me," she said gently.

Mateo took both her hands in his.

"You no longer have only yourself to consider," he said gravely.

"Mateo, I've known that all along – what's new?" she said, a note of impatience in her voice.

"Angeline," said the monk slowly and diffidently, "there is a new life within you, a new soul created by you and Paul – a gift from God."

She stared up at him uncomprehendingly, shaking her head slowly, and then looked at Alistair.

"Mateo, how can you know this? Our science could not detect life as…" Alistair hesitated, glancing sideways at Angeline. "… as early as this…"

"I sensed the new life: *La Guardia* has confirmed it - there can be no doubt," said the monk, absolute certainty in his voice.

Angeline turned to Alistair, her cheeks aglow.

"I must speak to Paul; he must know – he must be part of any decision I make in the light of this."

"Angeline, that is not possible until we leave this place – you know that," he said. Turning his head to Mateo, he gestured towards the screen and consoles. "*La Guardia* wanted to conceal this from us: how can we proceed on a basis of trust now?"

Mateo looked at them both, then turned towards the platform, raising his hand palm upwards in a gesture of appeal. The screen came to life, and the great voice filled the chamber.

"It is now time, Mateo. Angeline must be prepared for what lies ahead: Alistair must be made to understand."

"No!" cried the monk, springing up on to the platform, "They need more time – I need more time…" He moved rapidly towards the screen, but before he reached it, he was lifted bodily above the left plinth, spun around to face away from the screen, and deposited on the plinth, his body motionless, his voice silenced, his eyes closed. Alistair put his arm around Angeline, and gripped her trembling body tightly.

The light swirled out from the screen and enveloped the figure of the monk: another wave of light came and wrapped itself around the larger plinth next to him. Both consoles were alive with flashing lights and strange sounds, and Alistair felt an intolerable pressure in his ears. Angeline had slumped against him, and he supported her with difficulty, feeling his own sense of balance slipping away. He pulled her towards the base of the platform and they both sank to their knees: Alistair was now holding her with both hands, gently resting her body against the edge of the structure to provide support.

There were now two spinning pillars of light above each plinth: the form of the monk was invisible within the left one, but suddenly the light enclosing him lifted, detached itself from the plinth and move towards the column of light on the right, leaving the left plinth empty. As they merged, an agonised voice – the voice of Mateo – came from within the coruscating, swirling mass.

"Trust in me, my friends... do not be fearful..."

A strange odour permeated the chamber, animal-like, yet strangely reassuring; the density of the mass of light seemed to be changing – it was coalescing, and something was forming within it, moving, writhing.

Suddenly the light withdrew into the screen and as they saw the chimera rearing up before them on the plinth, a wave of terror swept over Alistair and Angeline.

About the size of a large horse, it was silver-blue in colour, hairless, the skin completely smooth; powerful muscles rippled on its body. It was supported by four legs, with six-toed feet that were clearly prehensile – more like hands than feet. A long, almost reptilian tail lashed back and forth at its rear, but the real shock of the creature was that, above the front of the long body, a human torso rose – a waist, a chest, two arms with six-fingered hands, a neck and a great head, with a mass of snake-like tentacles writhing on it. The sight that made them recoil in horror was that the head bore the features of Mateo, but devoid of colour, the great eyes blazing with an inhuman light.

The mouth opened and a terrifying, yet joyful sound came from it – the primeval cry of a wild creature released from a long captivity, exulting in its freedom and its physical power. Perhaps the most shocking fact was that, as it reared up on its hind legs, it was evident, from its whole physique, that the Beast of Moridura was female.

The creature sprang down from the plinth: in spite of its bulk, the movement was smooth and effortless, like a big cat. Angeline and Alistair stood up slowly and warily, trying to overcome their fear of *La Guardia* in her full, physical manifestation.

Angeline spoke cautiously, her voice trembling.

"Mateo – are you still with us?"

The creature moved to the edge of the platform and settled into a Sphinx-like posture. The great head bent forward and the huge grey eyes looked at her, then at Alistair.

"Mateo, as you knew him, is no more," it said in the alien voice that they had first heard in the chamber. "He is incorporated in me, and will never return. All that he knew, I know – all his memories are with me. His experiences, his loyalties, his affections, his temperament are incorporated in me. We are as one again, united as we have been countless times over the millennia since I created the first Mateo as my avatar. My name, the name my mother gave me aeons ago, is …"

The sound of the name that came from the mouth of the creature had an alien timbre and articulation – the closest approximation of the sound Alistair could manage was Arkimateo, and he and Angeline repeated it aloud simultaneously.

"Arkimateo…"

The creature gave a great laugh – it modulated gradually into an unmistakeably female timbre, but with the cadences and inflection of Brother Mateo. "You have correctly identified my sex as female; I feel you will be more comfortable with a voice that has female characteristics."

Angeline could not stop the flood of tears that came from her grief at the loss of Mateo and Alistair attempted to comfort her, looking reproachfully at the creature on the platform.

"Arkimateo – why did you do this? Why is Mateo no longer with us? He has come to mean a great deal to us in the time we have known him. Why did he resist you as you took him?"

"He clung to his human form, to his life, his friends – and he wanted to say goodbye," said Arkimateo. "But we have done this thing many times, Mateo and I, and when the time comes, it is best done quickly. Now he is at peace – I am at peace – we are at peace. We can only co-exist simultaneously in our physical forms for very short periods. When I created Mateo, I sacrificed my physical being for thirty-five of your years, and existed only as pure thought in the circuits of the consoles. So it has been, since I first found a creature whose genes could provide me with a suitable avatar. The Mateos can trace their lineage back to the earliest, tool-using being that walked upright on your planet – a pure, single bloodline that parallels the evolution of your species."

Alistair stared at the creature on the platform, trying to assimilate the incredible story that came from its mouth, in a gentle, but powerful female voice.

"Does that mean that Mateo also now exists as pure mind in the consoles, as you did?" he said tentatively.

The great head shook from side to side. "No, Mateo is wholly incorporated in my physical brain, my memories. He was my avatar: I am not his."

Angeline, in spite of herself, was beginning to feel a strange affinity with the female creature above her, and her grief and resentment were gradually ebbing away.

"You absorbed the physical body of Mateo and his memories by some kind of quantum process, Arkimateo, did you not?" she said.

"In a sense, yes," said Arkimateo, "...all of his memories, but only the essence of his physical being. I must retain that to create a new baby Mateo, if that is necessary."

"Why have you taken physical form again?" asked Alistair. "Why did you surrender your physical form in the first instance?"

Arkimateo looked down at Angeline. "I think you understand..."

Angeline nodded, and turned to Alistair. "I believe that Arkimateo can only survive in corporeal form on our planet for very short periods of time, and that duration may only be measured in days – perhaps only one or two at a time."

The great head nodded appreciatively. "You have great insight, Angeline Blade. There is another factor at work – can you divine what it is?"

"Your control of the processes incorporated in the consoles is limited when you are not in corporeal form: physical manifestation is necessary at the recurrent points in the cycle of the gravitational anomaly to permit full access and control?"

Arkimateo gave an oddly animal-like grunt of satisfaction.

"I have a question," said Alistair. "Did you create all the Mateos by the same process that you used to remove their physical form and incorporate them within you?"

"No," said Arkimateo. She turned her head and looked at Angeline; one of her front legs reached out in a tentative gesture that could only be described as a movement towards a caress, and Angeline instinctively reached out and touched the long fingers of the great hand. "The process you have just witnessed utilises something your scientists are presently searching for in their particle accelerators – that which you call the *Higgs boson* – the link between energy and mass. I could recreate the adult Mateo by that same process, but I would be destroyed, utterly and irrevocably. The Mateo you knew was conceived within my body, and he was born as a living creature is born, from within me. I have experienced the pain and the joy of motherhood, as you will, Angeline."

"But – but Mateo had no navel," said Alistair, confused, "and neither have you…"

Arkimateo laughed, a vast, joyful sound, but frightening to her listeners. "You are observant, but you are overlooking the obvious, my human friends. Am I not reptilian in appearance to your eyes?"

Alistair clapped his hand to his forehead. "He was born from an egg…" he said in astonishment.

Arkimateo sighed in satisfaction again. "The Mateos were all truly my children, yet were all truly human in their physical form. They had one father, of the human species: he is lost in the mists of time." Again the great laugh came. "He was unaware that he had donated his genetic code to create a unique race that would endure throughout human history…"

Angeline was fascinated. "How long were the gestation periods?"

"They were measured in weeks, not months – an artificially accelerated time scale - but were nonetheless fulfilling experiences. The sense of new life growing within…" Her voice became very quiet, and a note of sadness entered it. "I may never experience that again."

"How were the Mateos fed?" asked Alistair.

"I fed them for a few hours from the residual nutrients in the egg, then I left them near the earliest human settlements: human beings have lived in the vicinity of *La Copa* since earliest times, creating many superstitions and rituals around the site, which they regarded as sacred. Sometimes the baby Mateo was not found and starved, and I sensed his pain and his death. I grieved, and then I created another Mateo. Usually the baby *was* found and taken in by a family.

"When the child became a young adult, he was drawn to this place - to the Portal, to the chamber. From then on, he would become involved in the rituals, and was often regarded as a shaman or priest. Over the centuries, the people of the area came to expect, and look for the baby Mateos, recognising them as special children. The legends grew, and the earliest form of the Order of Moridura emerged. By the time of the schism in the Order and the formation of the Moriduran Brothers, only two members of the *hermandad* knew the secret, and the current Mateo would live a normal life, ignorant of his true nature, except when I required him as my avatar. At the time of the Ceremony, every thirty-five years, he was incorporated in me. After the great schism, the secret knowledge of the Mateos was limited to the Abbot and the Magus of Moridura, and they found and cared for each new baby, found a wet nurse from the village for him, and reared him as a child of the monastery."

"Arkimateo, how do you regard us? You are a living creature of another species, of great age: you have scientific knowledge beyond our imaginings. We must seem to you as the higher primates seem to us…" said Alistair.

The grey eyes looked at him, then at Angeline.

"No, that analogy is not appropriate. A chimpanzee can never achieve the intellectual level of a human being, but the only intellectual difference between us is one of years, and of scientific knowledge. If Aristotle, Socrates, Leonardo Da Vinci or Isaac Newton stood before you, would you feel superior to them because of your scientific knowledge? Your present knowledge is the summation of your culture, built on the achievements of those who went before you: do you doubt that these men could understand what you understand, achieve what you have achieved, given time?"

"What, no women available for your comparisons, Arkimateo?" said Angeline, her confidence growing.

"Their absence would have been paralleled in my matriarchal culture by an equivalent absence of males – our respective cultures ignored or restricted the achievements of one sex – it is regrettable, but it is so," said Arkimateo. "The future will be different for your race and your sex, Angeline. You are on the brink of the greatest scientific discovery of your time – the conquest of gravity and the development of a unified theory of physics. But before that you must either stabilise the oscillation of *El Corazón's* gravitational field or weaken it until it expands into nothingness – failure will result in it increasing to infinite mass, and then it will become a what you call a black hole."

Arkimateo abruptly reared up on to her hind legs. The effect was spectacular and intimidating: in the couchant position, her head was some metre and three quarters from the floor of the platform: rampant, as she now was, Arkimateo was over three metres tall, even though the rear legs were not fully extended.

"Come with me to the consoles and I will explain what we must do," she said, looking at the two white-faced creatures standing on the floor of the chamber, then, in the voice of Alistair's mother, "*That lassie's lookin' awfy peely-wally, Alistair!*"

Alistair laughed, a great feeling of relief and affection swept over him, and he took Angeline's hand. "*Peely-wally* means you're looking pale and unwell – it comes from the time when Glasgow imported Walloon chinaware from the Netherlands, which they called *wally* in the vernacular. Literally translated, it is *peeling Walloon*, that is to say, the glaze on your dinner service is flaking off."

"Unflattering but exotic," muttered Angeline, but some colour did return to her cheeks as they followed the incredible Beast of Moridura towards the glowing gold consoles. Arkimateo sat back on her haunches before the left-hand console, and they stood beside her, Angeline on her right and Alistair on her left.

A foreleg, or arm, slipped gently round Angeline's shoulder, and instead of being frightened, she felt warm and safe, feelings accompanied by a strange ambivalence about whether she was being embraced by Mateo or Arkimateo: she decided happily that it was both of them, and looked up at the great head, which was inclined down towards her.

Arkimateo's grey eyes twinkled and from her mouth came the voice of Alistair, causing him to start with surprise.

"Ma wee pal Angeline," said Arkimateo, in a completely authentic Glasgow accent, "we have work to do…"

Alistair bunched his shoulders and tilted his head, his eyes narrowing: he was annoyed at the appropriation of his term of endearment for Doctor Blade.

Chapter Twenty-Two

The thirty monks who would guide the members of the Ancient Order up the cliff path as they arrived by coach from Moridanza were assembled at the base of the path, waiting for Brother Mateo. Who else would coordinate their efforts but Mateo? For many years now, it was he who had organised the guides when any large group of visitors came to the monastery. They laughed and gossiped in the morning sunshine, with a sense of excitement and anticipation, feeling privileged that they would be part of the Ceremony and all the preparations leading up to it. After all, some monks lived and died in the monastery without ever having been present at a Ceremony: only a few monks would experience two ceremonies, and they were all over sixty years of age.

Footsteps on the path interrupted the monks' chatter, and to their dismay, it was Brother Gregorio who arrived in their midst, not Mateo. Gregorio motioned the monks to gather round him and they moved reluctantly into a half-circle in front of him.

Gregorio was unpopular among most of his brethren – he was regarded as a cold, imperious bureaucrat, and one who sought the favour of Don Ferdinand and the *confratres*, rather than cultivating the respect of his brother monks. Nonetheless, he had a small cabal of younger monks who looked up to him.

Gregorio launched into what he had to say without greeting or preamble, as was his way.

"You were expecting Mateo. He is engaged on other tasks for the Abbot: I will coordinate the visitors and guides," he said in his dry monotone. "The coach will arrive shortly with the first visitors; the driver, Cristobal Ortega, will then return to the village to pick up the next tranche."

Tranche, thought the monks: only Gregorio would have used such a pretentious word. "It means a slice of cake," whispered one of them, causing some strangled sniggering among the younger monks.

Gregorio stared at them with his severe expression, designed to carry the stamp of his authority, but it only caused more suppressed amusement.

"There will be a turnaround time of about an hour and a half; we expect several coach loads by early to mid-afternoon." he continued, "and you will conduct them up *el sendero de precipio* in groups of no more than ten visitors. I divide you into guide groups – thus…"

Gregorio strode forward with his left arm outstretched, and separated the monks into groups by placing his arm between the tenth and eleventh monk from the left, and then between the twentieth and twenty first.

"The first coach will carry Don Ferdinand and the senior *confratres* – they will be wearing their robes, but with the hoods thrown back, for safety reasons on the path. If some do not observe this precaution, and chose to keep their heads covered, it is not your place to counsel them otherwise, but be especially watchful of such persons – their balance may be affected on the path."

"… their balance and our safety…" grumbled one monk, attracting a glare from Gregorio.

"You will wait at the top of the path until the last pairing of the last group has arrived, then immediately descend to the plain. You will not enter the monastery under any circumstances. Brother Joaquín will conduct each group of visitors to the dormitory of the *confratres* as they arrive, and he will outline the arrangements that have been made for them during their stay, and for the Ceremony." Gregorio scanned the monks' faces for any signs of dissent: there was some murmuring and he decided reluctantly to take questions.

"Are there any points of clarification?" he said, his tone making it abundantly clear that a response would be unwelcome.

"Brother Gregorio – what shall we do as we wait on the plain? It will be some time before the coach returns…"

Gregorio looked coldly at the impertinent questioner.

"Pray. I will lead you in prayer until each coach arrives: on the arrival of the first coach, I will personally welcome Don Ferdinand and the senior members of the Order."

As he finished speaking, the first, faint sounds of the coach approaching came in the still air of the plain, and there was a ripple of excitement among the monks. Gregorio attempted to quiet them and pushed and shoved them into a relatively orderly group facing the road: he turned and watched the oncoming coach as it rattled noisily over the ruts. At last it came to a halt, and the figure of Cristobal Ortega could be seen through the front window, smiling and waving to the monks. He scrambled out of his seat, opened the door and jumped down, calling a greeting to the reception committee, and was pointedly ignored by Gregorio, who was staring straight past him.

A tall, red-robed figure emerged and paused in the doorway; the hood of the robe was thrown back, and the cold, haughty glance of Don Ferdinand de Moridanza swept across the faces of the monks, and instantly noted the absence of Brother Mateo. He stepped down from the coach, declining Cristobal's proffered hand, and strode across to Gregorio, who was bowing obsequiously.

"I bid you welcome, Don Ferdinand," said Gregorio.

Ferdinand made a slight motion of acknowledgement. "Where is Mateo?" he asked brusquely, and looking behind him, gestured to the figure hesitating in the doorway of the coach, waiting to descend. The bulky figure climbed down clumsily, and although his hood covered his face, Gregorio recognised the man known as Jaime.

"Brother Mateo is engaged with the Abbot on urgent business relating to the Ceremony," he said in reply to the Don's peremptory query.

"Is he?" said Ferdinand. "Does this urgent business relate to Mackinnon and his party?"

"I have no knowledge of the details," said Gregorio smoothly, looking beyond Don Ferdinand and silently counting the number of red-robed figures now shuffling about beside the coach. Almost all of them had their hoods thrown back, their faces visible. Among the exceptions were Jaime, and two men standing apart from the others, each carrying a long, flat case.

Gregorio counted a total of twenty-five visitors, including Don Ferdinand. He motioned to his first group of ten guides, and they moved forward in a gratifyingly disciplined manner.

"If I may request the first group of ten to come forward, Don Ferdinand, my brethren will escort them on the ascent in the usual manner."

Don Ferdinand ignored him, and motioned to Jaime, the two men with the long cases, and one other man, a tall, spare figure, with narrow shoulders, recognisable to Gregorio and the monks as Domingo, a member of the Grand Council, a brutal, frightening man.

"We will ascend as a party of five; five monks will accompany us in the normal pairing arrangement, and five will follow carrying our cases."

Gregorio was about to protest, but decided against it. He split his group of ten monks into two groups of five. The two men with the long cases were initially reluctant to surrender them to the monks who approached them, but an intervention by Domingo resolved the matter, and the five pairings set off, followed after a moment by three monks carrying small overnight cases, with two monks, Felipe and Antonio bringing up in the rear, each carrying an overnight case and a long case.

"Felipe, God has given us a heavy load today: what can these cases contain?" murmured Antonio.

"God knows of our burden," said Felipe, "but Don Ferdinand is responsible for it. My thought is that the cases contain weapons…"

On the plain, the coach had left for Moridanza, and Brother Gregorio led the remaining monks in prayer, kneeling facing them on the hard surface where the coach had recently stood, with the smell of fuel and engine oil still rising in the heat. As they knelt and prayed, they and the remaining members of the *hermandad* – who neither knelt nor prayed - watched the file of monks and members of the Ancient Order moving up the path, a snake with a body of red and black that became black towards its end, disappearing sinuously round the bend of the cliff. Just before the black tail vanished, Brothers Felipe and Antonio turned and made faces at their brethren on the plain, causing the chanted prayers to waver, to Gregorio's great annoyance.

He jumped to his feet and marshalled the next group of ten monks and ten visitors, and set them off up the path. Turning to the ten remaining robed and hooded figures, he invited them to join the monks in prayer as they knelt again. Six visitors did kneel with the monks, but four declined, and facing each other, began to talk in whispers.

When the tail of the new snake vanished around the curve of the cliff, Gregorio despatched the last group, then knelt in solitary prayer, asking God for the gift of humility, and for the strength to display more charity towards his brethren. His silent prayers were formal and structured: they were addressed to the Almighty, but also in part to an imaginary audience that would be lost in admiration at his devotional eloquence: but this time a passionate outburst from his deep inner voice interrupted the sonorous flow.

"Why don't they love me, as they love Anselmo, as they love Joaquín and Mateo?" he heard it cry: and the voice of the Lord seemed to answer him, telling him not to ask stupid questions, and that he already knew why. Gregorio brought his prayer to a hasty, perfunctory close, and stood up. Then he wept a little - sentimental, self-pitying tears.

At the top of the cliff path, Brother Joaquín stood beside the great gates, which were thrown open to welcome the *confratres* and members of the Order. He leant against one of the massive gateposts for support as a wave of weakness almost overcame him, but the first murmuring voices could be heard coming up the path, and he straightened with an effort and walked forward to meet the Magus Elect - Don Ferdinand de Moridanza - and his companions.

As they appeared, Joaquín noted that only Ferdinand and Domingo had their hoods thrown back: one of the three remaining men was Jaime – identifiable by his bulk even under the loose robe – but the other two hooded men were unfamiliar, and carried themselves with the poised, animal-like caution that signalled men accustomed to danger and violence. His eyes flicked to the five monks bringing up in the rear and to the long cases that Felipe and Antonio were carrying in addition to the overnight cases: the connection was made instantly in his mind with the two hooded men – they were the replacements for *los artilleros*.

He composed his features into a smile as Ferdinand and Domingo came towards him.

"Ferdinand – my brother Domingo – welcome" He shook their hands in turn, avoiding the flat, cold eyes of Domingo, and called a greeting to the three other men, but did not address Jaime by name – the anonymity of a hooded member was usually respected, although he could be addressed as *my brother* or by his title in the Order, if he had one.

"Señores, do you wish to wait for the rest of your party?"

"No," said Ferdinand, taking his bag from the monk who was holding it, and signalling to the others to do likewise.

"Then I will accompany you to the dormitory of the *confratres*; Brother Antonio and Brother Felipe will conduct the remaining two groups to the dormitory as they arrive," said Brother Joaquín.

"Brother Gregorio said…" commenced Felipe.

"I know, Felipe – that you must not enter the monastery – but you will explain the circumstances to him when you return to the plain. You have more than enough time – Cristobal and the coach will not be back for some time yet."

Ferdinand walked silently at Joaquín's side through the cloister towards the dormitory of the *confratres*. He cast a sidelong glance down at the monk beside him, listening to his inconsequential chatter and his friendly greetings to the monks working in the central area, and asked himself, as he had many times, how this humble, quiet little man could have become the Magus of Moridura. When Anselmo first revealed the identity of the Magus to him all those years ago, he had been incredulous. Yet here he was beside him, and this little monk would preside over the Ceremony and officiate at his elevation to Magus.

He had no idea of what opinion Joaquín had of him – whether he liked him or cordially detested him, thought him fit or unfit to succeed him as Magus: Ferdinand expected and demanded respect, because of his proud lineage. He wondered if Joaquín could interfere with his plans, even at this late stage. He quickly dismissed the thought: the key members of the Order were loyal to him alone: they accepted the token authority of the incumbent Magus, but, he, Ferdinand, represented the real secular power - he held the future in his hands, and they knew it.

They entered the dormitory, and Ferdinand moved directly to the place where he and his inner circle normally slept, near the far door. Tables with benches on either side ran down the centre of the vast room, with the beds at right angles to the walls. Joaquín had outlined the programme for the Ceremony by the time they reached Ferdinand's sleeping area; most of it was hallowed by tradition and familiar to Ferdinand from descriptions passed on to him by his father, by the Abbot and some of the older *confratres*. But he had a question for the outgoing Magus.

"Where is Mateo?" he asked bluntly.

"Brother Mateo is engaged on essential duties for the Abbot," replied Joaquín.

"I must speak to him," said Ferdinand, "I need his special talents for a task that must be performed before tomorrow."

"He may be detained by Brother Anselmo for the whole of today," Brother Joaquín murmured apologetically. "I, too, have things that I wish Mateo to do for me, but, alas…" He saw that Ferdinand found his reply unacceptable, and made sympathetic noises.

"Perhaps I can help – another Brother, a strong, resourceful, intelligent one – there are many to choose from…"

"There is no one who displays Mateo's special qualities – no one," snapped Ferdinand impatiently. "I must speak to the Abbot at once."

"Alas, I regret that Brother Anselmo will also be unavailable for most of today. Perhaps Gregorio, or I myself may be of service? We are, of course, at your disposal…"

"Gregorio is a stupid bureaucrat!" exploded Ferdinand, and then he met Joaquín's eyes, which were now impenetrable and flat, with no sign of their usual sparkle. He knew at once he had overstepped himself: the little monk was squarely facing him: the deference and affability had vanished, and he stared unblinkingly at him.

"You go too, far, Ferdinand, to speak of my venerable brother, the deputy of the Abbot, in this way. You will withdraw your remark at once."

The three hooded men stood like statues, and the cold eye of Domingo was fixed on Ferdinand: the newly-arrived second party, entering at that moment with Brother Antonio at their head, stopped abruptly, and fell silent, aware of the tension at the far end of the room. Ferdinand felt as though his father's spirit was hovering over him, sending a silent warning. His nostrils flared as he sucked air into his lungs.

"I withdraw my remark most willingly; it was crass, insensitive, and born of deep fatigue and the stress of anticipating our great event. My most esteemed brother and superior, accept my apology." He could feel the blood pounding in his ears, and his fingernails dug into his palms in frustration, every muscle in his body contracting painfully as he strove to master his rage.

His eyes met Domingo's for a moment, and he saw endorsement and approval in their cruel depths: Ferdinand relaxed with an audible sigh.

Joaquín beamed up at him.

"Delivered with a grace worthy of your esteemed father, of blessed memory. We are all exhausted and tense – our great day comes upon us, and the Good Lord tests our readiness for it," he said.

Ferdinand sat down heavily upon his bed; Domingo and Jaime followed suit; the other two men remained standing.

"Thank you for your offer of substitutes for Mateo. Of course, there are none. I will await the Abbot's pleasure, Joaquín," he said.

Joaquín bowed and turning, walked towards Brother Antonio and the second group. Domingo leaned across from his bed towards Ferdinand and spoke softly.

"Perhaps there is something in the legend of the vanishing Mateos after all, my brother," he said.

"Superstitious nonsense, based on coincidence," said Ferdinand, and the fat figure of Jaime on the other bed nodded. The two standing men turned their hooded heads very slightly towards each other and shook them almost imperceptibly: the reference meant nothing to them.

"I have had no breakfast: when do we eat?" asked Jaime plaintively, and slowly threw his hood back, revealing his bland, smooth features and slack mouth, his tongue running over his thick lips. His answer came from Brother Joaquín, who was addressing the second, and now the third group arriving from the coach.

"Please occupy bed spaces at the upper end of the dormitory to make way for the new groups as they arrive. Once you are settled go to the refectory, where breakfast will be served to you. Thank you, my brothers…"

Jaime began to struggle eagerly to his feet at the mention of food, but a look from Ferdinand made him sink back sadly on to the bed.

"We will eat after the others have finished – we have matters to discuss, Jaime, and must do so before the next coach arrives."

Domingo leaned forward, placing his hands together and leaning his elbows on his thighs. His eyes flicked contemptuously away from the fat man and he looked down at the floor.

"What task is so important that you need Mateo to carry it out, Ferdinand? He caused the death of our brothers – there must be a reckoning."

"There is no task – I want him close to me until the Ceremony is over: Mateo's loyalty is to the Abbot, and he is too friendly with Mackinnon and his associates: he is potentially a danger to us if we cannot keep him under observation and control his movements."

Ferdinand stood up and moved across to the nearest table, and was followed by Jaime and Domingo; the three of them sat down, Jaime and Ferdinand on the far bench, Domingo on the nearside, adjacent to their beds. The two artilleros remained standing, their postures indicating that they were awaiting instructions: Domingo pointed to the end beds behind Jaime and Ferdinand.

"Róger, Rubén - you will sleep there; remove the mattress from the third cot and place it underneath: no one will occupy that space – it must remain vacant."

The men nodded, and throwing back the hoods with relief, moved to the cots and laid their long cases on them.

Ferdinand placed his hands flat on table, leaned back and looked at his companions reflectively. One represented the political influence of the *hermandad*, with a key role in financial matters, as a bagman rather than an accountant; the other represented the *hermandad*'s iron fist, its capacity to instill fear, to intimidate, to discipline, and ultimately to send its enemies to God.

Jaime and Domingo were two of his three key lieutenants: the third, Severino, his counsellor, was absent from this meeting by design – he would arrive on the third coach later in the morning. Casimiro was Severino's deputy and would bring the American military tomorrow from Mérida; Vasco, who had been Jaime's deputy, had gone to God, and Amancio, who was Domingo's man, was still in the monastery infirmary. Ferdinand reflected on Severino's strong reservations about his recent policies and the execution of Vasco. Did he really need a counsellor? The role was hallowed by tradition, but…

Jaime, devoid of perceptiveness, blundered into Ferdinand's reverie.

"Should we not wait for our esteemed brother Severino? By the time we have eaten, the third coach may have arrived."

"No, we should not," said Ferdinand slowly and deliberately. "Severino's contribution was made fully when our strategic plans were laid: we are now considering our tactical responses within the plan. We will apprise him of our decisions and actions when he arrives."

"Hmm," muttered Jaime, "well, perhaps…" While he was usually impatient of Severino's calm and reasoned inputs to the deliberations of the *hermandad*, he was now uneasy that hard action was being contemplated, and he would bear part of the joint responsibility for it. Like all politicians, at such times he preferred to offload accountability on to an advisor like Severino, or at least spread the blame. In Mérida, he was always safely distanced from difficult decisions and violent actions, yet would boast about the things that he had caused to happen, but his first-hand experiences of violence on *La Copa* and in the chapter house had unsettled him: there had been the awful spectacle of the broken bodies on the plain

Domingo had up to this point ignored Jaime, but he was alive to the dangers that could arise from the fat politician's unpredictability; he had not forgotten that Jaime's outburst had precipitated the violence in the chapter house, resulting in the injury of his own deputy, Amancio. When he spoke, his tone was respectful and soothing.

"My brother, I understand your caution; we look to your mature input, in the absence of Severino, to broaden our appreciation of the implications of our actions. Nevertheless, act we must – Mackinnon and his associates must be neutralised, and the woman Blade must be secured." Seeing the look of alarm on Jaime's face, he shook his head, gave a dry chuckle, and glanced at Ferdinand, seeking his help.

"We do not intend to kill the chief executives of two major corporations just before or during the Ceremony, Jaime," said Ferdinand wearily. "The repercussions of such slaughter would be disastrous: leaving aside the fact that it would alienate our American guests, it would deprive me of the satisfaction of observing their chagrin when we dominate the new era of gravitational control. Casualties among the Moriduran Brothers would be equally devastating. The English consultant and the man Santiago could be disposed of, but even that is best avoided. No, we will simply prevail by our superior numbers and firepower – we have the 249s – the combat machine guns: Mackinnon and Lonnen are not fools – they will yield with bad grace. Besides, in the new era, we will need their expertise, contacts, facilities…"

Jaime looked relieved, and then became jocular.

"What a pity – I would have enjoyed seeing that arrogant pair cut in half by the 249s," he laughed. He was oblivious to the look of contempt on Domingo's face at his words.

"Our priorities today are these; first, we must find the Abbot, then Mateo, then the American woman; then we must obtain access to the diaries of Manuel's father, Eduardo Ortega," Ferdinand continued. "They contain information that is critical to us – the location of a passageway that provides access to the chamber beneath *El Trono*, and instructions on how to navigate it safely. There may be no living person who has used this access point, but I believe that whoever stole the core and the key, centuries ago, found and used this legendary, hidden route to the regulator of *El Corazón*." Ferdinand gazed up at the high roof timbers of the dormitory.

"We must seize the core and the key from Mackinnon and Lonnen and transport them, together with the American woman, to the regulator: we will then physically place the core back in its place. We have no need to place ourselves at risk from radiation by remaining there for an extended period. Doctora Blade would willingly sacrifice herself in pursuit of this fantasy of the Abbot's that *El Corazón* will destroy the world if its heartbeat is not stabilised, however, in reality, the supreme sacrifice will not be required of her: she will return with us, sign over her rights to the Blade Effect and be placed under contract to work for us. We need her more than we need Mackinnon and her father."

"Have we any idea where the Abbot and Mateo might be? Are they concealing the woman from us?" said Domingo, "Where do we start, Ferdinand?"

"I have considered these questions, Domingo – there are a number of possibilities. They will not all be in the one place, even if they are not engaged in different tasks; Anselmo does have a great deal to do before the Ceremony, and he may well have Mateo with him to assist."

Domingo shook his head. "I believe the Abbot is engaged with work relevant to tomorrow, as you suggest, but I do not believe that Mateo is with him: I think he may have been assigned by Anselmo to be the woman's protector. Mackinnon and the others will be acting as you have said, perhaps split into two teams – one roving, probably the

Scotsman and Manrique, the other remaining close to the hiding place of Blade and Brother Mateo, but trying to create an appearance of normality, as you suggest. As to where they could be – well, my brother, you have known the monastery since childhood – there are a thousand places they could be."

Ferdinand shook his head. "No single person knows the whole of the monastery – the knowledge is diffused among many. Men like Manuel Ortega probably know places that no monk has ever seen. Mateo, as a child of the monastery, with licence to roam in his boyhood – with the freedom and the anonymity of a boy at play – will know more of its secret places than anyone."

"What do you know of the sealed area behind the partitions in the guest wing?" said Domingo.

Ferdinand looked at Domingo reproachfully. "You know that it is forbidden to speak of that location – the topic is forbidden to all but the Magus, the Abbot and the Magus Elect, my esteemed brother. Only exceptional circumstances can justify even the mention of it."

"Are we not now facing exceptional circumstances, my brother? The Ceremony is imminent; *El Corazón's* heartbeat is erratic; the Abbot believes the end of the world is nigh; our enemies are among us and our new friends will be with us tomorrow, with high expectations. Do old taboos matter at a time like this?"

Domingo knew the risk he was taking with Ferdinand, but he was a man of fine judgement and totally without fear. Up to this point, he had harboured no ambition to lead the Order, at least not in its present form, with all its traditions and ceremonies, and its link to the Moriduran Brothers, but he had a vision of a *hermandad* that was divorced from the monks, from *La Copa*, a *hermandad* with centres of power in Mérida, in Madrid, in Rome, Paris, London – a truly European organisation, rivalling the great criminal networks of the world. The scruples of the monks, the family history of

Ferdinand de Moridanza – these things were obstacles that, till now, had impeded any real progress towards his vision.

"These old taboos, as you call them, are part of the fabric that binds the *hermandad* to the Moriduran monks, and they secure our complete control over unsophisticated people in the region," said Ferdinand.

Domingo decided not to pursue the debate: he realised that he could never change the mindset of the landed aristocrat sitting opposite him, and this knowledge brought a new clarity to his hitherto tentative thoughts about his own actions in the hours ahead. He thought of the secret knowledge he now possessed, and how he might utilise it.

"I bow to your deep understanding of our Order and its traditions, my most esteemed brother," he said, inclining his head respectfully.

Ferdinand swung his long legs over the bench and got to his feet, then began to pace up and down. Jaime looked anxiously at Domingo, but he was studiously examining the surface of the table, his hands steepled in front of him. Jaime looked behind him, and the two men beside the beds stared blankly back at him.

"Ferdinand…" he began.

"Stay silent, my brother – I must think…" said Ferdinand curtly. After a few minutes he stopped pacing, and faced them again.

"We need more time, and we need to eat. Let us head towards the refectory, my brothers."

They followed him down the dormitory in a line, Domingo matching the Don's long strides, Jaime puffing along behind, beaming in anticipation of food, and *los nuevos artilleros* gliding noiselessly in the rear of the little procession, their heads hooded again.

Chapter Twenty-Three

Anyone entering the library of the monastery would at first have thought it empty, but then the soft murmuring of voices might have caused them to look more carefully. Although the morning sun illuminated most of the library, the dark corner where two men were standing at a lectern required additional light from a large single candle on a heavy brass candlestick.

Brother Anselmo and Manuel, who was wearing the red robe of the *hermandad*, were closely inspecting one of the diaries of Eduardo Ortega. They had found a number of obscure references to a tunnel in the rock, to a link with "the path from the Portal", but they were buried in much inconsequential detail about the supply of provisions to the monastery, with no clues as to the location of the path. The elder Ortega, like many diarists, had delighted in concealing certain matters by the use of initials and simple letter contractions and substitutions. Brother Anselmo, given his acute memory for people and places, easily deciphered most of these.

"Can this be all, Manuel, my brother?" said the Abbot wearily. "What of this volume, with hollowed-out pages, presumably to contain some object? And why all this talk of wine? I wish your father had expressed himself more clearly."

"It used to contain a large iron key – but a key to what? I never knew…" Manuel laughed nostalgically. "As for wine, my father took great pains to be on good terms with every cellarer of the monastery – good wine was very close to his heart, together with good jazz."

The old man looked at him indulgently. "I prefer not to consider what your father gained from this close relationship with Brother Alfonso and his predecessors."

Manuel shifted uncomfortably, and pointed to the diary page of the twenty second of July 1935.

"Look, Brother Anselmo – at this point it refers to *the good wine near P.B.*"

The Abbot frowned. "P.B. – the initials of a monk, perhaps? Pablo B? But we never use two names for a brother. Can it be point B – a location? Is it one of your father's ciphers, Manuel? No, I have it – Padre Bernard! The resident priest of the monastery then was a Padre Bernard – I have seen his name on the records. But then we are still left with a puzzle; why *the good wine near Padre Bernard*? An instruction for the placement of wine at a meal?"

He shook his head. "No, this must be irrelevant – turn the page, my brother… No, wait! P.B?"

The hair on Manuel's neck stood on end, and his knees suddenly felt weak: he knew intuitively what the Abbot was about to say, but fervently hoped that he would not utter the words.

"*La Puerta de Bestia* – the old legend! It is located in the deepest recesses of the cellar, near the rear wall – where the fine wine is kept. The wine so much appreciated by Señor Lonnen…"

Manuel shuffled his feet nervously. "But surely that is only a legend – a myth, Brother Anselmo? Is it not?"

The Abbot shook his head slowly. "No. An old door or gate does exist in the rear wall at that point. Few have seen it, and it has never been opened in living memory. Some say it is not a gate at all – simply an ornamental feature. What *is* a legend – a myth, as you say - is any connection with a Beast. In fact, as you now know, there is no Beast of Moridura, no savage, malign creature with a penchant for destruction: only the being known as *La Guardia*, who spoke through the mouth of Brother Mateo in the chamber."

He looked at Manuel's relieved face, and smiled.

"You do believe that *La Guardia* is benevolent, Manuel? You are not still fearful?"

"Not of the reality, no," said Manuel, "but the old stories live on in my thoughts from childhood. How could I fear a creature with the voice and features of our beloved Mateo?"

"Our beloved Mateo," repeated the Abbot, his voice sad. "May God be with him, Señorita Angeline and Alistair Mackinnon."

"Amen," intoned Manuel fervently.

Both men gazed again at the diary pages in front of them.

"Why does Don Ferdinand think such a route exists? Why does it matter so much to him?' He looked anxiously at the old monk, and fingered his red robe uneasily. "How will the Don react when he sees me in the robe of the Order – how will Domingo react?" He shuddered involuntarily at the thought of Domingo.

"Your esteemed brothers will accept and welcome you – the rules of the Order demand that they do. I acted fully within my powers and the traditions of our Ancient Order in elevating you, my beloved brother. Wear your robe with confidence and dignity and fear nothing." The Abbot's firm tone reassured Manuel, and he drew himself up to his full height, felt the swirl of the red fabric around his body, and rejoiced in it.

The Abbot suppressed a smile. "You asked me three questions, and I answered the last: now to the first questions. Ferdinand believes that a tunnel to the chamber of the regulator beneath *El Trono* exists because old stories have always referred to it; one story says that the core and the key were stolen using this route. Your father kept such stories alive – he was a good man, but garrulous."

Manuel laughed in recollection, overwhelmed by memories of his father holding court in the café, in the square, in the refectory of the monastery, surrounded by eager listeners.

"Why is the possible existence of such a tunnel important to Ferdinand? Firstly, no one knows how *La Guardia* has accessed the chamber of the regulator over the aeons;

secondly, Ferdinand knows that some route must be used by those who replace the core and the key, and he wants to control that process; lastly, the legend says that it was an ancestor of Ferdinand de Moridanza who stole the core and the key. If this is true, he will want to remove this stain on his family name: the final thing that drives him is the need to show his American friends that he has a way of controlling the gravitational processes at the heart of *La Copa*."

"And he needs to abduct Señorita Angeline to assist him in replacing the core…" breathed Manuel, realising for the first time why the Don had coveted his father's diaries over the years, and the real nature of the threat to his friends.

"Returning to *La Puerta de Bestia*," said the Abbot, "Alfonso must have seen it many times recently because of Señor Lonnen's fondness for the vintage stored there: Mateo could certainly have noticed it, assuming that it is still visible, since he also has fetched the wine. However, that point in the cellar is the northern outer wall, and it lies against a depression in the inner perimeter rock of *La Copa*: if the door leads anywhere, it can only be to a shallow cavity in the rock. It cannot possibly lead to *El Trono*. In any case, Mateo would have mentioned it to me."

Manuel hid a grin; Brother Anselmo did not always fully appreciate the awe in which he was held by most of the younger monks, even by Mateo, who was closer to him than any Moriduran brother except Joaquín. The Abbot did not miss the suppressed amusement on his face.

"You do not believe that he would have told me?" he said, cocking his head.

"Forgive me, but no - I do not. Brother Alfonso would have told Mateo that it was forbidden to speak of it," said Manuel.

"Alfonso believes that everything that is not expressly permitted is forbidden, that is true…" said the Abbot reflectively. "Thank you, Manuel – I will ask Mateo when we see him."

He stopped speaking abruptly, and a look of pain crossed his face at the thought that he might never see the adult Mateo again – perhaps not even the new child. An image of the previous Mateo came to him, and then of the present Mateo as a boy, sitting raptly beside him in the library, turning the pages of a great illuminated manuscript in wonder. Manuel's voice caused the image to dissolve abruptly.

"How can we make sense of these things, Brother Anselmo? The things I have seen – in the chamber... How can I, a simple man, reconcile them with my belief in God?"

The Abbot looked at him blankly for a moment, struggling with exactly the same question in his own mind. For some reason, a buried memory from a history of the Greek Orthodox Church came to him, a memory of the 13th century monk, Gregory Palamas, of the monastery of Mount Athos, and subsequently Bishop of Thessalonika. He seemed to hear the voice of the long-dead monk, explaining patiently that one could know the manifestations of God, but not his essence, and that understanding could only come from the acceptance of paradox, and, ultimately, silence.

"Accept the contradictions, quiet your mind, my brother, and listen for the voice of God. His love and your faith will sustain you and grant you understanding," he said, and silently prayed that he, too, would be granted such insight.

They heard hesitant footsteps echoing in the library – the steps of someone tentatively exploring, searching. The familiar, querulous tones of the cellarer, Brother Alfonso, came from near the entrance.

"Brother Anselmo? Brother Anselmo? Are you there? Is anyone there?"

"Here, Brother – by the candle..." called the Abbot.

The ancient cellarer moved forward nervously, peering at the two men at the lectern. He recognised the Abbot at once, but not the red-robed man standing beside him.

"It is *el Americano* – he is calling for the good wine again. He is with the Englishman in the guest wing. What shall I do, Brother Anselmo…"

"Calm yourself, Alfonso – God has brought you to us at a fortuitous moment," said the Abbot soothingly, "You have been on my lips –and Manuel's – and now here you are!"

Alfonso looked confused, turned his head to the Abbot's companion, and then gave a start of recognition.

"Manuel Ortega," he said, staring in naked astonishment at the robe of the *hermandad* on the café owner's sturdy frame.

"Manuel has been elevated to the Ancient Order, Alfonso. He will be in a place of honour at the Ceremony tomorrow. He has rendered a great service to the monastery."

Alfonso's old eyes were round with surprise, and he made a half-bow to Manuel. "I am happy for you, Manuel Ortega – your father Eduardo will rejoice in heaven at your elevation. Who would have thought of such a thing?"

The Abbot reached down for the candlesnuffer and, stretching upwards, extinguished the flame on the tall candle. "Alfonso, Manuel: we will go together to the cellar and find Señor Lonnen's wine," he said, closing the diary and replacing it on the table with the others.

The old cellarer was flustered, and waved his hands in distress. "You do not need to trouble yourselves – I will go, I will fetch *el Americano's* bottle," he wheezed.

"We have an ulterior motive in accompanying you, Alfonso," said the Abbot, placing his hand on the monk's back and urging him gently towards the door of the library, "we want to inspect *La Puerta de Bestia*."

"Brother Anselmo?" gasped Alfonso, now totally bewildered by the rush of information. They left the library and moved towards the rear of the monastery complex, passing the entrance to the refectory. The early breakfasters were emerging, red-robed and red faced, their hoods thrown back, talking and laughing. Alfonso stopped at the cupboard along the way and obtained a small candleholder, a candle and a box of matches, muttering apologies for the necessary delay.

The Abbot looked back towards the group of visitors, who were now disappearing in the direction of the dormitory of the *confratres*, and saw another small party of red-robed figures moving in the opposite direction, towards the refectory: he recognised Ferdinand, Jaime and Domingo, but not the two hooded men at the rear of the group. None of them seem to notice the Abbot, Manuel and Alfonso, but as the five men moved into the refectory, one of the hooded figures glanced in their direction for a fleeting moment.

Brother Anselmo urged his little group towards the cellar, reflecting that two monks in black habits might have aroused no interest, but two monks accompanying another in the red robe of the Order might well do so. Had he glanced behind him, he would have seen the tall figure of Domingo reappear from the entrance to the refectory and stare at the their retreating backs.

Reaching the top of the cellar steps, Alfonso placed the candleholder in the niche in the wall, laid the candle beside it, struck a match and held it to the base of the candle, stuck it into place, and then lit the wick. He began to descend the winding steps, followed by the Abbot and Manuel. When they reached the heavy cellar door, he placed the candleholder in another niche beside the door and then began to pull the heavy door towards him, with assistance from Manuel. As it swung open, he retrieved the candle, and entered the cellar. The three of them moved through the cellar, past the new wines, towards the rear. Eventually, they reached the racks of vintage wines at the rear wall. Brother Alfonso started to retrieve a bottle of what he now thought of as the American's wine, but the Abbot stopped him.

"Not yet, Alfonso! First, we will look at this little gate or door."

It had been a decade or more since the Abbot had been in the cellar, and fifty years since he had looked at *La Puerta de*

Bestia, but it was immediately apparent to him that the door had been opened recently. The separation between its edges and the stone was clearly visible; there was no key in the keyhole, but the edges bore new scuff marks. He knelt down with difficulty and peered through the keyhole; he could see nothing, but felt cold air; he turned his head and placed his ear against it, and sensed the resonance of a large space. This is no cupboard in the wall, he thought, but where does it lead? He reluctantly accepted the possibility that this could indeed be an ancient path to the base of *El Trono*, to the heart of *La Copa de Moridura*, and he felt an unaccustomed frisson of excitement.

"My beloved brother Manuel – we may owe your father an incalculable debt," he said softly.

The air in the cellar, always cool, became suddenly colder and there was a movement in the air, a faint creaking sound, then the atmosphere returned to normal. Someone had either been in the cellar before them and had just left, or someone had just entered. Manuel didn't know which possibility frightened him more: the Abbot simply raised his eyebrows, and then he put his finger to his lips. They remained silent and motionless for a few moments, waiting. Eventually, Brother Anselmo spoke in a calm, unhurried voice.

"Get the wine for Señor Lonnen now, Alfonso, and we will leave – Manuel and I have work to do."

The old cellarer bent down, felt for the wine with a sure hand, lifted the bottle gently and straightened up again.

"I will take the candle and lead; take care, Manuel – the cellar and the steps present many hazards for those who are here as seldom as we…" said the Abbot.

And so they ascended the winding stone steps, wondering who the mystery visitor had been. Above them, Domingo moved smoothly and swiftly so that he would be out of sight before the Abbot, Manuel and Alfonso reached to top of the steps. In his pocket was an ancient iron key: the key and the location of the door that it opened were both unknown to the

Magus Elect. It amused him to think of Ferdinand's continued obsession with the diaries, and the Abbot's faith in the security of their hiding place. He headed for the refectory. Ferdinand, Jaime and *los artilleros* were seated at one of the long tables, being served by a nervous young monk.

"Where have you been, my brother?" asked Ferdinand testily, "Where did you disappear to?"

"I glimpsed Anselmo, the cellarer Alfonso, and Manuel Ortega, but I did not want to follow them or confront them without your approval," said Domingo, sitting down beside Jaime, who was oblivious to everything except food.

"Why did you not call out to the Abbot and tell him of our presence?" said Ferdinand angrily, "You knew that I wanted to see him…"

"I would think that he is already aware of that," said Domingo, "besides, I have more important news. Manuel Ortega was wearing the robe of the Order and the insignia of a Brother Elect and a *confrater*." He picked up a piece of bread.

Ferdinand stared at him, a look of utter incredulity on his face. "Are you mad, Domingo? A peasant – an innkeeper wearing the robe and insignia of a Brother Elect – a *confrater*! You must be mistaken…"

Domingo reached for a knife and cut himself a piece of bread. "Have you not already offered this peasant innkeeper membership of our brotherhood in return for access to his father's diaries, my brother? Why should Anselmo do less?" As he spoke, he felt the comforting weight of the iron key in his pocket.

"But at that level? And how could Anselmo do this without the approval of the Grand Council?" Ferdinand's voice was low, but the suppressed anger in his tone was evident.

Domingo paused with the bread to his mouth. "I have already observed that we are living in exceptional times, Ferdinand. The Abbot of Moridura has the right to confer such rank *in extremis* – to be later confirmed by the Grand

Council, of course." He bit the bread and chewed abstractedly, then gave a harsh, dry laugh. "Little Manuel of the Café Ortega – a Brother Elect and a *confrater* – truly, we live in an egalitarian age…"

Chapter Twenty-Four

"What in hell has happened to my wine?"

"Be patient, Red - play some music – it's too early to be drinking anyway," said Paul, moving from the big table in the guest wing to the pile of records and riffling through it. Santiago stood up and began prowling up and down, peering down the passageways and up at the landing above the two staircases.

"What's keeping that monk – what's his name? How long can it take to get a bottle?" Red grumbled.

"Alfonso," said Santiago as he returned to the table. "He's an old man and I believe the cellar is set deep in the far north side of the monastery."

"Well, he should be fit, going up and down the stairs," muttered Red. He looked across at Paul, who was placing a record on the turntable. "Not now, for God's sake, Paul!"

Santiago nodded in agreement. "We need to be able to hear any sounds, Paul – this is not the time…"

Chastened, Paul replaced the record on the stack. He thought of repeating that it wasn't the time for wine either, but decided against it - in Red's present mood, one word would have led to another. As he turned to return to the table, the sound of the door at the other end of the guest wing came to them, then the sound of the footsteps of more than one person.

Red stood up quickly, they all checked their weapons, and Santiago, positioning himself just to the side of the left hand passage, motioned to Paul urgently, indicating that he should move to the equivalent place next to the mouth of the right hand passage. Red stayed where he was, standing at the table and covering both points of entry and the landing above them, soberly reflecting that he was in the most exposed place if hostilities commenced.

The footsteps were now clearly coming from the right hand passageway, and each man placed his hand on his weapon but did not draw it: Manuel's voice was now audible, and everyone relaxed, just as the Abbot, Manuel and Alfonso entered the main area. The cellarer moved swiftly towards the table with the wine bottle, murmuring apologies for the delay to Red, who was gazing at Manuel, resplendent in his robe.

"Look at you, Manuel!" he marvelled, "It's a mercy you didn't appear first – I might have plugged you on sight, wearing that gear…"

Manuel blushed, but then recovered his aplomb, remembering his new status. "I hope you do not intend to shoot every member of our Ancient Order on sight, Señor Lonnen," he said, somewhat pompously. Alfonso was already opening the wine, and looked across inquiringly at Red Lonnen, to determine if anyone else might partake of his precious vintage.

"Oh, hell! Give us all a glass, Alfonso – we sure need it."

The five men sat down at the table; the Abbot declined the glass offered by the cellarer, but indicated that Alfonso should sit with them when he had finished pouring the wine.

"Yeah, sure, Alfonso – take the load off – have a glass yourself," said Red cheerfully. The Abbot nodded his approval in response to Alfonso's nervous glance, and the old monk sat down with relief, and poured himself some wine. Brother Anselmo reached for the water jug and treated himself to a less distinguished beverage.

Paul spoke first, standing and raising his glass. "I propose a toast – to Manuel Ortega, Brother Elect and *confrater* of the Ancient Order of Moridura – and our good friend. Congratulations, Manuel!"

They all stood, raising their glasses.

"To Manuel!" they chorused, gathering round him, slapping him on the back.

"To ma wee pal Manuel!" said a laconic Scots voice from the left hand passageway, and they all whirled round in astonishment to see the tall figure of Alistair leaning with one hand on the base of the staircase, holding up a phantom glass in the other. Red and Paul rushed across, peered down the passageway, and then seized Alistair by the arms.

"Where's Angeline? Where's Mateo?" Their voices clamoured urgently in his ears as they almost dragged him to the table.

"It's OK – she's OK!" he said, shaking free of them. "She's in good hands in a safe place – in the chamber with Arkimateo."

All except the Abbot looked at him uncomprehendingly: Brother Anselmo looked suddenly drained and sad.

"Then Mateo is gone," he said heavily, and sat down, overcome with emotion. "My poor Mateo…"

They all sat down again round the table and looked at Alistair, their eyes full of anxiety. Before he could begin, the Abbot went over and whispered in Alfonso's ear. The cellarer nodded, drained his glass, got up, bowed politely and left: Brother Anselmo resumed his seat.

"Where do I begin?" said Alistair. He launched into an account of the events of the morning, events so fantastic that he could hardly believe his own words as they left his lips. No man ever had a more attentive audience – there was absolute silence in the room except for his voice. At last he came to the end of his report, and drew breath, reaching for the wine.

Red was rubbing his forehead in agitation and Paul looked equally tense: Brother Anselmo's head was bent in grief at his loss: Santiago kept telling himself that, had any other man in the world recounted such a tale to him, he would have laughed in his face. Only Manuel seemed to accept Alistair's words with anything resembling equanimity, but then his friend was describing things entirely consistent with the legends and traditions that had always been part of his life.

"How do you justify leaving my daughter alone with such a creature, Alistair – *La Guardia*, or Arkimateo, as you say we must now call it."

"Her – not it…" corrected Alistair wearily. "I have made such scientific contribution as I am able to, Red, but only Angeline can complete this work. I hadn't realised till this morning the depth of her insights into gravity and singularities – her understanding is – it displays what I can only call genius: there's no other word for it. Arkimateo has perceived this from the start – she…"

"She – you say *she*, Alistair, but this is not a woman you are describing: by your own account it is something between a Gila monster and a centaur, and you have abandoned my daughter to it." Red's voice trembled with anger and incomprehension. Paul placed a hand on his arm in an attempt to calm him, but Lonnen shook it off angrily. Alistair leaned towards him.

"Red, I understand how you feel, believe me, I do. I love and respect Angeline, but I did what I had to do. Let me summarise my reasons once more: my scientific contribution was made – I had nothing more to offer them. Mateo, with all his respect and regard for Angeline, is now incorporated, body and soul, into Arkimateo. This creature, as you call her, is a sentient being of high intelligence from somewhere in the space-time continuum who has sacrificed everything to protect mankind – an alien species to her – from destruction. Her life has consisted of interminable tracts of time incorporated as pure mind in the circuits of the consoles, with occasional manifestations in corporeal form to perform hazardous tasks and give birth to new Mateos." He paused, looking infinitely tired and drained.

"What will happen in the next twenty four hours, in a context in which our very existence is under threat, will be the culmination of Arkimateo's lonely purpose over the millennia. Only Angeline can avert this imminent catastrophe. I *had* to leave the chamber to give you these facts and to implement, with the help of you all, other plans that form an essential part of the strategy to stabilise *El Corazón*." Alistair got to his feet.

"There is something else, for Paul's ears only, initially…" He motioned to Paul and they withdrew to the gramophone table and sat down. Those at the main table heard his low, intense Scottish burr but not the content of his words, and then they saw Paul go chalk white, and heard the exclamation that burst from his lips.

"Oh, God! Oh, my God! Angeline…" he said, grasping his friend's arm. Alistair succeeded in calming him, and then Paul stood up and motioned to Red to join them. There was another quiet communication between him and Paul; shock and disbelief showed on Red's face, then he hugged Paul, murmuring softly, and they returned to the table.

"Angeline is pregnant," Paul said, "Arkimateo was able to confirm this, even at this incredibly early stage – I have no reason to doubt *La Guardia* – why would she say such a thing if it were not true? I am confused, delighted, apprehensive – all the things you would expect me to be." He turned to Red. "In spite all the risks she is facing, Alistair says that Angeline has welcomed the news; she feels instinctively the truth of it – and I believe it, too. Red, you are going to have a grandchild…"

"The good Lord has willed this – from a single act of deep love, a new life has come among us. Perhaps it is a sign. I congratulate you both," said the Abbot.

In the emotionally charged atmosphere, none of those at the table saw a hooded man appear at the mouth of each passageway, each with a combat machine gun slung from his shoulder and levelled at the group. At the sound of the weapons being cocked, Santiago swung around and then froze; the others just stood there, stunned into silence.

"M249 squad automatic weapons - SAWs," said Santiago to Alistair, "don't try anything…"

"Good advice, señores – I advise you to heed his words," said the voice of Don Ferdinand: he came through the small rear door from the courtyard with Jaime, and walked towards them.

The Abbot looked at him aghast. "Ferdinand! In God's name, what do you think you are doing? Tell these men to put up their weapons – have you learned nothing from the events of the last few days?"

"Anselmo, I regret the necessity for this show of force, but we are dealing with four men of violence, men who bear arms at this moment." He looked in turn at Alistair, Red, Santiago and Paul. "So far, they are the only ones who have discharged firearms, with the intention of intimidating members of the Order: two of my trusted servants are dead. We are not the aggressors here, Anselmo, they are."

"They came to Moridanza and to the monastery in peace," said the Abbot, "and at the request of the Magus, although the manner of that invitation was altered and its intent perverted. Alistair Mackinnon had a firearm discharged at him in his own home, threatening him and his friends. Your trusted servants – God rest their souls – attempted to kidnap Doctora Blade; your intimates within the *hermandad* initiated the events on *La Copa* and in the chapter house. I deplore all recourse to violence – it is the way of beasts – but you initiated the cycle of violence. And there is the matter of the mysterious death of Vasco, a Grand Council member…"

Ferdinand listed impassively; he then raised one hand imperiously. "You are a man of God, Anselmo – I am not: render to Caesar the things that are Caesar's and to God the things that are God's."

"You are close to blasphemy, Ferdinand," said the Abbot, his tone cold and censorious. Jaime stepped forward, a sneer on his face.

"Mackinnon – surrender your weapon and tell your associates to do likewise; exercise great care, or risk a bloodbath." He made a sweeping gesture towards the armed men at the mouth of the passageways, and then stared arrogantly at Alistair.

"Firepower in a confined space creates complex dynamics and tactical options, don't you agree, Santiago," said Alistair, his voice light and conversational.

"Yes," said Santiago. He rested his hip on the edge of the table. "Combat machine guns, such as the 249s, are notoriously unpredictable in such situations, too heavy, particularly in inexperienced hands. They are designed to be fired from the ground, mounted on their bipod. If they are fired from a standing position, on automatic with a sweeping motion, they may hit unintended targets – you, for example, Jaime…" The fat man looked uneasily at the men across the room. "If they are fired without a sweeping motion, they must be aimed carefully. In inexperienced hands, the weight and recoil of the weapon can affect the aim."

Alistair gave a faint smile. "We have been through such an evaluation with the late *artilleros*, who carried less sophisticated, but more appropriate weapons. All things considered, Ferdinand, I must decline Señor Jaime's request: we will not surrender our weapons, nor will my colleague on the upper landing surrender his rifle, which is aimed at you."

Ferdinand's iron self-control prevented him from glancing up, but Jaime shot a panicky glance upwards to the landing. "I see no one, Ferdinand," he said nervously.

There was a discreet cough from the dark mouth of the upper corridor, and a distinct metallic click. This time Ferdinand did briefly glance upwards, but he could see nothing. He looked back at Alistair. "My men could fire upwards and penetrate the floor above with upwards of ten rounds per second of high-velocity bullets," he said.

"They would damage some fine old woodwork in the process," replied Alistair, "and they would both die from our bullets while their weapons were still discharging. As they fell, stray bullets might hit anyone on this side of the room. If they did not kill or incapacitate my rifleman with the first discharge, you, of course, would be dead, Ferdinand – or perhaps Jaime, who offers a larger target area." He laughed. "My concealed friend's weapon is only a reconditioned 1950s bolt-action .303 calibre, but highly accurate, with a reasonable repeat fire speed in his expert hands."

A long, tense pause followed, with Jaime's laboured breathing the only sound to be heard in the room. Eventually, Ferdinand spoke.

"Where is Doctora Blade?" he said, his voice strained.

Red tensed up, but Paul forestalled him.

"She is resting, Ferdinand - the events of the last few days have been very stressful for her."

"That does not answer my question…"

"Well, you and your question can go to hell in a handcart," snapped Red. "It's none of your damned business."

Ferdinand had recovered his composure, and most of his dignity. "I have the greatest respect for your beautiful, elegant daughter and her formidable intellect, Señor Lonnen. I assure you that I mean her no harm, but she has become central to our plans at this time. We must speak to her as soon as possible. By denying us access, it is you that places her in danger."

Alistair stepped in front of Red to avert another outburst. "Ferdinand, consider what's at stake for you, for the Order, for the monastery – you're placing everything that you value in jeopardy by this show of force. It can achieve nothing - please back off before something triggers a violent exchange between us."

"If you do not heed these wise words, Ferdinand, neither I nor the Magus will carry out our roles at the Ceremony, and I will advise the Magus to publicly withdraw his endorsement of you as Magus Elect," said Brother Anselmo, his voice grave and full of regret.

The tall aristocrat gazed deep into the Abbot's eyes, and saw there an iron resolution. "You are risking a breach with the *hermandad* as serious as the one that created the great schism in our Ancient Order, Anselmo," he said cautiously and deliberately.

"I know it, Ferdinand, but I am forced to take that risk by events of even greater significance. I urge you to withdraw – it will not resolve our differences, but it will give us both an opportunity to reflect, and consider our positions. Time is running out for all of us..."

"Out of respect for you, Anselmo, my most esteemed brother, I will do as you ask, but nothing has been achieved here. We cannot drift towards morning with these grave issues unresolved – please keep that before you at all times."

He bowed, and motioned the others to follow him through the door to the courtyard. The door closed behind them. Red slapped Alistair on the back.

"Holy Jesus! Remind me never to play Texas hold-em with you." The Abbot gave a wry smile at the casual profanity.

Paul looked at his friend in admiration. "Are you going to introduce us to your hidden rifleman?" he said. Alistair raised his eyebrows.

"What rifleman? I hope the guy up there is ready to show himself – I've no idea who the hell he is..."

They all looked up at the landing and Cristobal Ortega emerged from the corridor, white-faced and carrying a large adjustable wrench. He gave a weak smile, and waved to Manuel. "I was between coach trips and came up to see my father; I heard the voices when I entered at the other end, and thought I would move quietly upstairs and check what was happening – there was a sense of conflict in the voices." He came down the right hand staircase, staring in awe at his father in the red robe.

Santiago took Alistair by the arm. "How did you know it was someone friendly to us upstairs?" he said admiringly.

"I didn't," said Alistair, "I heard a noise – it was either their guy or somebody else, so I felt I had nothing to lose by the bluff."

As he shook his father's hand, Cristobal smiled across at Alistair.

"I released the jaws on my wrench – it is needed frequently for the coach – slid them apart then clicked them hard together – it seemed the best thing to do..." Manuel mussed his son's hair proudly and affectionately.

"Economy of means," said Alistair, complacent at the success of his bluff. "Sharp ears and quick wits! We're all grateful, Cristobal."

Cristobal shyly acknowledged the congratulations being showered upon him. "I must return to Moridanza – there is one more party to pick up." The Abbot smiled at the young man, and then sat down at the table.

"Cristobal, when you return, bring some overnight things with you. In recognition of the service you have performed, I invite you to stay overnight and join us at the Ceremony tomorrow. As an invited guest, you will be permitted to wear the red robe, and stand beside your father."

The Ortegas stammered their thanks; Cristobal waved his goodbyes and, as he prepared to depart, Manuel whispered in his ear to be sure to tell his mother of all that had happened. At last, he was going to be vindicated in Fidelicia's eyes.

Alistair sat down beside the Abbot and the others gathered round them; Manuel, now secure in his new status, was no longer embarrassed at being part of their deliberations.

"Angeline estimates that, by late afternoon, she and Arkimateo will have finalised their preparations for stabilising the heartbeat after the core and the key are replaced. Stabilisation of the oscillation is only one of three possible outcomes, as we already know," said Alistair.

"You'll have to remind me what the other two are," said Red. "One of them is bad, I remember that…"

"I remember Mateo's explanation – it made sense to me as a non-scientist, although Mateo was characteristically modest about it," intervened Paul.

Alistair spoke slowly, great fatigue showing in the lines of his face.

"*El Corazón* is some form of matter that arrived with the meteorite, and it lies there, independent of Earth's gravitational field, recognising only its own. The field strength that formed on impact is inherently unstable – it will either weaken or increase to infinite mass. The regulator has prevented the latter outcome, which would trigger a singularity – a black hole - but has been unable to weaken the field, which would cause *El Corazón* to expand into nothingness and remove the threat. To attempt to weaken the field, instead of stabilising the oscillation, runs the risk of going in the wrong direction. The regulator influences the number of oscillations of the field, but since the loss of the core and the key, it has been unable to react to insidious changes, the ones that have created our minor earthquakes – the vibrations we have all experienced."

"So only two options out of the three are acceptable," said Red. "Stabilisation maintains the status quo: a weakened field vaporises *El Corazón* and we then have the gravitational equivalent of an extinct volcano."

Alistair and Paul exchanged glances. "That outcome, desirable as it is, removes Arkimateo's *raison d'etre*," said Alistair.

Red looked puzzled. "So what? That's what it – what she – wants, as I understand it. So the Beast is redundant – should we shed tears? Arkimateo can go home, job done. My Angeline will be safe, not to mention the planet."

"Arkimateo has no world to go home to, Red," said Alistair. "What can she do? Return to being pure mind in the consoles? She can't exist for long in her bodily form; in any case, she would become a scientific curiosity – a freak to be examined, probed, exhibited…" He shuddered.

Red looked thoughtful. "If we enter the new era of control of gravity, Angeline will need her new girlfriend's input – we all will. What's the alternative, guys?"

Brother Anselmo, who had been silent during the exchange, now stood up, and paced slowly up and down. Watching him, it dawned on Paul and Alistair that it was not only Arkimateo that would lose her *raison d'etre* – the Ancient Order of Moridura would lose the living heart of its cult. Paul started to speak, but the Abbot had already read their minds, in typical Moriduran fashion.

"Thank you for your consideration, Paul – Alistair – but we will still have our faith and our God. All living things and all the institutions of men have their time, and then it passes," he said. "Perhaps Arkimateo will elect to go to her Creator…"

There was nothing to be said in response to the Abbot's words; they all fell silent for a moment, almost in a premature mourning ritual, then Alistair picked up where he had left off on the plan for the day, this fateful day that would determine everything.

"As I was saying – Angeline, with Arkimateo's help, will complete her analysis of how the stabilisation is to be accomplished, and that will include an evaluation of risk on a scale that no human has ever undertaken before, with the possible exception of the risk analysis that preceded the detonation of the first nuclear devices and the hydrogen bomb. In the late afternoon, Angeline will emerge from the chamber alone, and will signal to us from behind the panelling by knocking She cannot risk emerging without knowing that it is safe to do so – I took the chance, and in the light of recent events, I was wrong to do so. Angeline will wait until we open the door from the passageway."

Paul looked drawn and fearful. "What will the signal be, Alistair?" he said, but as he uttered the question, the answer came to him with an absolute certainty, and he smiled wanly.

"Of course – it can only be that..." he whispered, and knocked rhythmically on the table, a pattern of four knocks immediately familiar to all of them.

"I bet Angeline suggested that," said Red, shaking his head admiringly, "Fate knocking on the door – Beethoven's Fifth!"

"I wanted the Woody Woodpecker knock," said Alistair, tapping out the rhythm that the eponymous bird and another Bird, Charlie Parker, had made famous.

"Baroodelybebop," smiled Paul.

"Woody was only roodelybebop," corrected Alistair. "Angeline wouldn't have it – said it would trivialise the moment."

"I think Mateo would have voted for the jazz rhythm," said the Abbot sadly, and the living image of the young, smiling monk came to all of them, and they, too, were sad. Then another image came to Paul's mind, of a fearful, isolated Angeline, sitting alone on the trunk that contained the core and the key, behind the partition, in that eerie light, knocking and waiting.

"Alistair, I must wait for her inside the partition. She may need help and I can be a second line of defence for the trunk – for the core and the key," he said, in a manner that indicated that he would brook no disagreement.

Alistair looked at Santiago, and then at the Abbot – they both nodded.

"It makes good sense," said Santiago, and then he looked intently at Paul. "But you must not be tempted to descend the stairs to the chamber door, unless Angeline calls for help. Both of you would become very vulnerable if someone got behind the partition while you were down there." Paul nodded in acquiescence.

"Why can't Arkimateo come up with her and protect her?" asked Red, and then shook his head at his own stupidity. "I guess I know the answer to that: from your description, Alistair, the creature is too big to easily get through the partition – she might not even get up the stairs – am I right?"

"That's part of it," said Alistair, "but the main reason is that Arkimateo will commence her journey to the heart of *La Copa* by a route from the chamber that is too dangerous for Angeline, because it passes initially through the underground power source of the consoles. The tunnel was created aeons ago, when Arkimateo's own people implanted the chamber, *El Trono* and the regulator. It later intersects with a man-made passage from the monastery. From that point on, the main route is safer, at least for short periods, and a human being may follow it. The entry to the intersecting passage was apparently named …"

"…*La Puerta de Bestia*," breathed Manuel.

"How the hell did you know that?" asked Alistair in surprise.

"We have only recently discovered that the ancient legend of the gate of the Beast was a fact," said the Abbot. "It was the secret in the diaries of Manuel's father – we found it when searching for the access point."

'You knew of it?' said Paul.

"The last Magus died before he could pass the knowledge on to his successor, Brother Joaquín," replied the Abbot. "Many believe that the ancient thief who stole the core and the key was an ancestor of Don Ferdinand's – he certainly believes that, and regards it as a stain on his family name that must be removed. That is why he sought the diaries so eagerly from Manuel."

Alistair whistled in sudden understanding. "Aye - Manuel mentioned that… Ferdinand wants to make amends by replacing them himself – but he needs Angeline to assist him…"

"I'll kill that bastard if I have the chance," hissed Red.

Brother Anselmo sighed. "I know that you may find it hard to accept, but Ferdinand is not intrinsically evil; he is motivated by pride in his lineage, and ambition; he enjoys the exercise of power but he tries to act within the traditions and the spirit of the *hermandad* and the Order.

"He has the capacity to grow spiritually, but he has allowed himself to be unduly influenced by men who have no regard for any morality, such as Domingo, who represents the naked exercise of power through violence – an element that has always been present in the Order – and Jaime, a sordid, corrupt politician: Jaime is not his real name, it is a name given to him by the *hermandad*, to protect his anonymity."

Santiago looked thoughtful. "I have heard of this Domingo – he is a shadowy figure – the authorities are not even sure that he exists: a man with a reputation for ruthlessness – an enforcer."

"He exists, be sure of it," said Brother Anselmo, "you have sat across the table from him in the chapter house – the tall, thin man. He may have killed Vasco, Jaime's deputy – Mateo was suspicious about the nature of the fall."

"Is it too late to carry out your earlier threat, Brother Anselmo – to advise the Magus – Brother Joaquín - to publicly withdraw his endorsement of Ferdinand as Magus Elect?" asked Paul tentatively. Red, Manuel and Santiago looked at him in astonishment. Joaquín? The Magus? Alistair shook his head in exasperation at Paul's inadvertent revelation, and his young friend went red.

The Abbot made emphatic negative gestures - a lateral sweep of his right hand across his body and a shake of his head. "No – that would precipitate an attempt by Domingo to seize control by force, perhaps even to proclaim himself Magus of Moridura. Such an attempted coup would cause some of the younger Moriduran Brothers to resist – the violent parts of our history have influenced them, and they would respond to force with force. But there are a few others who would support him. His American military friends could find themselves in the middle of a riot, and Angeline's great task, and her safety, would be placed in jeopardy."

"Then you too were bluffing, Brother Anselmo?" said Red.

"Yes," said the Abbot simply, "I would not have followed through on my threat."

"Then what can stop Ferdinand and Domingo?"

"Arkimateo," said the Abbot, "and that possibility also carries great risk."

"You Moridurans are a bundle of joy..." Red shook his head. "Forgive me, but is there no good news?"

"Your daughter is our good news, Red," said the Abbot, then turning to the others. "Your meal will be served before Sext, and Paul may then take up his position behind the partition: from what you have told us, Alistair, we may expect Angeline sometime after None and before Vespers. All you can do is wait and remain alert: Ferdinand or Domingo will make some other attempt to find her."

"Remind me what those prayer times mean on the clock, Brother Anselmo," said Red apologetically, "I've been here long enough to remember, but I don't..."

"Sext is prayed at the sixth hour – midday; None at the ninth hour – three o'clock; Vespers at sunset," replied the Abbot.

"It's pushing on towards midday," said Alistair, "and we need something from you before you leave, Anselmo."

"One of you must be taken to *La Puerta de Bestia*," said the Abbot.

Alistair nodded and thought for a moment. "It can't be Paul, so it's down to one of the rest of us."

"Not me," said Red decisively, "I plan to stick around and wait for my little girl."

Alistair looked at Santiago and waited for his verdict. Before he could speak, the Abbot lifted his hand. "There is something else you should know: someone was in the wine cellar while we were there, and *La Puerta de Bestia* had been opened, perhaps for the first time in centuries. There may be danger ..."

"Then I must go," said Santiago. "Alistair and Red are needed here to give Angeline scientific support as well as physical protection when she arrives."

"Agreed," said Alistair.

"One thing," said Santiago, "I'll need a monk's habit, otherwise I will be all too conspicuous. Brother Anselmo?"

"I have anticipated your requirement, Santiago," replied the Abbot, and as he spoke, Alfonso emerged from the passageway carrying a black habit over his arm. Santiago took it from the bewildered old cellarer and slipped it on, and then struck a pose, head bent, hands clasped before him.

The Abbot smiled, and Alistair and Red laughed.

"Aye, you'll do fine, Brother Santiago – perhaps you've missed your true vocation," Alistair called out as the new monk departed with Alfonso.

"Manuel and I must leave now," said the Abbot, "All my efforts will now be directed towards the Ceremony, and Manuel will be my right arm in the work that lies ahead. I can offer no more help, Alistair – everything now depends on you, Santiago, Red and Paul to ensure that Angeline and Arkimateo can complete their tasks. May God be with you…" He raised his hand in a benediction then left with Manuel.

Red looked disconsolately at the empty wine bottle. "Let's hope Alfonso brings another with the lunch cart," he said, holding the bottle up, "or maybe Santiago will grab one for me in the wine cellar. And when you feel up to it, Alistair, maybe you'll tell me how long you and Paul have known the identity of the Magus. "

Alistair gave a brief explanation, and then the three of them sat silently with their own thoughts, until the familiar rattle of the cart came from along the passageway and the Magus of Moridura approached with their food, grinning cheerfully at the disconsolate trio.

Chapter Twenty-Five

The monastery chapel was full, the pews on the right filled with black-habited Moridurans and those on the left occupied by the *hermandad*, a sea of red, with the *confratres* at the front. In the front pew, on the left, reserved for the seven members of the Grand Council, sat Severino, Casimiro and Jaime. Conspicuously absent were Don Ferdinand, Domingo, Amancio and Vasco, who, it was rumoured, was dead. On the right, the Chapter of the monastery of Moridura occupied the front pew, with the equally conspicuous absences of the Abbot and Brother Joaquín. As the sixth hour was announced by the ringing of a bell, the low conversational murmur ended, followed by a moment of complete silence, and then the collective voice of the Ancient Order of Moridura was raised in prayer.

Even in the depths of the wine cellar, its faint echo could be heard by Brother Alfonso, and he fervently wished he was in the chapel with his brethren, rather than here with the man Santiago, who was using a small electric flashlight to examine the little door that aroused such dread in the old monk's mind. Alfonso didn't approve of electrical devices, especially in his cellar: who knew what effects they could have on the wines?

Santiago had successively put his eye and his ear to the keyhole, and his senses confirmed the Abbot's words – this was no shallow cupboard in the stone or the rock: behind it lay a large, resonant space. He took his knife from inside his habit, opened it and ran it down the gap between the door and the stone wall, down to the top of the bolt of the lock. He tried to manipulate the bolt at this point, without success, then inserted another tool from the knife into the keyhole, and attempted to use it as a lock pick, feeling for the tumbler. After a time, the lock yielded to his expert probing.

Brother Alfonso was becoming increasingly agitated.

"Please, señor, do not open *la puerta*," he pleaded. "It is forbidden…"

"Calm yourself, Alfonso – it is not forbidden: we have the express permission of the Abbot."

"Only the Magus may permit this – it is a violation," gasped Alfonso. "I will not stay! I will leave the candle - I can find my way in the darkness."

He began to back away, then turned and vanished soundlessly, and with surprising rapidity into the gloom of the cellar. Santiago shook his head, half-amused, half-annoyed at the cellarer's sudden departure: he used his makeshift lock pick to pull the door towards him. It swung inwards, and a cold blue-green light blinded him for a moment, a familiar light – the same glow that pervaded the chamber of *La Guardia*, or Arkimateo, as he remembered he must now think of her. All the conversations about radiation came back to him, creating a feeling of apprehension, but he quickly mastered his fears, knelt, and put his head through the doorway.

He found himself looking down a circular tunnel, over two metres in diameter, downward-sloping and curving to the left. The uneven surface of the black walls could be seen by the light that emanated from an invisible source. Santiago withdrew into the cellar and closed the door, and the light vanished; he looked through the keyhole and there was only darkness; he inserted his makeshift key and pulled it open again and the light returned.

He crouched there, reflecting for a moment. Unlike the walls of the staircase down to the chamber of Arkimateo, which were rough-textured but in a consistent pattern, and had clearly been worked by sophisticated power tools or lasers of some description, this tunnel had been hacked through the hard rock of *La Copa* with hand tools: it was hard to conceive of the back-breaking, interminable labour that had created it. He knew he had to go through the door, but remembering the Abbot's warning of an intruder in the cellar - and the missing key - he realised that when he did go through into the tunnel, someone with a key could lock the door behind him.

Looking around at the base of the wine racks, he eventually found a piece of wood that had broken off one of them. He held it against the bolt socket in the wall, marked it quickly with the blade of his knife, cut a crude plug of wood from it that would fit the socket, and forced it into place. It would delay someone who attempted to lock the door, but not for long. Carrying the piece of wood left over, he drew a long breath, crossed himself, and then he squeezed through the door into the tunnel, and, still crouching, turned and pulled the door shut behind him. He laid the piece of wood upright against the door so that he would know if it had been opened when he returned. He turned again and stood up slowly, not quite sure if he had enough headroom; there wasn't much, maybe fifteen centimetres. Stretching his arms on either side of him, he found about the same clearance from the fingertips of each hand – in fact, his open knife in his right hand almost touched the wall. He turned and inspected the aperture he had just come through.

He could see part of the rear wall of the cellar around the little door: it was part of the monastery foundations, constructed in a natural depression in the rock behind the inner ridge through which the tunnel had been driven. It was evident that the tunnel had been hacked into the rock ridge before the ancient cellar wall was built, and was of great antiquity. There could only have been one of two purposes in the mind of whoever undertook or ordered the arduous work, work that must have taken years - perhaps decades - to complete: to either drive the tunnel all the way to *El Trono*, or, as the downward slope and direction of the curve suggested, to intersect an existing route.

Walking down the tunnel had a disorienting effect upon him, caused by a combination of the black walls, the light and the unevenness and curvature of the floor beneath his feet; he frequently had to put his arms out to maintain his balance. As he walked, he remembered that he had left the candle burning, and hoped that it did not start a fire in the cellar. A vision of burning wine racks and exploding bottles came, vivid and disturbing, and he cursed his oversight: the vision expanded to include the entire monastery complex burning, and he cursed again. Attention to detail was fundamental to his nature and his training, and his omission gnawed at him.

The passage began to level out, and he found himself walking straight ahead towards a bright circle of light. As he came close to it, Santiago could see that his tunnel was intersecting with another: this had to be Arkimateo's route from the chamber, and the source of the light. He realised that the diameter of his route was narrowing like a funnel, and he had to crouch to move forward. He speculated that this reduction in diameter had been designed to stop the legendary beast entering the man-made tunnel. At the intersection, the exit point was less than one-and-a-half metres wide and high: he ducked through into a much larger, circular tunnel, over four metres in diameter, with the walls formed in the same regular pattern as that of the stairway to the chamber of Arkimateo. Straightening up with relief, he got his bearings.

Unless his sense of direction had failed him, if he turned left down the passage, he would eventually find himself beneath the chamber of Arkimateo, and going right would take him across the radius of *La Copa* to *El Trono*. This must be Arkimateo's route to the regulator, but who would transport the core and the key, now that Mateo had gone? The trunk was lying just inside the partition and it could not safely be taken down to the chamber. Arkimateo could not come up for it, and only Mateo had been strong enough to lift it unaided.

Something kept slipping and sliding at the back of his mind, an elusive concept that somehow held the solution to the dilemma, but he could not pin it down.

Relinquishing the problem for the moment, he reflected on whether he should reconnoitre further in either direction along the large tunnel, and decided against it. Nothing could be served by it, he decided – he must get back to the cellar and report back to Alistair. He turned and re-entered the small tunnel, and now, more sure-footed on its curved floor, moved rapidly back to the door.

When he got to the door, he opened his knife in case he needed it to force the door, but then he saw that the piece of wood was not as he had left it, but flat on the floor of the tunnel: he knelt and listened for a moment at the keyhole, then pushed it open gently: it was immediately pushed shut again from the other side.

Santiago drew back, ducked and launched himself against the door; it crashed open under his onslaught, and he forced his way through against a powerful resistance. A voice cursed in Spanish, then he was back inside the dark interior of the cellar. A figure lunged towards him, and it was only as the body struck him that Santiago realised he was still holding his open knife in his hand. The body slumped against him; there was a long, slow sigh, and his assailant slid down to the floor.

He saw the red robe of the Order, and, looking down at his knife, saw another shade of red. He bent over the man on the floor and placed his fingertips to his temples, then to his neck. He had dropped his flashlight, but the candle was still guttering on the rack. Santiago lifted it down and looked at the wide-open, staring eyes: the unknown man was dead.

"*Mierda...*" he said softly. He knelt on the floor of the cellar, followed his profanity with a brief, silent prayer over the corpse, and then groped around for the flashlight. The candle was still burning, and Santiago felt a sense of relief, but it was short-lived: there was a noise from the far end, a sudden change of air pressure, a cold draught of air, and then the voice of Brother Alfonso.

"Señor Santiago? Are you there? It is Alfonso…"

Santiago bent over and put his hands under the armpits of the body on the floor, and began to move backwards down the side aisle between the last two wine racks, calling out as he dragged the corpse.

"Brother Alfonso – I am still here!"

He laid the body on the floor again and edged past it back to the little door, just as Alfonso appeared, looking remorseful.

"I am sorry for my action, señor, born of old superstitions. As a man of God, I should know better than to believe in monstrous creatures lurking in the depths of the monastery. Please do not tell the Abbot of my cowardice."

"There are more things in this old world of ours than a man may know, Alfonso. Tell your confessor of your actions – I do not condemn you for your fear. I, too, am often afraid…"

The old man came closer, looking up at the tall, powerful figure in front of him. "I cannot believe that there are many things that you fear, señor," he said, lifting the candleholder. "The candle burns low; if we do not leave soon, we will be dependent on your little electrical light."

"I am ready to leave now, Alfonso," said Santiago.

Alfonso started to move towards the cellar door, but suddenly he paused. "My fears have not entirely left me, señor – I feel the presence of the Angel of Death." He shivered, shook his head, and moved forward again.

"Forgive a superstitious old man," he said contritely as they reached the cellar door.

Santiago parted from Brother Alfonso at the top of the cellar steps, thanking him for his help. On his way back to the guest wing he received curious looks from some of the monks; there were many tall, powerfully built Moriduran brothers, but none who walked with such a confident,

391

athletic stride. Santiago, aware of the curious glances, consciously slowed his pace, bent his head, and tried to blend into his surroundings. As he was passing the Abbot's room, Manuel appeared, and seeing Santiago, gestured to him to approach. As they both entered the room Brother Anselmo looked up from his desk, and stood up.

"This is fortuitous, Santiago – I have something to tell you that may be important. The *hermandad* member who unwisely held a gun to Señor Lonnen's head in the chapter house, and had his shoulder dislocated, has left the infirmary. His injury was attended to immediately on arrival; we suspect he has been feigning continued incapacity, and declining to leave – for what purpose, we can only guess. His name is Amancio – he is Domingo's man."

"Amancio…" repeated Manuel, shaking his head, "a dangerous man…"

"Singularly ill-named," said the Abbot. "Señor Paul would tell you that Amancio derives from the Roman *Amantius*, which means *loving* – not how I would describe him."

Santiago bent his head for a moment, and then met the Abbot's level gaze.

"You have already encountered him?" said Brother Anselmo, and then seeing Santiago's expression, dropped his gaze. "*Requiescat in pace*," he murmured, crossing himself. "When will it end?"

Santiago rapidly outlined the events in the cellar; the Abbot listened attentively and cocked his head for a moment as Santiago mentioned Alfonso's departure and return.

"Why did Alfonso leave you alone in the cellar?" he said.

"I think he went for another candle – the one we had was burning low," replied Santiago, uneasily skirting around the truth.

"This is the fourth death suffered by the *hermandad*; two of them were Council members. It is only a matter of time until they realise that he is missing; they know where his mission took him. I have to consider what Ferdinand will do…" The Abbot sat down again at his desk.

"He intends to use the route from the cellar to replace the core," said Santiago. "The man Amancio may have been sent to reconnoitre; he may have followed us to the cellar, then seized his chance when Alfonso left; alternatively, he may have entered, and seeing *la puerta* open, decided to imprison me within the tunnel. One thing is certain – the body must be removed."

"I will arrange that," said the Abbot. "Manuel, go to Brother Joaquín and tell him everything – he will know what to do."

"Thank you, Brother Anselmo," said Santiago. "I deeply regret that I have been the cause of another death: now I must return to Alistair and Red and bring them up-to-date." He and Manuel left the room together; before they went on their separate errands, they shook hands warmly and embraced. Passing monks and members of the Order nodded approvingly at this fraternal scene, symbolic, they thought, of the unity between the *hermandad* and the Moridurans, a unity that would reach its apotheosis in the Ceremony tomorrow.

Alistair and Red greeted Santiago eagerly as he emerged from the passageway.

"Where's Paul?" asked Santiago. Alistair pointed wordlessly to the mouth of the left-hand passageway.

"He's only separated from us by the thickness of a wooden panel, but he might as well be on the moon," said Red. He was ill at ease, pacing restlessly, looking at his watch frequently as though urging time forward.

"We had a bad moment when Paul tried to open the partition – it takes a lot of force and it's temperamental," grunted Alistair. "Mateo makes it seem easy, but it isn't.

Jesus, at one point I thought I was going to break the bloody thing, and then where the hell would we have been?"

"Yeah, and what will happen if it jams when they want out?" muttered Red. "I wish Paul had a fire axe or something like it in there."

"We'll just have to wait," said Alistair. "Let's hear from Santiago. Did you have fun in the cellar?"

"Not exactly – I killed Domingo's deputy – a man called Amancio, the one who held the gun to your head in the chapter house, Red."

"What?" gasped Alistair, "God Almighty! I thought he was still in the monastery infirmary with a dislocated shoulder…"

Red chuckled gleefully. "He's made a downshift to the morgue – he should've stayed put…"

Santiago explained the circumstances; Alistair rubbed the back of his neck in evident agitation. "They will know something is wrong all too soon, regardless of what arrangements the Abbot makes: when people don't show up where they should be around here it's natural to fear the worst. Ferdinand, Jaime and Domingo now have to rely on Laurel and Hardy, the guys with the combat machine guns…"

"… and they're hired muscle, red robes notwithstanding. The whole damned mess gets more volatile by the minute," said Red gloomily.

"We don't know what resources Ferdinand can call upon – and this guy Domingo is an unknown quantity to us. From what the Abbot said, they may have allies among the Moriduran Brothers," said Alistair.

"That's all we need," said Red. "At least up to now the enemy wore uniform – we had a colour-coding to go on…"

"While I was in the large tunnel, something came to mind – a problem," said Santiago. "When Angeline and Paul come out of there, how are we going to get the trunk across the monastery, down into the wine cellar and along the tunnels to the centre of *La Copa*? I would say that we have between eight and nine hundred metres to cover, maybe more, carrying a very heavy, bulky and conspicuous burden. Without Mateo's formidable strength, getting the trunk down the cellar steps will be impossible."

Alistair's brow furrowed, and he rubbed his neck again. "Angeline and Arkimateo mentioned something just after their mind meld…"

"Their what?" said Red, a note of menace in his voice.

"Don't give me any hassle, Red – you knew that something like that was going to happen – we talked about it before. It happened quickly – Angeline raised the question during one particularly complex scientific discussion between them; Arkimateo asked if she was ready, and she agreed. And suddenly it was done – I had no say in the matter."

Red chewed his lips in frustration. "What in hell do you mean, it was done? What did they do?"

"They didn't go up on to the plinths - Angeline simply looked up, Arkimateo held out one of her hands, they sort of shook hands, and it was done."

"How did Angeline react?" asked Red anxiously. "Was there any change in her?"

"She suddenly looked very, very happy and relieved – as if a great weight had been lifted off her mind. It was as though something had been made clear to her, a sudden scientific insight," said Alistair. "Really, Red, I don't think you have anything to worry about – she's still the Angeline we know and love."

"I'm sorry, I guess I'm just being a sorehead – but you know why…" said Red. "I guess you still think I'm a pain in the ass."

"Aye, I do, but Angeline loves you – she spoke about you and Paul the whole time we were down there – and that's good enough for me. I wish I had a daughter like her." He gripped Red's arm. "Given what lies ahead of us, there can be no time for disagreement – from here on in, it's got to be consensus all the way."

"Agreed – and thanks," said Red quietly. "*Pax*, as my future son-in-law might say."

Santiago was showing signs of impatience, and Alistair turned to him penitently.

"Sorry, Santiago, I've digressed yet again. As I was saying, Angeline and Arkimateo mentioned the problem of moving the core and the key. The consoles and the screen – they're not just control panels: they have the capacity to create and shape matter from pure energy – Arkimateo's people were manipulating the Higg's boson while we were still walking on all-fours. They have come up with a golden gizmo – Angeline will bring it with her."

"Like what?" asked Red.

"Like I think we're going to see a practical demonstration of what the future holds for the world – an antigravity device," replied Alistair.

Red looked keenly interested, and Santiago was about to say something but he stopped abruptly. There was a knocking sound coming from the passageway. The three men stood rooted to the spot, listening intently. The rhythmic pattern came again, distinct and unambiguous.

"It's Beethoven alright," said Alistair, and they moved as one to the entrance to the passageway. Alistair stood back to allow Red to operate the mechanism, but he shook his head and gestured to Alistair to go ahead. The panel clicked open a few centimetres, the narrow strip of blue-green light could be seen, but no one appeared.

"They're being cautious – they don't know who has opened up the partition," said Santiago. Red was about to rush in, but Alistair held him back. "You'll get your head shot off by Paul," he cautioned.

"Angeline – Angeline – it's Red," her father called out.

"Santiago and I are here too, Paul – it's OK to come out!"

The fingers of two hands appeared through the gap, and Red eagerly assisted in pulling the partition open; considerable force was necessary to raise the counterweight.

As it clicked into place, Paul's white face appeared cautiously, then the rest of him, his gun in his hand. He looked over his shoulder. "It's OK, Angeline," he breathed in evident relief, stood back, and helped a beautiful, red-haired monk in a black habit through the opening. She was holding something about the size of a personal compact disc player, made of pure gold and the rock of *La Copa*, and she held it with both hands, as one would hold a uniquely beautiful, delicate and precious thing.

Paul holstered his gun, and took the object from her with great care, so that she could embrace her father. He held her close, repeating her name softly: Alistair and Santiago pulled Paul aside to give them a private moment.

"Can it play mp3s?" asked Alistair.

"It's the future," said Paul complacently, "and Angeline tells me it's jog proof – and virtually indestructible - but we still can't help treating it like a clutch of eggs."

Alistair put his hand out tentatively and ran his fingers over the object, fascinated. Santiago, realising their vulnerability at this juncture, was in full guard mode, his weapon drawn and ready. Angeline was eventually released from her father's hug, and came over to embrace Alistair; she looked at Santiago, but he was not available for hugging. Red peered warily through the gap in the partition, half-expecting Arkimateo to appear, but then the trunk caught his eye, lying where they had left it.

"We have to get the trunk out, guys – I hope we can manage it without rupturing ourselves," he said.

"I'll get it," said Angeline airily, and before her father could stop her, slipped back through the partition. Those outside heard a tiny click, and suddenly the trunk appeared, hovering in the air, the gold and black gizmo sitting on top of it. It came soundlessly through the gap, closely followed by Angeline, holding a tiny control device in her hand. The trunk moved down the passageway and across the room, followed by its black-clad attendant, and then sank slowly and soundlessly to the floor. Angeline turned to the open-mouthed trio behind her, struck a pose and looked very self-satisfied. Alistair took a moment under the stairs to close the partition, and then joined them.

"I'm glad this didn't appear when Jimmy Hoffa headed up the Teamsters Union," she laughed, "or I would have been wearing concrete boots at the bottom of the East River."

The anti-gravity device fascinated Alistair and Red, and they took turns playing with it, raising and lowering the trunk using the little control.

"Will this work anywhere, Angeline?" asked her father.

"No – only within *La Copa*," she replied. "The Cup itself is acting as a huge dish aerial for the gravitational waves, in the same way as Alistair's rig at Ardmurran, but on a very much larger scale: to make it viable commercially will involve creating wave capture areas, probably with mast aerials, similar to cell phone masts. I have the theory firmly in place: from here on in, it will be simply a technological problem. The whole thing is roughly analogous to the development of worldwide radio coverage."

"What is the weight limitation of the device?" asked Alistair.

Angeline looked at him, and he saw a look of deep concern in her green eyes.

"There is no limit," she said quietly.

Paul stared at her in amazement. "But that means…. it means that…"

"Are you saying that if you put the device on any free-standing object that it will lift it?" said Alistair incredulously.

"Yes," said Angeline. She met her father's eyes and saw his worried reaction. She took back the control device from Red and pointed it at the trunk with the black and gold control still sitting on its lid. The trunk lifted about half a metre from the floor.

"Now push it, Red – but very gently! Alistair, get on the other side of it…"

Her father gently shoved the trunk with his hand; it moved off smoothly towards Alistair, who arrested its movement, then pushed it carefully back to him. It was like pushing a floating object in water. Paul gaped in astonishment, and even Santiago gave the phenomenon a little of his attention.

"If Alistair hadn't stopped it, what would have happened?" said Paul.

"It would just have kept on going until the initial impetus was exhausted, just like a child's boat in a pond," said Angeline.

Alistair and Red looked at the trunk, then at each other, and something unspoken passed between them. Paul took Angeline by the hand, looking uneasily at the device in her other hand.

"Angeline," said Alistair slowly, "I think Red and I have just had a mind meld – with apologies to you and Arkimateo – and we would like Paul, as a man who can lift us all to a less mundane level, to articulate for us what this device is going to mean to the world."

Paul was silent for a moment, and then squeezed Angeline's hand. "Set the trunk back down, Angeline – it's making me nervous," he said. As the trunk settled soundlessly and smoothly on the floor, he motioned them across to the table, and they all sat down, with the exception of Santiago, who maintained his surveillance of the four entry points from which a threat could come.

They waited expectantly as Paul collected his thoughts. He impulsively kissed Angeline on the cheek before turning his eyes to Alistair and Red.

"You two are the masters of the wisecrack, but this is a serious business, and I ask you to restrain your inclinations for a time, and give due weight to my opinions – OK?" He smiled at his own feeble witticism.

They nodded and waited.

"This discovery of Angeline's, and the technology that will inevitably flow from it will transform society, and that transformation will either be life-enhancing or destructive. The parallels with nuclear energy are obvious – a discovery that should have provided a cheap, environmentally-friendly, virtually unlimited energy source led to Hiroshima, Nagasaki, Chernobyl, half-a-century of nuclear standoff between the great powers, the problems of nuclear weapons proliferation, and a pollution problem that will remain for tens of thousands of years. The model we must aspire to must be something like the development of radio and television communications: in the main, positive in its impact on society, with few negatives."

He stood up, and stretched, then moved behind Angeline, placing his hands on her shoulders.

"We have as yet no single demonstration of the potential destructive power of the technology that will result from this, but nonetheless, in a previous discussion, Angeline recognised that she was in the position of Oppenheimer witnessing the first nuclear explosion.

"The possibilities I see, as a layman, are both positive and negative. Once gravitational field capture masts become relatively inexpensive, technologies that were previously hugely expensive and capital-intensive will become accessible to the poorest, most deprived areas. In transportation, construction, in every aspect of life, cheap environmentally friendly solutions will transform every task, every project.

"But that will threaten great industrial and political power bases – the automobile industry, the oil industry, aviation, shipping, construction, railways, material-handling – those who own and control these potentially redundant industrial empires will recognise both a threat and an opportunity, and a cataclysmic struggle to either contain or dominate the new technology will commence.

"The implications for the military and for governments, democratic and undemocratic, are evident, and we will have in our midst tomorrow the advance guard of one such power grouping, in the form of Ferdinand's military guests from America. Ferdinand, of course, is representative of another power grouping – the global criminal networks."

Paul paused, and looked at his audience; their expressions and their silence gave him permission to continue.

"We must recognise that we cannot go back. Pandora's box is open; the potential of the discovery is known to powerful interested parties. All we can do is try to control the release of the information and the development of the technology, at least in its initial stages. If this were a breakthrough in medicine – in pharmaceuticals – a cure for cancer, or for ageing – we could give it to the world by putting the details into the public domain, bypassing the power groupings and the individual profit motive: but gravitational control is of a different order. We can't put such a potentially destructive force in the hands of those who can and will abuse it.

"There are several aspects of the release of the discovery and the technology that we must control and influence: first, we must find - or create - an industrial and commercial entity powerful enough to develop it fully: next, we must implant in that corporation an ethical awareness – a conscience, if you like – that will inform its every action, rooted in the primary goal of benefiting mankind.

"To achieve all of this, we must create a powerful intelligence and security network of our own, to protect ourselves, and the discovery, from attack. And finally, in pursuing these complex objectives, we must beware of metamorphosing into the very thing we abhor, corrupting and betraying our own beliefs and ideals."

He stopped and sat down, avoiding the eyes of his friends, uncertain as to how his analysis had been received. Angeline had slipped her arm under his, and she was gripping him tightly and reassuringly.

Alistair exchanged a glance with Red; he stood up, looking with admiration and affection at his young friend.

"I always doubted the claims about the value of a classical education, but that was a masterly analysis, Paul; it summarises all that I feel and, I suspect, all that Red feels too. Here's my solution – and I'm arrogant enough to believe that I also speak for Red. We must be the ones to create the new corporate entity to develop the technology…"

He looked at Red, who gave a laconic thumbs-up. "I may have to postpone my entry to the contemplative life," he said, grinning widely. "My monkhood will have to go on the back burner…"

"All we need is a provisional name for the new corporation," said Alistair. "Any suggestions?"

"Arkimateo Gravitation," said Angeline unhesitatingly.

No one dissented, although Red looked as though he might have, had the suggestion come from anyone but his daughter.

Santiago had been silent up to this point, attempting to maintain his vigilance while listening to the analysis, but now he had to intervene.

"If we don't get the trunk to the cellar and from there to *El Corazón de La Copa*, there won't be any technology to develop," he said quietly, but with a powerful sense of urgency in his voice.

"You're right, as always, Santiago," said Alistair, springing to his feet, "we must get back to the task in hand. How are we going to get the trunk to the cellar, and who is going to accompany Angeline to the cellar, and from there, through the tunnels to *El Corazón*?"

"You guys can fight over who comes with me to the cellar and the small tunnel, but only Arkimateo will be with me in the journey down the main tunnel," said Angeline firmly. "She will know when I arrive at the intersection, and will come."

Paul became agitated, and he put his hand on her shoulder. "I'm coming with you all the way, Angeline," he said. "Whatever the outcome, I must be with you…"

She stroked his cheek gently. "Paul – I know you want to protect me and to be with me, and I want that too, more than anything else in the world. But you can't accompany me. Arkimateo can protect me from the radiation in the main tunnel and from conditions at the regulator, but she cannot protect anyone else: the mind meld did more than give me new knowledge, new insights, Paul…"

Alistair knew that she was struggling with an idea that she could not find the words to express. "What is it, Angeline? There is something else – something that you learned from Arkimateo after I left, isn't there?"

"Yes, there is something – I'm not sure I can explain it fully," she said reluctantly. "The regulator may now be within the event horizon of the singularity."

Paul, not quite understanding the significance of her statement, realised by the expression on her father's face, and by the sudden rigidity of Alistair's body posture, that they were both shocked by the import of her words.

"What does that mean, Alistair?" he said, a nameless fear growing in his mind.

Alistair looked at Red and then again at Paul.

"It has been generally held that nothing can escape from a black hole," he said, "but Stephen Hawking, the main proponent of that view, paid up on a bet and acknowledged that he was wrong."

Angeline shook her head. "He was both right and wrong – the answer lies in a quantum physics concept called *entanglement*, although as presently formulated, it is incomplete. I can only say this – I can enter the event horizon and emerge again, in our time, in our universe, as myself."

"Arkimateo has told you this, Angeline," said her father, his voice full of concern, "but how do you know it's true?"

She looked at him and then at Paul, Alistair and Santiago and they all suddenly realised that the Angeline they knew had changed in a fundamental way – there had been a transformation in the chamber that would forever separate her from the rest of her species. Paul felt a great sense of loss, and tried to fight back tears: this was more than a difference in intellect, of IQ. He had known from the beginning that Angeline was almost certainly more intelligent than he was, than any of them, but now...

"I know it's true, not because Arkimateo told me, but because she helped me to understand. I know it as a physicist, I know it in the depths of my very being," she said, and there was something in the way she said it that chilled the hearts of her listeners. Paul experienced the same uncanny valley moment that he had often felt in the presence of Mateo.

"Angeline..." he said, his voice despairing, "what has happened to you?"

"I am linked with Arkimateo at the quantum level, and she is linked to *El Corazón*," she replied, then pulled him close to her. "But I am *your* Angeline, now and forever, and our child is within me, Paul. Nothing that has happened can change that. Please trust me and believe me..."

Paul bowed his head for a moment, and then looked deep into her green eyes; what he saw there gave him hope. He started to say something, but she put her finger on his lips and silenced him.

"You will come with me to the cellar and through the link tunnel to the main tunnel, Paul, but not beyond that point. Santiago, will you ride shotgun on our stagecoach?"

Santiago nodded. "We must get a Moriduran habit for Paul. Then we must think of a way of camouflaging the trunk – a free-floating object might just attract undesirable attention. Ferdinand will be looking for the trunk; if we remove the core from the trunk, that will reduce bulk, but we must disguise it in some way."

Angeline lifted the gravity device off the lid of the trunk, and her father produced its key and opened it; the core gleamed as the light reflected off its surface. Angeline placed the device on its surface, stood back and operated her tiny control; the core lifted slowly and majestically from the trunk, hovered for a moment, then moved across towards her. She gently lowered it to the floor, and they all gathered round it, marvelling at its functional beauty.

"It will fit on the lower half of Joaquín's cart, providing its weight is nullified by the device," said Paul.

"My thought exactly," said Santiago. "We can cover it with a piece of cloth or canvas. Without the device, it would break the trolley, which isn't as robust as Mateo's cliff path cart."

"Red and I will hold the line here, and mount a diversionary activity, if need be," said Alistair. "Best be quick in finding the habit, Santiago – Ferdinand and Domingo will be up to something, we can be sure of that."

"Before we do anything, I must eat," Angeline said plaintively, "I'm starving – I missed lunch…"

Chapter Twenty-Six

"**W**here is Amancio?" asked Ferdinand in a low voice.

The dormitory of the *confratres* was full of members of the *hermandad*, and although they gave the group at the end of the room a wide berth, the voices of Ferdinand and his group had to be muted.

"Ask Jaime, my brother – He spoke to him recently," said Domingo.

Jaime looked uncomfortable, his eyes shifting from Domingo to Ferdinand. "I set him a task – he may still be engaged in it," he mumbled.

Ferdinand swivelled around. "He was instructed directly by me to stay in the infirmary until further notice," he said in a low, controlled tone. "Why did you countermand my orders?"

Jaime looked at Domingo in desperation, then back at Ferdinand. "You remember that Domingo saw the Abbot, the cellarer and Manuel Ortega – we discussed it over breakfast, Ferdinand."

"And?"

Jaime squirmed. "I did not want to bother you with it – a detail – but it occurred to me that they might be going to the cellar, since Alfonso was with them, and I wondered why." He looked nervously at the tall, thin man with the expressionless eyes.

"Domingo, you will remember that I mentioned my suspicions to you…"

"…and I dismissed them," said Domingo curtly. "What if they *were* going to the cellar? Ortega is involved with the wines of the monastery – he is a tradesman – an innkeeper. The Abbot often selects wines, especially when we have many guests."

"Well, I didn't treat it so lightly," said Jaime defiantly, standing up. "I felt that I should go to the infirmary and tell Amancio to go to the cellar area and see what he could find out. Domingo, I said I might do that …" His voice was petulant.

Domingo met the fat man's gaze with a cold stare, avoiding Ferdinand's suspicious glance. "I advised you against that course of action, my brother: my view was that, by the time you got to the infirmary and Amancio got to the cellar, Brother Anselmo would have concluded his business. You seem to have ignored my advice."

"I did not share your view, Domingo, but it is true that it did take me some time. The monks in the infirmary were reluctant to release Amancio – there was a long, heated discussion before they would let him leave." Jaime was now in a state of some agitation: he had antagonised both Ferdinand and Domingo, and Amancio was missing.

Domingo kept his counsel. The growing dissent between Ferdinand and Jaime suited his purpose. He was curious about what Amancio might have found in the cellar – he knew about the little door, but did not have the key. Domingo was also curious about his current whereabouts, but all that would emerge in good time.

"Do not be too hard on our brother Jaime, Ferdinand," he said, "as a member of the Grand Council he must use his discretion and initiative. Amancio may have gained valuable intelligence about the movement of Mackinnon and his friends, may even have discovered the hiding place of the woman Blade. Time is running out for us – we must achieve our purpose today: tomorrow must be devoted to our American guests and to the Ceremony."

Jaime looked at him in gratitude and some surprise; he feared Domingo and had never thought of him as an ally.

"Ferdinand, may I return to the question of what lies in the sealed area behind the partitions in the guest wing?" said

Domingo, and waited for the expected outburst, but there was only silence.

Ferdinand seemed to be experiencing some inner conflict: eventually he spoke.

"You know that I have sought the diaries of Eduardo Ortega, Manuel's father. This man, over his long life, acquired an unrivalled knowledge of the monastery complex. My father liked and trusted him, and confided many things to him. His diaries are a meticulous record of his observations and experiences of the monastery and the district of Moridanza."

"All of this I know, my brother," said Domingo. He turned to the two *artilleros*. "Leave us – walk in the cloisters; do not disturb or threaten anyone; do not engage in conversation with any person," he said, dismissing them with a wave of his hand.

"You know it, but its significance has escaped you, Domingo," said Ferdinand as the *artilleros* left. "Like many others, you underrated the elder Ortega when he was alive, as I may have underrated his son. Brother Anselmo does not confer the status of senior member and *confrater* on a nonentity. I am Magus Elect, but that status gives me no access to the ultimate secrets of our Ancient Order: only when I am confirmed as Magus at the elevation will I become privy to that arcane knowledge."

His intense frustration was evident. "Only the Abbot of Moridura and the Magus possess the hidden knowledge, and it gives them great power over the Order. The *hermandad* wields secular power – political influence, patronage, the power of money and naked force – but the old secrets confer an influence far greater than all of these."

Domingo maintained an expression of respect and deep attentiveness, but his inner feelings were of deep contempt for an educated, cultured man who could value such superstitions: these things were for the credulous and the fearful.

Ferdinand looked at the two men before him - one dangerous, ambitious and without scruple, of high intelligence, but devoid of a spiritual dimension, a man who lived only in the moment, with no concept of history and no respect for tradition, a man without any ethical or moral compass and the other a populist politician, without judgement or vision, a coward. Was the Abbot right? Had he become vulnerable to the influence of such men; had they corrupted his own beliefs? No, he thought - I need men such as these, but I control them and my destiny. Tomorrow, all will be mine, and my authority and power will be beyond challenge.

"Domingo, Jaime – my esteemed brothers: what is beyond doubt is that something very strange lies at the heart of *La Copa de Moridura*, something very old, very powerful and potentially very dangerous. You have both experienced its effects, in the vibrations and tremors that have so disturbed us in recent days. You have experienced the gravitational anomaly that it creates through your own senses. We know there is a control chamber, and that Mackinnon and his friends have the core and the key, brought from America by Lonnen. We must be the ones who compel Angeline Blade to replace them.

"None of us has observed the splitting of *El Trono* and the elevation of the Magus Elect. What I know is this – the guest wing of the monastery is an ancient structure, but it was built around a structure of even greater antiquity, a structure that covers a stairway – the Portal – that leads to something from the dawn of history. I do not know what that thing is – it may be an ancient relic, a rock, or a sacred place. Popular legend describes it as the lair of *La Bestia de Moridura*…"

He saw the faint, contemptuous smiles on the faces of Domingo and Jaime, and he controlled his surging anger with a supreme effort of will. Domingo spoke.

"Such stories are told around the fireside to children – we are all familiar with them, my brother."

"Are these stories any stranger than the reality of the regulator, the core and the key, Domingo? The old myths offer an insight into that reality. All legend - all myth - is rooted in some fact, some element of truth," said Ferdinand patiently, "and this myth tells of a path that *La Guardia* follows to *El Trono* and to *El Corazón de La Copa*."

"Why should the creature, if it exists, wish to go there?" asked Jaime plaintively. "What purpose can it have?"

"There is no creature, but in the old stories, its purpose is exactly the same as ours – to gain access to the regulator. Ortega's father's diaries contain the secret routes – the location of a man-made linking tunnel that intersects the legendary path of *La Bestia* to the regulator. I believe the diaries also contain information about the area at the heart of the guest wing, and how it may be accessed," said Ferdinand.

"If the core and the key are gold, why may we not keep them? They must have a high value," said Jaime, his eyes glittering.

Ferdinand gave him a look of naked contempt. "Because our Order exists to protect *El Corazón de La Copa* and because they will end the vibrations that frighten the credulous, and affect our reputation for controlling the phenomena. There is also another reason: I cannot go into in detail, my brothers, but please accept that the honour of my family is involved, and this is something that I must do personally before I am elevated to Magus. To the point – I believe that the American's trunk contains the core and the key, and that it and the woman have been concealed within the partition, in the forbidden place in the guest wing. There is nowhere else she can be – our people have searched every possible hiding place. If we do not act now, Angeline Blade and her associates will seek to move the trunk to the secret tunnel. If they succeed in this, our authority will be weakened and my elevation to Magus will be threatened."

Domingo stood up. "Let me go to the guest block, seize those of Mackinnon's party who are there, and find an entrance to this secret place – compel those present by force if I must. Jaime and *los artilleros* will assist me."

Ferdinand bent his head for a moment, and then rose to his feet. "I fear that you are right – there is no other way."

"Jaime, find the others, and bring them to the courtyard at the rear of the guest wing. Tell them to leave the 249s and bring only sidearms. Do not enter until I join you – do you understand?" said Domingo.

"You can rely on me," replied Jaime, and he waddled off purposefully.

It was the ninth hour and most of the monks and members of the *hermandad* were in the chapel at prayer. Those that were not looked with mild curiosity at two monks, of light build in comparison with most Moriduran brothers, one pushing a rickety, noisy cart and the other walking at the side of it, holding something with both hands - a devotional object, perhaps? Could they be new *oblates*? Both monks had their cowls pulled well forward over their faces, and their heads were bent. A more perceptive observer might also have noticed a tall, powerfully built monk at some distance from the cart and its attendants, moving in the same direction, constantly moving his head as though looking for something or somebody, his arms loose at his sides.

In the guest wing of the monastery, two men sat at a small table looking at old gramophone records. The sound of voices raised in prayer and song from the chapel drifted into the room, and the light from the great stained glass window reflected off the brass horn of the phonograph machine.

"Here's an old Paul Whiteman record with Bing Crosby – *From Monday On* – Joaquín must have picked it for the trumpet bit with Bix," said Alistair.

Red replaced the record he had been examining on the stack. "Jazz was never my thing – different generation, I suppose. As for Crosby – wasn't he completely supplanted by Sinatra – became old hat overnight?"

His companion sighed. "Sinatra was a towering talent, a great popular singer, but he was never a jazz vocalist. Bing Crosby, together with Louis Armstrong, virtually invented jazz singing - and modern popular song. Once the monks have finished praying, I'll let you hear this one, Red."

They both looked at the empty trunk standing on the floor.

"I have an idea," said Red. "Let's put the trunk inside the partition. If Ferdinand comes…"

"…*when* he come…" interjected Alistair.

"…when he comes, we don't want him to find the cupboard bare – let's give him something to think about."

"Good thought."

They crossed to the empty trunk, shut the lid, and carried it towards the end of the left-hand passageway. Alistair groped upwards for the wooden wheel. The small gap clicked open in the partition, and the two men went along, pulled it fully open to the lock position, and then lifted the trunk inside. They closed the partition and stood for a moment in the eerie light. Red looked at the stone structure in the centre of the space, a lonely portal to the chamber deep in the rock where Angeline waited to depart on her mission, accompanied by… He shuddered involuntarily.

"Let's get the hell out of here," he said, but something had caught Alistair's eye.

"Look at those stone blocks lying free at the side of the structure," he said, pointing at the base of the outer wall. "We can use them to weight the trunk."

They went across, selected ones that they could lift, and then carried a total of six heavy blocks across to the trunk in three trips. They placed them in the trunk and Red locked it.

"What shall we do with the key?" he asked, breathless from his exertions. "We won't need it again…"

"Unless you want to swallow it, throw it down the stairs to the chamber," said Alistair. Red went across and into the stone building, and Alistair heard a metallic clattering sound. When he returned, they both opened the partition again and went into the passageway. They paused at the end of it; Alistair groped for the wheel and closed the partition. As they emerged from the passageway, they saw Ferdinand and Jaime sitting facing them at the table, and simultaneously felt the muzzles of pistols pressed to their heads by the men on either side of the entrance to the passage.

"We learned a little from our previous encounter, caballeros, and abandoned our heavy weapons – you have our thanks for the lesson. Please join us…" said Ferdinand, standing up, and making a motion with his hand.

Jaime remained sprawled in his seat, a contemptuous, complacent expression on his face. Alistair saw a tall, spare man standing at the bookcase facing away from them. He turned slowly, closed the book he was holding, and walked slowly towards them.

"My name is Domingo. Permit my colleagues to take your weapons: they are professionals – please do not do anything rash."

Alistair held his right hand up, index finger and thumb extended, and raised an eyebrow. Domingo nodded, and Alistair reached slowly for his revolver and withdrew it, gripping it between finger and thumb. A hand reached across and took it from him. Domingo turned his cold gaze to Red Lonnen, and after a moment's hesitation, Red followed Alistair's example and surrendered his weapon.

"A Webley Fosbery .38 and a Ruger 9 mm – interesting choices of weapon," observed Domingo laconically, "one nostalgic, one realistic…"

They sat down at the table, facing Ferdinand and Jaime; the two gunmen moved forward and stood behind them. Domingo sat down at the end of the table, and there was a long silence. Jaime broke the silence, to Ferdinand's evident displeasure.

"They gave up easily this time," he smirked.

"Too easily," said Domingo, glancing at Ferdinand.

"You have abused your positions as guests of the Abbot by violating a place that is sacred to us," said Ferdinand, "a place that not even I, the Magus Elect, have entered."

"Aye, well, we're sorry," said Alistair, "but we did what was necessary. We Scots have a right to roam. No offence intended…"

Domingo asked the question that Ferdinand had deliberately avoided.

"Did you have Brother Anselmo's permission?"

Alistair pointedly ignored the question, and turned to Red. "I wonder how we can be of assistance to the Magus Elect and his companions?" he mused.

"What can we have that they want?" said Red, with heavy sarcasm in his voice.

Domingo made a slight motion with his hand, and the man behind Red Lonnen struck him hard on the side of the head with his open hand. The blood drained from his face in shock and anger, and he gripped the edge of the table, looking directly into Ferdinand's eyes.

"So, for all your pretensions of blood and family, Ferdinand of Moridanza, you are no better than a hood from the projects…"

The man across from him was impassive, and his face betrayed nothing - a superb example of self-control, thought Alistair.

"You are being too hard on Ferdinand, Red – you should look to the end of the table for a real thug," he said, and braced himself for the blow; it followed instantly and his head jerked under its force.

"The language of violence has its own precision, its own unique grammar and syntax," said Domingo calmly. "It is an effective medium for certain messages: was it not an American who coined the phrase *the medium is the message*?"

"Tell us what we want to know," said Ferdinand, "although I think we may already have the answers, or some of them at least. Where is Doctora Blade? Where is the core? Where is the key? Where are your associates Manrique and Corr? Where is the secret route to *El Corazón de La Copa*?"

"I'll answer all these questions, but please don't hit me again – I'm an old man, I might black out, and that wouldn't serve your purpose," said Alistair wearily. "Angeline, the core, the key, Santiago and Paul – they're all beyond your reach. As for the path to the heart of *La Copa* – through the rear door, across the courtyard and down the slope to *El Trono* would seem to be the most direct route." The ringing in his head had not quite abated, and he felt a little nauseous.

Ferdinand looked at Domingo, who was ready to order another blow, and made a tiny negative motion with his head, then he stood up, and Jaime also shuffled to his feet. "Open the partition please, Señor Mackinnon – we observed your movements when you came out, and we can find the mechanism, but it will be simpler if you do it for us."

"I'll be glad to," said Alistair, rising to his feet, followed by Red, "after all, it's your place, pal, not ours."

They went towards the passage mouth, Alistair and Red first, followed by *los artilleros* and then Ferdinand and Domingo.

"You do know that if we have to kill you, we will not hesitate?" said Domingo with a slight rising inflection in his voice.

"Indeed we do," said Alistair over his shoulder as he turned right under the stairs and reached for the wooden wheel. "Open, Sesame!" he said, and the partition clicked partially open. "Red and I must pull it fully open now," said Alistair. Ferdinand nodded, and both men dragged the heavy wooden panel open yet again. Domingo pushed past them, drew an automatic pistol from his robe, and peered inside cautiously, and then motioned to Ferdinand to come forward.

"Here is your sacred place, my esteemed brother," he said. "We must check what lies within that stone structure before you enter – Manrique and Corr may be there with the woman, armed and dangerous. I will enter with Róger; Rubén will remain with you until we return." He beckoned to one of the *artilleros* and they both went through the partition, pistols cocked. Domingo immediately saw the trunk and gave a thin smile of satisfaction. The two men approached the entrance to the stone building cautiously. Domingo signalled to Róger to enter; he reappeared after a moment, and waved, and Domingo moved across to him.

"It is empty, but there is a steep staircase with no handrail; I cannot see to the foot of the staircase, my esteemed brother," he said stiffly, unused to the form of address. They both entered the structure and Domingo looked down the stairs; it was impossible to see any end to them.

"Remain on guard here until I call you," said Domingo, "or raise the alarm immediately you hear anything from below. Stay out of a line of fire from the stairwell." He left the structure and went across to the gap in the partition.

"It is safe to enter, my brothers," he called out. "Send in Mackinnon and Lonnen first – I will cover them."

Alistair and Red were prodded through the partition at the point of a gun by the *artillero* they now knew as Rubén, and Ferdinand and Jaime followed. When they saw the trunk they both gave sighs of satisfaction.

"There is no one here, unless they are at the bottom of the steps within that structure," said Domingo. "It would not be safe to descend – it is impossible to estimate how far down they go. This is indeed a strange place, my brother – what can be the source of this cold light?" said Domingo.

There was no reply: Ferdinand was looking around the space, fascinated. It was exactly as the legends he had known since childhood had described it – the blue-green light, the little stone structure: he knew he was looking at the portal to the legendary chamber of *La Bestia*. He walked across and went through the doorway: the *artillero*, who had been peering down the aperture in the floor, straightened up and inclined his head respectfully. Ferdinand ignored him and looked down the seemingly endless stairs. He called out.

"Señorita Angeline – Señor Paul – Señor Santiago! If you are down there, please come up. We can resolve all our differences amicably – we share the same objectives…" His voice came echoing back to him, but there was no reply. He listened carefully for any sounds – there were none.

"Do you want me to go down and investigate, my esteemed brother?" asked Róger tentatively.

"No, my brother – remain here and be vigilant. Whatever happens, the woman must not be harmed; it would be better that you gave your life rather than risk her life," he said, looking directly into the man's eyes. Satisfied that Róger truly understood, Ferdinand turned and left the little building and rejoined the others.

"The trunk is locked, and they say that they do not have the key," said Domingo. "I have searched them both."

"Señores – where is the key?" Ferdinand asked softly.

"Santiago has it," lied Alistair affably. "He'll keep it until it is necessary to open the trunk. If you're thinking about forcing the lock, mind you don't damage the core."

Don Ferdinand moved to the trunk and grasped one of the handles; Domingo gripped the other, but they could barely lift it a few centimetres from the floor before letting it rest again.

"How did you move the trunk to this point?" asked Domingo in a tone of mild curiosity.

"Mateo did most of the lifting," said Red. "Without him, I doubt we could have moved it at all. Do you know, that guy brought my trunk up the cliff path and carried it all the way to the guest wing – by himself!"

Domingo looked at Ferdinand and they both moved some distance away out of earshot of the two men.

"What do you think, my brother?" said Domingo. "Something in their manner disturbs me. Are they lying?"

"If the core and the key are in the trunk, they are probably telling the truth; if the core and the key are not in the trunk, then they are already on their way to the passage to *El Corazón*, and this is a clever delaying tactic," said Ferdinand.

"We must force the trunk open, whatever the risk," said Domingo firmly. "Jaime, go and find something we can use as a lever – maybe a crowbar."

Jaime was only to eager to leave; the enclosed space, the blue-green light, the feeling of an unknown presence – all of these things frightened him. He disappeared quickly through the open partition.

Ferdinand was clearly ill at ease. "If they are already on their way to *El Corazón*, we may be too late," he said, his anxiety showing in his voice.

Domingo saw his opportunity.

"Then I must go back into the monastery and search for them. If they are trying to move the core, they will be conspicuous – one of our people will have seen them. You must remain here, my brother, with *los artilleros* in case the core is in the trunk and the others are at the base of the stairs or in the chamber – if there is a chamber…"

Ferdinand considered the options open to him: he did not wholly trust Domingo, but could think of no ulterior motive that he might have – what he said made good sense. Either he agreed with him or insisted that they wait until Jaime returned, losing more valuable time.

"Go," he said, and watched the tall, thin man climb through the partition. There was nothing to be done now except wait for Jaime to return. He looked at the inscrutable faces of the Scotsman and the American, with an uneasy suspicion growing in his mind that he had been out-manoeuvred. After what seemed an eternity, he heard a scuffling outside the partition and the clumsy figure of Jaime appeared, carrying a small crowbar and a heavy screwdriver. Ferdinand took them from him, and knelt in front of the trunk. He probed the keyhole of the lock with the screwdriver in the hope that he might be able to pick it, but without success. Eventually he laid down the screwdriver, and forced the end of the crowbar under the lid.

"For God's sake, be careful!" hissed Red, with a convincing show of agitation. "I didn't lug that thing across the Atlantic to have it damaged at this stage of the game..." As he spoke, he shot a glance to Alistair, who understood its import immediately. Ferdinand was occupied; one *artillero* was inside the structure at the head of the stairs; the other's attention was split between guarding them and watching Ferdinand's activities, and Jaime's bulky figure was now between them and the gunman. There would be a moment...

There was a metallic tearing sound, the lid of the trunk flipped up, revealing its stony contents, and Jaime moved forward to look, blocking the gunman. As Ferdinand cursed, Alistair and Red sprang through the open partition, and were almost instantly at the end of the passageway and under the stairs. Alistair groped for the wheel in the darkness above his head.

Rubén, the *artillero*, sprang to the partition, but his training and experience caused him to bend and put his head out cautiously before leaping into the passageway. At exactly that moment, Alistair turned the wheel to the close position. There was no interlock or safety cutout on the ancient mechanism – the weight dropped and the heavy partition closed swiftly, breaking the man's neck. He died instantly, his head lolling at a grotesque angle, his neck compressed, his tongue protruding from his open mouth, his eyes wide open and staring sightlessly along the passage. Inside the space, his weapon dropped from his hand and clattered to the floor.

Jaime stared in horror at the lifeless body hanging limply from the partition. Ferdinand put his hand to his forehead, his feeling of chagrin almost impossible to bear. He had been out-witted at every turn by Mackinnon and Lonnen, and now another man was dead.

"Support the body while I open the panel," he said, picking up Rubén's pistol and moving to Jaime's side. The fat man shuddered with horror as he put his arms round the body, taking its weight.

"Róger, come at once!" he called out as he began to pull the partition back. The other *artillero* came running from the door of the structure, looking uncomprehendingly at the bizarre scene in front of him. As the partition began to move, the dead man's head came free of the gap, and Jaime, unprepared, fell backwards with the body on top of him. He screamed in horror as Rubén's face came in contact with his and the dead eyes stared at him blankly; he scrambled frantically from beneath the body, gasping and panting.

"On guard, on your left!" commanded Ferdinand urgently, as he pulled the partition fully open and heard it click into position. The *artillero* sprang without hesitation through the gap in a crouching position, his weapon drawn. He looked up and then down the passage but could see nothing, hear nothing.

"They went to the left," said Ferdinand, "but they have almost certainly gone by now – they are unarmed." He looked contemptuously at the quivering figure of Jaime. "We must leave the body for the moment – follow me…"

Chapter Twenty-Seven

Angeline, Paul and Santiago reached the entrance to the cellar steps without incident, although they had attracted some curious glances. Santiago scanned the area then moved across to the cart with its precious burden. He gave Paul his pocket flashlight; taking the candleholder from the cart, he lit the candle, and went part way down the stairs ahead of them.

"Be careful of the robe when you descend, Paul – I know how treacherous it can be on the stairs…"

Angeline nervously operated her control, and the core, still covered by its cloth, lifted and moved out from the base of the cart and floated serenely a little above the floor. The prospect of navigating it down the stairs was daunting, and she desperately tried to recall Arkimateo's instructions; the buttons on the tiny control could only be felt, not seen, and she ran her thumb very lightly over them to position herself, terrified that she would inadvertently operate the wrong one. Paul was beside her, trying to shield her and the core from the gaze of anyone passing.

"Walk beside it, Paul," she whispered, "you can steady it and gently influence its direction, but don't push hard, or make any sudden movements."

Following the light of Santiago's candle, they started their descent, slowly and with infinite caution; at one point, Paul felt the hem of the habit catch on his foot, and stumbled, but then quickly recovered his balance. The cloth covering the core slid off, and the gold gleamed in the candlelight. Paul found that he could guide it with a very light touch, and his confidence grew, but he was aware that if anything went wrong with Angeline's device, the heavy core could injure him severely; the same thought had occurred to Santiago, who felt even more vulnerable as he looked up at the floating gold block.

At last they reached the cellar door and Santiago placed the candleholder in the niche at the side of the door and then pulled the door towards him. It creaked open slowly, and he motioned Angeline and Paul to enter; once they were inside, he moved behind them, listened for a moment, and then closed the door. Walking past them again, he held up his hand and put his finger to his lips; they waited as he moved down towards the end rack and the rear wall. The *La Puerta de Bestia* was closed. He looked down to where the body of Amancio had lain: it was gone – Brother Anselmo had been as good as his word.

"Come – it is safe," he called softly, waving the candle. Paul switched on his flashlight, and the little convoy moved towards him with difficulty down the narrow aisle between the racks. Santiago took out his knife and inserted it in the lock and pulled the little door inwards; the cold light from the tunnel shone into the cellar. He ducked through the door, then his head appeared again as he beckoned them forward. Paul backed through the door, and felt Santiago's hand on his head, protecting him from the stone arch; the core floated through, followed by Angeline.

Paul looked around him at the circular tunnel. "So, this is our slip road to the main highway - to *El Corazón de La Copa*," he said. "How far, Santiago?"

"Not far – follow me. Walk carefully – it takes a bit of getting used to – and remember, as with all slip roads, the hazardous moment is joining the highway."

They moved forward, Santiago leading, followed by Paul, then the core, with Angeline bringing up in the rear. Paul noticed that the tunnel was levelling out from its initial downward slope, and he could see a bright circle of light ahead of them.

"Be careful," said Santiago, "the tunnel narrows at this point – you will have to crouch to move forward."

He turned to face Paul, and backing through into the large tunnel, he indicated to Paul that he too should turn and face the core to guide it forward. Paul twisted round and placed his hands gently on the golden cube. Santiago moved to the side to let Paul guide it through the aperture. They were both totally focused on their task, and unaware of the tall, red-robed figure on their right, gun in hand. Angeline came through after the core, facing Santiago and Paul; a slight movement to her left caught her eye, she saw Domingo and froze, her body only part way into the main tunnel.

"Don't do anything foolish, my friends," said Domingo, stepping forward, "it would be unfortunate if anything went wrong now that we have come so far. Doctora Blade, please join your friends – you have nothing to fear."

Santiago was in agonies of self-recrimination; his concentration on getting his friends and the core through into the tunnel had caused him to fail to check the security of the area they were entering, a fundamental error. He reviewed his options rapidly, but they all risked gunfire, and the likelihood of ricochets from the rock all around them was too great. Angeline had reluctantly come forward and the three of them stood helplessly facing him across the floating core, instinctively placing themselves behind it, as though it could somehow protect them.

Domingo looked at the core, and at the device on top of it, and then at the tiny control that Angeline was clutching. A feeling of great satisfaction surged through him.

"So, it is all true – the golden core, the anti-gravity capability..." he breathed softly. He then motioned down the tunnel in the direction he was facing. "Please proceed," he said, "I don't want to stop your stately little procession to *El Corazón*."

They ignored his command, and he was puzzled by their expressions; they were staring at something behind him, Santiago and Paul with looks of utter incredulity and fear, Angeline with an expression of relief mixed with apprehension. He considered whether or not they were trying to trick him into looking behind him, but then a strange smell assailed his nostrils – a powerful, animal smell. Moving to his left, he placed his back to the wall of the tunnel, still covering them with his weapon, and then turned his head cautiously to his right. His blood ran cold in his veins at what he saw, and for the first time since his early youth, he knew fear: he instinctively pointed his weapon at the creature towering above him.

Angeline instantly recalled the warning about Arkimateo's automatic defence reflexes in face of a threat and the danger to those nearby; she moved quickly and pulled Santiago and Paul back into the linking tunnel, leaving the core floating unattended. Domingo looked up into the face of the creature, a face that was strangely familiar to him: he aimed his weapon at the great head and began to squeeze the trigger.

Crouching just inside the linking tunnel, Angeline, Santiago and Paul felt a sudden pressure in the air, similar to that experienced just after an explosion; it was followed by an awful cry of agony and a combination of horrific sounds that defied description, and then there was silence. Santiago waited for a moment before cautiously putting his head through into the main tunnel. He looked up at the face of the creature he knew from Angeline's description to be Arkimateo. The large eyes, glowing red, were not returning his gaze, but were directed at a shapeless pile of red cloth on the floor of the tunnel from which blood was oozing out in all directions. Santiago knew he was looking at what had once been Domingo – a compressed mass of flesh, bone and hair, mercifully covered by the red robe of the Order of Moridura.

"Arkimateo?" said Santiago.

"Santiago Manrique - I wish your first sight of me had occurred in different circumstances. I regret this, but my response to threat is autonomic – I have no conscious control over it when violence is directed at me, or my mission is endangered."

Santiago drew back into the link tunnel. Paul had his arm round Angeline's shoulder, and they both looked at him expectantly.

"Domingo is dead – apparently crushed to pulp by Arkimateo. She must have used some kind of gravitational field; the body has been compressed beyond anything that even a creature as powerful as she could have achieved by direct physical action. Paul, you and I will go through first, then Angeline can confer with Arkimateo."

Paul followed Santiago into the main tunnel, bracing himself for the sight of Arkimateo again, fighting back his instinctive fear of the huge alien creature. As Angeline entered the tunnel, Arkimateo moved to block her view of the remains of Domingo, towering over her.

"Arkimateo – what must you think of we humans?" she said sadly, looking up to the grey, lambent eyes, the red glow now absent from them.

"There is no time for regret, Angeline. Paul and Santiago must leave this place and return to the monastery – I cannot protect them from the radiation and the event horizon. We must go now: say your farewells quickly…"

Angeline hugged Santiago and kissed his cheek, then embraced Paul, kissing him on the mouth. They held each other tightly for a long moment; then Paul released her reluctantly and looked up at Arkimateo.

"Protect her – and our child…" he said simply, and then he went into the link tunnel, followed by Santiago.

"Angeline," said Arkimateo, "from this point on, we must maintain physical contact whenever possible – this contact is vital in protecting you from the radiation and in reinforcing the entanglement process that will enable you to enter and leave the event horizon with your physical body and memories intact. I will directly control the movement of the core, but hold on to your own control device."

Arkimateo flattened her great bulk to the floor of the tunnel; leaning her upper body forward, she reached forward with her upper arms, lifted Angeline, and, twisting round, helped her to mount her back, behind the upper torso.

Angeline struggled to maintain her balance. "What now?" she said nervously.

"Put your arms around my upper body, and hold on tightly," said Arkimateo, standing up and turning her head, giving a wide, Mateo-like grin. "Ready?"

"As ready as I'll ever be - I've ridden pillion on a motorcycle, but it was never like this!" As Arkimateo moved off down the tunnel, Angeline felt the powerful muscles moving beneath her, and she felt infinitely safe and protected. Even the Medusa-like tentacles on Arkimateo's head, which she had found the most terrifying aspect at the first manifestation in the chamber, now seemed like things of beauty. Close to, they seemed like tightly braided plaits, and when one of them touched her face, she did not find it repellent. To her astonishment, it caressed her cheek, and then others stroked her hair and neck. Arkimateo's voice came back to her, affectionate and reassuring.

"You are not disturbed by this feature of my anatomy, Angeline?"

"Not in the least," she replied. "It – they – are not hair; what function do they serve?"

"They are sensory devices, as important to me as my eyes and ears – they sense heat, and radiation, and they project control waves into my immediate environment: I suppose the closest analogy would be antennae. At the moment, they are controlling the movement of the core."

Angeline looked down and saw the gleaming core moving smoothly beside them on Arkimateo's right, then looked again at the tentacles.

"Did they also activate the gravitational field that destroyed Domingo?"

The tentacles moved suddenly away from her and coiled tightly on the great head.

"Yes," said Arkimateo, and for a time there was silence between them. Angeline tried to suppress her gruesome imaginings about the demise of Domingo, all too aware that Arkimateo could sense them in her mind. Eventually, a tentacle slipped back and touched her cheek tenderly.

"When you were a little girl, you wanted a pony," said Arkimateo.

"Yes – yes, I did…" stammered Angeline, startled by this knowledge of her past.

"… and as a teenager, you wanted a horse."

The old longings swept over her, and Angeline remembered her mother telling her sadly that they could not afford such things. Once she had become independent and had a reasonable income, Angeline had promised herself riding lessons, but the demands of her work had left little time for leisure pursuits. A great laugh from Arkimateo echoed in the tunnel.

"You could never have hired something like me by the hour from the stables, Angeline. But with a horse, you would have had a proper saddle, reins and a whip."

For some reasons, Angeline felt herself blushing, and confusing and contradictory emotions swept over her: her sense of loss over Mateo, her bonding with the strange creature on whose back she was mounted, her awareness of the child within her womb, her apprehensions over the task she had to perform, her fear of losing Paul, her father, Alistair and Santiago - all of these things combined to almost overwhelm her.

"Put away your fears, Angeline," said Arkimateo, "and believe in a positive outcome: together, we will complete our task and you will return to your father and friends."

"*We* will return, Arkimateo – we will return together."

A long, poignant sigh came back to her.

"I shall not return, Angeline: when we have stabilised *El Corazón*, my time here is over. There is no place for me in your world, no purpose – and there is no homeland to which

I can return. All living beings must finally face their end with equanimity – it will be a release from a long servitude for me."

"No, no!" cried Angeline, pressing her cheek against Arkimateo's back, "I can't bear to lose you – I want you to stay, we all want you to stay. We will make a place for you in our future, in our world: you belong with us now." She broke down in a flood of tears.

"I have no choice in the matter, Angeline – my end is pre-ordained. But I will find some way to make it easier for you to bear. You must believe that I will not fail you in this: but now we are close to *El Corazón* and must prepare ourselves. We are almost within the event horizon."

As Arkimateo spoke, Angeline realised that the walls of the tunnel could no longer be seen distinctly, nor could its roof: she looked down past the floating core to the floor of the tunnel, but saw only darkness. It was as if they were both gliding forward in a black cloud, a swirling, living cloud that seemed to be sucking them forward.

The voice of Arkimateo came to her, strangely distorted, as though from a great distance.

"Do not be afraid – be prepared for perceptual disturbances. We are on the edge of time itself, Angeline, and you will experience a temporal dislocation that may be frightening and painful for you. I am with you – do not surrender to the phenomena. Hold our mission firmly in your mind – I will protect you and your child."

Strange sounds clamoured in her ears, sounds such as she had never heard, beyond her capacity to identify or describe – sounds that seem to have multiple voices within them, voices that seemed to be trying to communicate something to her, but in no language that she could recognise. The communication was akin to the language of music – it had its own dynamics, rhythm and logic, and induced indefinable emotions in her, feelings of familiarity, recognition and progress towards some resolution. The experience was frightening yet pleasurable: there were sensory phenomena - odours, tastes and tactile sensations that tugged at the edge of memory, tantalisingly familiar, yet just beyond reach. She tried to focus on Arkimateo's great head, but found herself looking at a human head, the tonsured head of a monk, and her hands now seemed to be clutching at rough cloth rather than the torso of Arkimateo: the figure in front of her seemed smaller, and she could feel nothing beneath her. Her body felt as though it was floating freely in space, her legs dangling and her arms round the waist of a man.

"Arkimateo?" she said faintly, and her own voice sounded strange and remote.

The head in front of her turned, and she saw the face of Brother Mateo, unsmiling, his eyes looking through her and beyond her. The shock was such that only a supreme effort of will stopped her from letting go of the body to which she was clinging. As from a great distance, she heard the voice of Arkimateo, muted and faint.

"It is an illusion, Angeline – hold fast to me…"

The disembodied voices around her now began to concentrate into one, a voice with a terrifying timbre, imbued with deep menace, threatening her with something nameless, horrific. An overpowering sense of evil pervaded the space around her and the figure in front of her. She felt the presence of an inhuman entity, utterly without pity, bent on her annihilation and something was plucking at her body, as if trying to wrest her away from her protector. Beneath the sounds, smells and sensations assailing her senses there was, mercifully, an underlying note of redemption – a powerful bass line underlying the dissonance, serenely logical, promising that all was well, and that all would be resolved in time.

Suddenly, there was a sensation of almost intolerable pressure, and Angeline felt as if her very being was about to disintegrate, then it passed and she found herself on

Arkimateo's back in a chamber with walls similar to the great chamber beneath the guest block, but much smaller in size.

"We are now on the event horizon, just beneath *El Trono* and above *El Corazón de La Copa*," said Arkimateo, and she turned, reached out her upper arms and lifted Angeline down on to the floor. "We are in the chamber of the regulator - the core is home at last and we must replace it in its rightful location and activate it with the key."

"Beneath the Throne and above the Heart," breathed Angeline softly, looking at a smaller version of the gold consoles in the main chamber, with a rectangular void on the horizontal control desk that was clearly the home of the core. The lights and dials were similar to those on the great consoles under the monastery, and there was a screen in the centre, with no image showing, only a milky opalescence. She looked at the core hovering silently above the floor, and instinctively reached for her little control device.

"No, Angeline," said Arkimateo sharply, "we must exercise great care in replacing the core: the regulator has been locked in a control mode based on the last monitoring status, before its removal centuries ago. If we replace the core, it will instantly resume from that point, and will act on its memory of the old oscillation status, with catastrophic results."

Angeline moved close to the console. "We must find a way to persuade the regulator to read and evaluate the data it has collected since the removal of the core – am I right?"

Arkimateo grunted, and shifted about uneasily, her tentacles waving then stiffening in an attitude, and then waving again.

"The difficulty is – we cannot communicate with it until the core is replaced and the key activated…"

"That is really helpful, Arkimateo," said Angeline, "what we call a catch-22…"

"Is it?"

Angeline looked at her big friend with affection. "I'm sorry – I was using sarcasm – a bad habit of mine… It's in my genes, apparently."

"Aahh," said Arkimateo. "You do recognise our dilemma?"

"We must find a way to awaken Rip Van Winkle safely."

"Rip Van Winkle?"

"A man from my country who fell asleep for one hundred years – a fictional character…" said Angeline lamely. "I'm sorry, I must try to be more direct."

Arkimateo looked reflective. "A long sleep – the analogy is apt, and it gives me an idea. Rather than waken the regulator abruptly from its deep slumber, we must induce a dreamlike-state, then ease it into increasing awareness – lucid dreaming: it will then sense the danger and collect the accumulated data before taking control action."

"How do we do that?" asked Angeline tentatively.

The tentacled head shook. "I don't know," said Arkimateo slowly, "I just don't know…" She looked appealingly at Angeline, who suddenly began to giggle.

"Forgive me, Arkimateo, but you are thousands of years old and this has been your life's work! If you don't know, how the hell can I help?"

Arkimateo looked vaguely embarrassed, and the tentacles dropped around her neck and shoulders, giving her a despondent look, like a dog with its ears down. Angeline giggled again, but put both her arms out in sympathy. The upper arms reached down and lifted her up, holding her effortlessly in front of the great head, and Angeline leaned forward impulsively and kissed Arkimateo on the cheek.

"There, there…" she said soothingly, patting the other cheek, her legs dangling in space. "Now put me down and let me think…"

Walking around the core, Angeline could see no obvious electrical or electronic connectors of any sort, no plugs or sockets, no obvious sensor point – the two handles on the top seemed to be simply for lifting it in and out of its location, and the eight lugs on each side seemed to be simply locator lugs. She peered into the space on the console where the core would go and there were eight vertical slots on each side to accommodate the lugs – gold to gold.

Arkimateo, sensing her thought processes, came and stood beside her. "You are correct – these are simply physical locator points, not power connectors: the regulator will read the core fully when it is in position. It is in contact with the main consoles, but has had nothing to say for centuries. You must remember that these are relatively simple devices by comparison with the control consoles in my chamber – they are slave devices. We cannot communicate directly with either the main control devices or the regulator until the core is replaced."

Angeline looked up reprovingly into the grey eyes. "You knew all this before we came, Arkimateo – why didn't you discuss it with Alistair and me?"

Arkimateo looked away, and the tentacles writhed a little on her head. "I feared that you would not come because of the risk – or that your friends – your father – would not allow you to be exposed to such uncertainty. But I have faith that your human brain, and its intuitive understanding, will find a way around the problem. Your synaptic connections work differently to mine"

"Mmm…" said Angeline sceptically, "I sense flattery – not your style at all. Are the regulator and the core aware of our presence?"

"Yes, but only at a very simple sensory level, by vibration and physical contact; the central consoles will now also be aware that we are here, but we cannot communicate with them, nor can they communicate with us, only with the regulator. If we could communicate with them through the regulator, they could safely modify its response to the return of the core."

Angeline scratched her head then tapped impatiently on the gold surface in front of her. "There *must* be a way of communicating. When high technology fails, use low tech to get out of trouble. In our computers – primitive by your standards – we moved beyond an early input devices called a floppy disk drive, and modern desktops computers do not have them as original equipment, yet many users insist on installing them as a belt-and-braces option."

"Belt and braces?" said Arkimateo in a baffled tone, then reached into Mateo's memories and nodded in recognition.

"If only we could send a Mayday signal – an S.O.S. – to the control consoles…" said Angeline. She looked up apologetically. "There I go again – I'm sorry – these are distress signals used by aircraft and shipping."

She tapped three times rapidly on the gleaming gold surface, then three slower taps, then another three rapid taps. "That's S.O.S. in Morse code…" She broke off abruptly. Arkimateo's face now bore a wide grin, lights flashed in her eyes, and her tentacles waved jubilantly.

"That's it, Angeline – I knew you would find a way," she said, reaching down to muss Angeline's hair.

"But – but I don't know the whole of the Morse code – just the S.O.S bit…"

"But I can retrieve the whole code from Mateo's eclectic studies, and I can send at high speed," said Arkimateo, crouching down in front of the regulator. "The regulator and the control consoles do not recognise binary code, but I can trigger their responses in Spanish."

Her upper arms reached out and both hands touched the upper part of the console, then the twelve long fingers began to tap at high speed. Angeline could only stand, watch and marvel as the ancient and sophisticated entity used the basic alphanumerical code of Samuel Morse to get a message back to base. With a grunt of satisfaction, Arkimateo stopped her frenetic tapping and waited. The screen on the face of the console began to glow, and then a series of geometrical symbols flashed at almost subliminal speed. She turned her head and grinned, the big, wide Mateo grin.

"*We're OK, my bonny lass,*" she said, in an exact imitation of Alistair Mackinnon's Scottish tones, then, in her normal voice: "The main consoles know we're here – we can replace the core with confidence: the regulator will run a diagnostic routine and update itself before resuming its full control function. I can communicate with the central control in a limited way with Morse code, and you and I can use the regulator controls directly."

Angeline looked at Arkimateo in a way that prompted a question.

"Why are you so sad, Angeline?"

"You look so like Mateo," she replied, and then turned away, hiding her tears. "Let's get to work. Best re-state the problem - the critical initial strength of the field formed after the meteorite impact maintains a state poised between weakening to the point that the material we call the heart either expands to nothingness, or increases to infinite mass, resulting in collapse into a black hole. The removal of the core froze the regulator's control action, resulting in progressive instability. It is performing an infinite number of oscillations in a finite time period: we can either hope that the regulator will restore the field oscillation to the previous state, and accept the risk involved, or we can be pro-active and attempt to weaken the field and destroy the anomaly."

"If we must risk all, I prefer the pro-active route," said Arkimateo.

"I would rather die on our joint decision than on a throw of the dice," said Angeline. They both drew long breaths; Angeline pointed her little gold remote control at the core and lifted it slowly and carefully above the console; when it was poised just above its destination, she paused and looked up at Arkimateo. "You have a higher sight line than I have – guide me…"

"Slightly forward – a little to the left – a little more; now down very slowly, very gently! The final positioning will be initiated by the console."

There was a faint metallic sound as gold met gold and then the core slid smoothly and soundlessly down, to the accompaniment of a frenetic light show on the screen. Arkimateo gave a great sigh of satisfaction, and Angeline also exhaled nervously.

"We're still here," she said.

"We are – for the moment," said Arkimateo "but there is still the key…"

"God, I had forgotten about it," said Angeline, holding the little gold figurine up in her hand. "It's not a very good likeness of you, Arkimateo – you haven't got red eyes!"

"You haven't seen them when I'm angry. The key must wait – it offers us limited protection against getting our input wrong. It is a kind of enter key – once it is inserted and turned, the die is cast, and we cannot stop the processes thus activated."

"Shall I do it, or do you want the honour of initiating the process, Arkimateo?"

The broad hand came down and took her slender fingers in a light, gentle grasp.

"Let's do it together – then we are both to blame. If this does not result in disaster, we still have much to do, and the risk will be in our subsequent control choices. Look on it this way – if we fail, we are instantly obliterated, but in another, parallel universe we have made the right choice, and survive: we can therefore only experience success."

Their eyes met, then they both looked at the console as they turned the key. The level of activity on the console and the screen immediately increased, and Angeline could sense another vibration beneath her feet, as though something was moving smoothly and silently in the depths. Arkimateo began to hum softly, a tune that was profoundly Spanish in its rhythms and melodic structure.

"That went well," she said, breaking off her song, "and now we must actively influence the regulator's processes; if you tell me what you want to do, I will communicate in Morse code with the main consoles. I will interpret the console activity for you by using analogies with scientific theories and equipment with which you are familiar."

"How long will it take to complete all of this?" Angeline stroked her stomach. "I'm hungry – when will we next eat? I've already missed lunch today."

Arkimateo gave a short, harsh laugh.

"I have bad news for you – we must remain here until the splitting of *El Trono* – the final control actions can only be taken then. I can synthesise some basic nutrients for you using the console, but they won't be very appealing to your palate."

Angeline spluttered in astonishment. "But the splitting of the Throne doesn't occur until tomorrow – until the Ceremony! That means we will be here overnight!"

"Yes – until tomorrow." said Arkimateo, shrugging her big shoulders and flicking her tentacles from side to side fatalistically. "There is no alternative."

"But where will I sleep?" asked Angeline plaintively, looking around her. "There isn't even a chair, much less a bed. Can you synthesise a bed?"

"No," said Arkimateo, "but I can make you comfortable…"

Her tentacles waved, and Angeline found herself lifted, and turned to a horizontal position, and lowered; she seemed to be supported on what felt like a wonderfully soft, yet firm mattress and pillow. She looked down and saw that she was about eighteen inches above the floor of the chamber.

Arkimateo gave a self-satisfied grin.

"How's that? One of the many benefits of being able to manipulate gravity."

Angeline lay back and stretched luxuriously.

"This will put the bedding industry out of business – it's better than a water bed…"

"Enough – get off the couch and get back to work, Angeline." The tone was calm but with an undertone of urgency in it.

Angeline sat up swung her legs into space, put her feet on the floor and stood up. She looked at where the bed should have been, then, feeling foolish, turned to the console. As she placed her hands on it, a small aperture appeared and from it a small slab of greenish material slid out, about the size of a bar of chocolate. She poked suspiciously at the unappetising object.

"Surely the Higgs boson could have done better than this," she muttered, then tentatively took a bite…

"Domingo was a cruel, unprincipled man, responsible directly or indirectly for many monstrous acts of violence and intimidation in the district and beyond; his influence in the Order was pernicious, and it was growing. I believe he was largely responsible for the progressive decline in the character of Ferdinand. Ultimately, he would have tried to seize power from Ferdinand, and that would have had calamitous consequences. I cannot in all conscience mourn him, but I regret the manner of his death, and I will pray for his soul. The other man, the victim of the gruesome accident with the partition – I did not know him: God rest his soul."

The Abbot bent his head for a moment, then, lifting it again, he looked sombrely at the four men sitting across from him. Their respective accounts of the events that had led to another two deaths had taken him close to despair, an emotional state that he regarded as sinful in a man of God.

How did these men regard the deaths, he wondered? Red Lonnen was a hardheaded realist – he would not grieve for the men involved. Santiago would regard them with the detached attitude of the professional soldier, as casualties in action. Alistair Mackinnon had perhaps greater empathy with his fellow man than Lonnen, but he too was a pragmatist, with more in common with his business rival than he would ever admit. Only Paul had the emotional and intellectual depth to feel genuine regret that two more lives had been extinguished, and to question all the motives that had led to the conflict of the last few days. Red Lonnen's voice broke into his reverie.

"My prayers and my thoughts are reserved for my daughter and my grandchild in her womb. I am now the only one among you who has not seen the full, physical manifestation of the creature that she is with at this moment. What risks are she and her unborn child being exposed to? When will they be back? What can we do to help them? Don't tell me to pray. Whatever God's intentions are, He will expect us to get off our butts and do our earthly best for them."

Brother Anselmo smiled faintly.

"Indeed He will, Red. Let me offer what I can. She is at no risk from Arkimateo, in fact, Arkimateo is her only hope of surviving the hazards of the event horizon and of their joint task. I do not believe we will see them again until *El Trono* splits at the Ceremony tomorrow. We must help them at that point, their point of greatest danger."

Red stared at him in shock and disbelief; he turned his agonised gaze to Alistair, Paul and Santiago. Paul's expression mirrored his own. Alistair stood up and touched Paul's shoulder briefly as he moved behind Red. He placed both hands on the distraught man's shoulders.

"Accept what Brother Anselmo has told you, Red. Angeline will come through OK. We must rely on her to do what she has to – and she'll depend on us to do likewise."

In an uncharacteristic gesture, Red placed his palms on the back of Alistair's hands in acknowledgement, and then stood up abruptly, as though embarrassed by his action.

"It seems we have no choice. What about Ferdinand? He must be the most pissed-off man on the planet at this point – and he probably thinks Domingo is still around. What can we expect, Brother Anselmo?"

"We can expect the Magus Elect to prepare himself for the Ceremony – and to receive his American guests," said the Abbot. "He must exhibit the dignity expected of him in the great office he aspires to: Angeline is beyond his reach, and any overt display of violence on the day of the Ceremony would, in normal circumstances, be unacceptable."

"Nonetheless, he must display control and authority to the military visitors – how does he expect to achieve that?" asked Santiago.

"I would guess by displaying his role and status in the Ceremony, and by floating up to *El Trono* – am I right, Anselmo?" said Alistair, miming a man strutting self-importantly, then hold his arms up as if flying.

The Abbot suppressed a smile, nodded and then turned his gaze to Paul, waiting for the question he knew was inevitable.

"Any overt display of violence on the day of the Ceremony would, *in normal circumstances*, be unacceptable," said Paul, echoing the Abbot's words. "However, the circumstances are anything but normal – what are the implications of that fact?"

"On the day, the Magus and I are concerned only with the ritual itself: the Magus Elect is responsible for all other matters, including the maintenance of good order and the protection of those engaged in the Ceremony. Because of his own crucial involvement in the ritual, he delegates that responsibility to members of the Grand Council and Gregorio. He has already stated his view, to Joaquín and myself, that the four of you should be excluded from the Ceremony."

"I don't give a damn about the Ceremony – forgive me, Abbot, but my only concern is my daughter. I must be wherever she will emerge from the tunnel…" interjected Red. "I need you guys with me…"

"I must tell you that Angeline and Arkimateo may not return through the tunnel: their likely route back to the surface will be from beneath *El Trono*, just after it splits." The Abbot waited for the import of his words to sink into Red Lonnen's agitated consciousness.

"What? Why?" Red looked dazed by this new information.

"Because the chamber of the regulator is suspended above *El Corazón*, on the event horizon: when the natural, recurring geological phenomenon that precedes *El Partir del Trono* occurs, the chamber rises to avoid being destroyed. It is in effect the rising chamber that causes the splitting of the rock. Arkimateo has always been in the regulator chamber at this time, to monitor and control the phenomenon, and she sometimes emerges briefly, driven by a purpose that only she understands. The Magus and I are in accord in our view that Arkimateo will judge this the safest point to return Angeline to the surface – their work will not be complete until the splitting of the Throne; the nature of the process, called entanglement, that protects your daughter will almost certainly make this the least risky point."

Red was incapable of speech, poised between fear for his daughter's safety and an inchoate rage against those who had placed her in such danger. He made a desperate gesture with his arm to Paul that seemed to demand his input.

"Red, I know how you feel," said Paul " – it is how I feel – but try to look at it this way: if they emerge by this route, the main danger has passed. Waiting is the hardest thing to do, but wait we must…"

They all fell silent.

Chapter Twenty-Eight

"I haven't eaten this early in years." Jim gave a desultory poke at the eggs and bacon on the plate before him. Three of the four men around the breakfast table in Suite Four laughed – the fourth man, the bodyguard Nico, could only croak feebly: he was still suffering from the effects of Ferdinand's blow to his throat.

"You Army guys have it too easy - some time afloat would make you brighter at dawn." The voice of the U.S. Navy was unsympathetic.

"Come on, Larry – it's been a long time since you rolled out of a hammock at first light. Whereas, in the Air Force…" Peter – a Brigadier General in the youngest of the three services - looked slyly at his colleagues: an Army Colonel and a Naval Commander, and Pick Carter, who seemed only half awake.

"Of course, in the corporate world, you have a leisurely bite at eight, then a chauffeur-driven, Xalatera Merc takes you to the office by nine-thirty, and…"

"Can it," muttered the President of Xalatera Industries. "Get the grub down – Ferdinand's guy will be here any time now."

"I still think we should insist that Nico comes along," said Jim, "We don't know what we're getting into – we need some backup."

"I agree," said Peter, "Ferdinand's in no position to turn us down – his whole game's riding on our presence."

"It is not a bluff I want to call, Peter" said Carter. "When did you last have a business meeting with a guy who would try to crush the help's Adam's apple?"

Nico grimaced, both at the contemptuous reference to his role, and at the memory of the pain and humiliation. He was

Larry's man, assigned to ride shotgun with the brass on this strange mission: the incident had dented his credibility, and he badly wanted a chance to redeem himself.

"Pick, violence is our business – or defence, if you prefer. But I tend to go along with you – the Spaniard is a loose cannon: I believe that he wasn't bluffing. Nico, I'm sorry about what happened to you – I would like to kick the Don's ass too, but you had best stay here. Pick, I think maybe you owe Nico an apology, huh?" Larry's tone was calm, but insistent.

Carter made a contrite face. "No offence, Nico – I was out of line…"

Nico nodded, and waved his hand in acknowledgement.

The telephone rang, and Carter reached for it.

"Yeah? Yeah, O.K. – yeah, thanks."

He turned to the group.

"A guy called Severino is in the elevator now – he's a big wheel, not an errand boy: he's Ferdinand's *consigliere*."

"Why does he need the elevator? If these guys control gravity, he could have levitated up from the street to the window and waved," said Jim, to laughter from the others as they stood up, swallowing their last mouthfuls of coffee.

A polite knock was heard from the door, and Carter opened it, ushering into the room an elegant man in his late sixties, carrying a gift-wrapped bottle. His demeanour was calm and dignified; he had undoubted presence, but the machismo of Don Ferdinand was absent: in its place was the attentive stillness that signalled a willingness to listen and absorb the input of others.

"Gentlemen, may I introduce Severino," said Carter, "He says he doesn't want to confuse us with his extended family names, and Severino will do just fine: Severino is Don Ferdinand's *numero dos hombre*. Severino, may I present our guys – Jim, Larry and Peter. Army, Navy and Air Force respectively."

Severino bowed and shook hands with each of them, turned unexpectedly to Nico, who was standing quietly to the side, and looked at Carter. "I have something to say to Nico," he said.

Carter was flustered. "Gee, I'm sorry – yeah, this is Nico, our valued associate…"

Severino shook hands with the silent bodyguard.

"Nico, I regret deeply that your first experience of the Order of Moridura was one of violence directed against you. Please accept the apologies of the Grand Council. I understand that you appreciate fine wines, and I have brought a bottle of the finest vintage that Extremadura can offer. I hope you will accept this inadequate token of our regret."

He handed the bottle to Nico, who accepted it after receiving a confirmatory nod from Larry.

"That was a nice gesture, Severino – whaddya say, guys?" said Carter effusively. "Let's all sit down for a moment, shall we?"

"I'm afraid there isn't sufficient time," said Severino politely, "our transport is waiting and we must go now." His next remark left them lost for words.

"I wish to add that Nico will be most welcome as our guest at the Ceremony, if he wishes to come, and with your permission, of course…"

"Well, yeah – sure… Larry?" said Carter.

"If Nico feels up to it, we all want him onboard." As they headed out of the suite towards the elevator, Nico croaked into his boss's ear.

"How the hell did he know about me and wine?"

"You can be damn sure of one thing," said Larry, "it wasn't a guess…"

They went out of the hotel foyer and into the waiting coach: Severino introduced a youngish, thick-lipped man sitting in the driver's seat as Casimiro. He half-turned to acknowledge their presence, his cold, heavy-lidded eyes scanning their faces rapidly, and then he switched on the engine.

The first section of the coach consisted of three double seats on each side; the rear half was partitioned off. Severino opened the door in the partition and motioned to them to enter. The rear space consisted of two bench seats running lengthwise on either side of the coach and a narrow central table: laid out on the table were seven red robes.

"Señores – please be seated," said Severino. "We will move back to the more comfortable seats at the front of the coach shortly – this area is more convenient for the short briefing that I must give you: you will be well used to briefing - and being briefed - in spartan surroundings, I'm sure!"

The three officers and Carter sat down on the left bench, and Nico on the right one: Severino seated himself beside the bodyguard and clasped his hands together.

"Before I outline the protocols for our arrival in the village of Moridanza, and subsequently at the monastery of Moridura, may I answer a question that I know must be in your minds – why did I invite Nico to join us, in the light of Ferdinand's position on the matter after the incident at the hotel?"

The four men opposite him exchanged glances; Carter spoke first.

"Yeah, it did kinda surprise us, Severino – the Don was pretty firm in his refusal: what changed his mind?"

"He didn't change his position – I am acting without his knowledge and authority."

There was total silence, and Nico shifted uncomfortably in his seat.

"I guess you'll have to elaborate on that," said Larry.

"The situation presented to you by Ferdinand was that he and the Order had total control of the situation, and of the woman physicist, Angeline Blade and her associates. That is no longer so, indeed, it was never an accurate assessment of the situation at the monastery. Your safety cannot be guaranteed once we arrive. It was my judgement that you must be apprised of this, and that you must be allowed to protect yourself if necessary. Nico is armed, I am sure: I can provide each of you with sidearms before we get to Moridanza."

There was a long silence. Severino waited patiently for their reaction.

"I bet it's that bastard Lonnen, aided and abetted by Mackinnon," exploded Carter.

"On the contrary, they have been a stabilising influence – they were driven to use force, but have carefully judged its deployment to minimise the risk of escalation. Regrettably, there have been fatalities, most of them accidental."

Carter looked at the soft-spoken man in astonishment.

"People have been killed! How? Who killed them?"

"An associate on a mission to Scotland died by his own hand; two of Ferdinand's employees fell from the cliff path at the monastery; a member of the Grand Council, Vasco, fell from the outer courtyard; a bodyguard had his neck broken in an accident with a sliding door; another member of the Council, Amancio, has vanished – we believe that Mackinnon's security chief, a man called Santiago Manrique, may have killed him, either deliberately or accidentally."

"Holy Jesus," gasped Carter, shaking his head in disbelief.

"Let me get this straight," said Jim carefully, "There's Mackinnon, Lonnen, the woman, some little English consultant guy and this man Manrique – and you have the whole of the Ancient Order. Yet so far, all of the fatalities have been your people?"

"It is not strictly accurate to consider the Order as a unified force," said Severino. "The secular arm and the monks do not necessarily achieve consensus on all matters, and the monks are, for the most part, non-violent." He looked calmly at the men opposite him.

"I know that Señor Carter is a scientist, gentlemen – presumably you were selected as serving officers who also had a scientific background?"

Peter nodded. "That is correct – each of us majored in a scientific discipline. Why do you ask?"

"Because I have something else of a scientific nature to explain to you – the question of the nascent singularity at the heart of *La Copa de Moridura*."

Carter stared at him, shaking his head from side to side.

"A singularity? Do you mean a singularity as in…? No, you can't mean that…"

"… as in a black hole – yes, that is what I mean."

"I've heard some conversation stoppers, but that one sure tops them all," said Jim.

Carter produced a hip flask, unscrewed the top, and took a hefty swig.

"Je-sus," he said fervently.

"Ferdinand, I urge you to reconsider the path you have chosen. It can only lead to further conflict. Alistair Mackinnon and Red Lonnen are not our enemies – they are intrinsically good men, reasonable men. At this very moment, Angeline Blade is risking her young life to stabilise *El Corazón*. She is beyond your reach, beyond anyone's reach. If she fails, nothing matters – all life will be extinguished; if she succeeds, with God's help, then we owe her a debt of gratitude that can never be repaid."

"Anselmo, you exaggerate the dangers, as always," said Ferdinand wearily. "These people are foreign adventurers - international capitalists who wish to wrest control of the gravitational process from our Order. We are at the dawn of a new, glorious age for Moridura, for Extremedura, for Spain; if I do not act to secure our interests, the Americans will deal with Mackinnon and his associates; we will be marginalised, patronised, reduced to a sordid tourist attraction. We are bound to this land and this place by ancient ties, my most esteemed and beloved brother. We must demonstrate to our prospective American partners that we have ownership and control of the gravitational process and of the woman Blade. She must be compelled to formally recognise our rights to the development of her discovery – the so-called Blade Effect."

There were seven men in the chapter house. Ferdinand and Jaime were seated at one of the long wooden tables at right-angles to the stone table at the head of the chapter house; Róger, the surviving *artillero*, was standing behind them, his machine gun openly slung across his shoulder. Their red robes contrasted sharply with the black habit of the monk seated next them, his head bowed. At the stone table, Brother Joaquín, in the unique gold robe of the Magus of Moridura, was flanked by Brother Anselmo on his right and a red-robed Manuel Ortega on his left. The shafts of morning sunlight striking into the vaulted room seemed to caress and celebrate the red and gold vestments of the Order, ignoring the black habits of the two monks.

"Compelled, Ferdinand? How do you propose to compel this brave, intelligent, resourceful young woman to sign away her life's work?" said Joaquín.

"The life of her father and her friends will rest upon her decision," said Jaime contemptuously. Ferdinand looked straight ahead expressionlessly.

"Ferdinand, you cannot contemplate such a course of action," said the Abbot, "and you, Gregorio – how can you be a party to such an enormity?"

The monk next to Ferdinand raised his head slowly and met the Abbot's gaze reluctantly.

"Anselmo, I have prayed for guidance in this difficult matter, and I distresses me to challenge your authority, and that of the Magus – my brother Joaquín. But my conscience tells me that my allegiance must be to the Magus Elect, and to our ancient ways. The schism in our Order has been widening for many years, and it pains me to say that your lack of strong leadership in your time as Abbot has brought us close to the destruction of all that we value. In times like these, a man must choose. Many of the younger brothers feel closer to the ideals of the *hermandad* than to your concept of their role."

"If they become involved in this madness, then they will be expelled from the community of Moriduran brothers," said Joaquín.

"That depends upon who is Abbot of Moridura, does it not, Joaquín?" said Gregorio, with a sidelong glance at Ferdinand.

Ferdinand made an impatient gesture and rose to his feet.

"There is no more to be said – I must attend to my duties before the Ceremony commences," he snapped, indicating with a jerk of his head that Jaime and Gregorio should join him. They both stood up, and half-turned to leave, but Brother Anselmo's voice stopped them in their tracks.

"Ferdinand, Brother Joaquín and I are reluctant to challenge your status as Magus Elect on this day, but your elevation to Magus depends finally upon another judgement – the judgement of *La Guardia*. As for you, Brother Gregorio – my writ still runs. As of this moment, you are no longer a member of the community of Moridura. I expel you for open defiance of my authority in the presence of the Magus: arrangements will be made to transport you to Moridanza before the Ceremony commences."

The colour drained from Gregorio's face, and he turned to Ferdinand, who made a dismissive gesture.

"You are impulsive, Anselmo. Gregorio will ignore your words, since you will doubtless reconsider them after my elevation. He has my full confidence, and will remain with me until the Ceremony. As for *La Guardia* – I will not unduly concern myself about ancient myths, however frightening they might be to credulous peasants such as Manuel Ortega."

"You insult a senior member of our Order, and at another time, you will retract your remark. If part of your plan relies upon Domingo, then I must tell you that he is dead – God rest his soul," said the Abbot.

Ferdinand's face became an inscrutable mask as he strove to reconcile his conflicting reactions: he had lost a powerful ally – his strong right hand - but he had been aware for some time of Domingo's ambitions to seize control of the *hermandad* and the Ancient Order from him.

"Mackinnon will pay dearly for this," he said, "and for all the other deaths he has caused."

"Domingo was killed by *La Guardia*," said the Abbot.

"Anselmo, you leave yourself open to ridicule by giving voice to such nonsense," replied Ferdinand contemptuously.

He turned and strode towards the door of the chapter house, followed by Jaime and Róger. At the door, Gregorio glanced back nervously, and saw the Abbot, Joaquín and Manuel with their heads bowed in silent prayer.

"I am nine parts certain that we will be safe here," said Alistair.

"It's the tenth part that concerns me," said Santiago, peering cautiously over the low parapet of the shower building and scanning the courtyard below. The combined voices of the Ancient Order could be heard echoing from the chapel, a powerful, masculine sound. Red, Paul and Alistair were sitting with their backs to the water tank: all four of them were wearing black Moriduran habits. Alistair was performing card tricks with a dog-eared pack he had found among the books in the guest wing.

"Relax, Santiago, this is a defensible position: if we stay low, their only attack option is up the ladder one at a time – easily countered…" He brandished a long piece of iron he had found next to the tank.

"They could lob grenades, if they had any," said Paul, laughing.

Santiago looked around at them in irritation.

"Please keep your voices low, señores – however defensible our position, we do not want to attract attention."

Alistair held the pack of cards face down in his right hand and fanned the cards back progressively with his left.

"Tell me when to stop, Red," he said in a hoarse stage whisper, rolling his eyes towards Santiago.

"Stop!" grunted Red.

Alistair pulled back the top half of the pack and held it up towards the others, showing the bottom card.

"I cannot see it, but you can," he said dramatically, "but I can tell you it is the nine of diamonds!"

"So it is!" exclaimed Paul with exaggerated surprise: he had seen Alistair's trick many times before.

Red seemed more impressed.

"Not bad – do it again – but shuffle the deck first."

Alistair shuffled the deck furiously and then started drawing the cards back.

Red waited much longer this time before saying stop.

Alistair held the top half of the deck towards him, showing the card.

"Well?" said Red.

"Ace of Spades," said Alistair.

"A bad choice, Red," said Paul softly, and Red looked suddenly grim, his thoughts abruptly in another place.

"She'll be OK, Red," said Alistair reassuringly, glancing at Paul and shaking his head in reproof.

"Yeah…" said Red.

"We've been up here since eleven-thirty, and I need a pee," complained Alistair. "How will we know when they all leave the chapel, Santiago? We need time to get down the ladder and position ourselves to merge with the crowd."

"Any time now – they all have to get from the chapel to *El Trono* for the ceremony: When the singing stops, we move…"

The singing stopped.

"Now!" said Santiago, drawing his weapon and moving swiftly to the ladder. "I will stay and cover you until you have all descended – be careful you don't trip over your habits."

"I've been tripping over my habits for years," said Red, heaving himself up: Alistair and Paul followed him. Santiago helped each of them over the parapet on to the ladder, and then followed them down. They moved round to the blind side of the shower block, flattened themselves against its wall, and waited. Santiago knew that if anyone came through the courtyard gate, their cover was blown: he was relying on the Abbot's assurance that everyone would be in the chapel.

"I must pee," hissed Alistair and disappeared into the shower block. The sound of many voices and a multitude of footsteps grew gradually louder.

"I'll wait for Alistair," whispered Santiago to Paul. "You and Red must merge with the crowd as they pass: keep your heads down and don't engage in conversation.

"Damn him, why did he have to go now!" hissed Red. "We must stay together…"

The first wave of the black and red-robed figures began to pass on either side of them.

"Go! Go now!" said Santiago as he slid through the doorway. Paul grasped Red by the wrist and pulled him forward into the swirling mass of the Ancient Order of Moridura as they headed for open gate to *La Copa de Moridura*.

The little changing room was empty, but Alistair emerged through the open door from the shower area. Santiago put his finger to his lips and pulled Alistair towards the door: it was only when they were carried forward by the moving mass of people that Alistair realised that his need to relieve himself had cut them off from Paul and Red. He cursed his old man's bladder silently, and linked arms with his security chief.

Chapter Twenty-Nine

The sun was a blazing golden disc in the clear sky above the spear of black rock thrust into the heart of the Cup of Moridura: the assembled Moriduran Brothers, with their cowls covering their heads, sweltered in their black habits: the red robes of the members of the *hermandad* reflected more sunlight, but many of its lower-ranking members had unwisely worn their normal apparel underneath, and were equally uncomfortable. The *confratres* had chosen light clothing under the heavy robes and smiled complacently behind their hoods as they heard the muttered complaints of their brethren.

The Moridurans formed a half-circle on the north of the rock formation and the *hermandad* on the south side: the two groups were thus adjacent to each other on the west and east sides of the rock, but they maintained a gap between them of about two metres of open ground at these points. The front ranks of each semi-circle comprised the most senior monks and the *confratres*. On the south side, at the base of the rock, facing it, stood the Abbot, and Joaquín, the Magus of Moridura, resplendent in his gold robe, worn over his monk's habit, the hood thrown back: between them stood the Magus Elect, Ferdinand, also in a gold robe, his head bare.

Those closest to the seven metre high rock could see little of the Throne or the summit: those farther back could see much more, and the rise of the land meant that those at the rear of each group were looking down on *El Trono*. Over the centuries since the great schism in the Ancient Order, there had been much debate and some conflict over which group should occupy the favoured south ground, facing north, because this permitted the observers to see the front of *El Trono*, and the main actors in the drama in position at the base of the rock – The Magus, the Magus Elect and the Abbot. The Moriduran Brothers had yielded to the *hermandad*, consoling themselves with the fact that they could see the Magus and the Abbot when they moved round to ascend the stone steps to the summit, and, if they were far enough back, view the Magus Elect face on at his elevation – the climax of the Ceremony.

In the centre of the massed ranks of the *hermandad*, a group of seven red-robed and bareheaded figures stood out conspicuously because of the respectful space that had been left around Severino and his guests by the other hooded members on the slope. The Americans were ill at ease, not just because of the heat and the heavy robes, but because they were such a conspicuous target if violence erupted. The sidearms supplied by Severino gave a little comfort.

Among the monks on the high north side slope, Paul and Red were trying to find Alistair and Santiago without drawing attention to themselves, but in this, they were not successful: on the day of the Ceremony, some initial jostling for position was tolerated, but that moment had passed, and the two men attracted angry glances and remonstrations as they pushed through the monks, heads down. On the east side of *El Trono*, on the edge of the group, two tall monks remained in their chosen position, but kept looking back and scanning the Moridurans to the west and north of them, searching for movement.

"There!" said Santiago, gripping Alistair's arm. "At about twelve o'clock, halfway down…"

"Aye – it must be them – they're causing a commotion," whispered Alistair. He raised his arms and clasped his hands behind his head, mimicking one of Paul's favourite postures in the hope that it would be recognised. It was – the smaller of the two cowled figures turned towards them, placed his hands behind his head, mirroring the signal, and the two monks began moving down and across the slope towards them.

Alistair put his arms down. "They've got us," he said with satisfaction. His satisfaction was short-lived: the two monks suddenly halted, and both turned their heads abruptly to someone behind them.

"Someone's put a gun on them," said Santiago softly. "Whoever it is almost certainly saw us too."

"What should we do?"

Santiago drew a long breath. "I have to say that almost anything we do will make things worse: but we can try to get to them quickly…"

A soft, precise voice interrupted him.

"You will not be permitted to do that, señores – you are surrounded by my chosen brethren and we are prepared to use force to restrain you."

Alistair looked round in astonishment.

"Gregorio? Is that you?"

The cowled monk behind him inclined his head in confirmation.

It all came together in Alistair's mind – the Abbot's words about dissent among the brothers, the possibility of conflict – but Gregorio, the stiff, humourless bureaucrat? Then he remembered another humourless bureaucrat in steel-rimmed glasses, a figure from history, from the newsreels of his childhood – Heinrich Himmler, the head of the SS, a mass murderer. Hannah Arendt's phrase came to mind – the banality of evil. He looked at the hard-faced young monks who had formed a tight ring around Santiago and himself and speculated what weapons they might be carrying: probably knives or blackjacks, he thought: effective and silent at close range. His own revolver had been taken from him in the guest wing, and Santiago's machine pistol could not be used under the circumstances. Gregorio knew it, and made no attempt to disarm him.

Another phrase from a more ancient past came involuntarily to his lips.

"Father, forgive them, for they know not what they do…"

"You blaspheme, señor," said Gregorio, shocked.

"The sacrilege is yours alone, Gregorio," replied Alistair coldly, "you betray your God – you betray your superiors, the Abbot and the Magus – you betray your Ancient Order. We will not resist – nothing can be served by it now."

His eyes met Santiago's, and consensus was established. They both relaxed, and then faced towards the steps to the top of *El Trono*.

"Let's enjoy the Ceremony, Santiago. You too, Gregorio – we won't give you any trouble."

Further up the slope, Róger, the *artillero*, with his pistol jammed into Paul's side, was forcing him and Red across the gathering of monks and down to the western edge of the rock. It was clear from his awkward bulk that he was also carrying a combat machine gun slung under his robe. He made it clear that he would not hesitate to shoot those who had been complicit in the death of his *compadre*, regardless of the consequences of discharging his weapons in the packed crowd of monks. They believed him – his voice was that of a man freed from normal civilised constraints by hatred and a burning desire for retribution.

At the edge of the group of monks, Róger signalled to a corpulent figure among the *hermandad* that he had secured his prisoners. Jaime immediately headed along the edge of his group, down towards the point where the Magus Elect was standing between Anselmo and Joaquín. Red and Paul watched as he stopped close to Ferdinand and waited: Ferdinand turned his head, saw Jaime, and a signal was passed confirming that the father of Doctor Angeline Blade and the Englishman Corr were now hostages. He had received a similar message a few moments earlier from one of Gregorio's acolytes that Alistair Mackinnon and his bodyguard were secured. Ferdinand lifted his head and looked directly at Red Lonnen and then he made a gesture of recognition with his hand to Róger. The *artillero* waved back at him.

The murmur of the assembly gradually died down, and there was an almost palpable air of expectancy. Alistair and Santiago could see only the north side of the rock and the steps to the summit. Red and Paul, on the west side of the rock, had a clear side view of the three principal players, one in black, two robed in gold.

On the higher southern slope, the Americans looked uneasily at each other, and at Severino and Casimiro, not knowing what to expect; Nico had unobtrusively placed his hand on his automatic pistol, and was poised for instant action. The two Spaniards were looking at the summit of the black rock with rapt attention. The silence was absolute, and an uncanny stillness settled over *La Copa de Moridura*. No bird sang, no leaves rustled, the grass was still, and no breeze relieved the burning heat of the sun. Jim was reminded of the moments before the detonation of a tactical nuclear device in the desert many years before – a sensation of time suspended.

Nico felt a faint vibration in the hand holding his automatic, a steady, rhythmic beat, growing in intensity. The others felt it now, and looked to Severino for some reaction, some explanation, but his eyes were fixed on the rock. Larry opened his mouth to speak, but thought better of it. Peter reflected on how vulnerable they all were, surrounded by hooded figures, unable to determine who was hostile and who was not. Pick Carter fervently wished he hadn't got himself into this gravity thing in the first place, and hoped that the others would protect him if events got out of hand.

The ground beneath their feet was vibrating now, and some kind of heat haze seemed to be obscuring the summit of the black rock, and then a great rending, tearing sound filled *La Copa*, accompanied by another sound, as of some nameless force surging upwards from the bowels of the earth beneath them. A rhythmic chanting began from the assembled throng - *El Partir, El Partir …*

The Americans knew enough Spanish to translate the chant, and they felt relieved – clearly the assembly had expected the phenomena, however frightening they were to outsiders. Suddenly, the vibration and the chanting stopped and the haze above the rock cleared: from their vantage point on the slope, the Americans could see that the protuberance on the summit of the rock had split into two parts, and some kind of vapour was rising from the gap created by the split. They could see three people facing the rock at its base, one in a black monk's habit, and two robed in gold.

"The figures you see are those of the Abbot of Moridura in black; the taller of the two figures in gold robes is Don Ferdinand, the Magus Elect, and beside him is the Magus of Moridura. What you will now see is directly relevant to your mission, gentlemen – prepare yourselves," said Severino. His calm voice was reassuring after all that they had experienced, and they focused their attention on the tableau at the base of the rock. Ferdinand had stepped back from the others, and he raised his arms towards the summit of the rock as though in supplication. There was total silence, and then the figure of the Magus Elect began to rise very slowly upwards from the ground. A collective exhalation, a great groan, came from the assembly: the figure of the Abbot walked to the left of the rock and the Magus, in his glittering gold vestments, to the right of it. They both disappeared behind the rock as the ascending figure of the Magus Elect reached the top of the rock and glided forward on to the summit, facing the gap in *El Trono*.

As Brother Anselmo made his way round the base of the rock, something caught his eye among the densely packed group of monks. One monk suddenly jerked his head, allowing his cowl to slip back; his red hair caught the sunlight. The old man assessed the situation in an instant: the ashen-faced Paul standing next to Red and the grim monk immediately behind him – Róger, the remaining *artillero*. Anselmo made no sign of recognition but continued to move towards the base of the steps to join Joaquín, approaching from the other side.

Joaquín caught sight of Alistair and Santiago as he rounded the base of the rock, and the little monk also saw Gregorio and his band of young dissidents surrounding his friends. He made his decision instantly, without deliberation. Raising both hands above his head, he advanced directly towards them, causing the other monks to move back in astonished reverence to make way for him. Risking all, he called out to his friends, his voice full of warmth.

"Alistair, Santiago! Come to me, my friends!"

Gregorio and his followers remained in their position, defiantly confining Alistair and Santiago within a tight ring of twelve monks. The main body of monks had moved away respectfully as the Magus advanced, leaving Gregorio's group isolated.

"Gregorio, I command you to kneel before your Magus." Joaquín's voice was now resonant, commanding, and he stretched out his right arm, his finger pointing directly at the agitated monk. Gregorio hesitated, all his instinctive respect for hierarchy and vested authority compelling him to comply, his ambition and his fear of Ferdinand urging him to resist. Alistair and Santiago remained motionless, recognising the fragility of the situation.

The Abbot had now joined Joaquín, and stood with him facing the dissident group.

"My beloved brother, obey your Magus and respect your Abbot," he said in a tone of infinite gentleness. Gregorio gave agonised groan and fell to his knees, his hands clasped before him.

"Forgive me – please forgive me," he cried, his voice broken and pitiful. The young monks around him looked down at him with astonished contempt, then at the Magus and their Abbot, gripping their knives and small clubs uncertainly.

The main body monks around the dissidents moved swiftly forward, enveloping and disarming the confused acolytes of Gregorio: when they moved back, taking their rebellious brethren with them, Gregorio was alone, still kneeling, and weeping pitifully. Alistair and Santiago moved gratefully towards the Magus and the Abbot.

On the west side of the rock, Róger had heard the raised voice of the Magus, and he became aware of a disturbance among the monks on the eastern side: his attention was deflected from his prisoners for a moment, and in that moment, Paul turned and drove the heel of his hand upwards with great force under the *artillero's* chin. Róger fell unconscious among the monks around them, his automatic pistol still gripped in his hand. Paul quickly and unobtrusively retrieved it.

"Our brother has succumbed to the heat," he said in his halting Spanish to the concerned monks. "I fear he may have suffered a stroke – please tend to him – we will go for help," and with that, he and Red headed towards the rear of the rock to join the others, leaving the monks to discover the heavy weapon under Róger's robe.

The Abbot looked relieved as they appeared and were reunited with Alistair and Santiago. He turned to the Magus.

"Joaquín, although it is a radical departure from the Ceremony, I feel that our friends must join us on the summit, at *El Trono*. We do not know what other forces Ferdinand has mustered, and it is the safest place for them: Ferdinand would not dare confront them in our presence, and in front of the assembled Order."

Joaquín looked uncertain, then he smiled wanly.

"Let us hope you are right, Anselmo," he said.

"What in hell was that?" gasped Angeline as the great vibration and the rending sounds finally ended. She was standing at the console, with Arkimateo's strong hands gripping her shoulders, bracing her against the seismic tremors.

"That was *El Partir del Trono*," said Arkimateo. "The chamber we are in has lifted within the rock. Above us, the Ceremony will be reaching its climax with the elevation of the Magus.

"But that will be Ferdinand," said Angeline, "Surely the Abbot and the Magus will not permit him to become Magus after all that he has done."

"They cannot prevent his elevation," said Arkimateo. "Whoever stands in the central position when *El Trono* splits is lifted automatically to the summit – it is a natural consequence of the process: if a sack of potatoes was in that position, it would be lifted – but it would not become the Magus!"

"That's a relief," said Angeline shakily, turning and looking up into the great, wide eyes of her friend and protector, and then tears clouded her own eyes as she remembered that Arkimateo would not survive the ultimate process.

"I must now make my judgement on the fitness of the Magus Elect to assume the great responsibilities of the Magus of Moridura. That, Angeline, will be my last task, assuming that our work of this morning has now brought us to the correct final control actions. Are you ready to implement them?"

"May I kiss you first, Arkimateo?" Her pale face flushed to the roots of her red hair.

The great arms enfolded her, lifted her and held her for a moment, then pulled her very slowly and gently forward. She kissed the cool lips of the ancient being from another time and another universe with infinite tenderness. As Arkimateo put her down softly, she cried out.

"Please don't leave us!"

"I must, Angeline – but I will leave you something that will assuage your grief – and something that will stay with you for all of your life," said Arkimateo. "But now – to our task."

They both turned to the consoles and began the sequence of actions that would either cause the field oscillation that was *El Corazón* to expand into nothingness or collapse into the infinite density of a black hole, sucking everything into its maw. As the dials flashed and the screen blazed with light, Angeline gave the final control instruction to Arkimateo. She experienced a moment of fear, and then there was a great shuddering in the chamber, followed by utter stillness - the stillness and peace that come after a painful death - and then all console activity ceased.

"It is done," said Arkimateo sadly, "*El Corazón* is no more – we have achieved our purpose, Angeline. Now you must go quickly to the summit of the rock – to *El Trono* – there is very little time…" The urgency in her voice brooked no disagreement. A door opened in the wall of the chamber, and Angeline could dimly see a rock staircase leading upwards.

"Go, Angeline – you will be safe. I will follow…"

Angeline reluctantly headed for the door and the staircase, wondering whether she was being lied to: she looked back for a moment, and saw Arkimateo bending over the dead console of the regulator, tapping its surface at high speed: it came to life again just as she turned and began to ascend the steps.

On the summit of the rock, Ferdinand stood triumphantly, facing south, his arms raised, turning slowly from left to right, receiving the acclamation of the *hermandad*: he saw the American group, Severino and Casimiro on the southern slope, and smiled with satisfaction. A sound from behind him caused him to turn. Through the vapours that were still emanating from the sundered throne, a figure was emerging, rising from the darkness of the void in the rock. As Angeline stepped on to the surface, he strode forward swiftly and gripped her wrist, pulling her firmly forward to the southern edge.

"My people are holding your father, your lover, Corr, and Mackinnon and his henchman, Manrique," he whispered urgently. "Follow my instructions, Doctora Blade, and they will not be harmed: in a moment, Joaquín and the Abbot will join us, and I will be confirmed as the new Magus of the Ancient Order of Moridura. Once the Ceremony is over, you will sign an agreement that relinquishes control of your gravitational process to the Order and to myself. I have the backing of senior military, political and industrial figures from your own country. It would be an act of folly to resist. You and your friends will be a part of our future, and will share in the control and exploitation of the process – I am not a greedy man."

Angeline, still sunk in grief, did not resist, but walked up and down with him as the red sea of figures beneath them roared their approbation: on the north side, the monks, sensing from events that all was not well, were silent.

On the slope, Pick Carter grinned complacently at the sight and sounds of Ferdinand's triumph.

"I guess you were wrong, Severino," he said, "Don Ferdinand seems to have things under control after all."

A sturdy, somewhat squat, red-robed figure in front of them turned, and threw back his hood, staring at Carter.

"You are too hasty in your judgement, señor," said Manuel Ortega, and turning away again, put his arm around the shoulder of his son.

"Have faith in our friends, Cristobal," he whispered.

On top of the rock, Ferdinand turned to face the north, firmly pulling Angeline with him. He waited calmly for Anselmo and Joaquín to appear. A great silence descended on *La Copa de Moridura* as the red-robed figure of the Magus appeared on the right of *El Trono* and the Abbot came from the left of it. Their paths converged, and as they moved towards Ferdinand, he released Angeline's wrist, and, raising his arms, moved forward to greet them, but they did not meet his eyes, and walked around him to Angeline. Ferdinand turned slowly in shock, looking at their backs as they embraced her.

"You have succeeded, Angeline?" said Brother Anselmo softly.

Angeline nodded, and her eyes filled with tears.

As Ferdinand stared at the small group, his mind racing, he heard footsteps on the rock; he turned and saw Alistair Mackinnon and Santiago come from his right, and then Red Lonnen and Paul from his left.

"Stay calm, Ferdinand," said Alistair, holding up his hand "we can still work something out…"

Ferdinand's eyes met Red Lonnen's; he saw in them only implacable hatred for the man who had threatened his daughter. He turned over the options in his mind with lightning speed, and kept returning to one only, the traditional default choice of the *hermandad*, but he decided on one last attempt at the way of men before adopting the way of beasts. Forcing a smile on to his face, he turned around and moved confidently towards the Abbot and the Magus, who had their backs to him, facing Angeline.

"My most beloved and esteemed brethren – welcome! May we now proceed with my final confirmation as Magus?"

Anselmo and Joaquín turned, with Angeline between them, grasping their hands. Brother Anselmo's expression was one of great sadness, and it was reflected in the eyes of the Magus. The Abbot spoke, slowly and deliberately.

"You will never be Magus of Moridura. You have betrayed our Ancient Order, and by your actions have brought division and death to the monastery. Your only route to salvation is acceptance and contrition - leave us now and return to your home for a period of prayer and reflection, and then go to your confessor. You are now in the hands of God, Ferdinand."

The old man's words sent a chill through his heart, and Ferdinand felt a darkness of the soul descending upon him: it was replaced by a great rage, the anger surging up in him – a liberating, cleansing fury and a compulsion to action. He sprang behind the Abbot and seized Angeline by the neck, dragging her backwards almost to the edge of the rock: she did not resist, recognising the futility of struggling in his iron grip. Anselmo and Joaquín stared powerlessly at him, their eyes filled with horror: Alistair, Santiago, Red and Paul froze where they stood, poised for action but equally helpless.

Virtually every member of the *hermandad* could see the unfolding drama at the summit, with the exception of those closest to the rock: on the north side, only the monks on the higher points of the slope could see what was happening. It was evident to all that the Ceremony had radically departed from its prescribed ritual, and that something was seriously wrong.

Severino shook his head when Carter asked for an explanation.

"Folly – utter folly," he said, shaking his head.

"Is he threatening that woman?" asked Larry, reaching for his weapon. "Is that Doctor Angeline Blade?"

"It is," said Casimiro, looking anxiously at Severino.

Manuel and Cristobal were pushing their way down the slope to the angry protests of the members of the *hermandad,* as they unceremoniously elbowed them aside, anxious to protect their friends, but with no clear idea of what they could do when they got to the rock.

On the summit, Alistair and his party were advancing very, very slowly, inching their way forward, hoping against hope that Ferdinand would be preoccupied with restraining Angeline and that his view was blocked, at least partially, by the Abbot and the Magus.

Angeline managed to speak, in spite of the pressure around her neck.

"So this is what centuries of breeding and tradition have brought you to, Don Ferdinand – a crude assault upon a woman…"

Ferdinand flushed, but he made no response to her taunt.

"Anselmo – Joaquín – confirm me as Magus, in accordance with our ancient tradition or I will kill her," he said, his voice shaking. As he spoke, he looked beyond the two monks, his eye caught by a movement in the darkness between the halves of *El Trono*, and a sudden nameless foreboding overtook him. Something was rising from the depth of the rock, something that writhed and waved, snakelike and menacing: and then he saw a great silver-grey head and two huge eyes glowing red. His mind reeled, and all the fables of his childhood came rushing back to him, the tales of his nurse, of the servants, the pictures in the ancient volumes in the library. As Arkimateo rose from beneath the rock, and her huge body became fully visible, the name burst incredulously from his lips.

"*La Bestia!*"

His hands fell powerlessly to his sides, and Angeline immediately ran to her father and Paul: Alistair and Santiago joined them, surrounding her in a tight, protective phalanx, hugging her and whispering words of comfort. Anselmo and Joaquín began to move towards Arkimateo, calling her name, but she swept them aside and advanced upon Ferdinand. As the terrifying creature approached him, a great surge of adrenalin pumped into his system, and he reached for his concealed weapon.

"No, Arkimateo, no!" cried the Abbot, but it was too late. The great upper arms reached out and seized the Magus Elect, lifting him and pinioning his arms to his body; the air shimmered around them in their deadly embrace. The observers on the rock could only shrink back from the high pressure turbulence enveloping Arkimateo and Ferdinand:

from the heart of it came an awful scream, followed by a sound so horrifying that those who heard it would carry the memory for the rest of their lives – the sound of living flesh and bone being crushed by an intense gravitational force. When the disturbance in the air cleared, Arkimateo stood alone, looking down at the red and gold pulped mass on the rock at her feet that had once been Ferdinand of Moridanza.

Manuel and Cristobal, at the foot of the rock, had seen nothing, but had heard everything. On the slope, Severino looked at Casimiro, and they both bent their heads.

"God give his tortured soul eternal rest," said Severino, and Casimiro responded with a fervent amen.

"What in hell is that – that thing?" gasped Peter.

"It ain't a pantomime horse," breathed Carter, lost in admiration. "Jeez! These guys sure know how to put on a show!"

"I guess this kinda changes our plans," said Larry.

"I guess it does," said Pick Carter, deflating abruptly, "but Lonnen and Mackinnon are reasonable guys – there will be a place for me in their plans, I'm sure…"

"There is still the question of the Magus," said Severino softly, "all will depend upon who is confirmed in the office."

As if in answer to his observation, a terrifying voice of enormous power and alien timbre rang across La Copa, the voice of Arkimateo. The members of the Ancient Order of Moridura fell to their knees in awe and terror, leaving the Americans the only ones standing.

"Your brother Ferdinand betrayed the trust you placed in him and has now gone to your God. The man known as Jaime is complicit in the betrayal – deal with him as you see fit. Brothers of the Ancient Order of Moridura, behold the new Magus of Moridura!"

Manuel, kneeling at the foot of the rock, suddenly felt himself being lifted: he straightened up involuntarily and clutched at his son, but Cristobal was unable to halt his father's ascent to the summit of the rock and beyond. As he hung there in space, he felt himself turned in space to face south, then north, and his arms lifted without his conscious volition.

The monks and the *hermandad* rose to their feet and gave a great cry of acclamation as the squat little figure rotated slowly in the air

The great voice of *La Guardia* spoke again for the last time, a voice that penetrated to the very soul of those listening.

"Behold Manuel Ortega – Magus of Moridura!"

The terrified Jaime was seized by red-robed figures at the base of the rock and hustled away into the crowd. Cristobal moved to the spot where his father had stood and stared into the air above him, unable to comprehend what was happening, then he too was elevated to the rock and set down beside the Abbot and Joaquín, who had now removed his gold robe, revealing the black habit of a simple Moriduran monk. The floating figure of the new Magus sank gently to the summit beside him. The Abbot and Joaquín came forward, and, divesting Manuel of his red robe, helped him into the golden vestments.

Manuel looked at the Abbot with tears in his eyes.

"I am not worthy of this, Brother Anselmo – what will Fidelicia say?"

"She will be proud of you, Manuel, as I am – as we all are. Accept your rank with dignity."

The others came forward respectfully, grasping his hands and congratulating him. Only Angeline held back, her eyes on Arkimateo.

The lambent eyes looked at her for a long moment, and then the great head turned upwards towards the sun: the air shimmered, and then there was nothing. Angeline fell to her knees at the spot where Arkimateo had stood, sobbing bitterly. Paul and her father moved back to comfort her.

"We never said goodbye! She said she would leave me something – something to comfort me. Oh, Arkimateo!" sobbed Angeline inconsolably.

"She is free now, Angeline – her work is done, and her long servitude is over," said Paul, pulling her gently to her feet and stroking her hair. She buried her face in his shoulder, and then a sound from the gap beneath *El Trono* made her raise her head. Paul felt her stiffen, and at the same time he experienced a familiar feeling, his uncanny valley sensation, a feeling that had only ever been triggered by one event. He pulled back from Angeline and turned to look at the space between the halves of the throne. The figure of a monk was rising from below, a massive, powerful figure, features hidden under the deep cowl of the black habit, carrying something that caught the sunlight. The monk lifted his head, and Angeline sucked in her breath in a great gasp, and then, in a shuddering cry of joy and recognition, a name burst from her lips.

"Mateo – oh, Mateo!"

She rushed forward and then stopped, reaching her hands up to caress the young monk's face. He smiled at her, but his expression held confusion and disorientation as he looked around.

Paul and the others clustered round him, their delight at his return exploding in exclamations of welcome.

"Can it really be you, Mateo?" said Paul, grasping his arm.

The monk's gaze moved across the faces of his friends, as though seeking to confirm his presence in a reality that had slipped away from him. A great rumbling and grinding sound came from behind him as *El Trono* closed for the last time.

Mateo looked bewildered - he spoke their names slowly and cautiously, as if he thought they might disappear if he was too direct.

"Angeline – Paul... Brother Anselmo, Brother Joaquín! Señor Lonnen – Señor Alistair... Santiago – Manuel – Cristobal..." He shook his head, trying to clear his mind.

"I am sorry, my friends, my thoughts are confused; I feel as though I have just wakened from a deep sleep. How did I get here?" He looked around him and realised for the first time where he was, and then looked again at Manuel and saw the robe of the Magus of Moridura. The monk fell to his knees, and bent his head respectfully.

"Mateo, my friend, please rise," said Manuel, still ill at ease with his new status: as the big monk got to his feet, the little man embraced him warmly, placing his head against Mateo's chest. The monk recovered his composure and accepted the handshakes and embraces from his friends, still grasping the silver object in his hands.

He turned to Angeline, and held it out awkwardly to her.

"Señorita Angeline, I have to give this to you. I do not know who gave it to me, but there is also a message I must deliver to you..."

He suddenly slumped forward, and then straightened up, seeming to grow in stature: a familiar voice, warm and loving, came from his mouth.

"Angeline, my friend – I give you the gift of Mateo, a Mateo who will live out his life as a mortal man, a life that will be long and productive: I have also given him a navel, so that he may shower without embarrassment: Angeline, my true friend, I give you this token, from his hands, to remind you of me. It will protect you, your child and those close to you throughout your life. Angeline Blade, remember me always..."

Through her tears, Angeline looked at the heavy silver figurine in her hands, with its tentacled head and centaur's body. The large eyes glowed softly with an eternal love.

THE END